See these other books by Larry W. Miller Jr.:

Trials of an Archmage series:
Book I - Discovery
Paperback ISBN: 9-595-25758-5
Hard Cover ISBN: 0-595-65313-8
Available from www.iuniverse.com

Book II - Pern and the Giant Forest
Paperback ISBN: 0-595-30229-7
Available from www.iuniverse.com

Book III - The Mystic Library
Paperback ISBN: 1-905166-40-0
Available from www.amazon.com

Book IV - Ascension/
Circle of Darkness
Paperback ISBN: 0-595-41898-8
Available from www.iuniverse.com

Other Fantasy Books:
Long Live the Queen
Paperback ISBN: 0-595-27449-8
Available from www.iuniverse.com

Balance Lost / A Strange Friendship
Paperback ISBN: 978-1-4401-0693-4
Available from www.iuniverse.com

Science Fiction Books:
The Conquest of New Eden/
Sins of the Father
Paperback ISBN: 0-595-37561-8
Available from www.iuniverse.com

Droptroopers: Gauntlet of Fear
Paperback ISBN: 978-0-595-47591-9
Available from www.iuniverse.com

A Watery Crash
Paperback ISBN: 978-1-4401-8180-1
Available from www.iuniverse.com

Other titles in the works:
Fade to Gray (Book and Music CD)

LARRY W. MILLER JR.

The Last Wizard of Earth

EDITED BY ASHLEY M. MILLER

iUniverse, Inc.
New York   Bloomington

iUniverse books may be ordered through booksellers or by contacting:

iUniverse
1663 Liberty Drive
Bloomington, IN 47403
www.iuniverse.com
1-800-Authors (1-800-288-4677)

Because of the dynamic nature of the Internet, any Web addresses or links contained in this book may have changed since publication and may no longer be valid. The views expressed in this work are solely those of the author and do not necessarily reflect the views of the publisher, and the publisher hereby disclaims any responsibility for them.

ISBN: 978-1-4502-6975-9 (sc)
ISBN: 978-1-4502-6977-3 (ebook)

Printed in the United States of America

iUniverse rev. date: 11/05/2010

About the Book:

This was the first book that I ever wanted to write. The idea for it came on in a rush and I was unable to do anything about it. I had not yet developed the skills to get it down on paper. Now, however, with a few stories under my belt, I felt ready to undertake the grand adventure.

As usual, there were influences and support from those around me. Some were more active than others, but it takes everyone to take a project like this through to completion. I must first thank my editor and daughter, Ashley for her efforts on my behalf. I make enough errors as she well knows to require an outside view of the text to get it at least closer to presentable. So thank you and I love you. My family and friends were, as always, steadfast in their support and for that I am eternally grateful. I must mention a few of them here by name. (They will get a kick out of seeing their names in print. Who am I to get in the way of that?) Ramiro, you were always there to be a sounding board when I finished an exciting bit. Your grounding and support are truly appreciated. Ramazan Rushiti, a good friend of mine who asked to be a character in this book, I have promoted you to Commodore and given you a place in fictional history. Enjoy your lofty status. Garry, player, your input will be more valuable in "Fade to Gray" but I mention you here so as not to leave you out. Keep rapping and take care of yourself man. Roddy, you are an inspiration to me and I have tried to be one for you as well. The future lays before us like a golden carpet of glittering dust, waiting for us to walk across and leave our marks. With any luck, we shall take those steps in friendship and make a lasting impression. There are so many others that this paragraph would take over too much space, so I leave with a general thank you to the rest of you. This book represents a grand move forward and I hope you come along for the ride. No matter what your take on this project, enjoy the book.

Table of Contents

PREFACE

Who am I

This is my story. Who am I? I am the Last Wizard of Earth. Sounds special doesn't it? It really isn't. Actually I am an Elementalist. I bend and shape the powers of air, water, fire, and earth to my will. Where I come from, that is a common thing and I was not the best pupil in my class. In fact, I always struggled with concepts that other, more gifted and experienced casters grasped right off. It was fate that propelled me to this lofty and over-inflated position. Of course I am getting ahead of myself here. I was once known simply as Zack. My family, my adopted family, was poor and we had no family name since we had no land or title to the king. I was always hungry and dirty and my mother, bless her heart, never let it get her down. She would do backbreaking work to help Dad support us. Just thinking about it takes me back to the meadow and the old house, or rather the lean-to that we lived in. Dad had once been in the royal guard, but someone had done something to cause him disgrace and he could not get that kind of work anymore. He had scars that he wouldn't talk about. He kept mostly to himself and went about the drudgery of his life. He never knew how much it hurt me to see him like that. He refused to train us with a sword as well. He feared that we might follow in his footsteps and become as miserable as he was. So, we tried to ignore the sword on the wall and we went about our chores. The landowner we rented from had fruit orchards. All of the indigenous fruits were represented and he even had some that didn't normally grow around here. We would work for him to lower our rent when it was time to harvest. In exchange we got to take home some small portion of the wondrous fruit and some of the partially spoiled stuff that he couldn't sell anyway. We were grateful for it and never complained. My brother Joshua was older than me. He stood four inches taller and he took every opportunity to point it out to me. He was a bully, plain and simple. At least I thought so then. Now, looking back, I think he was worried about me and it made him lash out. All in all, we were happy. There were no major wars and we were too small to be noticed by anyone important. It kept Dad away from ridicule and we learned to live with the isolation. It looked like my future was pretty grim. I must admit that I never anticipated what happened later.

Now a lot of what I am going to tell you was told to me by my friend Casey. He is a specialist like me, but his knowledge is not of magic, it is of propulsion and maintenance. I did not know what those words meant when we met, but he is a good man with a huge heart and a quick mind. So don't get upset if I don't remember it all correctly. After all, I was not there. Okay, here goes.

THE END OF THE WORLD

Sparks flew as the small cruiser took the latest hit. The electronic noise that was supposed to keep the missiles from being confused had already faltered. John Riggins cursed as he bounced in the shock frame of his station. Automatic fire suppressors engaged and the flames were quickly extinguished without taking any of the crew's attention away from the battle. John continued his cursing. When he finally keyed the microphone on his headset, he had calmed down a bit.

"The Lizzies have figured out the new jammers Sir, and we are a sitting duck again." He said wryly into the pick-up.

The crew took this in stride. It was a message that they were now used to hearing. As the scanner tech, he was the eyes and ears of the ship. The human race had been running for its life. These scaly beings from outside of the colonized space had been relentless. No one even knows why they first attacked. The only obvious thing was that they intended to annihilate all humans.

The Captain looked at his tactical display. "Keep our power rotating from shield to shield. I don't want them hitting us in a weak spot or something. We need to plot the next jump and get the hell out of here." He ordered and the navigation officer, Maurice Dedrick, started feeding seemingly random vectors into the computer to plot. Captain Bryon Glass could do nothing more; all that was left was waiting for the crew to carry out his commands. The enemy ships were simplistic in design. They seemed to be just chunks of rock. They had no form to them that was recognizable. They had no engines on them. The scientists still wondered how they moved. In fact, the missiles that their ship was now trying so desperately to avoid were their own. The enemy had somehow turned them back against their attackers. In the history books, no one had ever fought a battle like this and here they were trying to survive their fifth encounter. The Fleet was now patchy at best. The original space Fleet had launched after the

1

enemy only to be blown apart by their own salvos. The chunks of rock did not even shoot at them in that first fight. So surprising was the attack from their own missiles that the enemy had no need to launch anything of their own. Since then, colony world after colony world had been obliterated. Now the enemy was heading straight to Earth. They were going to take out the human race at its source. The small craft bucked again as its own missiles struck home. Fires flared and were extinguished as more of the precious air supply was blown out into space. The ship began to yaw over as the power flashed and dropped. With the power signature gone, the missiles lost their lock and just kept running in on their last heading. Fortunately for the light cruiser, the last explosion had sent them drifting away from their former position and the remaining missiles missed them completely. The enemy stone ships moved past the now crippled human vessel without hesitation. It would be defenseless in the next attack and they had bigger fish to fry.

The enemy Fleet moved in silently in the vast darkness of space and Earth's defenses remained on full alert. The order that had been given was not to fire until they were in point blank range. The human Fleet had been all but destroyed, but massive defense platforms were poised to strike. The Lizard People paid them no mind. They continued in towards the shiny blue planet and all of the defenses fired at once. Nukes rained in and missiles and rockets of every type streaked out across the impossibly short distance. Laser and particle beams reached out to forestall the imminent enemy attack. The chunks of rock were actually taking a beating. The missiles all missed their marks. They had been directed back at the launchers. The beams, however, sliced into the enemy Fleet and caused at least some apparent damage. Then, the unthinkable happened. The enemy launched something of its own. It was some sort of pod and it was not launched at any of the defenders. It sailed in on a straight course, it ignored all types of electronic warfare and it began to burn upon entering the atmosphere of the defending planet, and the home of the human race. The pod continued its descent. The platforms starting blowing up as their own missiles struck them. The beams continued to strike the enemy, but the Lizard's ships showed no sign of slowing down or stopping. The pod fell to the earth and dropped into the ocean within a few miles of Hawaii. The splash was not overly large, but the wave it created headed out to decimate the small chain of islands. The pod continued its descent to the bottom of the ocean and unleashed its fury when it got there. The pod opened above a major fissure in the Earth's crust and the anti-matter that had been contained within caused a ripple of explosive energy that blew the core up through the crust and the Earth did something that scientists would have said was impossible. The planet stopped rotating and belched forth its contents into space. It was like ten thousand volcanoes going off at once in the same spot. The molten nickel core of the planet was ejected and the shell that was once a habitable planet caved in on itself and burst outward into a scattering of debris. The Earth was totally destroyed. The shock wave blew out all the remaining defenses and the enemy Fleet finally started backing away from the carnage. The moon was next to go as the wave struck it with unimaginable force. There was nothing left but gray rocks thrown everywhere.

The now lonely cruiser was adrift in space and a giant wave of awesome destructive power was rapidly approaching. They needed to move now. There was really no choice. The engineering crew was busily restoring power to systems. The back-up generators could get them moving once they were routed to the vital systems. They could not move yet, that was true, but they did have enough power for sensors. The bridge crew had just witnessed the destruction of their home. The whole bridge was silent and there were looks of shock, dismay, and horror on each and every face.

Casey, the lead engineer, broke the silence with his thumbs-up report on the propulsion systems. The navigator wasted no time waiting for orders, he arrowed the ship into the wave and announced to brace for impact. No one knew if the tiny ship could withstand these forces. All they could do now was pray.

With the power coming back on line, the computers began to process the requests that had been placed before the attack had disabled the ship. Frank Muskerini looked at the screen expectantly. Even as the ship bucked and heaved in the wave of the biggest explosion man had ever witnessed, he browsed for the information that he was sure could save them. The lights flickered and he hoped that the power would not fail again. The numbers and names continued to scroll up the screen and he paused as the computer found a match. He was so excited that he nearly forgot to print his findings. The acetate form spit out of the wall and he took it quickly. Then he turned to leave his quarters and headed to the bridge. The ship kept jumping and shaking as the long wave passed and he was thrown to the deck. Blood rolled down his cheek as he climbed back up and ran to the bridge. He got there just as all the trembling subsided. The ship had survived the wave. The fact that no debris caught them was only dumb luck. The captain unbuckled from his seat and strolled over to the commission plate and he ran his finger across the name engraved there. It read *S.S. Lost Cavalier.*

"Thank you, old girl, for keeping us alive again." He whispered to the ship and then he noticed the new crewmember on the bridge and immediately saw the blood on the side of his head and down his shoulder. "What is the meaning of this?" He asked in a tone of authority. The tone brought the rest of the bridge crew out of their shock and sent them back to their boards to update the status of the damage control.

"Sir, I think I've found it." Frank replied cryptically.

"You've found what? Don't you know what has just happened here?" The Captain yelled. He had needed to vent and this was the first opportunity. Even in the back of his mind he knew that it was a little unfair.

Frank looked around at the bridge crew, they were glaring at him. He didn't know why, but he was about to burst with his news. "Sir, I need to speak with you." He said at last. His optimism seemed to crack the shell of the Captain. "Can we go somewhere where I can explain properly?" He added, hoping to get away from all these prying eyes. The Captain pointed towards the briefing room and the two men headed there without another word.

The table was clear of any papers and the Captain strolled purposefully to the seat at the head of the table and sat down. His mood was still quite sour. The high-backed chairs were bolted to the floor and the carpet covered the floor and wrapped up half of the wall. It gave this room a softer look than the rest of the ship. The walls had sconces on them and light radiated up at the ceiling and flowed out into the space. It was beautifully arranged to bring a calming feeling. It was working for Frank, he was not so sure about the Captain.

"Sir, if I may, we have a chance to fix this situation." He offered and the Captain scoffed. "No! Hear me out." Frank continued and the Captain's look soured even more. "I have been searching the archives and I think that I've found the best place to get help." He said a bit triumphantly.

"Just where do you suggest we get help. The enemy Fleet is turning back from our destroyed planet. They will soon be looking for us to finish the job they started. The whole of the human race is lost. Don't you get it?" He asked, his voice rising again with the last sentence.

Frank shook his head. "It is true that we have lost this war." He paused for a moment to allow the thought to sink in. "We are all but defeated here. That is why we need to go elsewhere." He said with a trace of hope in his tone. The Captain began to shake his head.

The historian laid his printouts on the table before him. "I know that we cannot go very far, but we won't need to. The help we need is not in this system anymore. We need to go back." He said, trying to lead his superior to the proper destination on his own.

"Go back to where? You know that we have limited resources here. Stop talking in riddles." He ordered and Frank held up his hands in surrender.

"Okay, okay. What I am suggesting is that we use the sun's gravity to slingshot us around at higher than light speed. We need to go back in time and get the help we need to defeat the Lizard People." He said. It was like a bomb had fallen between the two men. It was a long couple of minutes before the Captain responded.

"You want us to go back in time to find someone to help us defeat the enemy Fleet that has just wiped us out?" He asked, it sounded crazy to his own ears as he repeated it. Part of him wondered if it was even possible. His reason told him that it was not.

"Sir, what I am talking about is going back for this man." He said and he handed the acetate form over to the disbelieving Captain. There was a hand-drawn sketch of a rather thinnish blonde man in a set of robes with odd symbols on it. He did not know the man, but he knew the costume. This man was some sort of wizard.

"What? You want *Merlin* to come with us to the future to fight the Lizzies?" He asked. "The man may have been good in his day, but he could not do anything to help us here. You know how far technology has come since then and you know that it didn't help us in the end. What makes you think this man can help us?" He asked in a challenging tone.

Frank stood up. He leaned over the table on his palms and locked eyes with the Captain. He never even flinched. "This is not some mythical magician like you suggest. Merlin was a real man, but his legend is mostly exaggeration. This man was a true wizard. He is from the final order of Elementalists that according to the ancient texts had the ability to bend the elements to their will and perform miraculous feats. If there is anybody that can help us, then it is him." He stated flatly. "You must admit that here, we have very little of a future left. If we go back for this guy, at least we have a chance to do something meaningful with the rest of our lives." He posed.

Captain Glass stood up and his tone was steel. "I don't think this will work. I cannot see what this man from the distant past could possibly do to help us with the enemy Fleet. Surely the magic is long gone. If it weren't then we would still have wizards now." He said and the challenge in his voice was undeniable.

"The elements are still here. We see air, water, fire and earth. All the pieces he would need to become powerful in our time. Even the enemy ships seem to be made of stone. He might have the ability to rip them apart with a few chosen words. This is knowledge that we have long ago lost. Who knows what he could do. This is the best and only chance we have to right this event. We could bring him back to just a few weeks ago and when the battle is fought, it can go differently." He said. His hope for the success of the mission was evident in his eyes. He honestly believed that they had a chance, no matter how slim. The Captain bit his lower lip as he thought about it.

"It is true that we have no recourse here. The situation is lost. That means that we have to find something else." He tapped his fingers on the desk, weighing pro's and con's in his head. "Surely it would not hurt to find out if it were even possible to pull this time travel thing off." He thought to himself. He turned his attention back to Frank who was waiting a bit impatiently. "Okay, take your figures to the navigation specialist and see if they can confirm your findings about traveling through time. I want a pass/fail and a best and worst case scenario in the next three hours. We will hide the ship from the enemy in the debris for that long. After that, we will have to abandon this quest in order to run. There are so few ships left that I don't think we will get very far, but I still want that choice. I am not ready to just give up to them here and now." He said and Frank nodded. Then the historian bolted for the door but it did not open for him. He turned back to the Captain.

Captain Glass pointed a finger at him. "Do not tell your story on the bridge. I don't want this crew to be given false hopes. They are fragile enough as it is, and to let them fall again…" He let the sentence trail off. "Be discreet and take care of this as quickly as possible. If we decide to go ahead and do this, then it will be time to tell them. If not, they will not even know that the plan existed. Am I clear?" He asked and Frank nodded solemnly.

"Yes sir. I'll get on it right away." He replied and the Captain pressed the button to open the door. Frank darted quickly through it and disappeared from view as the door slid back shut again. The Captain let his head fall into his hands as he leaned on the table. It was the worst day he had ever lived. He was not ready for another let down either.

A Desperate Plan

Frank had a vague idea of what was necessary to accomplish his desperate plan. He just needed to talk to the fewest people as possible so as not to upset the crew. He knew in his heart that this was the only way they could save the day. He just hoped that they could pull it off. He started down in engineering. He needed acceleration values and the weight of the ship and many other little details that had to be taken into account. He also understood that they were very busy right now just trying to keep the ship flying. With all of that working against him, he was still determined to take care of the requirements so that they could make the attempt. His specialty was not numbers, so he sought someone who could help him out with them. The only people he knew that were good with numbers were accountants and engineers. Since he was not looking to get his checking account balanced, he opted for the engineer. So it was with high hopes and a spring of purpose in his step that he entered engineering and stopped dead in his tracks at the turmoil he saw there. This was a small ship and there were always cramped spaces. But none of what he had seen so far had prepared him for this. Engineering was in utter chaos. Steam was venting from more than one pipe on the walls and people were dashing about with toolkits. Status boards were dead and the ones that did work were showing a lot of red lights. He knew that was not a good sign. He tried to flag one of the engineers down and they brushed him aside in a hurry to get to the next repair. The ship had taken a beating with the powerful shock wave and the lead engineer, the chief, was shouting orders as his hands danced across the keyboard before one of the terminals. Everyone looked, and truly was, busy. He backed out of engineering and headed back to his quarters. He decided to put his request through on the computer. Then he would be scheduled instead of just barging in on a shift with a heavy workload. His miracle answer would just have to wait.

After placing his original request, Frank continued on in the system and requested meetings with other specialists he felt he needed for the plan. He contacted Doctor Livengood to see if there were going to be side effects of time travel. He contacted Ken Livingston down in the computer section about computing the appropriate duration and speed required to even start time traveling. Then came the nasty obstacle of deciding when you have gone far enough. He had only a brief outline of when they needed to go. He did not have a precise day or even year. They might miss on the first attempt and have to work their way back. There were so many variables that they made his head hurt just trying to figure out what they were, let alone trying to solve them. He knew now that he desperately needed help. He had his requests all in, now he just had to await the appointments that he would receive back.

He had not heard back from anyone in two hours. The shift change had come and gone and his requests were still in the queue. They had not even gone far enough to flush the queue. This was bad news. The ship and its crew were really busy. Depression started to seep in and he felt the impending deadline creeping up on him. He started paging people on his list. He needed these figures quickly now. He had no more time to waste. Attempt after attempt failed. His messages went unheeded. The power went down and his terminal went blank. The lights in his cabin went out as well. He tried to leave his room and found that the door would not open either. It seemed like a system-wide failure. He heard later that the enemy had left the system and had not detected the small ship adrift in space. The engineering crew had shut down completely when the rock ships had come in close. There was no signature to give them away when the scans came. He had not known that death had been so close for them all.

When the power came back up, the Captain's deadline had passed. He decided to head over to navigation himself to try and get the numbers he needed. He figured that engineering would be too busy trying to restore everything. He stepped into the tiny office and saw that the principal navigator, Maurice Dedrick was seated at the console, typing away. The ship was about to make a small jump and there were a lot of last minute calculations to make to be sure things went off without a hitch. The stocky man kept his pudgy fingers flying across the keyboard and the screen kept filling with numbers. It was truly amazing that he could even read them that fast. He hit *enter* a few times and the numbers scrolled up off the display. Then he clicked on the *send* button and the file was off to whomever it was supposed to get to for proofreading. Maurice noticed Frank for the first time. He started and Frank backed up a step.

"Oh, you scared me." He said weakly. He had been so intent on his math that he had not even heard the other man enter the room. Frank held up his printout.

"I have a problem and I think you and your talents could be of help." He said, trying to engage the man's curiosity. "The Captain told me to come to you for this. At least he told me to come to the navigation section." He added, trying not to corner himself with a statement that could be tracked back to a lie. This man knew facts and figures and he would be the wrong man to upset now. He paused for a moment and then dove on into his presentation. He thrust the printouts forward and Maurice took them. "I need to know if we can sling-shot around the sun and time travel back to when the Earth was still there. In fact, I need to go back a good long way. I can't tell you everything, but I need to know if it is even possible to do this. The computer has a few theories about it, but we need someone with your particular gifts to verify whether or not we can pull it off." He said; the veins in his neck were starting to pop out. He was under a lot of stress. It was only partially relieved when Maurice opened the document and began scanning the initial findings.

"Okay, I can tell you that the theory is sound. I don't know if it has ever been tried, but the idea behind it is quite sound. The hard part is that the ship is not at full operating specs. There will be a lot more variables involved to see if we can do this. I will need a couple of hours of crunching in order to tell you how long it will take to reach a viable solution. We are talking theoretical here. I will start on it now. You can tell the Captain that much, but there will not be a quick answer." He started pushing keys again on the fresh screen. Then he looked over his shoulder to Frank. The poor historian looked deflated. "I don't suppose you can tell me why I am doing this can you?" He asked and Frank shook his head.

"I was told not to get people's hopes up too high. I am supposed to keep this plan to myself as much as possible." He replied and Maurice shrugged his shoulders. Then Frank found a possible motivation for the man. "If nothing else, you will be the first one to make these calculations. You will have secured your position in mathematical history." He offered.

Maurice let out a snort. "You must be joking. There is no one left to carry on a history for. We are basically it now. If we don't find a place to live, this ship will be our portable home forever." He said dryly. Frank had not even considered that fact. He had always assumed that they would resettle somewhere else. Thinking back on it now, he realized that the enemy would simply destroy any planet they tried to inhabit. This really was the end of the human race. The realization struck home and his hope and motivation died a quick, but painful death. Maurice noticed the change and shooed the man away. "You need to know that what you're doing is important. So do I. We need a new plan. If yours will work, then I am all for it, even if you cannot tell me what it is." He said and he winked at the distraught man. "Now go and tell the Captain that I am working on it." He said and Frank left the tiny office to comply.

*   *   *

The Captain sat back in his chair. He let his mind wander to avoid the duty laid before him. He had to write the latest log entry. How do you tell anyone that you witnessed the end of the world? He tried to start a couple of times, but when he went back and read what he had written, he deleted it to start again. The curser blinked at him and he hated it. The unfriendly little prompt was tormenting him now. He so wanted this to be done with, but he just couldn't wrap his mind around the scope of it all. When the door chime sounded, he felt relief wash over him, as the distraction was so welcome. He stepped away from the console and headed for the door. He glanced at the clock and realized that he had been at it for far too long. He pressed the button and the door slid open. He felt the presence like a punch to the chest. Frank stood in the doorway, he did not have his forms, but he looked like he was depressed. The Captain felt the hope drain away from his soul. He motioned for the historian to enter the compartment. Frank followed him back into the office and sat when prompted.

"Sir, I am supposed to tell you that Maurice is working on the figures for time travel. Apparently there were a lot of variables that I didn't even know of. He said that it will take a while before he can tell us if the idea is viable." He said and the sound of dejection in his tone was unmistakable.

Captain Glass saw the downtrodden man in front of him and his own feelings of dismay were reflected in this poor man. He suddenly felt sympathy for this kindred spirit being crushed by the monstrous weight of truth. He fumbled for the right words, but nothing came to mind. His own grief still had him clouded. He instead reached for a brandy sifter that was on the bar behind his desk. He pulled two glasses and set them on the desk and poured liberal amounts in the two glasses. Then he handed one to Frank. This was so out of protocol that Frank simply took the offered glass. He sniffed at it as the Captain sipped his. The bouquet was amazing. This was one of the rarest spirits in the known galaxy. He took a sip and the flavor burst onto his tongue and the sting of the alcohol burned his throat as the liquid found its way down. The warmth settled in his stomach and he suddenly felt just a bit better.

The Captain watched him closely for that reaction and he was ready to bring the conversation back when he saw it. "Let's say you tell me more of your plan. You want to go back to find this wizard. Or wait, an Elementalist you said." He prompted and Frank nodded.

"Well sir, I know that the details have been sketchy. I also realize that right now survival has been too important to enlist the crew in help of this plan. We had to avoid detection by the enemy and hopefully get further away from our demolished home." He said and a lump in his throat required a pause. He forced himself to go on. "What I am suggesting is that we go back further than medieval times. You had mentioned Merlin the Magician. He would have known a few things, but there were others way before him that knew a lot more. What we are most interested in now is finding that lost knowledge. The human race has forgotten something important. I believe that we have been given all of the tools necessary to ensure our own survival. Somehow we lost something key along the way. We were so interested in makings things faster and better that we forgot the old ways. Magic has been completely lost except in storybooks and movies. We need to find when it still existed and learn how to use it or at least bring back someone who can." He paused again. The glass in his hand felt warm to the touch since his own body heat had been transferring into it. The Brandy was making him a bit more talkative. He took another sip and this time, the burn was less noticeable. The warmth in his stomach remained though. "I think this Zack is the key to the whole plan. I found some translations of an ancient text that claims he could do amazing things with the wave of his hand. He had the knowledge and power we seek. He could defeat the Lizzies, I am sure of it." He said and his tone became more aggressive. He wanted to hurt the enemy. They had taken everything from him. They had taken his family, they had taken his home, and they had stolen his future. He had nothing left but the past. "If we can pull this off, we can return to before the enemy came and set up our defenses with the elemental magic and stop those ships from ever getting near Earth." He said with resignation.

Captain Glass swished the remaining liquid in his glass. He had sipped a few times while Frank spoke. He downed the rest and set the glass aside.

"Do you know when this Zack lived?" He asked, taking the plan a little more seriously than he had previously. It did sound like something from a fictional movie. There were no records of anyone doing what Frank had proposed.

Frank shook his head. "Not exactly sir." He responded. The records I found were recorded in the late thirteen hundreds. They are a re-telling of an older story. The reference was mostly obscure but it mentioned a lunar eclipse in the text that I have plotted. It has only happened as described about a dozen times in all of human history. I think we can find him if we concentrate on those times." He concluded.

Captain Glass, Byron, frowned. "Okay so you think you can find this needle in a temporal haystack and you want to pull this ship into the search with you. That much I understand, but how will you know he exists when you arrive at this earlier time?" He asked logically.

"Sir, the texts described some of his accomplishments. They talk of him changing the course of rivers and moving mountains and saving a king from a set of assassin twins." He said plainly.

Byron leaned forward. "A king you say? Who is this king, when did he live?" He asked, the details starting to fill in for this strange plan.

Well sir, the king was supposed to be one Reginald Bently. He ruled a small province in the late ninth century if the texts are to be believed. He is quoted as having ordered Zack, then known as the Master Wizard, to hold back an army of invaders lead by a set of twins. I could find no record of the invaders or the twins to find out who they were. It was simply a notation of an event. As you well know there are no really reliable records for back then. In an attempt to avoid missing our man, I propose that we jump back a little bit farther and watch for this wizard to come to popularity. Then he should be much easier to find." Frank said. The alcohol was starting to slur his words. He set the glass down carefully. He was surprised how much of the liquor was gone. Had he really drunk that much of the stuff? He looked at his hand and then around the room. His head was starting to swim. He was not used to drinking. It had been banned from starships for quite some time. He leaned back in the chair and watched the Captain for the next cue.

Byron looked at his crewman. The man could not hold his liquor, which was obvious. He was, however, normally competent. He was also gifted at the art of seeing beyond a problem to a solution that others might miss. The cockamamie plan might actually work. They were certainly desperate enough to try it. They just needed to get the right minds on the particulars. Frank had said that Maurice was already crunching the numbers. His past experience with the mathematician told him that it would not be long before they heard something. He eyed the man before him. The alcohol had amplified the man's depression. It had also loosened his tongue. He had found out what he wanted to know. He only hoped that it was not all a dream. He wanted to save the day. He wanted to put everything back to rights. He wanted desperately to play the hero. Most of all, he wanted his family back. His ship had been disabled and his defense had crumbled before the enemy might and his shame would not let him forget it.

The chime sounded and the Captain started out of his thoughts. Frank seemed to not even notice it. Byron stood up and stepped over to the door and pressed the button. Dr. Devin Livengood stood outside in the corridor. The captain looked at him twice before he caught himself and responded.

"How may I be of service to the good doctor?" He asked in an amiable manner. The liquor was doing some of the talking. He knew that the stuff was pretty strong, but his depression had made it even more so. "Please come in." He invited and the doctor stepped into the small room with a look of disapproval on his face.

"I got a message from Frank here and it intrigued me. He asked me what effects the crew might suffer during time travel. That request is not unheard of in the medical community, but it is quite rare." He answered and Frank stirred. The doctor looked at him and shook his head. He picked up the historian by his lapels and hoisted him to his feet. "How can you save us all if you cannot even stand?" He asked reprovingly.

Frank tried to focus his eyes. "Did I miss our appointment?" He asked and the doctor snickered. He had thought the man beyond all reason, but apparently there was still a small bit of intellect left. He admitted that it could just be reflex, but he wanted to believe it was something more.

"No, I came to find you. The computer said you were here and that you had been here for a while." He looked at the Captain. He was sure that the leader of the ship was responsible for the condition of his crewman. "We can talk about your plan if you are up to it. I want a little more information before I give you my prognosis." He said clearly and succinctly for the inebriated man he was holding up. "However, it is obvious to me that you will not be of much help for some time. You are drunk."

Frank pushed the doctor away and tried to stand on his own in defiance. He failed and fell back into the chair. If it had not been there, he would have gone to the floor. "It is not my fault; you do not turn away an offer from your Captain." He said with slurring speech. He was not really arguing, merely trying to justify his position.

The doctor nodded to him. "How about we go to the infirmary and try to get you sobered up. If your request is based on a plan or is something real then you may be more important than anyone thinks just now." He glanced at the Captain one last time in a visually scolding manner. Then he carted the historian out of the small room and down the corridor towards the infirmary. They bumped off this wall and that on the way down. Frank was really out of sorts. The Doctor only hoped that no one saw him like this. It would not do his credibility any good to be witnessed.

Despite his misgivings, the two men arrived at the infirmary without a hitch. No one else was in the corridors this late and there were no awkward questions to be answered. Devin administered an IV of glucose to help dilute the alcohol in the bloodstream. Then he readied his coffee pot. A compress on the forehead helped to forestall the upcoming hangover by keeping the blood vessels from restricting. Then he settled down to study the entries in the medical logs about time travel. He cut and pasted the relevant material into a new file and then printed that out for Frank to view once he was ready. The whole process did not take that long, but it was long enough for the coffee to finish and he poured a cup for his patient.

"Here, drink a few sips of this and then tell me what you have in mind." He ordered and propped up the man on his examining table. "We have a lot to talk about."

Frank did as he was told. He did not much care for coffee but he admitted that the strong flavor awoke something inside of him. His mind started to clear a little bit and the caffeine started offsetting the alcohol. His eyes tried to focus but the bright clinical lights were too blinding and he squinted terribly. "Can we talk in the dark?" He stammered and the Doctor laughed.

He stepped over and turned the lights down about forty percent and Frank found the change to his liking. "Is this better?" Devin asked. His uniform was spotless as it always was. He had just carried a man to this room and not a seam was out of place. His smile seemed genuine and his eyes showed that he knew more than anyone ever gave him credit for. Even in the reduced light, his manner was evident. He was on a mission of his own. Frank had triggered something in this man with his request. He had an adventurer's side to him. He wanted to do the things that stories talked about. Time travel was a big step towards the hero status he craved. Doctor Livengood sat down opposite the table. "Perhaps you could tell me what this plan of yours is; then I could tell you if the crew is in danger or not." He suggested. It didn't really sound like a suggestion, it sounded like an order. Even so, the man's smile never slipped from his face.

Frank looked at the doctor and wondered what he could say that would not violate the Captain's orders. Then he realized that a doctor had an oath to protect the secrets of his patients. He felt a little bit better. "What I must tell you, you cannot repeat to anyone else aboard this ship. The Captain has ordered me not to tell anyone who does not directly need to know this." He said and Devin nodded that he understood. He had a coffee cup in his hand too. He had a pang of excitement bubbling up inside of him. If the Captain had forbid gossip; that meant that the plan had some real hope to it. He tapped his foot expectantly. Frank decided that it was all right and plowed on. "I have asked the captain to take us back in time to find the last great wizard and either learn what he knows or bring him here to fight the Lizzies before they destroyed Earth." He said all at once. The doctor's eyes grew wide.

"That's fascinating. How do know about a wizard in Earth's past?" He asked and Frank waved off the question, sighed and then shook his head in resignation.

"I am a historian and a student of human culture. I have been looking into the power and hoping to find a link to it. It is long lost information that we seek now. Our technology has obviously failed us here. The enemy turns it all against us. We need to try something different. If we can do this, we will have saved everybody. We might even be able to erase the destruction of the colonies and maybe prevent the entire war. We can turn this situation around completely." He said with a flurry that was infecting the doctor.

"If we manage to travel in time, why not simply move the initial contact ship away from meeting up with the aliens in the first place?" He asked logically. He looked at the man before him as if he were a child. He sort of loved this position of devil's advocate.

"We know when the first reported sighting was, but not the first actual contact. We also don't know if any of our colonies were attacked before an actual ship stumbled across the enemy ships. It may be that we cannot stop the first meeting from happening." Frank said. His drunken swagger was now gone. He was serious about this. He had done at least some research on the subject before placing his request to the Captain. "We have to find a way to fight this enemy. We know that their ships are made of rock so it is possible that an Elementalist can command them." He added. Devin looked confused.

"What's an Elementalist?" He asked.

Frank paused for a moment, perhaps he was gathering his information in his mind to answer the question, or maybe he was just a bit confused from the alcohol and stimulant battle waging war inside of his body. He took a sip of coffee and then proceeded. "An Elementalist is a wizard that controls the four main elements. They can control wind, fire, water and earth to make things happen. Since rock is of the element of earth, it may be that an Elementalist is just what we need to defeat the Lizzies once and for all." He said with a small amount of pride. "The only problem is that Elementalists have been extinct for a long time." He almost fell over as his energy began to wane. The doctor caught him and steadied him, never releasing the arm. "We need to go back to before the times of knights and honor to the times of mysticism and magic. Then we can find this man who can save the world."

The doctor looked at Frank skeptically. "What kind of power does this man have that he can defeat the enemy of the human race?" He asked, his patience all but gone. "Tell me what one man can do to stop the people that our entire race could not defeat." He pleaded. Frank's demeanor was slipping. The alcohol was starting to win the battle and the end result would be sleeping it off. Doctor Livengood knew this, but he was so desperate to find the answers that he did not care. He shook Frank. "Tell me!" He screamed.

Frank looked at the doctor; the shaking was throwing him even further down the dark tunnel his eyes were already forming. He tried to stay coherent. "He can do anything. I don't know the spells, but he can move mountains. He can cause tornadoes and waterspouts. He can manipulate the elements themselves." He said the last line trailing off as his consciousness left him. He went limp in the doctor's hands. Devin lowered the drunken man to the bed and turned out the lights. The coffee cup was restored to the counter and he left the infirmary feeling only marginally better than he had before. There was indeed a plan hidden there somewhere, but he did not hold much hope that it would succeed.

* * *

Morning came as it did any other day. The crew was on a two-shift rotation. That meant that everyone had down time for the night shift, but only half of them went to work for the next eight hours, then the first shift went to work. The other half would go in about eight hours. Frank awoke in the infirmary and his head hurt. His throat was dry and his tongue felt like leather. He also had the slight after taste of coffee on his breath and his stomach felt queasy. This was not going to be his day. He stepped out of bed only to find a cold floor instead of the carpeted floor in his quarters. He froze in place. He knew that he was not home. Where was he? There were no lights on, but a panel in the grayness in front of him looked impressive. He put both arms out in a feeling maneuver, trying to find something that could orient him and help him to determine where he was. He found a wall. It was the standard ship's bulkhead wall so there was no clue there. It was, however, a good starting point to finding a door. He traveled along the wall until he found a set of switches. It was the luck he was searching for. He hit the first switch and the lights came on. He saw the bed that he had been laying on in the middle of a sterile room. He was in the infirmary. He didn't remember getting here. His clothes were still on so he had not been here all that long. He checked himself for injuries but found nothing other than this thudding headache. He dialed down the lights somewhat to relieve the throbbing they were causing. He checked his watch and found that he was in the morning shift. His duties did not restrict him to one shift or another, so he was used to not having to be somewhere when the shift change came. No one was expecting him at some little cubicle aboard this ship. He saw a coffee cup on the counter and he moved towards it. He hoped to jog his memory a bit. His head was swimming so he decided to sit down on the bed instead. The cup would have to wait. He pressed the call button but no one came. He was confused. Wasn't someone in here supposed to be monitored? His indignation flared. He was unhappy at the system that let him find his way here. He was angry with the empty room that seemed to be his prison. The door activator switch was turned off. He could not leave. Now no one would come if he called for them. He was cut off from the rest of the ship. He could only wait and try to remember what had gotten him here in the first place.

* * *

Maurice had been crunching numbers for hours. The files related to time travel were exhaustive. No one had as yet done it, but the speculation ran high on just how it could be done. The most dangerous part seemed to be getting close enough to the sun to use its gravitational pull to accelerate beyond what the ship could accomplish on its own. The ship was used to fending off the absolute zero cold of space. Now they were going to ask it to take temperatures that would defy the instruments. He had fuel masses and ships' tonnage calculated in and he was waiting for updated figures for the mass of the cargo and personnel as he continued working on the acceleration curves and plotting the best course. By the numbers he calculated, this plan was showing its first signs of hope. The requirements seemed to be within tolerances for the ship they had. He checked and re-checked his figures as the possibility began to infect his mind with enthusiasm. Hope was something that he would have sworn was impossible in this dark time, but nevertheless it was true. He took another sip of the coffee that kept him going for projects like this. There were three other empty cups already on the shelf near the terminal. He paid them no mind at all. The latest set of projections came up on the screen. The computer had been working on them for over twelve minutes this time. The arcs displayed as the graphical interface plotted the path around the circle of the sun on the left side of the screen. The right side was a column of scrolling numbers. He looked at it carefully as the stresses hit the ship and the icons stayed green throughout the journey around the sun and back to Earth. It was wonderfully reassuring. He settled in and checked the findings and the data that the projection generated. He took the animation frame by frame, looking for anything that might cause a problem for the flight. There was nothing untoward there. It was a clean run. He would double-check it with the mass figures when they arrived. It looked like he had a solution though.

Maurice went to page Frank. The man did not answer at his terminal. He queried the main computer for a location and the sensor logs told him that his quarry was in the infirmary. That seemed odd, but the good feelings of having reached a possible solution required him to tell *someone*. The excitement was building and he knew that it would become overwhelming. He also knew that he could not tell anyone else. Other people would ask too many questions. He didn't even know what the project was about. He copied his findings onto a memory stick and headed to the infirmary.

* * *

Repair crews had been working non-stop now for a couple of shifts. In truth, the work put many a crewman's mind at ease. They all knew what had happened. They all felt the weight of extinction closing in on them. They felt the hopelessness of their plight. The busy work had only temporarily supplanted the grief that was surely to come. The distraction had paid off. Most of the ship was back up to full operations. The status boards were now all green and all that remained were minor details to be worked on as time permitted. The major repairs had been completed in record time. Trying to avoid the inevitable flush of emotions, the workers began to look for more work to do. One of them, Casey Fulton, sat at the engineering terminal and checked the requests for another assignment. There was always something to do, but right now there were more than ample volunteers to do it. He thumbed the controller on the side of the screen to scroll through the list. Most everything he saw had been assigned. He sighed and continued his search. He ran across a message from some Frank Muskerini. He opened the non-descriptive entry and glanced at the request. There was nothing in the message that said exactly what he was looking for. Casey shrugged his shoulders and accepted the job. He pulled up the schematics of the ship and queried the sensor relays for Frank's whereabouts. The man was in the infirmary. He shrugged again and headed that way. There was no time like the present to get things done.

* * *

Frank was still lying on the bed when the door chimed. He pulled himself upright and looked expectantly at the door. He could not open it from the inside; maybe someone else would open it from the outside and let him go. He stepped over as the chime sounded again. He hoped that whoever it was would check on him by opening that blasted door. The indicator on the door changed from red to green and the door slid into the side wall. Maurice stood in the doorway and Frank felt the urge to shake the man's hand.

"Thank you; I have been trapped in here for hours." Frank explained. He wanted to bolt past the man and out into the freedom of the hallway beyond. He resisted the urge to do so, but only just barely. Instead he waved towards the corridor. "Shall we proceed to someplace where you can tell me what you found out?" He asked. Frank had not missed the excited look in the man's eyes and his constant fidgeting. He could tell that Maurice was ready to burst. He led the mathematician/navigation officer down to the lifts and then to his quarters. They could speak privately there and maybe he could get some good news for a change. If there was any indication in his companion's mannerisms, it was a positive one. He hoped that he was right. They reached his doorway and Frank was relieved when his thumbprint activated the door like it should. He ushered Maurice inside and bade him to sit down in the only chair. Frank sat on the bed. "Okay, tell me what you've found." He prompted and it was exactly what Maurice had been waiting for.

"You wouldn't believe how hard it was to get some of these figures." He began. The look on his face suggested that he marveled in the success of his own work. "The course plan seems solid and the margins are good. I think your plan for time travel is possible and even doable for us." He blurted out.

Frank sat back and let out the breath that he didn't realize he had been holding. It was the news that he only dreamed of hearing. He wanted to pinch himself to see if he was awake now. He felt that it would have looked bad though so he kept his hands at his sides. "Great, why do I sense that there is a 'but' coming?" He asked, feeling his skeptical side emerging in the face of this apparent success. The throbbing in his head could have caused such a mental stammer.

Maurice looked at this man carefully. Frak was good at second guessing things. He was good at reading body language as well. It was almost uncanny. "There are a few tests yet to run. I need real data for the mass of the ship's crew and cargo. I don't foresee any real problems there, but I intend to run the simulation again once those facts are available to me." He said. His smug smile was almost irritating. "When this all gets out to the public, I shall be famous." He said at last.

Frank looked at him cock-eyed. "There is no public. We are all that is left." He scratched his head and then ran his hand through his hair. It was pretty dirty now and he made a mental note to get cleaned up before going to the Captain on this. "If we don't succeed, there will be no more human race. There will be no future for anybody. We will have our own lifetimes and they will most likely be cut short by the Lizzies as they hunt us down relentlessly." He leaned back on his hands. The weight of his own words was dragging him back down that spiral of depression. He shook his head and sat back up again. "What you have is our only hope. I am somewhat relieved that you think it will work. I suggest that you cross check your work with another specialist. Pick one that will be able to see things from a different angle than you do. Let no one else know what we are up to. If this gets out, we may upset the rest of the crew." Frank cautioned.

Both men looked up when the door chime came. Frank stepped over and pressed the open button for the door and it slid away. A grimy looking engineering type man stood in the doorway. He had a toolkit in his left hand and a dispatch notice in his right. His coveralls were covered in black grease and oil. His smile was warm and his rough and calloused hand set down the tools and reached out in offering of a shake to Frank.

"You requested engineering support?" He asked and Frank took the offered hand and pulled the man into the already cramped room.

"Yes, you are just what we were looking for." Frank responded and both Maurice and Casey looked surprised. They did not get the chance to voice their confusion though. Frank barreled on into his next point. "Maurice here needs some of his figures checked on a possible flight plan. I need someone from engineering to check this out and tell us the feasibility of the plan." He said, not divulging too much to this newcomer.

Casey looked at the two eager men. He admitted that this was not the emotion he was expecting. This whole ship was suffering from depression. It seemed odd that these two were somehow immune. He looked from one to the other. "What plan?" He asked simply. Maurice shrugged his shoulders and Frank turned red. Casey looked at Maurice incredibly. "You don't even know what the plan is?" He shook his head. "Then how do you know it will work?" He asked. Maurice started to answer and Casey held up his hand to forestall that reply. "No, I'm sure there is an operational reason why you don't know." He looked directly at Frank. "Am I to assume that your security measures also apply to me?" He asked bluntly.

Frank nodded. Then felt that a verbal answer was required here. "Yes, the Captain ordered me not to divulge the details of the plan to anyone. I am to find out the feasibility and then report back to him. Maurice here has done some preliminary calculations and they appear to be favorable. I would like you to review them and give us your opinion. You have an engineering background and he has a navigational background. There may be more variables that have not been considered. We need to be absolutely sure of ourselves before presenting our findings to the Captain." He said with a professional tone that belied his inner feelings.

Casey considered the two men for a long moment. He wondered just what he had gotten himself into. He realized that this type of project could keep him busy for a while. He decided that busy was better than sitting around thinking. "Okay, give me your findings and a terminal and I will do what I can." He said and Maurice handed over the memory stick. Frank directed the engineer to his own terminal in the crowded room and then Frank sent Maurice back to his own quarters so that he wasn't hanging over Casey's shoulder. It was a nice touch and a good move for their relations.

Casey dove into the first string of setups and he immediately got a clue as to what they were trying to do here. This was time travel. He looked up at Frank and the man's face gave no indication of his inner feelings. He wanted to delve into this some more. "Why don't you go get something to eat for us? I will get started and hopefully I can have some kind of answer for you soon." He suggested and Frank left the small space to retrieve the food.

Casey took the opportunity to dive in fully. The calculations were pretty extensive. The idea was to accelerate towards the sun and slingshot around it to achieve a faster than light velocity and open a temporal rift in order to travel back in time. The calculations did not say where, or actually when, they were going. It only covered the feasibility of the journey. The odds looked good based on these numbers. He added a few variables for hull integrity and potential structural failure. Things that he cared about and others took for granted. Then he added some more accurate numbers for the acceleration curves that were projected. He did not have mass numbers for the crew and cargo, but he did have more precise figures for the mass of the ship itself and its displacement ratio. Those would prove invaluable during the trip through the sun's corona. The hydrogen gasses there would be like racing through the upper layers of an atmosphere. The friction and drag coefficients would come in to play. He added as much as he could on the fly. Then he started paging through schematics and pulling numbers he did not know offhand. The calculation tree was growing rapidly. He kept plugging away and adding figures whenever he saw something that needed more. This was an ambitious project and the numbers presented had really only scratched the surface. Hull and architecture should be called in too. He knew that the security wouldn't permit that. He sent a few inquiries out and hoped that they would respond without too many unanswerable questions. Then he forced the computer to run the simulation again. The acceleration continued on, but was more irregular this time. The drag coefficients took their toll on the simulation just as they would in real life. The ship started the dicey slingshot maneuver and started to decay the orbit into the outer edges of the sun's corona. The heat index climbed rapidly and the mission ended with the ship crashing into the sun's surface. He frowned at the numbers that the ship ended on. Even if the ship had survived, the crew would have been cooked inside like a pressure cooker. He adjusted the flight plan to sweep in a little more gradually. The new arc would start the turn before the gravity took a real hold on the ship. Then the slingshot would already be started as they dove into the fire. He watched again as the ship followed the course. He witnessed the wider arc and he smiled as the temperature readings remained above normal, but not fatal anymore. Then the ship started its turn and the sun caught it like a shortstop making the turn to throw to first base for the double play. The ship slipped through the mists and the heat and rocketed out the other side. Then it wavered and blasted into faster than light speeds. The computer ended the simulation with a 'success' message and Casey smiled at the screen. He had done his best to make sure that everything was accounted for. There would be more information coming in. He would add it when it did. For now, though, he was pleased with the results. He was watching the simulation again when Frank came back with the food. Two trays and a couple of drinks had pressed the man to the limit of his personal balance. He set down the first tray and gratefully grabbed the remaining tray with both hands. Then he settled down with it on the bed.

"Oh, I see you've run the simulation." Frank noted. He was not close enough to see any detail and he had not seen it from Maurice at all. So he was unaware that it had changed somewhat since it was first run. He leaned forward for a better look. The ship swung wider than he expected and it made the turn with amazing speed. Then the simulation reported successful transition into faster than light speed. He nodded his approval and sat back down. "So what did you think?" He asked Casey.

Casey chuckled as he thrust a sandwich into his mouth. "It needed a bit of work. I have done some of it already, but I think the original theory is sound and that with a bit of fine tuning, we can make this work." The speech was garbled through the chewing but Frank was listening closely and he made out what was said.

"So you have others that need to see it before it is ready?" Frank asked as he nibbled a carrot. He didn't much care for them but his diet usually lacked some of the essential nutrients one needed to maintain for a prolonged space journey. Since there were no longer any closer destinations, he figured he'd better catch up with the program.

Casey thought about the question. Did someone else need to see this? "No." He answered finally. "The Figures that I have asked for should make a pretty good likeness to reality here. Once they are in and firing, I think we can safely say that we have a good plan here." He said and he took a sip of the red liquid, it was cherry, so that he could swallow the bite that seemed to dry out his throat. "I am assuming that this is only the first phase of a plan. Are you allowed to tell me more?" He asked, ever conscious of security and shipboard gossip possibilities.

"No, I'm sorry, but you can't even mention what you know now to anybody. The Captain has requested that any specialists involved know only the bare minimum before he is ready to announce it to the crew." Frank said. His face showed no emotion during the response. He was like a robot repeating responses that had been pre-programmed in. Casey nodded his understanding.

"Well, when you do come out with this, I am curious to hear it. Please make sure I get at least a little credit for this." He smiled and it was Frank's turn to nod in understanding. They were both switching their concentration to the meal. They were finished before too long and an awkward silence stretched on as they realized that this meeting was over.

It was Casey that broke that silence first. "When the figures come in, I will return to finish what I started. Then you can go to the Captain or whoever you have to have this approved through. I wouldn't suggest doing anything before that." He warned. Then he stood up and collected the two now empty trays and his tool kit. He hit the button to open the door and left. His last words rang through Frank's mind a couple of times and he looked again at the simulation. His own dream was there before him in all its mathematical glory. He decided to page Maurice back to see what was done to it. He was pretty sure that it was different. It didn't quite match his mental image. Either way, Maurice deserved to know what was going on.

*   *   *

An enemy awakens

The great stone ship searched the surrounding area for debris. They had fought the interfering animals that had slaughtered their ancestors so long ago. Now they were following the orders and eliminating any survivors. There had been a sense of satisfied revenge when the enemy home world was destroyed. Sure, there was a catastrophic loss of life. But it was also a symbol of strength. They had broken this enemy's back. They would annihilate the rest of them and be forever rid of this human vermin. It seemed that these people had found almost every nook and cranny to hide in. The eradication process was taking longer than had been forecast. The Lizard Leader looked at his surroundings. His people were busily searching and putting these wretches out of their misery. They found no spirit left. These people were weak and useless. Their machines had done very little to the stone battle Fleet of the warriors. Their place in the universe was now forfeit. The resources that they were consuming now belonged to the victors. This was war after all; humans were now the vanquished and downtrodden. They were the losers. The supreme commander would be pleased. The only problem with that was that so far, he didn't know what was going on out here. There was no communications equipment that could help them. The lookouts were still pointing out pockets of humans and they were lining up weaponry to take them down. It was the gruesome, but necessary task that had been given them to do. With machine-like efficiency, they blew another small pocket of enemies out of existence. The sensors showed no more signs of life so they moved on. The spiral pattern they took would cleanse the system and then they would move out to the further infestations of colonies. The initial destructions had taken place according to the battle plan, now was just cleanup. A power surge in the distance caught notice and the stone ship veered to the new course to track it down. It was only a smaller craft, but orders were orders.

Commander Zarg's tongue flicked out expectantly as he prepared to savor another kill.

* * *

Frank awaited his chance to show the Captain the plan and he now had high hopes that it would be approved. The numbers looked good and the simulation ran flawlessly time after time. Maurice had come by and acknowledged the changes and he was impressed by the engineer's input. The course correction made perfect sense to him as he read the new parameters. Casey had stopped by and plugged the latest figures in and now they could account for the mass readings on the ship as well. A manifest had given them the numbers they needed. They had ignored the inquiries about why they needed these figures. If all went well, the asker would find out soon enough. The new plot was perfect. The ship would slingshot around the sun and pass by without any real damage. The velocity would peak at much higher than what they actually needed to break the time barrier, intellectually speaking. It all looked good. Casey even said so as he left Frank to his thoughts with the simulation running on a loop in front of him.

Frank decided that it was time to bring this before the Captain. There had been enough delays. The human race was still becoming extinct out there. They needed to move fast. He took the updated memory chip and switched off the terminal. Then he checked the computer sensor logs for the Captain's whereabouts. It was a short distance from his current location so he headed out to meet with the man who controlled his destiny.

Frank tapped on the door standing shakily outside the small cabin. There was a shuffle inside and then the door opened. The Captain sat in a chair, his clothes were disheveled and the young woman he was with was wrapped in a blanket. Frank's face turned red as he realized what he had just done. He apologized and backed back out of the doorway. The door slid shut and he cursed himself for not being more careful. He started down the hallway slowly at first. His mind was in shock at his own stupidity. The odds of gaining the Captain's favor had just dropped sharply. His frustration was rising as he knew how important this was. He hit the wall and then quickened his pace before someone responded to that as well.

A few moments later, the Captain stepped from the room and smiled at the girl on the bed. She was still just wrapped in a blanket and it made his mind go over all that they had done there. He stepped clear of the doorway and the metal door shut and cut off his view of the young lady. Then he looked up and down the hallway. No one else had seen anything. He just needed to take care of the historian and his activities would remain unnoticed. He headed with purpose to his conference room and the terminal in there.

Frank had gone to the lift and not known where to go next. His entire existence right now was dedicated to the mission he had worked on. Now he had that presentation and a fuming captain to bring it to. It didn't seem fair. He rode the lift to the top. The observation deck was there. He looked out at the stars through the multiple windows that allowed them to see the entire night sky above them. He still held the data chip in his fist and his palms were starting to sweat. He put the precious chip into his pocket and forced himself to calm down. He had just gone into a breathing exercise when the beep came. The Captain was calling him to his quarters. Frank gulped and headed back to the lifts. The ride seemed to take forever and the hallway seemed to stretch out before him as he traveled the relatively short distance to his fate. He rapped on the door and there was a sharp response to enter. The door slid aside and he stepped in, not sure what to expect from this meeting.

"So, you have a problem with authority." The Captain said and Frank looked confused. "You have interrupted me and I cannot have that happening again. How should I deal with this problem?" He asked and Frank was afraid that this was the end of his career. He remained silent and the Captain shook his head. Then he sat down and looked at Frank with a deathly serious glare. "You saw nothing." He said plainly and his tone was dangerous.

"Yes sir, I saw absolutely nothing." Frank responded and the Captain nodded. "What I actually need is to show you the numbers for the mission." He tried to focus the man back on work. "We need to act quickly on this before the window of opportunity closes on us and the human race is doomed." He added, hoping to be safely past the last conversation. The Captain looked thoughtful for a moment and then he made direct eye contact again.

"You want to go all business, I can deal with that. Show me what you've got now." He ordered and Frank pulled the memory stick from his pocket. "Here are the findings. There were three of us that worked on this and we think that it is complete now." He ventured. The Captain took the stick and placed it into the socket on the table. The screen displayed over the table. It was projected from lenses in the glass tabletop. The left side was the scrolling numbers, and the right side was the simulation with the ship slipping around the sun and into history, literally. "So this is what you've come up with?" He asked and Frank nodded.

"Yes sir." He added when the older man glanced at his lack of response. "We think that not only is it possible, but it is necessary to go quickly before the location of the sun and ourselves make this course invalid."

"So this is a 'hurry up' mission? I don't like that." Captain Glass responded. "I want some time to make my speculations on this data. I may even ask in a specialist or two of my own before I take your word for face value." He said and Frank looked just a bit put out. The he realized the safety of the ship was involved and it all made sense to him now. "Okay, so if we go ahead with this plan, how long would the preparations take to get under way?" He asked seriously. He had a look of doubt on his face.

'From what I gather, the main delay is not the ship. It is in telling the people what we are about to do. The possibility of reversing the current disaster can be real. They need to understand that and be dedicated to the mission. We're going to need everybody at their best if this is going to have any chance of working." He proclaimed directly. "The calculations show that we may just pull this off. You know better than I what that could mean. I had no family left here. You had some on Earth. We can bring them back. Surely it is worth the attempt." He lost his steam at that point. He had treaded a dangerous line trying to evoke the Captain's feelings. It was a card that maybe he should not have played. This time, however, his gamble paid off dividends.

"Okay, we can do this." The Captain said as if Frank had just planted the words in his mouth. "Inform the station heads that we are to start the preparations now. We need to be out of here when the chance is at its best." He was building up his energy in order to inform the crew. Frank could tell this and he just smiled back supportively.

The Captain had mustered himself sufficiently. He stood up with authority and led Frank out of the cabin. He went straight to the bridge as Frank turned back to engineering to await the announcement. He wanted to be available in case any questions arose about his plan.

*　　*　　*

The Captain reached the bridge and everyone came to attention. He waved them back down. He strolled purposefully to his command chair.

The officer in it stepped aside quickly and released control of the vessel to his superior officer. Captain Glass looked out at the bridge and he leaned forward and hit the communication systems activate button on his board. It was set to broadcast and an alert chime rung out all over the ship. All decks and stations stopped what they were doing and looked up at the speaker boxes set into the walls around the ship. He cleared his throat and that was the first thing broadcast to the crew. Then he used his full voice and spoke to everyone as if he were in front of a large crowd. It was not all that far from the truth.

"We have a mission before us. You know what has happened. The enemy has beaten us and the Earth has been destroyed. The colonies were not spared either. Our race is about to die a horrible death at the hands of an aggressor we were ill-prepared to face." He said in somber tones. He let the moment hang there for a few seconds longer as the crew thought of people they had lost. Then he drove forward towards the announcement. "We have a plan that will give us a chance to repair the damage that has been done here. I won't lie to you. The chances are slim. However, they are real. We can go back in time and set things right." He paused for a couple of seconds as the shock swept across the ship. "I know that nobody has attempted this before. I also know that we cannot find an answer in the here and now. It is too late here. We need to find the answer elsewhere, or rather elsewhen. I think that this plan has the one and only chance of keeping our species alive. We are to go back in time and bring forth a wizard. The magic that has long been lost to us is the only thing that will prevent the Lizzies from killing us down to the last individual. Preparations are to being made immediately and we need to get underway while the conditions are favorable. Plus there is always the danger of being located by that enemy Fleet out there combing the system for stragglers like us." There was another pause as the real danger underscored the need to leave right away. "You must all know that this mission will be dangerous. I have weighed the risks involved and have determined that the consequences of not going outweigh any personal risk we could be taking here. I need each of you to go above and beyond what is normally expected of you. Do not be afraid to point anything out. The more we learn along the way, the more chance we have to actually do the unthinkable. I know that you have the spirit of heroes in you. It is now your chance to show it. Know that if we are successful, then the rest of humanity will never even know that they were in danger and that we intervened. It will just go along as it always has, blind and happy. Our duty is before us and our destiny awaits. Good luck to all of us as we undertake this monumental journey. That is all." He said and he released the broadcast button.

Hopelessness had begun to creep in all over the ship and now there was a new hope. The mental energy level aboard the ship rose sharply. The initial shock started to ebb away and a new determination was being born. People had something to do now. Casey had prepared for this and had downloaded the plan to the main computer. Now the specifications showed on all of the displays and everyone on board could see what they were about to attempt. The engineering crew scrambled and the reactors were all brought online. The navigational numbers were fed to the helm and soon everyone started strapping themselves in as the ship shot forward. It came to the proper heading and began its run. The sun came into view on the main screen and the beauty of it caught the bridge crew for a second. The sound of the engines on full was all that was heard as the people were all silent in the moment. Then a flashing and beeping light pulled the attention of the tactical officer.

"Sir, we have a bogey on our tail." He announced. They were channeling all of their power to the engines. The electronic shielding would not be available. They were a sitting duck. Albeit a rapidly accelerating duck, but one without any kind of protection.

The Captain gripped the arm of his chair. "Who is back there?" He asked; he already knew the answer as the computer began to take them through the flight plan toward the sun's corona.

"Sir, it is an enemy ship, one of the big ones. It is the stone battle cruiser that we faced before based on the laser scoring we put on them. They have begun to pursue, but they are quite a bit behind us. I think our acceleration curve caught them by surprise." He offered.

The Captain gritted his teeth. The timing was bad. They needed to get out of this time now. He could not turn to engage the enemy ship. He was committed now to the course. He called to the engineering department for more speed. To their credit, the engines peaked about thirteen percent higher and the enemy fell back a little more quickly. They were now out of the attack range of the enemy weapons. The sun was now larger. They were still heading towards it, they were about to veer a bit to the outside and then enter the channel to sling around it using the gravitational pull. The ship's icon looked just like the simulator. The only difference was that there was a following red icon as well. All they could do now was wait as they shot through space faster and faster.

* * *

The Lizard Leader looked on as the enemy ship started to run away. Humans had fled before his might before. It was not all that uncommon. He ordered his ship to follow and it began to accelerate as well. As he watched, he noticed that the enemy ship was getting smaller. They were actually running away successfully. He could not let this one escape. He demanded more movement from his ship. The stone behemoth obeyed and they slowed the shrinking ship a bit. They were still losing it to distance. The humans seemed to be running towards their own sun. It made no tactical sense. They would need their shielding to prevent from being cooked inside their metal conveyance. His people could kill them easily then. Of course the enemy was fleeing madly. They could have lost their senses. Maybe they were committing suicide instead of being slaughtered. He decided to watch for a bit to see. It was always interesting when someone decides to end their own life in order to avoid embarrassment. In truth, it was a more honorable death than he would have given them. It made him wonder if there were true warriors among these filthy humans.

The human ship continued to go faster and faster. They were now streaking away from his stone ship and he was getting unhappy about it. A sound from the side made him look over. His second showed him an arc with his finger in the air. The leader knew then what the enemy was doing. They were using the gravity well of the little star to shoot themselves so fast that the faithful could not follow them. They would not succeed. With the arc course in mind, they veered off of the current course in order to cut the ship off as it cleared the other side of the sun. The giant stone ship launched and spikes of stone like giant lances hurled towards the spot where the ship would be once they finished their run. Then he waited and watched as his shots moved rapidly towards the enemy's destruction.

* * *

The *Lost Cavalier* shook and began to heat up as it dove behind the sun. The enemy could not get a lock on them now. That was small consolation to the heat they were now experiencing. The creaking and groaning from the ship's hull made more than one crewperson nervous. The speed was incredible and the ship shot out of the sun's corona and out into open space again in a blinding flash. Great spires of rock sailed towards the tiny ship as it came around the sun and fate stepped in to avoid the catastrophe.

A large solar flare erupted from the surface of the sun and pushed the ship off course and away from the incoming fire. Part of the dorsal fin on the ship was burnt away and their speed shot up higher than even the best projections had predicted. The ship was moving so fast that time stood still. Colored light distorted around the perimeter of the ship and it danced and strung out behind the vessel like a torn rainbow. Then the stars disappeared. Light could not penetrate the continuum. They were on their way into history.

The enemy leader witnessed the impossible. The ship vanished and a wispy light trailed it into oblivion. He stopped the stone ship and thought about what he had just seen. Had the enemy ship imploded? He had not seen such a thing before. They exploded for him usually. His display showed only small amounts of debris. They had not been destroyed then. It was incredible that these animals had somehow managed to elude him. He set his ship back to the original course the enemy took. They would move fast to try and find what the enemy had done and follow them. Orders were still orders. His task force was busily eliminating other threats. Only his ship and his brother's were available to chase this missing enemy ship. His brother had brought his ship up to the first one in order to provide support and witness to the kill. The two stone ships started the passage. They applied speed faster than they ever had before. They followed the arc to the degree and the sun's gravity caught the ships and slung them around the curvature just as they had seen the enemy ship do. Then they too began to get the color distortion of light around their ships and both of them vanished into the void as well. The leader looked on and his crew was frightened. His look was not of fear; it was one of a hunter after a particularly difficult prey. The chase was on. He was now glad that his brother had come too. It would be the perfect witness for his final victory. He licked his chops in anticipation of the glory and adulation of the home world. His eyes saw only the blood rage. Oh yes, the hunt was truly on.

THE MIRACLE OF LIFE

The trees in these woods had stood forever. The timeless nature of them blended well with their inhabitants. The elves of the highest trees communed with nature at a level that was never truly understood. The vines and branches were their roadways in a vast network of arteries that formed the Elvin community. Green moss and tree bark were common adornments and also offered wonderful camouflage for the protectors of the forest. Proudest of the elder races, the elves often sought seclusion from the rest of society. Their long life spans and low birth rates made them especially susceptible to extinction. They were fiercely aware of this fact and it drove them to maintain their isolation. A new disease could wipe them out. War could ravage them to a point that was unrecoverable. For all that, they were great fighters and healers. Life was so precious to them that they celebrated each and every birth among them. This was an extra special day. An expectant mother lay in her humble home giving birth to twins. This was so unheard of that everyone was anxious to hear the news of the actual delivery. The shaman had already blessed the mother and the domicile, all that was left was for nature to take its course.

The inside of the home was warm and inviting. The humble abode was lined with trinkets that the mother, Allarya used as an herb gatherer and mixer. Medicinal herbs hung drying all over the place and the few individuals present were cramped in the small space. Old Narcilla, midwife of the clan, watched closely in the almost darkness. Her low light level vision was extraordinary, even for the elves. Her sharp pointed ears could catch the slightest changes in heartbeat of the unborn children. The pains had been coming regular now and everything was proceeding normally. Trevend, the expectant father, stood by to help in any way he could. He got the impression that Narcilla only tolerated him. He watched his wife closely. His vision was also keen and he could see the effort she was going through. Her brow was dripping with sweat and she gripped the coverings on the bed as she gritted her teeth. She made no sound and the midwife tilted her head as she caught the skipping of a heartbeat that meant that the child was ready to emerge. The first one had already dropped and rotated in place a few hours ago. Now it seemed ready to go. She leaned forward and looked into Allarya's eyes. The gray eyes of pain looked back at her.

"You must push now child, the baby is ready for you to." She instructed in one of the softest voices that Trevend had ever heard. It was all amazing to him. Allarya tensed and bore down for a few seconds and released again. The pain did not fully subside this time. It was really time for this to happen. She took three deep breaths and then pressed again. The pain shot up and she clamped her chin to her chest as she pulled herself upright by the bed covers. The first child's head appeared and in that miracle of birth, popped out into the open air. There was the briefest of moments delay as Narcilla pulled the newborn male child from the womb and wiped his nose and mouth and then struck him sharply on the rump. There was a startled cry out of the baby and she bundled him up for warmth right away. Then she listened again to the mother and child's heartbeats. She hurriedly cut the umbilical cord and tied the end off with a natural twine that prevented infections. Then she handed the child over to his father as she concentrated on the next child. Allarya was already bearing down from the natural instincts of an expectant mother. Narcilla nodded her approval and leaned forward again. "Your son is beautiful, now let's see what else you have in store for us." She said softly and then the pain shot up again. Allarya was already sore from the last birth and now she thumped her head against the wall of the tree they lived in. Then she took those quick breaths and bore down. Trevend marveled at her strength. He watched her as she again performed the miracle that was rare enough here. She birthed a girl. Narcilla picked up the child gently and repeated her previous actions. In seconds, there was a second cry out and then the warm wrap. There was some clean up to do and she began to inspect Allarya for damage. It was not unheard of after a child-bearing. Fortune was on the mother's side though and she was fine. She was simply exhausted. Narcilla placed the girl child on her mother's breast and both parents cooed softly to their children as the midwife excused herself from the family. Outside were many of the villagers and she smiled at them. She leaned in close to the crier and his face lit up as well.

He looked out at the expectant waiting elves and he held his arms out to encompass them all. "We are blessed with two healthy new children. It is one boy and one girl." He said and the whole tops of the tree erupted in applause and shouting for joy. Narcilla let it play out for a few minutes, and then she raised her slender hand for attention. The obedient crowd silenced and she nodded her appreciation to them. "The naming ceremony will be three days hence." She said aloud and the entire crowd erupted again. She waited patiently this time. They were due this celebration. "They shall be joined to the spirit tree and become members of this clan." She completed and the true celebration began. The festivities went on long into the night.

*   *   *

Elsewhere in the kingdom, there was news of a different kind. King Jerome Leopold sat upon his throne. He had his advisors before him and one of them was troubled. The astrologer looked on as the witch made her strange signs and wards. There was little he could do to belay the fears that this woman was about to put into the king. He had also seen the black marks on the future of the monarch. He had just not been able to discern what was wrong. Somehow, this witch had. She finished the dance; it was a blend of eroticism and arcane knowledge. She finished up kneeling before the king. She held the claw of a chicken and held it out for the king to see. It was twisted and bent. She slithered forward and whispered just within the man's hearing.

"Sire, your kingdom will fall. You will be slain without heir and your name shall be lost to the memories of history." She said and the king's eyes went wide. His own ego would never allow such a turn of events to come to pass. His brows lowered and he set his jaw.

"Tell me what you know." He commanded and the witch flinched at the ferocity of the request. She did a few steps of the dance she had just completed to regain her composure and then she slithered back into place to pass on her knowledge to her sovereign.

"A pair of twins shall come from a far off land and they shall bring chaos and destruction to your peaceful kingdom. The signs are that this will take place a few years from now, but now is the time to strike. If this is to be avoided, you must act now. These twins have already been born. They are alive and somewhere outside of your kingdom. Their souls are strong and dangerous." She hissed and the king stood up abruptly.

"Bring my scholar. I will send a proclamation to the kingdom. This must not come to pass." He said. He stepped past the witch to the other advisors. The astrologer caught his eye, the first of the four men standing there in the half-circle. "And what do you say about this vision?" He asked in a demanding tone.

"Your majesty, I cannot see as clearly as she does, but there is a definite blot on the horizon. The moon passes into Aires and soon it will reach a summit and this foretells of doom and foreboding. The Gemini constellation has been interfering so it could mean that twins are involved. I cannot tell for sure. It is still too soon to interpret all the signs. I do, however, have a deep fear within me that what she says is true." He finished and the others nodded their agreement.

The king glared at them. He didn't like the idea of his subordinates knowing more than he did. That was why he had them here, but it always made him uncomfortable. "Do you all concur this finding? Am I doomed to die from the hands of these twins from a far off land?" He asked and the men bowed to him and withdrew a few steps. The king leapt forward and struck the robed man on the end on the top of his bowed head. The doomed man fell to the floor and the sound of his chin breaking on the polished marble was unmistakable. "How dare you not tell me of impending doom when you discover it?" He screamed at them.

The astrologer stepped forward, daring the king to strike him down next. "Sire, we met in council about these very findings while the witch contacted you. It is our belief that if she had not contacted you, we would have very soon anyway. We do not come to you with half-truths and guesses. What we present must be verified and double-checked before it is put before the royal ear. To do otherwise would be remiss in our duties. We serve only you and we live for that purpose alone." He said and he bowed dangerously close to the enraged king.

Jerome took in the scene and his rage started to die down a bit. The explanation made sense to him. He needed to get out of the throne room for a bit. He had thinking to do. He needed to draft his proclamation first and then he would think on this prophecy, a lot. He knew that the only one that could prevent this disaster was he himself. "You must be gone for now. I will summon you again when I have figured out what to do. Then I will get your opinion on that course of action. If there are any changes or developments I want to hear about it right away. I want to hear it even if you don't know what they mean. We are all in danger now." He harrumphed and headed back to the throne where he plopped down heavily into the overstuffed chair. The high backed wooden frame bore his weight easily and the cushion let out a puff of air and dust flew from the impact. The advisors left the room and the witch was the last to leave.

She looked back at her king and she felt pity for the poor wretch trying to avoid his destiny. In her experience, it never worked like that. He would only bring pain upon himself for these efforts. The guard closed the huge doors and she could see him no longer. She headed back to her bones and potions to try to determine who these mystery twins were and how she could locate them.

The next people into the audience chamber were the scholar and his scribes. The king felt the new eyes and he looked up from his thoughts. "Ah good, you are here. I need to release a proclamation to the kingdom. I have just been given terrible news and it is now up to you to make sure that it does not come true. The proclamation should be sent to all of the neighboring kingdoms as well. I want all twin children put to the sword. Twins are such a rare occurrence that we will not lose too many citizens for this and my reign will be assured. Also put it to my guard captain that I am not to be visited by twins at any time." He ordered and the scholar looked at him in terror.

"Kill children sire?" He asked, hoping that he had somehow misheard this man of power. "We don't actually want to kill children do we?" He asked for emphasis.

The king glared at him. He was not used to his commands being questioned. "Send the proclamation as I have commanded. I will not be slain by a set of twins from a far away land without an heir. All twins shall be put to death to avoid this horrible prophecy." He said louder and more forceful than he had the first time. His anger was growing and that would only spell doom for these groveling citizens if they pushed him further. The scholar realized this and he bowed before his king making sure not to take his eyes off the man.

"It shall be done as you command." He said to supplicate the angry man who held his life in his hands. "We shall do it immediately." He added to make sure that there were no questions as to his loyalties. The scribes took down all that was said and they now closed their books and headed for the door. The scholar took his leave as well. The king watched them go. The fire in his belly was still there. It needed a place to vent. He needed to hurt or kill something. It was not the persona he put forth for the people. It was the person he used to be as he fought for one lord or another in the defense of this same country and kingdom he now commanded. He had earned his post on the battlefield. He was an animal inside with the instincts of a hunter and the skills of an assassin. He was a monster in a gold embroidered outfit and a crown. He was a caged beast and his frustration would require some serious physical activity to simmer down. He stepped away from the golden throne and headed for his sparring field. He had personal trainers and he had already decided that they needed a few bruises to keep them on their toes. A slight smile crossed his face at the thought. He left the confines of the aristocratic room and entered the arena of combat. Here he felt more at home than anywhere else in the world. His workout started and the bodies flew from his might as he began his therapy. They would need the healers later on this day.

* * *

Before the dark decree could be released to the general public, another life-changing moment was shared in the Village of Mountainbrook. The humble residence of Karl and Romana Slovney was aflutter with activity. The time of their first born was drawing near and the preparations drove Karl out of the small hut. He paced about outside unable to see through the pane of the window to his own cottage. The sounds he heard were not all that encouraging. He heard his wife scream and then he heard a child scream and then he heard his wife scream again and there was commotion inside. He wanted to bolt in there but they had warned him not to interfere. So he shoved his hands into his pockets. It was cold outside. His hut was located outside of town on the northern side and he could see the shifting hills off in the distance. He had long ago grown used to their constant movement. It played tricks with the eyes and he was not ready for that just now. He turned away and looked at the firewood that he had already chopped. The bucket of water was almost frozen and he set it closer to the hut in case they needed it. Then he paced around some more. The talking kept on going and the last sound he would remember forever, the sound of weeping. He could stand it no more. He burst into the room and saw the midwife and her servant crying over his wife. There was blood everywhere and he nearly gagged at the sight.

"What happened here?" He bellowed; the shock was starting to take away his strength. "What happened to my Romana?" He screamed and dove to her side. Her skin was still warm but her breathing had stopped. She was already turning blue. He looked around at the two women and they stepped back from him. His eyes turned dangerous. "What happened here?" He demanded.

The midwife knelt down. She was holding the baby. "You have a son." She said weakly. "Your wife had trouble. The inside of her was all broken up and she bled everywhere. She is lost." The lady said solemnly. She handed the baby boy over to his father. "Have you a name for this child?" She asked and tears welled up in Karl's eyes.

"Romana wanted to name him Zachery." He replied. The moment was one of the finest and one of the worst he had ever experienced at the same time. He had gained an offspring, an heir. He had also lost the love of his life and his pain began to turn to resentment. This helpless infant had taken from him his one and only love. He handed the baby back to the midwife roughly. "Take it away. I do not want to see it again." He said and stormed to the back of the hut. He grabbed the sheets that his wife had woven and he wrapped his beloved in them. Then he dragged the body out of the hut for proper burial. His grief blinded him to the women and they left him with the babe in their arms. They feared for the newborn's life if they left the boy there.

That would be the last time that I saw my father. I don't even remember him. I was raised by my uncle. He became my father. His wife, my aunt, became my mother. He was a good man, but he was always worried about things that I considered petty. Still, he worked hard and we had food to eat and a roof over our heads. So it was all in all pretty good. He had a son, Joshua, so I was just another child in a busy house. I ended up cooking and cleaning when I was old enough. I was able to help the woman that was my mom now. Oh yeah, and that Zachery business, call me Zack. I've never gone by Zachery and I don't intend to start now.

I guess the most important thing to remember is that I never fit in where I grew up. I know what you're thinking; no one ever fits in. It is always harder for us than anyone else. Well, that may not actually be the case, but if felt like I was alone my whole young life. In fact, it was not until I was twelve that my life gave me a nudge in the right direction. I remember that it was a summer's day and the wheat was about chest high. We would be out cutting it down soon enough and there were always chores to be done. I was fetching water when the cloaked man approached the walkway to our little house. I stepped up my pace, risking splashing the water and having to go back to get more. I really wanted to see who was visiting. You see we hardly ever got visitors. They were mostly customers who bought the food we grew on Uncle's lands. We were far enough removed from town to not even think of it. By the time I got to the house, he was already inside. I took care to wipe my feet and I placed the bucket next to the porch where it was supposed to be. Then I entered the house timidly. I peered around the door and saw the two men sitting at the little table that uncle had made years before. They stopped talking when they heard me enter. I closed the door and stepped into the main room. The house only had two rooms. There was the main room and the sleeping quarters. My lanky form must have looked unsightly to the man. If so, he didn't show it. His eyes looked cold and gray at first. His face was impossibly old. To a twelve year old, he looked a hundred. His robes were obviously of fine weave, much better than even the women from town wore. There was gold stitching on the hem and around the wrists. The garment looked to hang loosely on his form.

"So young man, come and let me get a look at you." He said, his tone much warmer than his eyes would have suggested. He looked at me as if he were looking through me. It was most disturbing. "You are to be trained. Do you know what that means?" He asked. I didn't know and I shook my head.

His eyebrows rose a bit. "You don't know who I am, do you?" He asked. His tone started to get a twinge of impatience to it. "I am a wizard." He said flatly. My mind went into shock. I had heard the other boys talking about great magic and fierce battles with monsters and swordsmen of godly skill. Surely he could not be one of those.

"Sir, I did not know that wizards were real." I replied in my child innocence. He let out a belly laugh that shook the windows in their frames on our small house. He was genuinely amused and I felt embarrassed. My face turned red and I'm sure that only fueled his laughter even more.

"Let me assure you that they do exist." He said at last. "In fact, you are to become one like me." He said in a tone that was so serious that all laughter had been forgotten. He made it look easy to swing through emotions and then get back on to topic. "You will come with me to my place of study and you will learn how to read and write. The arcane arts require a strong discipline and I shall teach you that as well. It will be hard work and the rewards are something you will not understand for years." He said to warn me. He leaned closer and I could see a swirling mist in those gray eyes. He had more depth there than I had ever imagined. "You will be tired, hungry and frightened. In the end, you will be stronger for it all and you will be a great wizard." He said directly. I did not know what to think. It seemed so unreal.

"Yes sir." I replied. It was the only thing I knew to say.

The wizard looked at uncle. "We will leave this afternoon and you will be given the standard compensation for your efforts." He said. I didn't understand it then, but I had been sold to this man of magic. Uncle no longer wanted me, or the money was good enough that he wanted it more. I remember weeping at nights while I considered that. Eventually, I gave up on my old life and embraced the studies.

Studies, what a funny word for the slave I became. Clean the floors, scrub the walls, trim the hedges, and polish the tableware. It seemed there was no end to the menial tasks to be performed in the boarding school that the old wizard brought me to. The work was not unlike what I was used to at home, so I figured that everyone lived like this. I had been there for about two weeks when the first moment of excitement came.

The day was hot since summer had come into its own by now and I was busily sweeping the front cobbles in the massive front yard to the complex. The stonework had been placed around the perimeter to keep people out I guessed. The work was pleasant enough and while I was out there, the bullies could not pick on me. The other students had arrived earlier than I had so they felt superior to me and let me know about it daily. My hair was shorn to almost bald to prevent infestation and I was issued robes. They were rough and heavy. They were also just like everyone else so it gave me a sense of belonging. While I swept, a carriage approached. The horse pulled it along with a regal gait and I stopped only briefly to marvel at it before my better sense told me to look busy. I worked the cobbles with the broom vigorously while the carriage stopped and the driver climbed down from his lofty perch to open the door for the passenger. It was like right out of a fairy tale. I had never read one since I could not yet read, but I had been told stories in the bedchambers. The woman who stepped from the carriage looked frail and thin. Her posture was one of superiority and she stepped down with only the merest of assistance. Her white robes were lined with golden glyphs that were somehow different from the ones I had seen the master wear. These looked much older and she stepped on the cobbles like she was floating above them. She stopped when she got to me and her soprano voice was like music when she spoke.

"Is your master in?" She asked and I looked up to see the most beautiful face that I had ever laid eyes on. Her golden brown hair was nearly to her waist and her long thin hand reached out to touch my head. She waited patiently while my mind tried to function again. Then she started to chuckle and I turned red. "Please tell him that I have arrived." She instructed and I left her to the path as I ran to comply with her order. I carried the broom with me; her amusement continued as I tripped over it in my haste. I scrambled up and dove into the main entrance and shouted for the headmaster. An acolyte stopped me and shook me to calm down my rush.

"What do you need?" He asked in scorn. This was a breech of protocol to go shouting in the main entrance and I realized it too late. I tried to give him the message and my words were cut short. His hand struck the side of my face so hard that I sprawled to the floor. The impact with that solid marble floor was worse than the initial hit. "You should not have come in here. You know that you trainees are not allowed in these hallowed halls." He said with venom in his tone. He raised his foot to kick me and a flash of light blew him away from over me and he skidded unceremoniously across the floor. I tried to look up but my vision was blurring from the throbbing in my head. I tried to speak and I croaked out that we have a visitor. By then there were more acolytes here and they ignored me for the new visitor. The lady had made it into the entrance. She was fast enough to see what had happened and I felt ashamed. The acolytes were bowing to her and she sent her driver over to pick me up off the floor.

"I have just witnessed an injustice within these sacred halls. Someone will have to answer for this." She said. Her singsong voice cut through all resistance and I felt big rough hands lifting me. He took me to the vision of a beautiful woman again and she reached out and touched my head. The throbbing subsided and she spoke some words that I couldn't understand. In moments I was able to see again. She wiped the blood from the side of my head. I hadn't even known that I was bleeding. "You were only obeying my instructions and I am honored by your personal commitment. We shall see each other again. I think I can find your master myself now." She told me and then I was released; I bowed to her and her driver and then I picked up the broom and went back to my work on the cobblestone path outside. I did not know who she was, but I imagined that she was important. She had done something I didn't understand. She had healed me. That was amazing. When the work was done I went back to the sleeping chamber to clean up before the evening meal. The other boys there kept their distance, but they were all eager to say something. I could feel their stares as I went about my business. I started to leave and one of the older boys stood in the doorway.

"What did you do?" He asked. He sounded like he was fighting a mixture of curiosity and jealousy. The curiosity won out in the end. "The acolytes are all abuzz about you making contact with a visiting witch. They say that she even cast a spell on you. What happened?" He asked and the other boys all closed in to hear the answer. I looked around and realized that I was not going to get out of this one without telling them.

"Well, I was out sweeping the cobbles as I was told to do this morning. The carriage came and stopped at the end of the path and a woman in white robes stepped out. She is like an angel. She told me to inform the master that she had arrived and I hastened to comply. When I came into the great hall I was hit by an acolyte." I said and they all gasped.

The larger boy, Gavin I think his name was, looked at me in horror. "You went into the great hall? You're lucky to be alive." He marveled and I nodded to him that he was right. I understood that I would have to describe it to them later. Right now they just wanted to know about the witch.

"Anyway, when he hit me I hit the floor pretty hard. I couldn't see and my head hurt. I think he was going to kick me or something when she stopped him. I couldn't see what she did but I know that it was some kind of spell. She was too far away to have physically struck him down. She had me brought to her and she touched my head and it stopped hurting. Then she released me from her command and I went back out to work." I concluded and they all looked on amazed. "I am hungry, can we go now?" I asked and they all backed away a small amount. Gavin slid aside to allow me to leave and I thanked him accordingly. Several of them were with me as we walked the old worn halls to the eating chamber. The dusky room was utilitarian gray and the large wooden tables were old and scored. The tin cups and plates were easily cleaned and the gruel they served was slopped into them from a large ladle. It was all very efficient and nutritious enough. It was also very boring. I vowed to someday eat fine food. Surely a caster of spells could be well fed. We got into line and waited for the process to grind us through. In a few minutes we were all seated and spooning up the slop. Then we left in an organized manner and rinsed the plates and cups in a large barrel and hung them up on a rack. They would be scrubbed later; it was just to get the larger pieces off. We headed back to the sleeping chamber and there was a surprise there waiting for us as well.

The headmaster had heard of what had transpired and he was none too pleased. The older trainees were lined up at the end of the beds and we fell into place alongside them. He paced the length of the long room and then turned around. He had been counting us. He knew how many were supposed to be here. He seemed satisfied and he then started looking at faces.

"I heard that a trainee violated the great hall and was struck down for it while in the presence of our honored guests." He said and his tone was unpleasant. "I am also to understand that this trainee was simply following orders and therefore was justified in this instance. It is therefore my decree that this incident is over and there will be no punishment given for this offense." He said and his eyes sparkled a bit when he next spoke. "There will be a special exhibition of skill in the courtyard on the morrow. There will be seating for the acolytes but you may also attend if you wish to stand. A special section has been reserved for you to witness the spectacle and power of the witch from the elves. You are not to do anything that will disgrace us so be on your best behavior. This is an honor that first year students rarely receive." He turned to go. Then he turned back when he reached the doorway. "Remember that you are representing me out there. Be there at two bells sharp and be clean and orderly." He left the room and everyone seemed to be in shock. The excitement would crescendo all night. A couple of the other boys congratulated me for avoiding trouble and I tried to melt back into the crowd to think and dream about the next day and seeing that lovely woman again. The Headmaster had said elves. Could it be that she really was one? She had been thin and slender. She had been so radiant. Perhaps she was a mystical being from ages past. I went to sleep with a smile on my face after the chores were done.

*   *   *

My First Magic and the Grand Display

The morning chores went by so fast that they were all done well before the two bells. All of us trainees were cleaned and dressed and excited about the prospect of a break in the monotony that was our life. The promise of a school of magic had almost been forgotten. Now it was the primary thought of all of us lowly trainees. The courtyard was completely packed. The grandstands had been erected and the acolytes were crammed into them to the point it looked like it would collapse at any moment. It was hard to believe that there were so many students here. The area that we had to stand in was small in comparison. We lined up as instructed and the view was dramatically less than stellar. I was still excited though and the rest of us strained and craned our necks to see what little we could. We had no idea what to expect anyway. Would the display take place on the ground? Would it happen in the sky? We knew nothing. None of us had ever uttered a word of arcane power. We had no skills other than manual labor and as yet, no background knowledge that would prepare us for what was to come.

Trumpets sounded in the distance. There were no trumpeters so we were confused and elated by the blast of sound. They made a regal fanfare and the crowd of acolytes erupted in applause. At this point, we still could not see anything. The sun began to heat us all up along with the excitement. As tightly packed as we were, it was getting sweaty and itchy in our robes. Now that the show had started, no one even noticed anymore. The chariot that I had seen before sailed in from above the trees. It was really flying! We watched with our mouths open as it gracefully cruised in and settled down in the open yard before us. The driver climbed down as he had before. I fully expected the radiant woman to exit the carriage through the door in its side, but that was not in the plan this time. She burst through the top of the carriage her body aglow with amber light as she lightly twirled around as she ascended. Her robes fluttered around her as she reached a height that was dizzying. Then she spread her arms out from her body to stop the spin. Her ascent also halted and she hovered above the field and looked down upon the spectators. The winds were whipping around as they held her aloft. She moved forward and pointed down to our section of the field. We all looked around to see what was going on. The driver trotted over to us. He seemed to be scanning the faces. His eyes met mine and he smiled.

"You are to join me out here now son." He said as he did the impossible. He reached through the crowd and dragged me out by the arm. In truth I did not resist. "You are a part of this show today. The Mistress has a special plan for you." He said as we walked out to the carriage. He pointed to a spot on the ground and told me to stand there. I did as he told me. My eyes were still fixed upon the heavenly beauty above us that so resembled an angel, even more so now. He settled back in the driver's seat of the carriage as she mesmerized the crowd with aerial acrobatics. The winds swirled and lifted her in all directions and she rode them like a wild horse or a trusted animal. Then she commanded them to set her down and she stepped gracefully on the soft grass. The grass grew up to reach her. The blades leaned in towards her as if they wanted to be with her. Then vines sprung up at an unnatural rate and unfolded around her like a protective cocoon. Then she reached her palm up towards the sky and fire erupted from her palm. It shot up in a rolling ball and dissipated into the heavens. The fire was nearly fifty feet high and she swung her arm around in a circle. The flame ball became a thread of fire in a spiral over her head. The vines mimicked the spiral on the other side and formed a double helix of power about the amazing witch. Then the fountain in the yard began to react. A waterspout formed as the winds blew the water into her desired form. They danced just as the vines and fires were. There were now three double helixes of power in the courtyard and she stepped out of the one above her head and strolled over to me. She smiled as she got closer and her eyes showed recognition.

"Ah, my young champion. Are you ready to cast a spell for me?" She asked. I jumped. I had never cast anything. I had not learned even one word of power. I tried to tell her so but she knew what I was thinking. "You need no skills for this casting. All you need is to trust me." She paused a moment. "Do you trust me?" She asked.

"Yes Madam." I replied. I was still under her spell of beauty. Perhaps she knew all of that too. It was not until now that I noticed her pointed ears. She really was an elf. Her deep eyes showed no evil and I felt completely safe in her presence. "What would you have me do?" I asked, ready to take this next step.

She smiled even wider. "No fear in you. That is a promising start to your career." She said and then she handed me a small stick. It was sanded smooth and painted gray and purple as if by berry juices and sand. Somehow I knew this, but did not understand why or from where. The tip of the thing looked charred, like it had been in a fire. It was light but instantly felt good in my hand. I knew nothing about such things but decided that it was better not to point it at anybody. I lowered the tip to the ground. She nodded her appreciation of the small act and she leaned close to my ear. "You must say the word of power to activate the wand." She said and I looked at her confused. She just smiled and waited for me to do something. I looked at the wand and thought about the word. She was not going to tell me what it was. I had no idea what the wand could do so I got no clues from its function. I imagined the wand in my mind. I wanted it to do something for me. I held it out in a safe direction. Then I surprised myself.

"Please, wand of power, tell me what your purpose is and how I may fulfill it." I said to the wand and I heard a voice in my head. The voice said only two things... It said 'tempus confuto'. I looked at her to see if she had heard the voice as well. She did not look all that inspired. She was simply waiting for me to figure it all out. I pointed the wand at the fire and vine helix and uttered the words. The double helix halted in place. It was locked in time while the other one continued on its merry way. I had frozen time for only one of the towers of power. The elf witch looked at me with pleasure written on her face. I pointed at the wand again and said 'tempus refero' and the tower was released from its halted spin. I then handed her back the wand. It was more than I wanted to do for today. The applause from the bleachers reached my ears and I realized that it was now for me. I blushed red and the lady witch knelt down to look me directly in the eyes. She was looking for something. I don't know what.

"You will one day be a powerful wizard. I know that you are young, but you have the gift. You have the sight and the hearing to embrace the ways of the ancient magic and that is a rare thing indeed. So it was not merely chance that you were out sweeping yesterday morning. We were meant to meet and you needed this nudge towards your true potential. I will speak with your headmaster and ensure that your studies are accelerated. The world cannot wait for them to get around to training you. There is too much work to be done. This will be difficult for you, but you must be strong. I know you have it within you, do not falter and save us all in the end." Then she stood up and waved her arms. The magic all dissipated and then she sent up both arms palms together to launch a flash display that lit up the whole sky with golden birds that flew out among the crowd and dazzled the minds of all present. Then she retreated to her carriage and left me standing there, just as dazed as the rest of the onlookers. Her driver snapped the reigns and the carriage flew off back over the trees and left our sight. Apparently the show was over. When the daze ended, the whole crowd applauded again. The sound echoed back from the tree line and then we were ushered back inside the massive school building. I was directed away from the other trainees. They took me to a chamber with fancy tapestries on the walls and a woven rug on the floor. There was a writing desk and parchment in the middle of the room. An elderly man sat at the desk and scribbled his perfect text onto the page. I could not read the writing, but then I could not see the pages from where I stood anyway. This seemed to be just a holding place for now. This was not my destination. The headmaster stepped into the room and I got immediately nervous. I had not caused any if this; I was simply along for the ride. Now I may be expelled for breaking their traditional path of instruction. He didn't look angry, not exactly. He looked more confused and maybe agitated than directly angry. He motioned for me to follow and I obeyed. We left the solitary man and his ceaseless writing and stepped up the stairs to an office of massive proportions. There were paintings on these walls and the large desk held so many things on it that the eye could not take them all in. It just looked like clutter. The headmaster strolled to behind the desk and sat heavily in the overstuffed high-backed chair behind it. He grabbed a long bulbous pipe and lit it with his outstretched finger. He puffed a few billows of smoke and then he returned his attention to me.

"You seem to have made an impression." He said almost casually. "I need to know something though." He said and his tone turned dangerous. "How did you know how to use the wand?" He asked and I started to shrug my shoulders. I stopped myself before finishing that blasphemous move. I straightened my back and looked directly ahead.

"Sir, I asked the wand how to use it and heard a voice in my head tell me two power words." I said and I thought back to what it had said. Somehow the words were not in my memory. A look of confusion spread across my face. "I can't seem to remember what the words are now." I admitted and he nodded as if he understood.

"Words of power are like that. You use them and they vanish from you. It is as if they are consumed in the casting. Still, what you did out there was impressive. Your peers did not let us know that you had this potential. Can you explain why this is?" He prompted.

"Sir, I didn't know that I could do that. It was not until the lady handed me the device that it occurred to me what to do with it." I answered plainly. This was all still so new to me. I had no answers for myself, let alone for him.

"Well, you have done something that is unheard of in these halls. You have passed from trainee to acolyte in the first year. Nobody has ever done that before. You will still have chores and tasks to perform, but you will also receive instruction in magic. If you cannot handle anything, let me know immediately. It is no sin to admit that you need more training before doing something difficult or maybe even impossible. That is what magic is for, doing the impossible. You will be reassigned living quarters into the next wing and you will have to deal with the resentment that will naturally follow you into this accelerated training program. Your new peers will have paid their dues to get where you have been placed. Respect them and understand where they are coming from. It will make it easier for you to gain their acceptance that way. I am told that the witch will return to check on your progress in a couple of months so work hard and don't let us down." He told me in that stern voice that signaled the completion of the speech. So, dismissed as I was, I left the room and found an acolyte standing there waiting impatiently for me. So it was that I started my actual magic training.

*   *   *

Travel through Time

The *Lost Cavalier* streaked backwards through time. Its path was constant but the difficulties were mounting. The ship's stabilizer had since broken off and the ship's mass was now different from the calculations. There was also the problem of knowing how long to remain at warp for the desired effect. This was almost all guesswork at this point. Captain Glass looked out from the command chair. He had long since lost any of the amusement he had gained from the streaking lights. Now he was ready to see the stars normal again. The problem is he did not know when to slow down. The preliminary calculations suggested that they needed to be at warp for about two hours. He looked down at the timer and it told him that the two hour mark was still four minutes away. He pressed the communications button and warned the crew that they were about to decelerate. Then he paused until the timer hit two minutes away. He looked up at the helmsman.

"Take us down to the threshold of warp please." He instructed and with slight variations in thrust, the ship began to slow down. The streaking lights danced and changed with the speed differences. They formed complex patterns and dazzled the eye anew. The timer now had fourteen seconds left and the Captain ordered the ship to drop out of warp. The throttle was dropped down to half and the ship drifted at warp. Now the engines were being reversed and the lights streaked out as if being grabbed and they pinpointed back into the stars they represented. The ship had successfully warped. The only question was where, or rather when, were they? The Captain looked around the bridge and the crew seemed to be sighing in relief. He couldn't blame them.

"I want a damage report and let's get ourselves to Earth to see what time it is here now." He commanded and orders were issued all over the ship. He stood up from his chair. The crew paused for a moment for him to speak. "Well done people, now let's see if we can do this mission or not."

He said and then he paraded from the bridge. The normal duty officer for this hour stepped over to the command chair and sat down.

"I have the bridge." He said to the electronic log.

The ship passed all of the diagnostic tests and they were soon off to find Earth again. It was a long way from home and it was home at the same time. The very idea of it was hard to wrap your mind around. It seemed almost laughable that they were going to the past to save their future. Still, they had made their first big step in that direction. The shiny blue and green marble came into view and they looked on in awe. The first thing they noticed was that the defense perimeter did not exist. They had successfully traveled at least to before the space Fleet had been formed. That was a good sign. It still remained to be seen where they had ended up. But at least they had traveled. The engineers were even now updating their data on the trip and they hoped to determine when they were in order to more accurately predict any future jumps. It would have been foolhardy to believe that they had reached the correct time with that first jump. They also had the added problem that the enemy had seen them before they vanished from time. No one knew what the Lizzies could do. Could they track the ship and realize just what had happened? Had they simply thought that the ship had been obliterated by the solar flare and the subsequent missile attack? There was no way to know. They entered Earth orbit and the science specialists started to get excited.

"Sir?" One of them piped up. The duty officer looked at the young woman with interest.

"Yes; what have you found out so far?" He asked in a sensible tone that helped to quell the excitement she was having difficulty hiding. "When are we?" He asked directly.

"Well sir, we are obviously back in time quite a bit. There are no industrial toxins in the atmosphere. The ozone layer is still fully intact and much of the landmasses are undeveloped. Not all though. Based on some of the architecture in the European sector, we are at least in the seventeen hundreds somewhere. There are old fashioned wooden ships down there. There are no automobiles and no skyscrapers. The North American continent seems mostly undeveloped as well. There are fires and settlements dotting the eastern coast so we could be near the revolutionary war era. We can check for the British ships when the orbit comes around again." She said in a rush. She was obviously excited with what they had accomplished so far.

"Very good. Let me know when you have been able to verify your findings. If what you say is true then it is probably better that we do not land this time. We will make another jump backward in time and try to find this wizard." He said reasonably.

*   *   *

Elsewhere on the ship damage control teams were inspecting and repairing what they could around the ship. Casey had climbed up to the dorsal fin on the ship and the melted metal stopped his ascent. His pressure suit warned him that the atmosphere was gone here. He had closed all the hatches behind him as was protocol and now he was glad that he had. There was a hole in the top of the ship. The dorsal fin was gone. There was only an open stump there. He understood immediately what that meant. It meant two things. One, the pilot would have one hell of a time bringing the ship down into an atmosphere without the vertical stabilizer the fin had once held. The second problem was even more dangerous. With an open wound, the ship could not come close enough to the sun to try for another time warp. They would need to repair this before they could attempt it. The interior bulkheads were never designed to handle the stresses of the heat of the sun. The exterior plates were a just barely situation as it was. He cursed their luck. Then he laughed. He expected luck with the situation they were in? It was just so unbelievable. The outside plating could be replaced, but it would be almost impossible in orbit and they would not have enough of the raw materials to fabricate the entire fin. They could just do a patch job out here. They needed to land and get some ore to be processed into the materials needed. He climbed back down and went through protocols to avoid venting anymore of their air as he could. Then he keyed the microphone in his suit.

"Sir, this is engineering team four reporting." He said with his professional voice. He hoped it masked his own disappointment. He waited a moment and then he repeated his message. "Sir, this is engineering team four reporting." He said into the pickup. This time he could hear his own impatience in his voice as it echoed back to him electronically.

There was static on the line and then it crackled to life. "Team four, we are receiving, proceed with report." It said and he thought he recognized the voice. He decided not to mention any names in case he was wrong.

"The vertical stabilizer is completely gone. We will have to adjust the computer to compensate for this on re-entry to the atmosphere." He said first. The officer of the day looked perplexed. He wondered why they would have to land at all. They would just jump again and fix it there. He started to say so, but the report wasn't finished. Casey continued his report. "The hole left behind from the missing fin is open to the outside and our shields will not protect it from the heat of the sun. We cannot do another jump until we fix the hull at least. We can do only a temporary patch here in space. We will have to land and acquire more metal to fabricate the fin. Only with the ship complete will we have a good chance to complete our mission." He said and the man in the command chair gulped.

"Then what you are saying is that we are stuck here until we fix this?" He urged. He was hoping that he was wrong. Somehow he doubted it though. The Captain was not going to like his report.

"That's affirmative. We will need to complete repairs before we can move forward, or rather backward, with our mission. We need to set down somewhere that we can mine some ore so that we can process them into the components needed to complete the repairs." He said. His tone was flat, emotionless. "I would suggest that we get a second opinion on this. I really don't want to be right here, but the way I see it, we need to land somewhere near mountains. That would give us the best chance to expose a vein of ore and lessen our down time. Or the ultimate would be finding an existing mine that we could get into and out of before anyone knew that we were there." Casey offered and the duty officer looked thoughtful, if unhappy.

"Noted in the log. See what we will need and I will pass your recommendations on to the Captain." He said in that professional tone that meant washing his hands of the whole problem. Casey made a note of the change and responded in the affirmative.

Captain Glass was sitting up in bed. His head hurt again. He could not get the image of the Earth from his mind. The disaster had been complete. There should be no coming back from that one. He was doing all of this in order to cheat the fate that had befallen him. His mind would not let him sleep. The people that he had lost still haunted him. He was always tired now. He would probably always be tired from now on. He hadn't truly believed that this time traveling thing would work. Sure the theory was there and had been for some time. Now they were back in time quite a ways and his doubts were slapped in the face. They were actually doing something. Hope began to flicker in his subconscious. Maybe this *could* be done. He shook his head to keep himself on the reality of the situation. This was a long shot. In fact it was one of the longest shots he had ever heard of. A wizard was supposed to save them? It sounded crazy even to him. Still, they had taken that first step. If nothing else, the crew had something else to focus on. Maybe they had sleep problems too. He could check with the doctor, but he felt it better not to bother the man. They had gone back far enough in time to lose the damage that human civilization had done to their planet. Even in the worst-case scenario, they could live out their lives here in the fresh and pristine environment below them. All they had to do was stay out of time's way and live hidden away from the general populace down there. He frowned at the thought of their equipment falling into the hands of people that wouldn't understand it for centuries. Still, the thought of time travel and the ramifications were always in the forefront. They would have to destroy everything and start afresh. It would be most rewarding. There would be a lot of hard work, yes, but most rewarding. He rolled over to try to find that elusive sleep he needed so badly.

*   *   *

A Battle for the Past

What the Captain and his crew did not realize was that their travel through time had left a trail of shifted temporal particles behind. It was like a distorted ribbon of color behind them and the Lizzies had no trouble following it as they followed the tiny ship back through time. The trail ended abruptly and the Commander ordered his ship to slow down. His brother followed suit and the two mammoth stone ships appeared before the red planet near the target planet of the humans. The small red globe obstructed their view of the prey so he ordered them to maneuver around it. At this distance, the metal box of the humans was invisible. They had to be there somewhere though. He decided to cover both sides of the green and blue planet. He sent his brother to the far side as he headed in directly. They easily outmatched their prey and it would not be long before the mission was complete. The weapons were ready and his bloodlust was rising unbeckoned in his soul. His mouth turned into a snarl and the rest of the bridge crew felt the shift in mood. They wanted to see this kill too. It was why they were here. They were warriors after all. The hunt was drawing to a close. Victory was to be savored and the chase was equally as important. These humans knew how to run. That made them exciting. Millennia of instincts drove the hunters as they closed in on the unsuspecting world before them.

* * *

The news that they needed to land somewhere was not welcome to Captain Glass. He ranted and he raved and then he considered the mission and acquiesced. He was just considering where to put down when the radar went active. The display started flickering as the updates pulled computer power from their current calculations. The tactical station took the priority and then everything stabilized. The crew took a sharp breath as the large stone ship headed towards them. The Captain saw the screen for himself, but he wanted a second opinion. "What do you think tactical?" He asked in a brisk tone. Because of the distances involved in space combat, decisions needed to be made very quickly and then once made they took a long time to play out. So it was imperative that they get all the information that they can quickly to make the right choices since there was rarely a second chance on this sort of thing.

"Sir, they are coming in basically ballistic as they usually do. They have not changed course to intercept as yet so we may not have been spotted. I do not expect that to last for more than the next few minutes. Then I expect that they will launch and send everything they have at us. Our envelope of opportunity is very small. We probably won't be able to make planet-fall undetected. They destroyed the Earth before; they could easily do it again. We need to lead them away from here or our own future will not have existed and we will most likely disappear." She said. It was more of a report than he had expected and he nodded to the woman as he considered the words carefully.

"So what we need to do is disable that ship and get safely down to the surface to affect our own repairs before proceeding back for our quarry." He said aloud. The crew did not know why he spoke aloud. The reasoning seemed sound to them, but as of yet, no one knew how to disable one of the enemy ships. It had never been done. He continued on, to everyone's surprise. "Okay people, our situation is critical! We have a world below us unable to protect itself from this threat. In fact, it is the late 1700's down there and they couldn't have defended against us if we had half a mind to attack them. We need to lure the enemy away and disable them as quickly as possible. Does anyone have a suggestion of how to do that?" He asked. The floor was completely open for the first time in any crewmember's memory.

The helmsman answered up first. "From what I can tell, running is the only option we have. We need to run away from Earth to drag them away. They are after us after all." He said in a matter fact tone.

The Captain's eyebrows rose and he chuckled. "You have a point there, but if the Lizzies discover humanity in its more infant form, they could save themselves a lot of trouble by eliminating them now. We may not be enough of a draw to prevent them from blowing this planet Earth up as well. How do we make sure they follow us?" He inquired more directly.

One of the more quiet bridge officers, John Riggins, the targeting and weapons specialist, spoke up and everyone swung around at their stations to see who had spoken. "Sir, I believe that we need to redeploy our weapons. We don't want to shoot the enemy ships. We want to destroy their ordinance in flight. So we target their projectiles while flying an extremely evasive path towards them. Once we get close enough, we can punch a hole in that ship with our beam weapons. They are the only things that the enemy hasn't turned against us. If he hurt them, they have to answer us before they can move on to destroy the second Earth." He said and Captain Glass was glad that this man spoke rarely. He seemed to have waited until he had thought the whole thing through before bringing it up. He considered the survivability of this plan and it looked grim.

"What's to keep them from blowing us out of the sky? If we launch missiles and they turn back on us, we could be destroyed by our own munitions." He said flatly. The idea was rather unpleasant. They had crippled themselves before with the enemy's surprise move.

"Sir, we disable the electronic tracking system on our birds and guide them using the on-board computer here. The enemy seems to have jammed the missile's own target acquiring software. If we don't use it they should be immune to the enemy's defenses." He offered.

"If we can use our missiles, then why don't we just shoot them at the enemy ships?" The Tactical officer asked in shock.

The Captain looked over and then back to the weapons specialist. "A good question that one, do you have an answer?" He asked, reinforcing the tactical officer's surprise and supporting his crew.

"Yes sir, if we launch our standard missiles against the stone ships, they will not cause enough damage to penetrate the stone shells of the enemy ships. We would expend our salvo with little or no effect. The beam weapons seem to penetrate by melting the rock in small spots and venting the ships to space. I have a plan to drain ship's power into a single beam with intent to slice at least a portion of the enemy ship off. I have hopes that this may disable at least some of their systems. Even if we don't try that, we can cause them enough damage to pull them away from the fragile world below." He answered in conclusion.

The Captain rolled the words around in his head. "Have you brought these theories up to anyone else before?" He asked and John lowered his eyes.

"No sir, I was working on the problem while we were repairing the ship. I figured that we would eventually run into them again and I wanted to be ready when that happened." He replied and the Captain looked sternly at him.

"If you had mentioned this earlier, we may have had more than one mind on the problem and thus be further along in the development of it. The idea has merit, but now we must deploy it in desperation. There will be no tests. There will be no second chances. We need to do this and now." He said and then he looked out at his bridge crew again. "If any of you come up with anything, report it to your supervisor and we can all analyze the merits of the idea. Prepare for battle, sound red alert and take us away from Earth, but slowly and casually. We need them to engage us farther from the planet. Tactical begin working on some fancy maneuvers to save our hides while we try to cut the enemy down. If we can even open a small fissure in that ship, I want a missile plugging into that hole to blow it up from the inside. A firecracker in an open hand causes a burn. If you enclose it, the hand is blown apart. If we can cause a big enough explosion inside the ship, we may just get out of this alive. You all know the stakes. I want firing solutions on my plot as soon as they are ready. This is gonna be tight people. Let's get to work." He commanded and all of the stations began cranking out their data.

*   *   *

Commander Zarg, leader of the two hunting stone ships, felt the adrenaline spike as the human ship came into view. They had gotten lucky and now the quarry was close. He gripped the arms of his chair as he looked out at the marked ship. The feeling was infectious in his whole crew. The bloodlust rose up in all of them and they waited for their leader's next command.

"They are not running, so they may not know that we are here." He speculated. He wanted to chase them down directly and end the scuffle quickly with his decisive victory. He could not give in to his instincts though. He was the commander. He needed to keep control. "Bring us in nice and quiet. The longer they remain slow and dumb, the closer we will get before we spring our trap. Prepare to launch upon my command. I want a clean kill on the first try. Then we can take the tales of our hunt and victory back home." He said and the patriotism of his crew brought them around to tactical thinking again. Their yen for recognition overrode the initial depression of not charging in. It was true that they were all nearly identical. They used their status to separate themselves from the masses. It was what drove them to be warriors in the first place, the need to be above and apart from the rest.

"We will take this ship as a trophy and present it to the supreme leader. It is a symbol of our completed mission. Then we will all enjoy a hero's welcome home." He said and all of his crew were on board with that. The stone ship edged closer, it altered course towards the enemy, but did not change speed. The waiting was the hardest part, but they were now committed to this course of action. He sent a thought message to his brother to bring the second ship from around the planet to the far side of the enemy ship.

* * *

Tactical made an announcement. "Sir they have altered course towards us." She spoke up in that fine soprano voice of hers. The Captain looked at his own plot. It had just updated with the new numbers for the enemy ship out there. He rubbed his chin and smiled.

"They appear to have seen us, but they evidentially believe that we don't see them. They have not increased speed. They have not launched weapons. They must be trying to close the distance before using any of their ammunition since they would have trouble restocking it here. The thought occurred to me as well. We are in for the long run though." He shifted in the chair. It had suddenly become uncomfortable. "Keep sharp for their launch. They will not delay forever. For the time being, they are making our job easier. The closer they get, the less we will have to close to use our beams on them." He said. His smile was hiding his true feelings. He was nervous now. The earlier battles had not gone well. In fact they were disasters. They could not afford another such now. They needed to succeed at all costs. In any normal circumstance he would have turned tail and run now. He was resisting the urge to order it even now. They had to get this enemy away from the fragile planet behind them. He definitely felt like a prey animal. This hunter was stalking him and the thought was not all that comforting. What he hoped was that this prey animal had teeth. He wanted to hurt these Lizards for what they had done. Revenge was a dangerous path, but he so wished he could hurt at least this one ship. Now the future depended on him doing just that. He followed the various departments as they went about their preparations. The Weapons officer now seemed to be the key. If that failed, they were lost. Either way, they would find out in the next thirty minutes or less. He sat back and tried to look calm, nearly oblivious to the hectic frenzy around him.

* * *

"The humansss have not run yet," was announced over the still bridge of the mighty stone ship. Commander Zarg's brother had reported in that he was on the way. He would clear just after they had engaged the enemy at the current closing rates. The prey had not seemed to notice the great stone ship as it bore down upon them. They were like sheep. It was so disappointing after the brilliant chase that they had started earlier.

"We cannot wait forever for them to notice usss." He said aloud. "What is our dissstance to them now?" He asked and the crew checked the plots.

"SSSSir, we are only 400 measuresss out. They could not be sssso blind as to not ssssee ussss by now. We show ssssome damage to the top of the ship, but we should be visible even if they went and looked out a window now." The voice replied in desperation. The bloodlust had them all shaking in place with involuntary twitches. It was a form of hell they had grown to know.

"Very well, launch our attack and let them know that we are here." He ordered and a wave of relief swept across the bridge.

"Aye ssssir, we are firing now." He said as the ship belched forth more of the rock spires that were their primary weapon. The battle was at long last engaged. The jitters swept away with those projectiles and the bloodlust rose in each of them to a crescendo. Their eyes saw only red now. The prey was at hand and the victory would be glorious.

* * *

"We have weapons launch." The tactical officer said clearly over the microphone pickup at her station. The plot before her began to update with the stone shafts and she began to count them. "We have twenty inbound spires." She reported and the weapons officer rubbed his hands together. This was what he had been waiting for. He targeted the incoming spires and made sure he had positive locks from his console. He had to update the missiles from his station since the on-board guidance systems were disabled. The missiles hit the tubes primed and ready. He glanced back at the Captain and with a nod of approval, he pressed the firing stud and the ship bucked as it expelled the newer and dumber missiles. He fired twenty of the precious missiles after the twenty spires. They pulled away from the ship with full thrusters and then they locked onto the signal that was being broadcast to them. The missiles did not streak back towards the *Lost Cavalier* as many had feared. They kept on course and the computer updated them every couple of seconds. The spires began to shatter under the fire of the missiles. Fragments of rock were spread to the solar winds as the weapons were neutralized. The *Cavalier* then started its own attack run. Full power applied to the thrusters as it danced and weaved towards the enemy ship. They were close now, closer than anyone had a right to be to the enemy ship. Surely it was closer than anyone else had ever dared to go. The beam weapons were now fully charged and the batteries were peaked. The emitter sang out as the first beam was generated. The lasers shot out first and scored hits on the stone ship. Their concentrated heat bore holes into the outside of the ship. They were not big enough yet to fit a missile, but the process had started.

More spires leapt from the stone ship as it tried to adjust to the new aggression of the enemy. Missiles streaked out and obliterated them as well. The bridge crew of the *Cavalier* held their breath as they waited for what would happen next. The only ones moving were the weapons specialist and the helmsman. John Riggins smiled as he pressed another button. Grasers were brought to bear as the distance closed even more. The particle beams ripped into the earlier holes and enlarged them as the molten rock oozed out of the way. The weapon officer saw his opportunity and he launched one ship-killer missile. The missile was devoid of its normal guidance system, but the ship had ample computer space for him to guide it all the way in. The hole in the stone ship glowed red from the heat as the rock spilled out into space. The missile streaked into the hole and a timer started. It flew in for point three seconds more and then it exploded. The mighty ship of stone tried to contain the fury within itself, but the stress cracked and powdered stone blew out form the blast. The intense heat melted a section of the interior and a large chunk of the ship flew off and spiraled end over end away from the main portion. The shout of triumph aboard the small ship was brief and intense. The Captain stood up in his excitement and ordered another missile. Lieutenant Riggins replied aye and sent another into the enemy ship. Debris littered the area as the second missile hit the inside of the exposed ship and the remaining portion of ship split into two distinct parts. It drifted off as if there were no power or control. The *Cavalier* spun around and bolted towards the planet. It was now a popular belief that they had just won the battle. Given the damage that they had inflicted, the assumption seemed reasonable enough.

* * *

Commander Zarg clung to life as he tried to contact his brother. His ship had been blown apart around him and the fragmented stone was beginning to break down. The force of that blast inside his ship had been terrible. His crew was lost. If he had not been pinned down by debris from that first blast, the second would have killed him. His leg had been caught and was fairly badly injured. He called in anguish and his brother was bringing the other ship up for the rescue attempt. The enemy was still between them and there was a chance that his ship could bring the other down. Zarg began to fade from consciousness as he made his request.

Commander Phylus sat atop his stone command chair. He was worried in the back of his mind about his brother Zarg. This concern did not relieve him of his duty though. He needed to destroy the enemy ship before he could do what his heart demanded. He needed to get to that broken ship and fast. His crew was on full alert and the news of the destroyed stone ship brought a grim overtone to the standard activities of his bridge. The metal box had struck and struck hard. The prey had turned the tables on the hunter and that meant that they were more dangerous than had been originally anticipated. His weapons were ready and all he needed now was a visual on the human scum to fire. He had a target specialist on his ship and the stone would guide to the enemy ships by mental control. The fight should be short and deadly. The metal box came into view and he tensed as he gave the order to fire. The shafts of rock leapt forward like a porcupine shooting its quills. The enemy ship came barreling in at high speed. He did not know what tactics they were using, but he was ready to counter anything. He sent a second launch even before the first one got to the target.

* * *

Captain Glass sat stone still as his tactical officer announced the second ship. The stone spires were already in transit and the weapons officer, John was already predicting that they would be hit this time. The enemy had simply sent too many of the weapons to be destroyed by his fire control. They saturated his net. He did what he could and many of the rock weapons were turned to harmless fragments and dust. The *Cavalier* was struck three times and the piercing weapons caused havoc across the board. The beam weapons were still online though. They opened fire as the two ships passed each other. A nasty gash opened down the side of the stone ship from end to end. It was a hole about a foot wide from tip to tip and many of the lizard crew was killed even as the humans were sealing off areas from their battle damage. Lives were lost on both sides and the two ships kept moving on their previous plans and did not circle back to each other.

The *Lost Cavalier* was puking smoke and air badly as the automatic hatches closed. They were heading towards the Earth so they simply continued on in. The atmosphere caught them and the heat began to rip through the exposed bulkheads and if there had been any survivors in those holds, they would have been fried in there. The ship listed to the side as the spires altered its aerodynamics. They screamed in over an ocean and as they tried to veer northward away from civilization, the stabilizer gave way. The ship began to plummet down almost uncontrollably. Captain Glass's knuckles were white as he gripped the arms of the command chair in apprehension. He sounded the collision alert and ordered everyone to brace for impact. Fires started across the ship as the heat found its way through the damaged areas of the ship. The crew fought the fires even as they tried to strap in for the crash. A coastline became visible and the ship screamed in way too fast to make out any detail. They needed to bleed off a lot of speed if they had any chance of survival. The engines were unresponsive and the helmsman pulled up hard to bring the ship's nose up and use the wind resistance to stall the ship. The broken and twisted metal screamed in the wind as the ship lost more than two hundred miles an hour of speed. They were now traveling only slightly faster than a jumbo jet on cruise. The countryside below was mostly trees. The video display had flickered out and the helmsman was guiding the ship simply by infrared sensor displays that were being run on auxiliary power. He picked a cold spot and angled the ship into it. The battered and broken ship hit the water and skipped nearly seventy feet to hit the surface again. Then the water took hold of the ship and it stopped amazingly fast. The crew were tossed around inside. The strain was similar to landing a jet on an aircraft carrier. The *Lost Cavalier* was no longer flyable. They would need to get repairs underway as soon as possible. That is, if it could be repaired.

*   *   *

AN UNLIKELY ALLY

Captain Glass shook his head. They were alive. He didn't know how many had survived. But they were still alive and the mission could try to continue. He unbuckled himself and starting checking members of his bridge crew. Main power was down so leaving the bridge was currently impossible. There was a manual override, but the wall it was on looked twisted and he didn't think he could move it by himself. There was a gash in the opposite wall and the sounds of a river could be heard through it. There was light there too. It allowed them to see in the darkness around them. There were bodies everywhere. He hoped that they were merely unconscious. The bridge crew had been mostly strapped in so they fared better than would the rest of the ship. Captain Glass had the emergency kit out and he was waving smelling salts under the noses of his crew. They were startling awake and he was glad for the company. He had a sinking feeling about the mission now. The top fin problem had just taken a back burner to getting this ship airborne again. There had been only one casualty in the crash aboard the bridge. The weapons specialist, John Riggins was pinned to his station by the console that had shifted upon impact. He had destroyed an enemy ship and another had killed him back for it. It all seemed so unfair. There had been so much death and destruction already. Bryon looked again at the wreckage that was his command. They needed a plan now. He was going to have to come up with it. The first order of business was getting as many of his people back up and running. Then they could ascertain what the ship needed. If it was even possible, they would then have to start fabricating parts and perform the actual repairs. This would not be an easy mission. If the ship could not fly again, the whole mission would fail. He couldn't let that happen. They had to finish this and get back out into space. The ship listed a bit; the river that it was in was still pushing it. It rested uneasily on the sandy bottom. This was the past too. There were all kinds of warnings about how to proceed in such a volatile situation like this. There were so many temporal possibilities that it hurt the brain just to try and think of them all.

The bridge doors were sealed. The auxiliary power unit did not help the situation since the doorframe was also skewed a bit. The hatch was not going to open without some major work. The refugees from another time climbed out onto the hull through the gash and stood up on top of the ship. The river was relatively wide and the ship was nestled into the western bank. The land was mostly unspoiled woodlands here. The sun was patchy through the dense growth and they traveled back down the hull to another hatch. It responded to the codes due to a battery powered console and the remaining bridge crew members dropped back into the ship to search for their comrades.

*   *   *

Casey Fulton stood on the remains of his engines. The in-system drive was a pile of rubbish. The twisted metal and splattered lubricant were skewered by one of the offending shafts of stone. He and one of the other engineers were cutting it out in sections in order to see what kind of damage was behind it. They had been trapped down in engineering with about four other crewmates and they were all busily repairing and patching things as best they could. Surprisingly, the upper portion of the drives was still intact. The boosters were still working, but they still needed main power to do more testing. The reactor was automatically shut down when the impact unsettled its radioactive components. The seals had held and the radiation had not leaked. It was pretty much all that had saved the engineering staff so far. If it had ruptured, then they would have died almost instantly. The right side of the ship had another of those shafts through it and there was still the missing top fin problem to be addressed. The board was showing red lights on the bridge as well. The links were all down and there was no sign of life or power that way. They all feared for the worst. The work was all they had and they were determined to do it. Corridors were bent in the middle of the ship and conduits needed repairing. Cables needed patching. Then they needed a head count of survivors and sooner or later someone would be asking them for the miracle of flight again. The task seemed insurmountable. Each of them looked at one little piece of the big puzzle and worked feverishly to maintain some sort of order. There were no longer fires aboard though and that was good. They could vent to the outside for air reserves now, so they would not be overloading the life support systems.

The backup generators were not designed to handle a full crew of repairs so they would have to work in shifts or lose power to all.

Footsteps on the other side of the hallway brought Casey out of his own thoughts. He shined the portable light down that way and saw people dropping into the ship from an emergency hatch. It was the bridge crew! His own joy must have been apparent on his face as they all smiled at him. The Captain dropped last and Casey saluted the man.

"At ease." The Captain replied. "Report." He ordered.

Casey looked around at the destruction he was trying to correct. "Well sir, we have lost main power and the in-system drive engines. There are still two more stone shafts to be removed and the damage checked. The bridge…"

"I know about the bridge." The Captain interrupted. "Just tell me how many people are still alive aboard my ship." He commanded.

Casey felt his heart skip a beat. "Sir, we have not yet made it to every section, but we show that there are at least twelve deaths among the crew. There are still several people unaccounted for out there somewhere. Perhaps you could add your bridge crew numbers to our own and help boost morale a bit." He suggested.

The Captain thought for a brief moment, and then he came to the realization that this engineer was much more valuable repairing his ship than chasing around after bodies in the wrecked spacecraft. "You go and see to the repairs. I will handle the personnel problems. I will want a more complete report after there has been a chance to accumulate the data for it. In the meantime, get my ship working again." He ordered and Casey nodded and left the Captain and his bridge crew to return to the conduit he was patching. Upon completion, the doorway opened up before them. The hatch system was back up. This was good news for the Captain and his deputized search crew. Now they could get into all of the compartments and hopefully save a life or two. There was still the threat of local populace. They had crashed somewhere. Someone may have seen them. Time was now the enemy and they had to work fast or be discovered. The timeline could be irrevocably damaged. They needed to get to the historian and find out when and where they were.

* * *

Miles looked on as the loud noise screamed overhead. He was attached to the Virginia Militia and his feet hurt. They had been patrolling for some time. His unit was guarding Point of Fork and the munitions there were of paramount importance to the war effort. British invaders had not as yet come this far, but the paranoia was still in full swing. If they had something that could tear up the sky, then all was lost. He grabbed his musket and ran towards the crash. His breeches made scraping sounds as he tore through the brush. He knew that the Fluvanna River was just over that way. Maybe whatever it was hit the river instead of the trees. His musket felt like a part of him now. He had carried it for weeks. The July heat was still making him sweat these runs. He longed for the cooler temperatures of fall. Of course, he dreaded the cold of winter. His powder bag was slung over his shoulder and he had his knife at hand as he carved his way through to the river. He stopped short when he got to the bank. The thing in the water looked like a beached metal whale. It was damaged and smoke poured out of it. Pulling out paper and charcoal, he started to draw the thing so he could report what it looked like. His strokes were crude, but he was overall satisfied with the results when he put the charcoal back in his pocket and eyed the paper that was so valuable a commodity out here. Then he started to head back to his unit. The general would want to know about this, he thought to himself.

He didn't get very far. A well-timed lunge brought cold steel to bear and Miles was pinned by it. The sword was running from the hand of the bearer into Mile's stomach where it caused severe indigestion and internal bleeding. The British scout smiled as he looked into the face of his latest victim. His job was to see that nobody could give the warning that the British Army was coming. He had just silenced another rebel and the feeling of close combat carried its own adrenaline rush with it. He held the sword firmly as the man died before him. Then he gave a quick twist and pulled it free. The blood splattered the leafy ground and he wiped the blade off carefully like a professional should. He quickly went through the man's effects and he took note of the drawing. The metal thing was right there in the river and he looked at it and then at the drawing and nodded. He folded the paper and put it in his inner pocket. Then he took the enemy musket and broke it against a tree. The powder he took with him. It was a rare commodity out here in the thickets. Then he headed back onto his course. They would take this Point of Fork soon and LT. Col. Simcoe promised him a promotion for the successful completion of this mission.

He left the scene and the *Lost Cavalier* was left alone to its own demise as the world around it continued on in its own struggle. It was war and the lines of both sides were currently in transition. The Virginia of 1781 was bloody and dangerous. The Fluvanna River pulled at the metal hulk and the craft started slowly working its way downstream. The settlement and storage facility was close now. The young officer did not know how close, but he was ready for whatever he found. He slipped back into the shadows as he made his way forward. When he got the chance, he would report this metal object to his superiors. Until then, he had a mission to complete.

* * *

Frank had been tossed around in his quarters during the crash and he had a good-sized lump on his head to prove it. They were obviously down now. The power was off so he had no light whatsoever. He tried to peer into the darkness, but his eyes could not even show his hand in front of his face. He knew his room pretty well and he felt that he could manage to navigate it. He stumbled into something else in the dark and his knee told him that he was not as clever as he thought he was. He tried to orient himself and tried again. He hit yet another obstacle. His hands groped around the object and he realized his folly. The ship was sideways. He was standing on a wall and trying to follow the floor plan. That wouldn't work very well. He thought about it and set the image in his mind of where he was and how everything must look. Then he made his way to the doorway. It had been on the wall before, now it was in the floor. There was no power so he couldn't use the normal button to open the metal door. He dropped to his hands and knees in order to look for the manual release. There were no sounds from the corridor beyond, so he didn't know if there were any other survivors yet. He hoped that there were. He could not do this mission alone. In fact the orientation of the ship worried him more than he would have admitted. He found the wheel and began to turn it. The door unsealed and shifted just a little bit. There was no light there either. He continued to turn the handle. He could hear the gears in the wall turning and he could hear a soft scraping sound as the door slid obediently aside. When the handle stopped, he let go and reached for the edge of the opening. The hall was not very wide, so the fall to the other wall wouldn't be so bad so long as the opposite door was not already open. He decided to test it first by dropping a pen down into the hole. It fell for less than a second and clattered against the far door. Relieved, he lowered himself into the hallway and released from his full extension. He fell the short distance without incident despite his own fears.

He trod carefully as he headed towards the front of the ship. The emergency lights were even out so there was no battery power in this section of the ship. He wondered how long he had been out, lying in his room. Why had no one come for him? His mind began to conjure up images of the most terrible kind. He pushed them away. He didn't have time for that now. He slowly worked his way forward and got his first stroke of real luck. This wall had an emergency medical kit mounted on it. He pried it open and found what he was looking for, a small flashlight. He switched it on and looked around the corridor. It was a bit unnerving at first, seeing the corridor on its side like this. It had been what his mind had expected but it still threw one off when they saw it. There were no bodies in this section so he let himself feel a little bit of hope. He made better time and gained access to the front hatch. It had been automatically sealed just as the power was dropping out. It was still only halfway closed. He squeezed through and slid down along the curved wall toward the side of the secondary bridge. His light danced on the walls as he tried to control the fall. He caught a foot on the plaque on the wall and tumbled over for the rest of the trip. He cursed himself for the sloppiness of the entry. Then his wonder took over and he played his light over the various positions. There were no bodies here either. If anyone had come to this auxiliary bridge, there was no sign of it now. He went to the engineering console and flipped the switch to try and power it up. Nothing happened. He let out a sigh. He hadn't really expected that to work anyway. His specialty was history, not engineering. The side wall did not have an exit to the room. He needed to climb the far wall. He looked around for some cable or cording that he could use to lasso the handle next to the hatch. But there was nothing available here. He tried climbing manually and made it to about halfway. The wall grew steeper and steeper as the curve sharpened. He was trapped in this room now. He settled down to wait until someone restored at least partial power. He switched off his lamp to avoid killing its meager battery. In the darkness, the best thing to do was sleep.

* * *

Maintenance crews had been scouring the ship for survivors and repairing things as they could. The ship's attitude made things more complicated and they had difficulties getting around in places that were normally considered easy access. The engines were brought online and emergency power came on for about half of the ship. This meant that life-support would come on for those sections as well. They couldn't right the ship yet, but at least they had some semblance of power. With this small amount of positive feedback, the crew's morale began to recover. It would probably be some time before the computer was brought online, so the internal sensors were unmonitored, even if they had been powered. That meant that they were down to searching manually. The locked doors were frustrating since they could only be opened from the inside with manual releases. The crew quarters could not even be searched. Casey was working on a bypass to route some of the emergency power to the door system. There were still unaccounted for crew out there that might need help. Lord knows they would need everybody to have a chance of survival. He fashioned a logic probe into his conversion box. The probe's access to the circuits allowed him to 'ghost' the door system into the life support queue and thus route power to the door automatically. The only problem was that it required him to go to each door and plug the probe in to activate that particular door. That and the simple fact that it hadn't worked here yet, kept him working at it feverishly. He grunted and tinkered and the light on the top of the probe switched from red to green and the door engaged and swished open. He pressed the lock button to stick it in the open position and removed the probe from the socket. He smiled and kissed the small metal box.

"Okay, let's go get our people back." He said to no one in particular. Then he made his way towards the crew's quarters. That had the highest concentration of locked doors. Then he would spread his electronic magic throughout the ship. At least now he had a plan.

*   *   *

Once back on the bridge, the lights started to come on. Power had been at least partially restored. The Captain looked at the read-outs across the board. It didn't look good. Most of the systems were offline. The most notable exception was life support. He was thankful for that at least. He knew that he had a good engineering crew. They were still fighting. They were still trying to keep them alive. It made him proud. The *Cavalier* looked pretty bad from his point of view. The mission was definitely in jeopardy. The worst part was that the enemy ship, the second enemy ship, was still out there somewhere. It had been damaged, he was sure of that. Eventually they would be back though. He needed to get his ship working again and get back out into space in order to have any chance to continue. They could destroy the Earth at any time and all of the minutes from now on would be borrowed time. He had seen several of the maintenance crews doing next to impossible tasks to try and keep his ship together. He understood the difficulties. The problem was that there were no alternatives. There was no back-up plan. His only shot was this one. The rest of the universe would have to get on without humans if they failed. This was survival on a species level. There was no way to underestimate their own importance. The history of mankind was about to end. It would require heroes and more. They would have to become legends. They still had to travel further back in time. They just weren't far enough. He could not tell how much farther they needed to go. The computer was still offline and he could not pull up his own logs either. He was picking up pieces of debris as someone with a welder was working on the massive gash in the wall. The sideways bridge made him remember everything about the desperate flight. He felt the weight of responsibility as it pressed down upon him. He had taken on more than any one person could hope to support. He had to be strong. That was all that there was to it. He sat on the side of his command chair. He made a mental note to get his ship oriented correctly as soon as it was possible. It would be a good first step to putting everything right again. He sighed and lost himself in his darker thoughts.

* * *

Frank was lying on the wall when the lights came on. He felt a low rumble in the wall beneath him. The engine had turned on. His eyes popped open and he could see the room he was in. It didn't look damaged at all. Of course the secondary bridge was inside the ship deep in the center to prevent loss to all of the command crew to a lucky hit on the primary bridge. He made his way to a console and checked the lights. Most of the ship was still dark and sensors were not working. He saw activity in engineering and more on the bridge. Systems were coming back online. He marveled at the work. It must have been under the most extreme circumstances that anyone could imagine; yet it was being done. He checked his own location and the life support was on here. He had lights and he was not freezing. Of course the world was outside and it could regulate the ship at least somewhat. He could now see the far away hatchway and his determination to reach it redoubled. He opened an emergency compartment and found cable and a carbon dioxide cartridge launcher with a spike. He aimed above the hatch and fired. The sound of the cartridge was loud in the empty room and the "thunk" sound as the spike penetrated the metal wall was reassuring. Both sounds echoed back to him a couple of times in the round room. He began to climb the cable. His hands were taking a beating, but his ascent was slow and steady. His feet were walking up the wall and when he reached the open hatchway, he swung his legs into it and dumped himself into the forward hallway. The hallway was still without power, but the open door allowed light to trickle into the dusky looking place. He stood up and brushed himself off. Then he headed forward again. The ship was not all that long and he knew that at the front edge of it were stairs that he could use to reach the main bridge. That was where he had decided to go. He really wanted to go outside and see what was going on there. The thought of seeing the Earth in its pre-industrial era was a powerful compulsion. At this rate he figured he would reach the bridge in another fifteen minutes or so. He was starting to feel hungry as well.

*   *   *

The ship sat in the water and was unaware of the turmoil around it. The British army was advancing on the Virginia Militia and the unsuspecting American Colonial forces were about to get a rude surprise. LT. Colonel Simcoe led his troops towards the Point of Fork settlement in order to destroy the stores there that were supplying the rebel forces. His scouts had found the location and he was bringing up his small company to make the attempt. Simcoe looked on as his men readied themselves for the advance. Their red and white uniforms flashed in his mind as he imagined his own future. He would be a war hero. He knew this to be true. His ego would not allow otherwise. Cornwallis had told him much the same. Each mission was vital and cutting off the insurgents from their weapons and powder would greatly help the war effort. It was hot here. His men were grumbling about the grueling pace. Let them grumble, he was still in charge. He would arrive within the day and the American scum would know what it was like to be taught a lesson. His horse followed his lead without hesitation and he made his way through the men to the front. He wanted to see what was ahead of them before sending his men forward for the final leg of their three-day journey. Once this was dealt with, he had orders to continue on to Yorktown and settle the unrest there as well. He knew that he was understaffed for that particular action, but he understood that others would join him for that assault. Now he needed to take the supplies out and bring his men back in one piece to present his trophy to his commander. This close was the most dangerous part of the mission.

Without the element of surprise, the fortification could possibly hold. He wanted to make sure that they wouldn't. His advanced scouts had cleared the path before him and now they had the enemy in sight. He knew that the moment would be here soon. This country was beautiful. He regretted that he was here to kill people. He would have liked to visit under more ordinary circumstances, but fate had proved that it just wasn't meant to be. He settled back in the saddle and swept back to his troops. They would not get there if they didn't get going. Daylight was a commodity that they couldn't control. They had to make their march under the light skies and hit the enemy after the sun had set. They would switch to quiet advance when they got closer. It was slower but may just let them sneak up. It was less military than he liked, but these people were determined to stop him and his small company. He needed every advantage he could get. He ordered his troops forward and the whole company spread out into the woods and marched out to meet their destinies.

* * *

Commander Zarg felt a wave of atypical emotion as his brother stepped into the compartment. Phylus had brought his ship in to rescue his brother and commander from the void. The two lizard men looked at each other and not a word was uttered. They embraced quickly and then Zarg stepped over to the threshold and boarded the second ship. His had been a complete loss. He looked at the crew that was expecting his next words. He could see it in their eyes.

"I am in command of thisss vessel." He said in his slithering voice. "We will hunt these humanssss and kill them for the glory of the hunt." He said and the fire in the blood rose in all of the crew in the room. He held up his fist with a ceremonial knife blade in it. The twisted edge looked as lethal as it truly was. "Successss!" He screamed and they all repeated it back at a shout. He looked at them with fire in his eyes. The prey had hurt him. He wanted his revenge. Killing the planet to destroy his enemy was not good enough. He had to kill them with his own hands. He would rake his claws through their flesh as he savored their deaths. This human vermin must be eradicated and then they could return home victorious. Nothing else was acceptable. He headed to the command chair and sat. This completed the ritual and Phylus stepped back into the shadows in order to prevent anyone thinking that he was interfering with the change of command. It was unusual for a commander to be replaced that was not dead. But now they had a battle seasoned veteran and a serious hunt for an elusive and obviously skilled prey. This would be a hunt of legendary status. The glory, oh the glory they would reap. The stone ship headed back towards the enemy planet. They would search for their quarry on the ground. Failure was not an option.

*   *   *

The maintenance crews managed to free up all the doors with Casey's help. The crew was accounted for. There were fourteen casualties and the bodies were temporarily put off the ship for burial. A small scouting party swept out from the ship. The river had it pinned to the north bank. Ropes were tied to the heavy trees and with almost everyone's help, the ship was turned using logs rolled under the hull along the river's bed. Even though it was a small ship, it was almost too much task for the small crew. It was agonizingly slow, but the ship rotated under the forces applied and when the ropes were tied off, the ship was back to its original up and down orientation. Now the repairs would go easier on the inside. The only problem now was that parts were running dangerously low. They had a full fabrication unit for smaller parts, but the materials needed would have to be gathered. A brief survey of the surrounding area netted a surprise. There was a body and a broken musket not far from the ship. The mud along the bank of the river showed footsteps leading away from the craft. It was a sure bet that someone had seen the *Cavalier* now. This was getting dangerous to the timeline. The pieces of the broken musket were brought aboard for Frank to inspect. His eyes lit up at the prospect and the engineers were anxious to get at the artifact to see if there was something there they could cannibalize to repair the ship.

Frank swept his hand over the elongated barrel. It had been broken against a tree. This was presumably because it was too heavy for the killer to carry away so he had taken it out of action to prevent the enemy from using it. It was sound military strategy. The craftsmanship was crude. This weapon had been hastily made. The pan was angled away from the weapon and the metal had broken like the liberty bell at the point of impact. If it had been intact, it would have made an excellent memento of the trip through time. As it was, he turned it over to the engineers and they started running metallurgical analysis on it. They got excited almost immediately. It was crude, yes, but it had the right metals in it. There were trace elements of further use from such a weapon as this as well. They were just impurities to the smiths at the time. But combined in a different way and in enough quantities, they gave the first hope of actual repair to the downed spacecraft. More of these would need to be found.

Frank used the weapon as a guide to tell when they were and he was startled by the answer. They were in a hotspot of historical significance. This meant that they would have to be even more careful than was originally suspected. The timeline would be fragile here. A wrongful death could change all of history. The world was in flux as the young nation of America fought for its independence from Great Britain. He knew these terms in a general way only. It had happened so long before his birth that it had seemed like myth. It was a story they taught in school. He didn't understand the lesson at the time, but now they were here. There were people dying around them. The fighting for freedom might just run over them if they weren't careful enough. Worse yet, it looked like they needed things from here. That meant that some of the crew was going to interact with the locals. In peacetime, the main threat would be the authorities, now it would be armies of men who would shoot first and not bother with questions. They were supposed to have put down in an isolated spot somewhere. This had not happened. They were in the thick of history and now they would have to deal with that. The idea scared him more than he would like to admit. He decided to look up the proper dress for the time period. If they didn't stand out so much, they had a better chance of succeeding.

He dialed up his personal data device and remembered that it did not have power yet. The main computer was still offline as well. He felt suddenly impotent separated from his records of history. His edge was now gone. He would have to think on his feet and come up with another solution for the crew. He left the ship and headed for the leading scouting party. If he could help them, then maybe, just maybe, they might be able to find something useful. He wished that he understood these people more. He would have to wing any negotiations and sound convincing. A seed of doubt crept into his mind. The need was too great to ignore though. They needed costumes and metal goods. He tried to keep quiet as he headed in the direction of the group. He had a tracker and they were not too difficult to locate when he concentrated on it. The problem was that he was unused to moving through wooded brush. He kept tripping and scraping his feet. He would have let out a string of curses, but fear kept him quiet.

There! Movement up ahead of him and he strained his eyes to see what was going on. A gunshot rang out and there was a lot of shouting. He waited for it to die down before he moved forward. He stepped up carefully and he was surprised at the scene he discovered. One of the crewmen was down and injured. There were two soldiers there. They were dressed in brown breeches and tan shirts. They had powder bags over their shoulders and muskets lay on the ground in front of them. The scouting party had taken them and they were on their knees with their hands on the backs of their heads. A lieutenant kept a handgun on them and they were looking at it in surprise. None of the captives had been shot. Frank stepped up and pulled the shirt away from the fallen man's wound. The ball was right near the surface. With a quick spray from the emergency medical kit, he disinfected the area and with a quick motion that brought a startled cry, he popped the musket ball out of the wound with a tiny thin metal tool for picking locks. Then he applied pressure to the wound as he readied the skin patch to cover it. He sprayed the adhesive and clotting agent and then he held the patch in place until it bonded with the skin around the wound. The skin patch began to adjust color to the man's skin and in a couple of minutes was almost invisible. Frank put the items back in the kit and handed it back to the man who had been assigned to carry it.

The Lieutenant nodded to him in appreciation. "You're pretty good at that." He noted and Frank nodded.

"We had to deal with things ourselves in the outer rim colonies so I learned early on how to treat minor wounds." He replied and the explanation seemed to satisfy the group. "I would like to join you and head out looking for supplies." He said to the group, making special care to address the Lieutenant almost directly. "We need period clothes if we are to blend in here. I am not exactly sure where we are yet, but this is a war. There has to be supplies somewhere out here. These men are clothed and fed. They can't be cut off from their support." He said pointing at the two captives.

"You have a good point there. We can take these men's clothes and maybe infiltrate a supply depot or some other such. That is, if there is one around here." He reached out and grabbed the hair of the closest prisoner and pulled the face to his own. "You wanna tell me where we are?" He asked and the man looked at him in fear. His training, such as it was, did not include interrogation and resistance. Even so, they were not ready to give out any information to strangers. These people did not dress like redcoats, but they talked strange and were obviously foreigners of some sort.

"We'll tell you nothing!" He replied in defiance. He got a quick blow to the shoulder for his efforts and he felt and heard the crack as it broke under the amazing hit. He pulled in a big breath and clenched his teeth against the pain. His eyes were watering and he tried to be strong. The stranger knelt down to his level and looked him in his clouded eyes.

"You don't understand me." The man said. "In my eyes, you are already dead. How much you suffer makes no difference to me. We are going to find out what we need to know. How long that takes is up to you." He said in a calm voice that somehow seemed even more dangerous than yelling and screaming would have. "You are at war to fight for your country; we are at war to fight for the existence of all humans everywhere. I'd say that our need is greater than yours." He said, still maintaining that frightening tone. "How about helping us and you out?" He asked and his tone turned playful. That scared the man even more. It made him seem somehow crazy and worse yet, it made it look like he enjoyed inflicting pain.

"I, I can't tell you more." He said. Even as he said it he knew that it was a wrong answer. The other man's hand pressed down on the broken shoulder and the pain was more intense than he could have imagined. He screamed and a hand slapped him across the face hard enough to loosen a tooth.

"You still don't understand. I didn't even break anything else yet. You are feeling more from the original hit. I have all day to keep this up if you want me to. We have drugs that will prevent you from passing out and make sure you feel it all." He grabbed the man by the head and held the eye contact again. "Tell me where we are." He instructed. It was no longer phrased as a question. The pain never quite died back down again. He knew that this was going to be his last day of life.

"We are in Virginia." He gasped out. His shoulder felt like it was on fire. The man in front of him took the answer and prompted for more. "We are stationed in the Virginia Militia and our current assignment is to protect Point of Fork. The enemy is supposed to be coming to take the stores there and we are to prevent it from falling into their hands."

Frank knelt down next to the man. The Lieutenant backed off ever so slightly. "You say that you are assigned to a supply depot?" He asked for clarification. The prisoner nodded. It hurt to do so and he winced at the fresh pain.

"Yes." He said weakly.

Frank nodded. "Good, then tell me, how far away is this depot and in which direction?" He asked and the group listened intently as the man gave away his military secrets. They were soon off on their way towards the depot. They had taken the clothes from the two men and left them tied up in the woods. The hopes were that someone would find them and rescue them. Two random deaths were undetermined in the timeline. They just didn't know if it was dangerous or not.

As it turned out, Point of Fork was a storage depot for almost all the things they needed. It had the muskets and clothes they needed and woolen blankets and powder and just about everything the war effort needed to continue on. Frank understood now where they were. He was nervous to be sure, but now he knew that there would be an answer for him. He got one of the uniforms and he led the way when they approached the base. The remainder of the group held back out of sight and just Frank and Lieutenant Ken Livingston walked up to the camp as if they had been spooked by something. They looked around at noises that weren't there and they hurried into the gate of the small fort. The wooden construction looked crude and it would not have held up to modern fire. But for the era, it was solid looking enough. Frank stopped at one of the guards just inside the perimeter.

"They are right behind us somewhere." He said in a worried tone. "Seal us up and don't let anyone in." He ordered and the two guards closed the gate and slid a sturdy looking board across the back of the gate to strengthen and lock it in place. It was definitely crude. Ken and Frank helped them do it and headed into the camp under the guise of reporting what they had seen. Frank had researched a little bit before all of this, but he felt out of his element here. Ken seemed solid and no-nonsense. Between them, the mission had a chance of success. They were inside of the fort now. Several men were busily preparing for an assault. The enemy was really close. The history books told how Point of Fork would be abandoned due to the threat of an overwhelming force from the enemy. The preparations here did not suggest that. Frank was a bit worried and Ken didn't know what was about to happen. He needed the supplies and he was wondering why they hadn't gone to inspect them yet. He was about to suggest just that when Frank looked at him and relieved his worry. "We need to get to the supplies and make sure it's what we can use." He said, mimicking the thoughts of his comrade.

"Right, I think it would be best to check there in the middle of the compound." He said, gesturing with a nod towards what looked like a barn with a thatch roof. It didn't look like the soundest fortification, but it was situated in the middle and thus the most protected part of the fort. They took to walking again. This time it was with purpose that they strode. There was only one bored guard at the supply depot itself. They nodded to the man and he looked up at them. No one had bothered to relieve him in quite some time and his own fatigue was obvious. Frank caught the feeling from him and stopped himself from smiling. This was too easy.

"I am here to relieve you." He said and the man's eyes popped open wide.

"Really? I thought that they had forgotten me here." He replied, somewhat better of spirit than he had been. "I haven't even been to mess in a while. Thank you for coming. I am going to go to bed." He said as he picked up his musket and powder bag and left, his feet dragging through the dust as he headed to the barracks. Frank took up the position in front of the supply house and Ken went inside to do an inventory. There were blankets and clothes. There were the muskets they needed and the powder. Thread and linen were sectioned aside and kept dry. There were a few pieces of metal there that were presumably for making more muskets. This obviously did not happen here, they did not have the facilities for it. This was just a storage facility and this was a valuable commodity. There were bags of grain as well. Cotton was here too. It was most impressive. Ken took down the numbers and headed back out to report to Frank.

"They have what we need right here. We just need to get it out of here without anyone knowing it was us." He said under his breath just in range for Frank to hear. He busied himself by taking up position on the other side of the door from Frank. Then he whispered across the opening. "Got any ideas how to do that?" He asked and Frank smiled. He read the smile correctly and he smiled back. "I hoped you would say that." He said frankly.

Frank made Ken start with his next statement. "We need to talk to Von Steuben." He said and the Lieutenant did his best not to gawk at the historian.

"You told me he was the commander of this fort." He answered, straining to keep his voice down in his surprise. "How do you propose we talk to him and not threaten the timeline?" He asked, truly afraid for the first time this mission.

Frank stepped a step closer in order to keep his own voice down. "We need to convince the man that the enemy force is vast. If he thinks that the enemy will overrun him badly enough he will abandon this post entirely. Then we can take what supplies we need and the British will come and destroy the rest. History will remain unchanged and we will be able to carry on with our mission." He said and Ken thought about it for a moment.

"I don't know what happened here. I will have to take your word for it, but I think talking to this man is dangerous." He said and his mannerisms did not reflect his internal struggle. He wanted to shake Frank and make him see reason. The sad part was that the man's words made sense. Despite their inherent danger, it seemed like a good avenue to take. "Where will the commander of the fort be now?" He asked, giving in to the logic of the plan.

"He will be easy to find. Leaders always have lackeys around to do the menial tasks for them. We watch for someone bringing food or drink and follow them to the commander. When they get close, we will sneak in and talk to this man. Our report earlier should have filtered down to him by now. He will think that the enemy followed us all the way to the gates. They remain closed at this time. I hope that they remain so until we are all evacuating this fort. The body near the ship tells us that the British soldiers are close. We have no time to lose here. We need to get these preparations for war turned into packing up and leaving if this is going to work." He said reasonably. The sparkle in his eyes suggested that he loved this planning and scheming. Ken made a mental note to keep on eye on this historian from now on.

"Okay, we need a guard to come here and hold this post while we are away." He said and his voice turned grim. "They left that other fellow here a long time without relief. My guess is that we will not see another relief in the time you suggest." He offered.

Frank nodded to him. "You're right about that. I will leave you here and I will go talk to the Baron. Then you will be close to the stores we need and I can return once the deed is done." He said almost smugly.

"I don't like the idea of splitting up, but I can see that you have this all thought out. I just hope you're right about this." He said in acceptance.

"Me too. There are a lot of gaps in the history books. We must do this and move on before history records us. That would be wrong and most dangerous." He said and before Ken could say anything else, he slipped away into the darkness. He found the mess and sure enough there was a lad carrying a pot of boiling water. He followed the young man away from the building and across the compound. He made sure not to draw attention to himself. There were not many people about, so he kept to the shadows for concealment. The lad went to one of the back houses. It looked like a log cabin, as did most of the compound. There was a stone fireplace and it had candlelight making the whole thing look cozy and inviting. The boy carried the pail all the way to the door and knocked three times and then two. The door opened and he was ushered in. Frank waited and watched. In a few minutes, the boy exited again. The bucket was empty now. He headed back without the load in higher spirits and Frank smiled at him as he turned a corner and was gone. It was time to make his move.

Frank hopped down from his vantage point and crept up to the house from the side. There were no windows on this wall. He peered around the back and it was window free as well. There was a door and there were two crates in front of it. It was a small barricade perhaps. Frank would have laughed if his needs were not so grave. He tore at his uniform. He rolled around on the ground to dirty it up some more. In the safety of a hidden alleyway behind this small house, he made his appearance look dismal. He even smacked the side of his face on one of the crates. He stopped when he heard the sound. He didn't want to make the commander inside suspicious. He backed to the side of the house and then he dragged himself to the door as if he was only barely able to do so. He thumped his fist on the door and shouted. "Let me in, the baron must know, let me in." He shouted and his pounding would have awakened the dead. Of course the three men inside the house were not even asleep. A surly looking man in a much better uniform and officer's stripes opened the door and his stern look suggested that if alcohol was involved that there would be a hanging.

Frank eyed the man and immediately knew that he could manipulate him if he tried hard enough. "Sir, you must know the enemy is almost here. They are coming. I saw the red of their coats and barely escaped with my life." He stammered and Captain Richard Napier pulled the wounded man into the cabin and closed the door.

"What's this about the enemy?" He asked in a brusque tone and Frank nodded to him.

"Sir, what I have seen shakes me to my marrow." He said first to get the proper tone for his story. He had only come up with an outline of it before this moment. "I was going to find out what that noise was earlier today. There was a crashing sound and I went to investigate it. I went all the way to the river to find what I was looking for. All I found was enemy scouts. Thinking quickly I hid and remained unnoticed for some time as they made their way past. I hid mostly to see who they were scouting for. Luck was on my side and the scouts never noticed me. They continued on towards the camp. I knew that I needed to raise the alarm here, but without knowing how many men were coming, I felt the report would be insufficient. I waited for the sounds of more men coming and it was not long before I heard it. There were more men than I could count initially. They were wearing the red coats. They had weapons and horses and even cannon were being brought to bear. I knew then that Point of Fork was in trouble. It looked like an entire brigade coming towards us. I started to run but several of them saw me. I knew that I had to get back in order to warn you. The darkness had started to set in and I hoped that it would shield me somewhat from the enemy eyes. Muskets fired and I heard shots hit trees as I ducked and weaved through them. My side hurt and I fell more than once. They are coming and we are in danger. I know the men are ready to fight, but we are so outnumbered I fear for us all. If only my warning could allow you to save yourself, then all would not be in vain. Sir, I fear we are all going to die this night." He said and he deflated as if thoroughly exhausted. The three men looked on, weighing the words and the appearance of this man. Could he be right? Is the enemy on their doorstep with cannons and more men than they could ever hope to defeat? Were these meager supplies worth finding out? These men could help the war effort elsewhere.

Baron Von Steuben looked at his commanders. These were his go-to men and they looked shaken. He knew then that this campaign would have to be fought elsewhere. He stood up and addressed all assembled. "We are to retreat from this stronghold and set up a skirmish line just beyond the Indian village to the south. When they come we will cut them down and take back what they have stolen. The British will learn that they cannot come here and order us around. We will drive them back to the sea." He said. Historically he was just full of hot air, but the goal had been achieved. The Captain saluted and left the cabin. He had orders to fulfill and men to marshal out of there. Point of Fork was officially lost.

The remaining man in the cabin was someone that had not been introduced. He was a soldier of course, but his rank was hidden from view. He had dangerous eyes and an easy balance to him. He looked like some kind of assassin. He made sure to keep an eye on Frank and the Baron paid no attention to either man. It made Frank's skin crawl just being watched by this man. He lifted himself up and saluted the Baron.

"Sir, if I may be excused, I need to prepare for our departure." He asked and the salute was returned.

"As you wish, our duty requires us to do what we must. You have earned your keep this day. What was your name again?" He asked and

Frank felt a twinge of worry. This was where history would record him and he wanted no part of that.

"Sir, I'm just a poor soldier who wishes to help. I am only glad to be of service." He said, and he staggered a bit for emphasis. "If I may, sir, I must go now." He beseeched.

"Of course, dismissed." Von Steuben said and Frank made a hasty exit and once clear he breathed a sigh of relief. He could already hear the sounds of packing and breaking down. The troops were no longer sharpening swords and cleaning muskets. They were evacuating the place and he felt his plan click into place. There was still hope for the *Lost Cavalier* and its crew. They would get the supplies they so badly needed. Now they just needed to get them out before the British Army really came.

* * *

A Confrontation in the Past

The stone ship made its way to the surface. This ball of green and blue was actually quite beautiful. It was not as beautiful as the golden sands of their beloved home, but it had a charm all its own and lots of life. They settled in, following the trail of the enemy. The metal box had been crippled and it had crashed somewhere in the northern hemisphere and somewhere on the western continent based on standard geography. So they aimed for the middle of this continent and decided to spread out their search from there. The stone ship nestled in near a gulf to the southeast and open land to the north. The trailing piece of land headed south and east and the main portion of the continent lay to the north. They were warriors, but they were also accustomed to desert climate. The temperature here was fine. They felt the heat of the local sun on their green skins and it felt warm and inviting. The land to the north would be cooler as they progressed. The enemy so far had hopefully not realized this. They could hide from the true people, as the Lizard race thought of themselves, in the icy mountains or the polar caps. It was simply too cold to follow there. But the metal box had been driven to the ground. It had not been piloted. There was enough battle damage to take away things like landing spot selection. They simply went down. Commander Zarg looked out at the openness of the land as he stowed his gear in the little pouches he wore across his torso. His towering height and his almost regal stature made him stand out from his troops. The group headed north.

* * *

When Frank returned to Ken, Ken was a nervous wreck. The alarms had sounded and retreat had played. Everywhere he looked troops were busily gathering what they could and leaving the fort. The front gates were now open and people were filing out. Frank smiled at him and his nervous face when he approached. The two men stepped into the storage barn and looked around. There was no one present. Frank pulled Ken down to a crouch behind some crates in case someone happened this way. "Go ahead and contact the crew. We need these supplies moved now. We don't know how long until the British arrive to sack this place and we need to get the stuff out before they do." He said needlessly.

Ken keyed the communications device hidden under a flap on his shoulder. "We have the supplies and need assistance for immediate evacuation before we get in history's way." He said into the pick-up. There was a pause and then the only message that either of them expected came.

"Hold the fort, we are on the way." It said on the other end of the line.

Both men nodded and fortunately ken remembered it was only audio communication and he responded with "affirmative."

Frank poked his head back out into the courtyard to see how far the evacuation had progressed. There were only a few stragglers here and there, and they were bossing the remaining troops around to get them out. He chuckled softly to himself. No matter how long the military lasted, there were always those who pushed and those that needed pushing. He pulled back into the safety of the barn and hoped that they had enough time to do everything they needed to do. Every minute brought the British closer to this place and he didn't want to be here when they did come. He had gone out on a limb to bring about this retreat. He knew that it was historically accurate. But he also knew that it had been taking a major chance of destroying his own future. The thoughts around time loops were endless in themselves. He had no wish to live through one of them. He just wanted to be back in space again so that they could try again to reach the correct past. They still needed to save the future world. They still needed to defeat this enemy to prevent the loss of everything human. This quest was still far from over.

* * *

It was only a couple of hours later that the ship arrived. Frank did a double take. The ship was flying! It was amazing. They had fixed enough of it to get airborne again. It was amazing what people could do when they had no other choice. The *Cavalier* landed inside the closed gates of the compound. They had been sealed to slow down the enemy sacking of the place.

The ship hovered in and set down lightly in the open courtyard and Frank and Ken each grabbed armfuls of provisions and headed at a trot towards the ship. Crewmates came out just as fast and the resupply was well under way. They lifted off again, having cleaned out most of the provisions. They left behind a paltry sum and flew off to get out of history's way. They went east over the ocean and then turned southeast. They had a lot to do and the threat of enemy contact was a constant reminder of just how desperate the situation was.

Captain Glass sat upon his command chair as if it were a throne. His ship was flying again. His engineering staff had switched things around a bit, but he had control again. They couldn't go out into space yet. They needed a lot of work on the hull to complete that. The most noticeable improvement was not on the ship at all. He had hope again. His brighter mood was infectious and the crew had a lighter step as they went about their business. The computer was running at reduced capacity, but now they could begin calculations for the eventual warp transit again. That kind of forward focus did wonders for the morale of the crew. The only dark point was the ceremony for the fallen comrades. It would have to wait until they were ready to depart. The enemy was still out there somewhere. In fact, this flight was dangerous. They could not flee to space and the enemy could find them easier in the air. The danger of interfering with history was real though and they chose to flee such a hostile and volatile situation before irreversible damage resulted. They had two other minor problems. They had two prisoners. They were men of the Virginia militia and they were currently in lock-up in the brig of the ship. Lord knew what they were going to do with them. Maybe they could be convinced to become crew, but they were completely untrained. They hadn't even given names yet. They were too frightened to be of any use just now. Maybe Frank could help them transition to a modern ship, but somehow Captain Glass doubted it. The *Cavalier* continued on its way. They were crossing a vast desert even now. They were heading to the other hemisphere. They were uncertain to where. They still needed minerals and metal so the basic idea was to find a mine somewhere that had been abandoned and land there. Nobody could think of one, but the sensors were on again with the limited computer power, so they were scanning the ground looking for pockets of ore and no human life signs. It would be slow work, but the payoff could be huge. Captain Glass sipped his coffee and watched the screen as the ground went by below them.

* * *

The Lizzies did not share the concern about the timeline. They had landed in a rather unpopulated spot but their search brought them face to face with human savages that they had never seen before. These people were deep red skinned and their reddish tint suggested that they were always angry. They were cunning warriors and it was good hunting sport for the lizard men to take them down. Of course the technology advantage was vastly on their side. Still, the sport of it made the playing field more even. The hunters ventured out in pairs and left their energy weapons behind. The prey used arrows and spears. They also wore war paint and the Lizard men felt a comradeship bond with these ancient warriors. If only the humans had not evolved past this point they might not have been at war. They seemed to understand their environment and they worshiped spirits. The green invaders did not slaughter them to the last man. They tired of the sport and left the rest to fend for themselves. It had been most entertaining and also most intellectually rewarding to know that they had such potential within the species. Perhaps that was why this particular prey was turning out to be so challenging. The thought brought a smile and Commander Zarg and his brother gazed out at the desert land and they moved further north. This land needed to be searched and he still faced the need to bathe his claws in the blood of the prey.

"Sssir. We have a power signature easssst and north of here." One of the techs told him. He whirled around from his vantage point of the desert outside that so reminded him of home.

"Sssset our coursssse accordingly. I want that prey found." The red eyes and the look of bloodlust were unmistakable and it brought a corresponding reaction from the tech. Satisfied, Zarg swung back around to watch the desert go by as the craft veered away from the old course to track the new power signature. They were close now. The prey could not elude them forever. He could almost smell the blood.

* * *

The *Lost Cavalier* swung over Africa and continued over yet another ocean. The scanner kept finding people whenever it found mineral deposits. The current command was to find somewhere that people weren't. They hit the coast of Australia and the sensors swung into overdrive. They needed something now. The land below was covered in a blanket of snow. They crossed over half of the continent with no luck and then the computer pinged. A mountain range in the southern portion of Australia met all of the criteria and the ship settled down onto the top of a mountain. The vista below was amazing and the small amount of research they could do told them that it was called Mount Beauty. The name fit. There were ore deposits right near the surface and no one around for miles. The engines were shut down and the ship was put on minimal power use. There were still repairs to be done, but the metallurgy needed their attention first. The engineering staff was put on double shift to accomplish the melting down of the muskets and the determination of how much raw ore they would need to rebuild the missing fin and patch the holes on the hull for an extended warp flight. The race was on. They did not know where the enemy was and they needed to get out of this time and back even earlier to pull this long shot of a mission off. No one was ready to give up on this. The entire concept was just too grave. Everything everywhere depended on them now. The weight of responsibility was enormous and no one felt it more than the Captain. He looked at the boards as the power shut down to low levels to conserve what precious amount they did have. His crews were stepping up and he felt a wave of support from them as they went about their difficult and unusual tasks.

The countryside was as beautiful as the name implied. The ship was nestled down between two smaller peaks just short of the lofty spire of the top of the mountain. The natural crevasse was exposed and a vein of gold was showing in the seam of rock that had been exposed. Of course the value of gold was not a concern here. They needed it for its electricity conducting qualities. The muskets were being melted down and the engineering crews had taken all available personnel in order to speed the process along. Sheets were laid out to cool the metal on and forms were applied. The metal was mixed with other alloys to give it the rigidity and the heat shielding they would need to return from space. There was also the high probability of coming a bit too close to the sun. Ceramic tiles were being fired up as well in kilns that brought the clay to temperatures that would have been impossible during this era. Slowly, the ship was being put back together. It would look rather piecemeal, but it would work.

Meanwhile, on the inside, more repairs were under way and the busy work had kept everyone active. This had allowed them to work through this second setback. Frank was busily helping to stoke a fire and Ken had been employed operating a lifting crane that used giant iron tongs to lift the assembled hull plates to the correct position on the ship. There, technicians welded the plates in place. The base was still intact for the dorsal fin and now there was a skeleton of support beams in place awaiting the application of these same hull plates. The open wounds the ship had taken on the sides were almost repaired now. The new metal did not match the original and it made the gashes look like scars down the side of the craft. The job was definitely patchwork at best. But if it held, they were still in business. In ideal conditions, the work would have been painted with the IR reflective paint. They had the correct paint in storage. The time was just too short to worry about it now. They needed to get back into space and away from this time as soon as possible.

The scanners showed the entire area clear of human activity. It was cold up here. The kilns provided enough heat to keep the work moving along. The snow and ice at the top of the mountain was beginning to melt from the runoff heat. For now, it was not a problem that they needed to address. A little water running down a mountain in 1781 could hardly be dangerous. There was no one else around to be in danger.

So the work continued and the fin was rebuilt. It looked raw until the tiles were placed onto the metal skin. They were plastered in place with molecularly modified polyurethane that would accept the extreme temperatures and not let go of either the ship or the tiles. It was a good job, even for rushed work. When the Captain saw it, a tear formed in his eye, broke free, and rolled down his cheek. They had worked so hard for this. The ship was provisioned again and now it was also whole again. The whole process had taken two weeks and everyone was both tired and relieved. This had been a major project. They prepared to depart.

*   *   *

Commander Zarg had done his best to follow the prey, but they had gone to the frozen side of the planet. He had to order his troops to withdraw. They could not function in that cold. He wondered how the puny humans could withstand those temperatures. He had watched on his scope how they had a heat source. He thought about dropping in his troops directly onto that heat source. They may have been able to pull off a strike, but if the humans had somehow sensed them and turned off the heater, then the lizard warriors would be frozen in place and in enemy hands. That would have been unacceptable. He pulled his people and his ship back up to orbit above the humans and their metal box. They would have to come to him eventually. He had the patience of a game hunter and they were still the prey. He was going to make them pay for his earlier loss of face and they were all going to die for the sake of his vanity. His lip curled at the thought to tearing through that metal box, rending and clawing through the enemy bodies as he aimed to reach their leader. That is the one death he would savor most. It was the one individual that had hurt him and destroyed the ship he had brought here. It had left him helpless in space. If his brother had not been close enough for the bond to bring him, it might have been the end of the line for him. The thought of how fragile life really was raised even more rage from him as he continued planning the death of this meddlesome human. He would not be denied again. He had ordered that the sensors be manned at all times and that whenever anyone saw anything change, he was to be informed no matter what time it was.

He got a call as he was falling asleep. The caller was a nervous crewman. "SSSir, we have movement on the enemy metal box. They have taken to the sssskiesss and we will bring them to range within a few minutessss." He hissed at the commander. Even though sleep had been about to take him fully, he sat bolt upright in the bed and he looked at the man that had been calling his name softly for a while now.

"What? What is it?" He sputtered

"They have lifted off and are heading towards usss." There was a pause for discipline, "What are your orderssss?" He requested formally.

"Take us on line to the enemy craft and prepare our weapons. I want to disable it and board it out here in space. They will be helpless before our might!" He said. All thoughts of sleep had vanished with the onset of bloodlust. He was a killing machine and his only regret was that it got released too damnably seldom. The battle was about to begin and his victory was close. He so longed for the corridor-to-corridor fight that was about to ensue. War at a distance was no fun. He needed to get his claws dirty. He needed to smell the fear and taste the blood as he vanquished his enemy. It appeared that this day was for glory, his glory.

*   *   *

The *Lost Cavalier* drifted up and away from the mountain that had sheltered it. The sleek craft had been patched and at least spot painted and now it looked much better. It was also a bit more powerful. There was a small side effect to the ore that they had mined there. It was more concentrated than anything that remained in the future. That meant that the qualities of the metal were stronger. It had allowed the teams to repair and even upgrade a few smaller systems. The fuel was stronger now with some of the natural ingredients that they were forced to add. The engine efficiency was up to one hundred and fourteen percent. They were ready to attempt another time jump. In the sky above them though, was an ominous dot. There was a common sharp intake of breath when the screen focused on the dot and magnified the stone ship. It too had been patched and now the enemy was closing in on them. The ship was only just pieced together. They could ill afford another clash now. But it seemed that was what they were going to get. A quick calculation showed that they could not evade the enemy completely. They could make a run for it, but the long distance rock spires would be able to harass them all the way to the jump coordinates. They may not be able to absorb that much fire during such a tricky maneuver. They needed an option and fast. They had closed before. That would not work again. The enemy would fire long before they could get into range with the beams. There was little time to come up with anything, and the ideas simply weren't coming. The two prisoners were brought to the bridge. They were fresh eyes and it was hoped that when they witnessed the enemy, they would decide to join the crew in defense of the human race.

They were escorted directly onto the bridge and they stopped short when they saw the main display. It showed them the stars and an enemy ship barreling in on them. It was not a good feeling. It was a safe bet that these two men had never left the planet before. In fact no one from that era had. They took it pretty well considering the situation. They stood there frozen as the captain asked a few questions.

"Gunner, can we use those missiles of yours here?" He queried.

"No sir, we are too far out for unguided missiles to have a chance to hit. We would have to close another four thousand miles to reach extreme range," was the grim reply. It had been delivered dry and emotionless. He was thinking about his arsenal and what would work. He only answered the question out of reflex and he kept browsing his inventory. There had to be something that would work. They had come so far.

* * *

Commander Zarg felt the frenzy zero in on the corners of his mind. The enemy was now in sight! He had his weapons, but he wanted to take them hand to hand. This hunt was proving to be the most difficult of his life and its glory would wash over him like a warm blanket. School children would tell his tale as legend. His sharp teeth showed as his evil smile lit up his face. They could not escape him now. He had them. He would even share his glory with his brother. The two warriors would be angels of death. They would strike fear into the hearts of the weak and timid. They might even erect a statue in his honor. His mind drifted off to the future and the glory he so deserved. The metal ship shifted its course. It began to pour on speed. The enemy was fleeing! Like a scared rabbit, they ran for shelter. Unfortunately for them, in space there was no shelter. It was just cold and death among the unblinking stars. He gripped the arm of his chair and his claws dug into it as he commanded his ship to follow. He wanted his weapons aimed, but not fired. The legend would make better reading if he boarded the prey ship and took care of business himself. In his mind, he was already that legendary hero. His own ego had already solidified his self-image into that god-like creature. He stood up and glared at the view before him. He pointed at the enemy ship.

"I am coming for you." He said and the words were a curse. "You are going to die by my clawsss today." He told the fleeing ship and then he whirled around to see his crew. They were anxious and eager. They too longed for the hunt and he knew that they wanted to be in the boarding party. He pointed at two of them and they jumped up to follow as he left for the airlock. The rest of them looked dejected but they were still professionals and they would track the enemy and keep the ship on course for the fateful juncture. They wished that they were there, but their part in this legend in the making was just as important and they were ready to take their parts and build their own myths.

* * *

"Sir, they are turning and closing with us." The helmsman said. The *Cavalier* was shuddering as the engines cranked out more than they ever had before. The new repairs seemed to be holding up and they started the run towards the past. The captain gripped the arm of his chair tightly as he watched the plot on the main viewer.

"Have they fired on us yet?" He asked and he was surprised at the response.

"No sir, they have not fired. They are trying a cut off maneuver. They have position on us and they may well be able to pull it off. Our increased speed is giving them pause to worry about the intercept. Otherwise, they seem content to try and dock with us." He said at last. The idea of that was just as staggering and mind numbing as the fact that they needed to live or everything else died. The Captain could not believe his luck.

"If they want a close battle, then we'll have to give them one. Continue on our course and pour everything you've got into the acceleration curve. I want at least a good shot at them before we hit the turn around the sun." He ordered and the helmsman nodded.

The *Cavalier* streaked out towards the sun and the gravity well of the star helped to draw them into even more speed. The stone ship of the enemy was still closing on them. No one even knew how it moved, let alone how fast it could go. The airframe shook as the ship went speeds that its designers had never intended. The nose of the ship began to glow as the gasses collected on the front. The outer edges of solar activity were now striking close to the fleeing ship. The stone ship came in with complete disregard for the super hot ball of gasses. It ignored the sun almost completely. The focus was so great to catch this one fleeing ship.

"Distance to target?" The Captain asked and the answer came quicker than expected. The tactical officer had been readying this calculation so that all he had to do was hit "enter" for it to run.

"Sir they are nine hundred miles back and closing at about one hundred and fifty yards per second. They will reach us just as we make our turn." He replied and the whole bridge crew took a deep breath.

"Very well, I want all the power you can spare routed to our chaser laser. I want to make that ship veer away from us as we make our move. If we can stop them from following us, we may be able to find the wizard without their interference." He said and the weapons officer started hitting buttons and routing the power that he could muster. At this rate of speed, almost everything was being used to drive the ship forward. There was scant little to divert at this time. He didn't want to touch life support. He decided to use two of his missiles straight back to keep the ship out of their ion trail. The ship bucked as the two missiles streaked backwards. He hoped for the best but it would still be over a minute before he knew if he hit anything.

*   *   *

The stone ship was tense. They were closing on a prey that had proven the ability to strike back. The loss of the other ship had proved it. The commander was lost to his bloodlust and would not see this. He was ready to launch himself into the void and join in the glorious battle. The metal box was close now. It was really close. Not close enough to board yet, but really close in space terms. The weapons were all primed and no one fired them. At this range, there was no way that the enemy could survive their attack. Yet, the ordinance was still lying inanimate in the bay. It seemed wrong somehow. The metal box used fire like a candle to move through space. If they extinguished the candle, then maybe it would stop and they could take the ship the way the commander wanted to. Now they were in high-speed pursuit and things were becoming frightening. If anyone had said so, they would have been criticized for their views and maybe even spaced. With the commander no longer on the bridge, his brother was holding the command chair as his own. It had been his before and it still felt comfortable. His brother was a dreamer, a romanticist and that was dangerous in command. The course was now familiar. The enemy was trying to travel through time again. It was amazing that they had repaired their metal box enough to try that again. The previous fight had sent their spires ripping right through the metal skin of the enemy vessel. It had even crashed on the planet and now it was back in the skies again. No matter what you thought of humans, their ability to adapt had proven itself during this encounter. Even faced with imminent defeat, they were still running and they probably had a plan to try and turn this encounter around to their benefit.

Suddenly the enemy launched two of their weapons. The small fires behind them showed that they were active and the short range made evasion very difficult. The stone ship began to adjust its course to avoid the missiles. The hulk of a ship felt the hit as the first missile struck them. It ripped into the stone but the penetration was not there. Chips flew as the corner of the ship blew apart and it dodged the second missile with more elaborate motions. It looked panicked as it danced around behind the tiny metal box. The humans would not be able to catch them again. Down on the decks below, the commander was being tossed around the small room. He was ready to leap out into the void. This maneuvering was not part of his plan. He cursed at whoever was responsible, but he held on tight to the railing and he watched for his chance to leap into history.

* * *

The *Lost Cavalier* did not dance around. It did not spin, it kept flat and straight and it would have been a sitting duck. That is it would have been had the enemy ship been firing. Instead it was racing straight into history.

The turn came up and the stone ship was practically alongside the *Cavalier*. The open hatch on the stone ship showed a suited up boarding party ready to launch and the gunner smiled. He had been waiting for a target and the guns on board were already primed and ready. He put the crosshairs on the stone ship and he fired into the hole. The two chain guns were linked to the one control and the rate of fire was ludicrous. The commander dove for cover as the rounds raced into his open hatchway and turned the back wall into Swiss cheese. Three other members of his boarding party were not so lucky. Their bloody carcasses were strewn about by the sheer violence of the attack. The compartment beyond held the air or they would have been thrown out of the open hatch living or dead. He looked back out the opening and he readied for the leap. It was insane to be a boarding party of one, but his rage and his ego made him consider the impossible. He stepped back away for a running start on his leap. Just then the hatch closed. He raced forward and hit the hatch hard. He screamed in anger and frustration. He slumped to the deck, exhausted and furious. "Someone is going to pay for this." He said as he contemplated his next move. The enemy ship was as close as it ever would be. This was their opportunity. He knew that the glory had just been snatched away from him at the last second. He pressed himself up off the floor and made his way back into the ship. They would have to follow this enemy ship again. He was certain they were traveling through time again. It was the only explanation that made sense. This crew had better find them again or he would slaughter them all for their disgrace. He would not tolerate failure, not again.

*   *   *

The *Lost Cavalier* made the turn and the enemy ship fell back a bit as it adjusted its course to match. Then the slingshot maneuver started and both ships began to build up serious speed. The enemy was still so close that it made everyone nervous. At least they were going to warp again. The heat shielding was taking a beating as the sun's corona began to eat away at the new material and flecks were beginning to fly away. The hull shook as the ship started slipping into faster than light speed. It made it there once and then dropped back. Then it got its second wind and lurched forward. The stars disappeared into the inky blackness and they were traveling back again.

Based on the previous jump and the rough calculations, they had a target goal to shoot for. They would need to remain in warp for two hours and forty two minutes and about twenty-six seconds to get close to this person they were searching for. At least that was their best guess. The counter began as soon as they hit warp. The ship stopped telling them anything about outside. The void was just that, a void. No light, no gravity wells, no anything. The vastness of space seemed cramped when compared to the infinite beyond. The ideas circulating around about it would have made a good paper for the literary and scientific circles. That is, if they still existed. The Earth and its subordinate colonies had been destroyed. Now there was no one left to read that paper, so there was no point in writing it.

The time passed slowly aboard the ship, as there were no reference points in the void. The time outside was rolling back at an amazingly fast rate. The stone ship was right alongside, but since there was no light here, the ships could not see each other. Unlike the *Cavalier*, the Lizzies did not know how long this trip was supposed to last. The void outside was something akin to madness. This prey was going to pay for this second trip through time. When the commander returned to the collective den, he would have a grand story to tell. This was something beyond legend for the hunt. The glory would be fulfilled and the entire crew would become heroes. They just needed to complete this hunt and head home. It didn't sound all that hard, but it was getting more worrisome by the moment.

* * *

Training and Growing up

Zack felt the pull as the amulet danced in front of him. He had spun it before, but it had failed to come to him. Now the power was flowing through him more freely and he reached out. His fingers were held out longingly as the gold trinket danced just out of reach. The distance was so small now that surely it would jump to him without too much trouble. He watched and then he closed his eyes. He envisioned it in his hand already and the amulet shot up to his hand and he felt the cold of the gold and the warmth of the magic at the same time. He liked the feeling and he opened his eyes to see what he had accomplished. Sure enough, it was now in his hand. He had not reached any farther, so it must have come to him. He let the magic ebb away and its departure brought a small level of dissatisfaction to him. He only felt truly happy during the casting of magic. This was an exercise in air elements. The amulet did not actually fly. It had been carried by the air to him. He had been working with water for a couple of weeks when they suggested that he work with air. His muscles ached from the strenuous work. He did not mind though. His body was actually getting in shape from all of this physical effort. The work that trainees were forced to do now made perfect sense to him. They needed to build up stamina in order to get through these lessons. He smiled at the truth of it. There was even more to be learned by the cadet's aggressiveness to the work. If one of them did everything he was asked and nothing more, he was more than likely just going to follow orders and not create anything of his own. If the cadet tried to get out of the work all the time, they would not be ready for the greater challenges that came later and they might get held back from the art of magic class. If the rare worker showed up that would take on additional responsibility, they were immediately promoted and moved onto bigger and better things. Magic was not all that complex, but it was demanding on the student and teacher alike. This had been a good session and the acolyte that was doing the instruction nodded to Zack.

"Not bad. You have been practicing." He said in an almost offhanded tone. "You still have a long way to go though." He warned and Zack nodded his understanding. The amulet went back into the box and he closed the little catch on it. It was valuable after all. Zack felt that he would see it again sooner or later. He was not sure what it did, but he was certain that it was more than just a piece of jewelry. "I need you to go and study now. There will be more tests later. Remain vigilant and you will do well." He instructed and Zack thanked him and left the stuffy room.

He headed back to his little quarters. The training had been going on now for six months and his skills were a little above average and he was starting to believe that this was all actually possible. He was the youngest acolyte in the wing and one of the youngest ever taught here. His acceleration into the program had stepped on a lot of toes and he had to watch out everywhere. His work ethic had turned most of the negative energy and convinced them that he was supposed to be here. He had turned a corner with the instructors too. They were now willing to help him when he struggled. He never gave up on a task and he had suffered much for his stubbornness. Now they all knew him and there were actually smiles for him in the corridors and byways of the ancient school. Zack was overall happy and he was still unaware of his destiny.

That's right. I didn't know what was to happen in the future. We had not learned about things like that because the future is a scary thing that is open to interpretation like no other magic art. I hate talking about myself in the third person, but it seemed easier for you to understand me more. My other friends were growing up too. I shall tell you about them next.

*   *   *

Fourteen summers had seen the elfin twins grow long and lanky. They would have looked awkward except for the natural grace of the elder race. Maxillen was running through the woods with the grace of a deer. He had his first bow in his hands. He had made it himself and it was crude by elf standards. Still, it was functional and his later masterpiece was still yet to be made. He had trained the tree with the right roots and his grand bow would be finished in another few years. A good elf bow was not made; it was grown in the right shape. The tree had to be coerced into making the perfect shape. It was an art form that took many years to fully develop, but the elves lived long and they took much pride in their craftsmanship. Right now though, He was racing towards a glimpse of his destiny. His bare feet trod lightly in the light underbrush and the wind of his passage blew his sandy brown hair behind him as he crossed the familiar terrain. The White Witch would be returning today and he was sent to escort her in. He had left his sister, Florena, at home. She had pouted about it, but the responsibility was his and his alone. The rendezvous was rapidly approaching and he knew that he should not be late. He could feel the pain as his lungs complained about the effort and strain he was putting on them. The songs of the birds above him continued unabated at his passing so he knew that he was not making too much noise with his panting. He jumped a particular log that was in his path and found that he didn't know the terrain as well as he thought. He had misjudged what was beyond it. He fell and fell as the small ravine played out below him. He scanned the wall for something to grab onto and he found a few vines. He reached out as he fell; trying to keep his mind focused and avoid the panic that was trying to kill his thoughts. He grabbed at the vines and just snagged one. The pull on his shoulder was hard. It hurt badly and he almost lost his grip. He swung his bow around the vine and pulled it to his other hand. He paused for a moment; the panting of his breath was now strained with the pain in his shoulder. His hand was still clenched on that life-saving vine though. He started to climb. He wrapped his legs around the vine and pinched it between them with his legs crossed. Then he pressed upward and let go of the hand that hurt him. It was a long way down and he really didn't want to see what was down there close up. Now he cursed the fact that he had made his sister wait behind. She could have pulled him up easily. He was the more nimble and she was the stronger of the two of them. He pulled with his good arm and slipped his legs up and pressed again with his torso. Then he reached up again. He slung his bow over his back and let the hurt arm dangle. This was going to be hard enough without it getting in his way. He continued his ascent. When he reached the top, his brow was caked with sweat and he was dirty. He looked down at himself and knew that he had just blown this meeting. He was now late and he was not presentable. He skirted the ravine and continued on anyway. Maybe, if she waited at the rendezvous point, he could still do his duty and escort her back. He knew that there would be words and disciplinary action, but he would face that if he still completed the mission. He went back to his run in an effort to get there in time. He bolted from the woods and into the clearing at a full run and the horses started. He froze in place and the woman in fine white robes looked at him first with a frown and then, to his surprise, with a roll of laughter.

Maxillen was angry at her reaction, but he realized quickly that her sense of humor could save him a lot of grief. He decided to go for humble here. "Many apologies your highness. I have fallen upon hardship en route to you and beseech your forgiveness in my tardiness." He said and he bowed low, but not evenly. His shoulder protested the movement.

"I see that you have some kind of trouble. Your shoulder is not working and your arm hangs loose from it. You cannot fire a bow that way to protect me. So right now the situation is unacceptable." She dismounted with a graceful slide down from the horse's back and glided over to the dirty lad and her smile remained in place. The poor boy wondered if she smiled when she smote down her enemies. He hoped that he would not find out. But she did not strike him. She held out a hand and he lifted his good arm up to take her hand. It was soft and sweet and he felt his heart race a bit just at the small contact. She pulled his hand to his opposing shoulder and told him to hold it in place. Then she grabbed his hanging arm and with a sharp jerk pushed it back into the socket. The pain was intense, but brief and his good hand actually felt the joint snap back in. His face showed his surprise and the woman in white smiled at him warmly. "You bore that well, you are truly a warrior." She said in a supportive tone.

The attention made him blush and she looked away to save him any further embarrassment. "Then miss, if you are ready, we can leave for the village." He offered and she shook her head.

"No, I will not travel further until you have demonstrated your archery skills for me." She said. His shoulder felt sore, but he could move his arm again, at least a little. He pulled the bow from his back and went to pull the string back. His shoulder screamed at him. It was too tender to apply that particular force to it. He winced and let go of the string.

She looked at him just as if he was a young child. "You cannot expect it to work like new after just being put back. You will be sore for a couple of days. The fact that you can pull the string at all is encouraging. Take it easy and enjoy my camp for a bit. When you are ready, we will go." She motioned for him to sit by the fire. The horses had since settled down and the camp looked undisturbed again. Max sat down almost heavily. For him, it was a bit of a change. He had always tread lightly and been Fleet of foot. He suddenly felt tired and heavy. His eyes were already closing and the White Witch pitied him. He had run a long way only to find that he was mortal after all. It was a lesson that many had to injure themselves to learn. She was just glad that the injury was not permanent. She would protect him through the night. Then maybe in the morning they could move on. Staying in place too long was even more dangerous than moving along with a disabled archer.

*   *   *

Florena was reading in the ancient texts. The village masters had introduced her to the writings in hopes that she would understand some of the more indistinct ones. She was, after all, a gifted reader and she was also a member of a set of twins. That meant that she was more attached to the spiritual side of their culture. She had been able to fill her time away from her brother with these studies. Suddenly, her shoulder hurt. She looked up and saw nothing. The book fell from her hands and the sage looked at her with a sideways glance.

"Is something wrong child?" He asked and she held her shoulder as she tried to understand what was happening to her. Her eyes clouded with the pain and she started to fall. The sage was old. He was older than most of the members of this community, but he was still agile. He scooped her up and placed her down gently in a soft bed of leaves. She whimpered there and he tried to pull her hand free to inspect the damage. She was strong. He pulled it away using almost all of his strength. When he observed the shoulder, it looked fine. It was obviously causing her a lot of pain. She was suddenly very weak. "What are you doing child?" He asked her and she gritted her teeth.

"I am sending him my strength." She replied. Her voice was strained and it tried to squeak on her. "He is in danger. He is hurt and he is afraid of falling somewhere." She said and the sage looked troubled.

"Who is afraid, young lady?" He asked and she shook her head. He tried to hold her still, but she began to thrash. He watched her and the motions looked familiar. She was climbing a rope. At least it looked that way to him. He called for his assistant. He tried to hold her arms and legs still, but they were tensed in a mortal struggle. Then, as if she had reached the top, she collapsed into exhaustion. Her eyes returned to the present and the sage looked at her in curiosity.

"He is out of danger now." She said. Her smile was genuine, but her eyes looked tired and still a bit worried. "He is hurt, but he will live now." She said and the sage put his hand on her shoulder.

"Tell me child, who is hurt?" He asked and she locked eyes with him.

"My brother is. He is trying to get to the White Witch and escort her here. Now he is hurt and scared in the forest. Worse yet, he is worried about being late for his mission. He is defenseless now that his arm is hurt." She said, as if reporting to a field commander.

"So you know what is happening to your brother from here?" He asked and she nodded that she did. He pulled the top of her shirt back and observed the bruising on her shoulder. If there was an injury on her brother, she shared it with him. He stepped away and produced a salve to remove the tenderness of the wound. With luck, it would help her brother as well. He knew that the White Witch was due back. He also knew that these two children were twins and thus were subject to some bizarre side effects of their maternal bond. Now he had documentable proof of this phenomenon. He began to take notes as she drifted off to sleep. She had to sleep for them both just now. Or maybe her brother was also asleep now and they needed to share this as well. He would have to question the young man when he returned. For now though, he had plenty to observe. He would monitor this one child and make sure that all was well.

The witch had told him that they were somehow special and that their lives would be in peril more often than was customary for anyone to have to endure. He had taken his oath to protect these two children seriously. It had taken him quite a bit to let Maxillen go on this mission alone. Now he realized that the boy was never alone. As long as he kept one of them with him, the children would be able to be protected by him. It may not be a perfect solution, but it brought him a sense of relief for the time being. He would deal with their protests later.

*　　*　　*

Max slept lightly, but his body was healing at a remarkable rate. He was unaware of his sister's connection to him and the care she had received for his benefit. He knew that he needed to get strong enough to protect the witch. He knew that they needed to get moving before anything evil found them alone in the woods. He knew that his ward had put magical protections around their camp and that many of the creatures would pass them by unnoticed. He also knew that these same protections would not work against anything truly dangerous. There would be stories to be told about this mission and he knew that his part would sound bad. He had been careless and he had been injured by that carelessness. He was lucky though and he had survived to attempt the mission. He hoped that his efforts would help him remove the stigma of his own stupidity. He felt only support from the amazing woman in white. She watched over him as he slept and he felt a wave of comfort and bliss wash over him. She had placed a magical ward over him to help him rest and recover. She also understood that they needed to move on as soon as they could. The world was not a safe place and those that sought power would always threaten those that had it. This elegant woman was no exception. She was powerful enough to make them pause though and that was all they had just now. It was not enough protection to be sure, but at least it was something. Max dreamed of grand adventures and mighty beasts. His bow was lying next to him and the quarrel of arrows he had made was slung over his good shoulder. Other than that, he looked like a small child cuddled up warm next to the fire.

Night finished without an encounter and when the first rays of the sun began to stretch across the blue-green grass and light the morning dew, Max awoke feeling quite rested and his arm moved a lot more easily. He picked up the bow and tested the string. It pulled easily. His strength was not at full, but his recovery was not bad at all. He set the bow back down and looked around he camp. The woman in white lay peacefully in her travel robes. A wolf skin wrap kept her from shivering in the night air and the fire had long since died out. Max stepped away and gathered some small sticks to rekindle it. If they could get some warm food in their bellies, then maybe they could get back to the village today. He hoped so. He had a suspicion that his sister needed him to be back. He was unsure why he felt that way, but no matter the source, the feeling was real. He dropped the sticks by the fire and took the small pot to the nearest creek for fresh water. When he came back, the beautiful woman was looking at him. Her gaze not so speculative, she was more than curious about something. He set the pot onto the sticks propped it up over the fire and with a small incantation, he caused the sparks to ignite the sticks and soon they would have hot tea. Then he turned his attention to his charge.

"I trust you slept well?" He queried and her face showed that he was acting out of the norm. She was a mixture of concern and surprise.

"How is it you can carry firewood today and haul water around when your shoulder was out of place just yesterday evening?" She asked. He shrugged his shoulders.

"I don't really know, but I suspect that my sister has something to do with it." He said and the white robed woman was surprised again.

"You share your experiences?" She asked and her tone suggested that this was new material for her.

"Sometimes I know when she is in trouble. I only assume that the reverse is true. She has come to my rescue before when a bully was trying to flatten me. She is much stronger than I am." He blushed a bit at the admittance. Still the information was true and the witch knew it. "Anyway, she must know when I am in trouble too." He fidgeted a bit as if he were uncomfortable with the path this conversation had taken. It was customary for the males to be the stronger ones. Of course that was the male perception of the role they were to take. It rarely reflected the truth of the situation. In fact, women were often stronger at least in spirit than the males of the tribe. This one had a strong spirit though. What he lacked in physical strength, he would easily make up for in spiritual and magical power. His will was almost unstoppable and his soul was bright and pure. She was sure that he did not know any of that, but his potential was greater than anyone she had ever met among her people.

"We must break camp soon and then we can be off to the village. We must talk with your sister about what she experienced during your ordeal. I believe that she has sent you some of her vast strength in order for you to recover more fully than should be possible. You are lucky to have this sort of connection. It is a very rare thing and the ancient texts only hint at the power available through it." She stood up and her glory was revealed. Her robes were sparkling white and her hair flowed as if the wind were blowing it. She held her hand aloft and the sun shone brightly upon her palm. The light danced around her as it played through the camp. The dew dried almost instantly and the water came to a boil faster than it would have. She lowered her hand and stepped forward. She didn't seem to walk; she glided across the ground and lowered her hand to the pot. The water was now tea. Max had seen no leaves crumble into it. Instead, she had made tea from the golden beams of light. It was all startling and somehow elegant. She poured a cup for each of them and then set the pot back down. Max took a sip and the tea flowed into him like golden energy. He felt revitalized and soothed at the same time. This was not some tea, it was warm nectar and he loved it. He found it difficult to just sip it. Of course the temperature made him do that. He wanted to just gulp the stuff down and then ask for more. This was amazing and he had never had anything like it before. Sooner than he would have liked, the cups were empty and the two adventurers broke camp. They were still on a mission. They needed to get back to the village and Max felt ready when they did start off towards that goal. He had his bow in hand again and this time, his steps were cautious. He would not make the same mistake while leading this expedition back home. He would make sure that she got home and then he would see what needed doing next. His new self-confidence made him bold and he wanted the chance to prove himself again.

She smiled and shook her head as he led the way like a stag deer. He was so full of himself and his minute abilities that she almost found it laughable. Still, she let him hold that image since it was useful for the current circumstances. There would be time later to correct him and make sure he improved.

*   *   *

Right or Wrong

The king had ordered all twin children to be put to death. It caused him a great deal of strife all across his kingdom. The normal guard detail was re-dispatched and their new black armor stood as a symbol of the dark deeds they were committing. The penalty for disobedience was death so they were as much victims as the children they were sent to slay. The cries and aftermath were avoided mostly by leaving as soon as the deed was done. They questioned midwives and medical personnel in their search. They hoped that the madness would end before too long. A prophecy was taken seriously around these parts and the abatement they hoped for never came. Children were hidden at birth if there was a chance of being discovered. They were separated and quieted away to prevent discovery. It didn't matter. The detail had a sorcerer with them. He would point out the offending children and the order would still be carried out. It was definitely a dark time.

After one of these missions, the group got together to discuss the future and to drown their own sorrows of their gruesome duty. The captain of the guard, Milas Fjord, looked over the tankard of ale he gripped and the images of his foul deeds passed through his head. His mood darkened even more than his armor. The innkeeper kept well clear of him and his group. They were all silent, lost in their own personal hells. Their manner was worse than a band of mercenaries. He looked out at his comrades.

"How have we fallen so far?" He asked in a soft voice laced with frustration. It was a thought they all shared. He slammed the tankard down on the table and the wench came to refill it. He shooed her away. He didn't want to forget through the liquor. He wanted to remember and somehow atone for his misdoings. He stood up and the other men watched him carefully. "This mission is evil. We are bound by contract and honor to continue it, but my heart demands more than this. We must disobey our directives and not slaughter any more innocents." He announced to the group. They were all in shock. It wasn't that they disagreed. In fact they all felt exactly the same way. It was just that he was openly defying the king. The sorcerer always seemed to know what was going on. The Captain's life was now in danger. They knew it, but were unable to bring themselves to stop him. Instead they simply looked on.

"We need to get back to the castle and I will personally tell the king that we are guards, not butchers. He will probably have me killed for this, but I will at least die having tried to clear my conscience." He said. He wavered for a brief second and then he lifted his tankard up high. He was going to tilt it back and empty it the rest of the way. At least that was how it appeared.

This was all a ruse to get the sorcerer to lower his guard to attack. The dark spell caster had foreseen this outburst and he was ready to carry out the king's instructions and kill this upstart before he shattered morale beyond his ability to recover it. He pointed his ring at the man in the black armor and muttered a few words. His breath caught as the dagger plunged into his chest. The Captain had not continued with the tankard. He had kept his other hand on the hilt of his parrying dagger and drawn it slowly. In his effort to cast the spell, the sorcerer did not see the slow hidden movement. His spell died unfinished as he slumped to the floor. The sorcerer's hand reflexively moved to withdraw the weapon and the pulling out of it ripped his chest open even further. His blood was now flowing to the wooden floor and the pain in his chest told him that he was finished. He could not draw a breath either. His arms flopped to his sides and he fell forward. The impact broke his nose. By that time, it didn't matter anymore. He was dead.

The black-clad men all turned to see the dead man and hope surfaced in them after so long. Their dark demeanor turned to a positive note and the Captain actually smiled at them. "I mean what I say and we need to return to the king now." He said and he stepped over and retrieved his dagger. He wiped it off on the fallen sorcerer and then tossed the innkeeper a few coins for the mess. The man looked surprised. Then he surprised Milas. He tossed them back.

"No sir, if you are truly defying that dark decree, I'll clean up your mess for free." He said proudly and he got his mop to start the process right away. Milas nodded to him and led his men out of the inn and back out onto the street to retrieve their horses. They rode out of the town and back towards the castle.

Word spread of the honorable Captain and his defiance and soon it reached the ears of the king. Somehow, the word spread even faster than the men could ride. Of course they could not use magic to relay the message and others could. By the time they reached the fortress of gray stone, the entire remaining guards were posted outside to prevent them entering the fortification.

Milas reined his horse in and looked on. He lifted his visor and smiled at the guards along the wall and at the closed gate. His job now was to inform the king of his insubordination. It appeared that the job had already been done for him. Still, his own personal honor code required him to continue on and do it anyway. The old man on the throne needed to be told that his greedy and personal request was wrong. He set about the task. He drew his sword and readied his men for a charge.

*   *   *

The king huddled in his throne room. He knew that his kingdom was in disarray. His latest set of decrees had made him very unpopular. Still, he was the king and they would do what he said or they would die! His anger rose unbidden and he calmed himself down only with great effort. Now he had a disciplinary problem with his guard captain. This was not good news. The man had always been loyal before. Some outside influence must be acting upon him. This made him dangerous. He kept his seer close and the impending sounds of doom continued. He hoped that his soothsayer would tell him that the captain would not get into his fortifications, but alas the witch-man had told him the opposite. The captain would get in and there would be a confrontation. He hoped that it would not be one of violence. His battle years were behind him by more than he could count. He still had his ceremonial armor on, but it would not hold up to this man and his dark armor of king's service. He spat at the thought. King's service, what a joke. This man wanted to kill him. He kept the power close and no one would take it away from him. The anger rose again. The king drew his sword from the hand rest of his throne. It was in this pose that he expected the traitor to come. When Milas did not enter the room right away, he dropped the tip of the heavy sword and it tapped the floor and came to rest there. The king sighed and dragged it back to his seat. There would be time enough to fight. All he could do now was wait. He was the most powerful man in the kingdom and waiting did not suit him. When this man came, his anger would empower him to kill the upstart. Order must be maintained.

*   *   *

Milas sat atop his horse and the gate stood before him. He had been in on the design of this gate and it would not fall for a few men on horseback. It would, however, open if the right circumstances were applied to it. He circled around a bit, checking for a particular buttress in the wall above the massive gate. He found what he was after. He quickly sheathed his sword and drew his crossbow. He dismounted the horse and dropped to one knee. He aimed carefully and with a sigh, he loosed the bolt and it arced up to the buttress. The bolt struck the stone and ricocheted into the compartment beyond. It stuck into a wooden gear there and pinned it in place. To the overly complex mechanism, it was like locking the door in place. Everyone inside the structure was now locked in. They were officially under siege now. Milas smiled again and he put the crossbow back into the sling on his horse's back. Then he drew torches. They were strips of cloth soaked in pitch. He lit one from an existing torch on the wall and then flung it over the wall. The torch left a trail of black smoke behind it as it sailed end over end over the wall and onto the grain-shed roof. The fire caught immediately and the alarm was raised to put out the blaze. The food supply for the castle was stored there. It had been an excellent throw. He backed away with his horse and they rode off together to go for the other side of this castle. There was a secret exit for the king that was quite a distance away from the main barricades. He would wait for the man to panic and come to him. So if he couldn't get inside of the castle, then he would simply bring the king out to talk to him. Once he was clear, he drew a trumpet from his pack. It was used in battle to order the troops around. He blew three high notes and a short run in a decrescendo. It was the battle song for an overwhelming force and the order to beat a hasty retreat. He blew it several times to make sure that all heard it. The only one that mattered was the king himself.

*   *   *

The king was still in his throne room when the trumpet calls came. He was instantly enraged with the audacity of the move. The aids had already told him that the food stores were destroyed and that the gate would not open to get more. He knew about the secret exit so he was not worried personally. He needed time to get away though. This guard captain was going to be relentless. He just knew it. His seer was no help at all. The man looked frightened himself. There was nothing alive that he feared for he could tell the future and thus avoid anything harmful. This shook the king to his foundation. He feared for his life now. He picked up his sword and told his seer to follow him. They would leave this place and escape to fight another day. He had three personal bodyguards as well and they led the way through the seldom-used tunnel to the emergency exit. The hatchway had been grown over and so when they reached the end of the tunnel, it took two of the three bodyguards to move the door. For the moment, the king was thankful that he had brought them with. He could not have opened the door himself. They emerged and looked around. Shafts protruded from their chests as the waiting black guards peppered them with arrows. They had been lying in wait and now the moment was at hand. The two men fell back into the tunnel and the third guard tossed the king away from the opening. An arrow sailed into the hole and the seer looked down at his own chest. It was lodged right next to his heart. This was the image that had made him so afraid. Now that the moment had arrived, he embraced it and fell over in peace. The last bodyguard started to usher the king back away from the attackers. He felt the stab as the arrows filled his back. They penetrated his armor and that same armor that usually protected him suddenly became very heavy as his own strength left him. He dropped to his knees and his armor made a clanking sound as they hit the stone blocks in the floor. The king gazed at him in horror. He gaped at the intruders and he knew them. He knew all of them. They were once his guards. The Captain led the way and the king pulled his sword up in readiness. The whole situation was so laughable.

Milas lowered his weapon. The crossbow was not loaded anymore anyway. He smiled at the frightened man before him. "Look how low we have both sunk." He said in that small space and his voice echoed in the tunnel. "Your majesty if you would accompany us to the surface we can talk with a bit more dignity than this small space affords us." He said and the king knew that he was vastly outnumbered. He lowered his sword and nodded.

The king stood among his former guards and he knew that he was not a liked man. They had the evil in their eyes. He had tainted them with his commands and they were probably here to avenge themselves upon him. At least he knew that he was a dead man. They had killed his advisor and that was an offense punishable by death in itself. He wanted to take his revenge upon them, but he knew that it would be futile. His only hope was to stall them until reinforcements could come. Unfortunately he didn't even know if any were coming. His heart began to feel the despair that had truly befallen him. His situation was lost.

Milas sat down the crossbow and knelt before the king. In truth, the king did not know what to expect next. "Sire, I have been your loyal servant for many years. I fought beside you in battles of valor that would rival legend. I pledged my sword to your service and my heart still longs for that to be so.' He said and the king's brows rose with the everlasting fealty he was feeling from this man. Perhaps he had misjudged the good Captain as an outlaw. "You must know that what you have sent us to do is wrong." Milas said, pulling the king from his thoughts. "You sent us to kill innocent children in order to protect you from a ghost." He made eye contact and Milas' eyes were stone cold. "We did this deed of yours until we could stomach it no longer. This butchery ends now." He proclaimed and the king grew suddenly angry.

"How dare you tell me what is and what is not. I am king of this land. Your lives are forfeit to me as I choose. This prophecy is strong and I have had it verified by more than one seer. There will be twins and they will bring the end of my rule. That much is certain." He said in a huff. Milas was unaffected by his outburst.

His tone dropped to a dangerous level. "If prophecy tells you that your rule will end, then it will. Your rule, like everything else in nature, is a finite thing and has to end someday. That is why you have offspring to carry on your family line. We will not continue on this dark course. Your grip on your seat of power is fragile at best. You have made the people fear you. That is what makes it work for now. When they decide that they can no longer live with your horrible actions, they will come and behead you. Then your rule will be finished for sure. I would protect you in that hour if you revert to the kind and benevolent king you used to be. That man I would support unto death and beyond if it were in my power to give. For a tyrant as you have become, I hold nothing but contempt." His words were scathing and the king thought this knight would turn and spit after uttering them. He did not.

"My rule is good for the kingdom. I have brought my people up from their humble beginnings. The trade routes have been fully established and commerce with other kingdoms is now possible. No one is starving in my kingdom either. People are working for a better future. Is that not what I have done?" He asked, his manner suggested that this was a challenge to his rule and he had spent some time making sure his arguments were iron clad and rock solid. He was a person for the people. That had been true once. Now he wasn't so sure, but he needed to be so he put on that persona to placate this knight and his deadly sword.

"It is true that you have done much during your rule." Milas admitted. "It is also true that hunger has been dealt with at least to some degree. Clothing has been provided for others and your community-minded efforts are known from border to border." He said and the king swept his arms wide to encompass the land around them.

"I have done much to raise my people to where they are today." He said, taking credit for all of the reform. In truth, he had instigated the reform and was responsible for most of the work being done.

"I will admit that you have done much for this kingdom. It is why we are talking now and you do not currently have a belly full of steel. "I think that you can be saved. That good man you once were is still in there somewhere. We just need you to find him and revert you to your former self. Then the land can once again move forward and strive to become a major power in this entire region instead of hiding in their homes in fear of their own leader and his minions of doom." He said and the king looked at him anew.

"You mean you want to go back to the glory days. Back to the days of good guys and bad guys; the days of chivalry and kindred spirits?" The king asked and Milas looked a bit uncomfortable. "I never wanted those days to go away, but they did. I have been trapped in my towers, trying to find the spirit that would save the day. Now I have found at least a part of that." He said and Milas looked confused. "Surely you don't think that this deed can go unpunished?" He asked, a bit of amazement in his voice. "You have contradicted a direct command from me. I cannot allow that to go without some recourse. It would set a precedent that would crumble the command structure and allow everyone to be equal under the new lawless land. You need to bow down before me in public and admit that your actions were wrong in capturing and confronting me. Then I can get to work on this transformation you believe is needed." The king said. His eyes gave away nothing as Milas peered into them.

"No milord, I cannot admit to wrongdoing for this act. I can, however, admit to wrongdoing in following your order in the first place. If that will suffice, then I would be only too happy to comply with your directive. Then the kingdom can get down to healing and recovering. Please, let us help you to regain your social standing with your people. Allow us to appear in public helping people. It would be an act of atonement for past deeds. It would also go a long way if you made some form of compensation for the families of the slain children." He said and the king actually seemed to listen to the suggestion. His face showed a war going on inside as he weighed the two sides of the argument. Milas held hope until the king shook his head.

"No, if I admit any wrong, it would show the people that I am weak, fallible. They must see me as right and strong. I must be invincible in their eyes in order to command their respect. If I cannot have that respect, then I must use their fear to maintain control." He said and his look turned to that of a predator. "You must comply and bow before me or my other troops will hunt you down like a dog." He said directly and without emotion. His eyes were turning red with the hatred that was bubbling up from beneath the murky water of his mind. "If you will not do this, then run away. Go somewhere that my men will never find you. You cannot be allowed to interfere with my power. There is no clear heir and the land would fall into disarray without me on the throne. You know this to be true. You must walk away now or serve me without question."

Milas shook his head. "I'm sorry sire, but I cannot follow you now. We will take ourselves away and not bother you any longer. I had hoped that there was still a chance to save you, but now I can see that the power has corrupted you beyond reason. You will not have to worry about us anymore. We are no longer citizens of your kingdom." He stood up and took off the black gauntlet on his right hand. He threw it to the ground before the king. "My service to you is at an end." He said formally. And he turned to leave. The king's rage continued to build as the scene played out before him. He gripped his personal dagger so tight in his hand that his knuckles were white.

He now stood up quickly and lunged forward. "Die traitor!" He shouted as he moved forward. His dagger flashed in the light and the sound of a bowstring twanged. The cry of anger turned to a surprised shout of pain as the king fell backward, staring at his arm. His hand no longer held the knife. The shaft of the arrow had gone through his forearm and his fingers would not work. The shock prevented him from feeling much of the pain. Unfortunately it would wear off soon enough. He staggered back and fell to a sitting position in the grass. He stared at these men who had killed his guards and his seer and who now had the power to kill him as well. They turned as one and left the startled man sitting in a field of grass. He cursed at them but they never turned back to look at him. They left the black armor behind and they headed out of the kingdom. It was one of the saddest days that they had ever experienced. Milas led his men away and they were all relieved to have this dark episode of their lives be done and behind them.

*   *   *

ELEMENTS AT RANDOM

I had been doing my work diligently and my studies had gone well. I was not as fast as other students, but my work ethic continued to serve me well. Sometimes it made the other students angry with me, but I quickly became one of the favorites of the instructors. Magic had been such a flighty goal at first and now parts of it were making sense to me. I was working hard on my air studies and the small particles in it. There were so many ways to manipulate them that the spell combinations appeared to be endless. There was a special pair of glasses that allowed me to see the particles for brief periods of time. They danced and sparkled in the air as I watched. The price was a monstrous headache. I was so enthralled by them though, that I continued to borrow and use the glasses. I found that if the particles moved in currents they could be used to build energy. Some of the cryptic words of the spells began to make sense to me. The mind did not like to lock onto those words, but now the meanings of the words were forming images in my head. I could link the images to form the correct words. It was a major step in the initiation of an acolyte when he constructed his first spell. That is not when he cast one, but when he created one. I could see this as being one of the best parts of the whole training. I was looking forward to using this power. However, looking back, I was really not ready for what came next.

It all began so innocently. I had been late to a meeting in the common area. Of course I paid the price by staying behind and helping the master clean up after his demonstration. The display had been neat though. He had combined air and fire elements to make a controlled explosion. The rolling ball of fire had danced around at his will. It seemed to consume anything it touched, but he had it so precisely controlled that it did not do any real damage. We all felt the heat, but none of us were burned. It was an amazing display of skill and control. I would have mentioned this, but I had not yet been spoken to. Instead, I was sweeping ashes from the floor and then I would stack the books and transport them back to the master's tower before they fell into some wrong hands.

The master had been bored with me recently and it may have made him drop his guard a bit. I worked in peace as the wisps of fire began to form. I really didn't notice them at first. They began to swirl above me in the high-ceilinged chamber as I concentrated on the floor. Then the wind picked up. We were inside. I looked around and the stone floor began to melt. I called out in surprise. It was not my bravest moment, but it may just have saved my life. The master looked up, ready to chastise me for my outburst. He saw the fire as it swept down for me. The floor opened up and a geyser of hot water erupted from the opening as I felt the pull of the wind upward. The fire began to burn me. Fear rose up in me like I had never felt before. The wind caught my robes and I was off of the floor as the tendrils of fire lashed me over and over again. The scars would be terrible I thought, wondering if I would even survive. Rocks sputtered from the water and struck me. The wind was knocked out of me and I could not speak anymore. That eliminated any chance of spell casting out of this mess. The master was running now. I could just see him through the pain. He was waving his arms and casting something big. The wind slammed me down to the floor and the melted rock solidified, holding me in place. The rocks continued to pound me and the fire lashed out at me over and over again. I thought I would go mad. Then the worst part came. The water rushed over me. I held my breath, but I could not get out of the floor. I then knew that I was going to die here.

The master pulled both arms back and swept them forward. The winds he called pressed the water away and I took another desperate breath in the short respite. The water sloshed back over me again and at least the stones stopped hitting me through it. The fire was also cooled under the water. For that at least I was thankful. The broom had been destroyed under the unforeseen attack. The floor began to crush my back. The elements were all working against me. The master swept the water free again and I took another badly needed breath. This time, though, my mind was working. I shouted the time stop command and the elements all froze in place. It even stopped the press on my back. I tried to squeeze free as the world around me seemed to be a snapshot of utter chaos. I managed to wriggle free and stepped out of the hole that had been my burial place. Then I commanded time to continue.

The master froze for a second and he realized what I had done. Then he and I both put our hands forward and cast the banishment spell. The elementals fought the compulsion, but in moments they were all sent away and the room returned to its former state. The hole was gone and the air was completely still again.

I felt tired. Okay it was more than tired. I felt drained. It felt like the whole world had come to get me and they had almost succeeded. The master looked at me with a new respect.

"How did you know the time-stop spell?" He asked and I reminded him that I had cast it from the wand during the visitation from the White Witch. He said that he understood that all I had done was to find the power word for the wand. I shrugged my shoulders.

"I didn't know that the power words were limited to the item they belong to. I thought they were usable anywhere." I replied and he took me aside.

"You are a remarkable young man. The witch saw something in you that we have as yet not seen. I wish to know more about your theories. We can talk regularly and I will help you with your studies as well." He said and I nodded my thanks.

"If you will pardon my ignorance sir, but what was that we just experienced?" I asked and he shook his head.

"There is no crime in ignorance; there are only answers yet to be sought." He paused, as if putting his next words together properly before speaking. "You have just been attacked by random elements." He said quietly. "There are elements living among us all the time. We have a good relationship with them most of the time. We do not destroy their habitat and they grant us our powers. When some of the elements feel that we have not held up our end of the bargain they become disgruntled. Such an element by itself is annoying at best. It is when they combine that they can start to wield true power. My guess here is that you either have set them off or that you will do so in the future. Elements are not constrained to a linear view of time. They can see pretty much all of it at once. They live outside of it all like observers in our world but with the power to affect things here. They help us as part of their amusement and to maintain this lifestyle that they love so much. If you do something in the future that is so important as to launch all four elements at you, then we must make sure that you are prepared for this future. Your training will be advanced again. I don't know what you are or where you are going, but the world has singled you out as special. We cannot stand in the way of that." He said as if addressing a young prince. "You need to be able to protect yourself from these attacks. This is the earliest that I have witnessed such a thing.

You have not even had time to develop a dislike among these creatures as yet. Neither have I seen an attack so focused. Whatever it is that you will do, it is going to be major."

I looked at him as if he had grown wings. I'm sure that it showed on my face that I was surprised. There was nothing in my past that could have prepared me for this turn of events. I had already been bogged down with the studies and now they were going to speed those up. Somehow I doubted that it could even be done. I wondered what else would change and what was coming for me next. Those elements had nearly killed me.

"Sir, I don't mean to sound ungrateful, but how will I be advanced further? I mean, I can barely keep up now." I said, a bit shakily. The old man looked at me with a wry grin.

"Quite right you are. If you didn't feel burdened, then I would have been worried. Rushing the training is dangerous. There are things that are usually remembered through repetition and you will have to find another way to do it. You do not have the time to do things the normal way. The witch sort of warned us about you, but there is obviously more here than either of us can see just now. You must do all that you can. I have spoken with your teachers and they all agree that you have diligence enough to make up for the accelerated schedule. They worry as I do about gaps in your training and we will guard against that as best as we can. We are not trying to produce a super-mage here; all we want is for you to get the basics upon which you can expand yourself. Your classmates will be more powerful than you most of your career. It seems you will always be playing catch up." He looked troubled. "But alas there is more to tell. Usually we have students select an element to master. You have not been far enough into the program to be told this. There is no way that anyone can master all of the elements. The elements themselves fear anyone who tries. It gives too much power to a single individual. It is this course that I think you must follow. We do not know how you will be challenged, so we must prepare you for any contingency. You will be trained in all four elements. You are used to being tired and hungry, this will not change. The long nights of studying are just now beginning and your pursuits will have you on different eating and sleeping schedules. We have masters of all four elements here and we will give you to them one at a time for personalized training." He paused for a moment. "That is, as soon as you have mastered the basics." His robes were damp from the previous fight and he looked more haggard than the casting he had done would suggest. The two of us walked together out of the chamber and back to the living quarters. "You must remain here until you are summoned. Keep diligent on your studies while you have this time. Meals will be brought to you and a ward will be placed on your room for protection. Once we have secured the area again, we will come for you and you can rejoin the classes. If this takes too long tutors will be sent to you. Treat them with respect. They are trying to help you. This is most irregular and you will simply have to adapt to the changing circumstances. Is that clear?" He asked. There was no humor in his voice at all.

"Yes sir, I will remain here and practice hard. I understand the need to be prepared and I will cause no trouble for you more than what has already been revealed." I replied, hoping it would be the right thing to say. He simply nodded to me and left. The door closed behind him as my quarters were magically sealed. From the look of it, I was not to even see the other acolytes anymore. It would be lonely I figured. I was wrong.

It was not long after I had been left that the first tutors showed up. They made some warding signs as they entered the room. I was busily practicing my air conjuration. The elements had answered the call, but it was a limited thing. It was less than half the result I would have gotten before the attack. Something had really messed them up in my corner of the world. I thanked them for the effort they did give and I disbanded the spell when the tutors arrived.

It was two men that I had never seen before. They were upper classmen in the acolyte training program and they looked at me as if I were an infected corpse. They really didn't want to get all that close to me. I could not have convinced them that I was innocent of any wrong doings. In fact, if your future self is involved, there may be no deniability anyway. I greeted them accordingly with their rank in the guild. They did their best to make sure that I learned something. It was more about how uncomfortable they were than actual magic use, but I did my best to comprehend not only their teachings, but also the messages hidden behind them. It was not until the master came to me that the real progress started being made. We went to a workout chamber. There were hot coals in a large air furnace and a water trough on the other side. The ceiling had an opening to the sky and the floor was dirt. It was perfect for our use. Of course that was what the room was meant for, but the comment still holds true. I stepped up to the marker in the middle of the room and awaited my first instruction.

The master stroked his beard as he considered the first test. He stepped behind a protective barrier and then he called out to me. "Okay young man; show me what you know of water elements." He instructed and I quickly ran through what little that I really did know about the element in question.

"I do not know much, but I will do as you command." I announced and then I started the spells. The water trough began to boil and froth. I pulled the power from the water and shot the column into the air. It went straight up and then hit an unseen barrier and spread out in all directions. It looked like an umbrella from what Casey told me when I described it to him. The water sheeted down and around the central column and then broke into ribbons of moisture. They turned back in on the trough and returned to their normal state when the spell finished. There was nary a drop outside of the trough when it was done. Then it was time to show the last spell that I had learned. I brought up both hands and spoke the words of the shield spell. The water swept up out of the trough and arced over to me. The sheeting action surrounded me as I concentrated on the spell. A perfect ring of sheeting water encompassed me and then I spoke the final words. The water froze in place and I was then trapped in a cage of solid ice. The ice was not natural though. A hammer could not have broken it. Magical hammers had a chance of cracking it. It would have to be a non-standard attack to penetrate this particular barricade. Of course at the same time, I could not send anything out of the shield spell. The ice was clear enough to allow me to see, but that was the extent of my contact with the world outside of the spell. I could not hear or smell anything. I could not cast outside of the shield even though I could see the target clearly. It was like a self-imposed prison. This spell also would not allow you to move. So escape from an enemy would be impossible. It was like being in a fortress of glass. I held the shield for a few minutes and then I dissolved the ice back into mist and then wafted it over to the trough to redeposit it where it began with a wave of my hand. The master looked pleased with the cast.

"I can see that you have been paying attention in your classes." He said and I could tell he somehow meant more than what he said. I did not understand it at the time, but he was actually proud of me. "Now, show me what you know of fire." He instructed and I felt queasiness in my stomach. I had not used fire all that often. It was the most popular element but I had an inherent fear of the art. I took a deep breath and pulled the image I wanted from my mind. The coals did not have any open flame when I started. I fanned them to flames with a small gust of wind and then the real spell started. Flames danced and frolicked about as they rose into the air. The room became quite hot as the flames built a wall before me. I sent the image I wanted and they formed into a vast bird of fire. It had been an image I had seen sketched into a book. The whole thought of it scared me. It was this that I wanted the master to see. I was facing and indeed using my own fears to complete the conjuration. The bird soared overhead and circled around in the vast amount of space in this high chamber. Then I swept my arms around and pointed at a stone altar. The bird swooped down and landed on the altar. Then I tried my most powerful spell. I commanded the bird to split into two. It hesitated and then did as it was bid and I soon had two smaller birds of fire perched on the altar, awaiting my next command. I sent them up into the air again and they performed a ballet of deadly power. The dance was quite beautiful but I had to maintain my concentration. Then I started to feel weary from the spell and called them back to the coals. They flew into them as if they wanted to crash into the ground. Instead of an impact, they simply diffused into the coals as soon as they touched them. Then I removed the gusts of wind and the flames died back down to their previous glow. I didn't realize it, but I was breathing hard now. I looked around and saw the master nodding. I hoped that was a good sign.

"You have learned much from what I can see. It is amazing to me since you are still a first year acolyte." He said, pulling on his beard in a thoughtful pose. "Who taught you to split the phoenix in twain?" He asked and I bowed my head.

"I saw it in a book." I replied. His eyes opened wider.

"You have access to books of magic?" He asked. His tone was dangerous and I could feel the anger rising from him. I knew that I needed to defuse him before he exploded into rage and stopped my training.

"No sir, I was looking at a book of fantasy as a child. I could not read then, but there were sketches and I thought that those pictures would create an impressive display." I added in a hurry. His face changed right away. Now it looked more troubled than angry.

"So let me understand this. You saw this fiery bird in a book and made it happen from your mind alone without knowing the proper spell for it?" He asked and it was obvious that the answer he was seeking was no. He *wanted* to be wrong about this. Of course the only problem with that is that he was right. I had wanted to impress him and I thought it would be the best thing to use. Now I was unsure of my next move.

"Sir, is what I did wrong? I just wanted to make a good light show so that you would see I've been learning. I didn't want you to think that you are wasting your time with me. I wanted to please you so desperately. Perhaps my error was in judgment, but if so I apologize humbly." I replied and I dropped to my knees in a bow. I hoped that it would be enough to show that I meant no disrespect. I had misread the man almost completely.

"You have done well. In fact, you have done far better than you should have been able to do. Part of this intrigues me and part of it makes me worry. You felt the heat of the spell?" He asked and I nodded that I had. In fact, I had been sweating during the entire conjuration. "You did not make a fancy lights display. You conjured an elemental beast and furthermore, you made it split into two such beasts. That level of power should be beyond your control and yet you allowed them to fly and then were able to bring them back to the coals. It is truly remarkable." He stepped down from the platform he had been observing from. "I see that you are tired now. After what I have seen, I don't blame you for this. It was inevitable. We shall continue this after you have had some time to rest. Do not study this night. In your weakened state, the elementals may take advantage of you and that would be a sorry situation here in my school. Get some good rest and eat a good meal on the morrow. Then come back to me here. The protections will remain on the hallway and will track with you. You should not be detected while on your course. Of course you must avoid contact with any of the other students or faculty. They could be manipulated into something dangerous against you." He paused to let all of that sink in. His expression told me that he expected me to understand everything. Fortunately this time I did. He wanted to keep me safe until I could be trained further. I did understand that. I nodded to him and stood back up. Then I left for the room that I had been confined to. It was now the safest place to be. He told me later what had transpired after I left.

* * *

The master looked around the room that had just been used to house two phoenix conjurations. He knew apprentices that could not have mastered the skills to conjure just one of them. Now this young acolyte does it for show. He knew that something was wrong here. The elementals had attacked the boy and the White Witch had given him some cryptic warnings about this same boy. Zack had been watched closely. He was a diligent worker almost to the point of extremism. He had power. He was not the most focused child that had ever wielded the magic, but he had vast amounts of energy at his disposal. He had controlled things that should have required much more training of the mind in order to understand. He needed to speak to the witch again. He knew that it would be difficult, but he also knew that he would have trouble protecting the young man by himself. There were bigger players involved here. He left the chamber and headed for his own personal study. He had a scrying bowl there and maybe, if she was in a good mood, he could establish a link to the witch and ask her more about the puzzle in his charge.

He pulled back the curtains from around his conjuring chamber. The worn floor was still comfortable to him as he sat in the center of the runes that were scribbled so painstakingly on the floor. These were words of power in the ancient language. He had protections and intrusion glyphs etched out about him. He was almost invincible inside this fortress of magic. He knew that the threat was real. He knew that the young man knew nothing of his own destiny. The witch had sent for him to be brought to the school. She had made sure to come and meet him when he arrived at the school. Now she would be interested in knowing his potential. The master knew this to be true. He hoped that her curiosity would override her anger at having been scryed. He filled the bowl with water from a gourd he had set aside for just such a task. He dropped a few drops of some liquid metal into the bowl as well. Then he commanded the winds to blow. They needed to link him to the distant location in the elven forest. She had been heading back there all those months ago. Hopefully, the winds could find her without too much trouble. Once they were linked, then the bowl would allow him to see her and if she had a water source around, she could see him too. He started the chant that would allow the winds to stay linked as they bridged the gap over the land. It was like water in a pool reacting from a liquid dye being poured in. The connection spread and covered more and more area. The only difference was that it was focused in a specific direction. It was like an arrow streaking out over the landscape and searching for the distant forest so far away. The wind was fast. It bridged the long gap and the bowl formed the image like a reflection on the still surface. The master peered in and noticed that she was already looking back at him. Her face did not show anger though. It showed more of an 'I told you so' attitude and it annoyed him ever so slightly. Still, he put that emotion away before it could show on his face.

"Greetings milady." He said and he performed a small bow without taking his eyes off of the water. If he broke the concentration now, it would kill the spell. "I trust that the journey was pleasant for you?" He asked. His tone remained light and casual.

"I live for the journey. The land and I are forever linked. We elves belong to the world and it to us. It is not a matter of a good or bad journey." She said as if addressing a slow student. It was a speech that he had heard before.

"Of course, I meant no disrespect." He replied as he had always done in the past. "The reason that I am contacting you…"

"Is that you have seen what the child can do and you were wondering how it can be and how did I know about it." She finished for him and he looked startled.

"Am I that transparent?" He asked and she chuckled. He loved the light melodic sound of it.

"No, we are just on a pre-determined journey the both of us. You have been given the supreme honor of training the savior of our world." She said and he looked startled again.

"He is the savior of our world?" He choked out. "You mean this small boy?" He asked incredulously. "He is still untrained and unready for the power he can conjure. He conjured two phoenix birds to display what he knew of fire for me today." He offered and the White Witch smiled at him.

"Did he lose control of them?" She asked and it was obviously a sore spot for the master.

"No, he did not. He commanded them to fly and then back to the coals. It never looked as though they would attack him. His will was complete and intact even as they tried to eek away at his mind." He said and she nodded to him.

"Of course, he had brought them into existence. They owed him their lives. You know what can happen if they believe that they can undermine their master. He has such a vast potential that you will be amazed over and over again as the training continues." She told him and he just sighed.

"So are you willing to tell me more about him? How does he save the world?" The master asked. He knelt forward in case she answered softly. He did not want to miss any useful information.

"I am troubled over that image. I cannot say what he does that saves the world. I can only tell you that he will not do it for more than five thousand years. The spirits have shown us that he is somehow special and that they will come for him. I do not know further than that." She looked to the side for a moment and it became obvious that someone was telling her something outside of the link. Then she turned back as the master waited patiently. "There is one more thing I can tell you. When they come for him, they will bring death and chaos with them. Some kind of demon will follow the saviors through to find your young man."

The master tried to absorb this information but it was just so far fetched. Who lives five thousand years? "Who will come for him?" He asked and the elf witch shrugged her delicate shoulders. Even this far away and viewed through a scrying bowl, she was strikingly beautiful.

"The spirits have not made it clear who is coming, only that they will come." She answered. Her face showed that she wished she could offer more. The fate of the world was at stake. She knew that as well as anyone. But there was no more to give. It was so frustrating. She had taken precautions. "I must go now. There are plans set in motion and I must ready our kind for them. You must do as best as you can to prepare the chosen one for his trials. It is all that I can tell you now. If I see more, I will give that to you as well." She said and he nodded his thanks to her.

"I thank you kindly and wish only health and long life to you and your kind." He said formally and she waved her arm and the spell broke. He was left with even more questions than he had before the contact. This boy was more important than even her earlier messages would have led him to believe. He decided to sleep on it. With any luck, he would know what to do in the morning. He crept over to his sleeping mat and as tired as he was from the spell, he fell asleep almost instantly.

* * *

ANOTHER TIME; ANOTHER PLACE

The *Lost Cavalier* stayed on its course and the enemy ship was right there beside her. Neither of them dared to fire anything in this faster than light space of nothingness. They both readied themselves for a life and death struggle as soon as they dropped out of warp. There was no way to evade the enemy now. The reduced human crew had to face the enemy and their race would live or die with their efforts. It was a heavy burden for them to bear. Captain Glass was already feeling that massive weight. He sat in his briefing room. The plots were set before him and he knew that the Earth would be powerless against the enemy force in the time period they were heading to. The best calculations would put them in the fifteenth or sixteenth century. According to their historian, that was when the king ruled that they needed to find. It was still the plan. He knew that they couldn't fail. They had no options anymore. Everything hinged on this one thing. They had to succeed. His hand shook as he tried to come to grips with the responsibility. He was, after all, the Captain. He needed to be invincible and unshakable. He found that living up to the ideal was harder than the manuals would have predicted. He grabbed hold of a locket that he kept with him all the time. It had belonged to his wife. She had been on one of the first colonies hit; she had been visiting others in the family. Their primary residence was still on Earth. He knew that she would want him to succeed. She was the reason that he was doing this. He wanted her back so badly. The gold locket and the frail chain would have been cold if he had not been holding it so tightly. Now it was warm and comforting. Her image was on the inside and he held it up for a better view of the striking lady of his life. Her gaze looked somewhat sad. She had not liked the picture at all. He liked that feature of it most of all. It showed her more naturally than some studio presentation. He held the picture up for a moment more and then he closed it. The present needed his attention. The countdown clock told him that they would be dropping out of warp in about fifteen minutes. The weapons were charged and the enemy was close enough to score a major hit with their beam weapons. His only hope was to disable or destroy it before they fired in return. His poor ship couldn't take another beating like the one it had already suffered. It was all patchwork and welds now. He got up and left the briefing room. He didn't even bother to switch off the screen. He knew that his business would be concluded one way or another on the bridge now. So he headed straight there. When he walked onto the bridge, he smiled at his first officer. The man was just hitting the comm. button to page him to the bridge. It was a nice sentiment, but he knew what time it was. It was time to meet his destiny. If there were any records of this mission, history would call this a pivotal moment in their story. He strolled over to the command chair and the first officer vacated it with the appropriate log entry to hand over command back to the Captain.

"Give me a situation report." He ordered and the crew gave their status by the numbers and he nodded to each one in turn as they related all the pertinent information to him. His ship was ready for this fight. He had reservations about her sturdiness, but not of his crew. These people were all professionals. He took in the sights and sounds of the bridge as they all watched him, at least out of the corners of their eyes. He tapped his fingers on the arm of the chair. There was a worn spot there from him doing so for so long. "Good, then we might as well get to it then." He announced and the crew braced for his next order. "I want us to drop out of warp and fire at the place where the enemy will drop out. We have both of our courses laid out so simply project where they will be given a twelve second reaction time. Then send everything we have into one volley to arrive just as they decelerate." He said and looks on the bridge were a mixture of horror and respect. This was a bold and desperate plan. The targeting was plotted and a thumbs-up told the Captain that they were ready. He took a deep breath and let it out slowly to calm his racing heart. Combat still made him nervous. He hoped it would always be so. "Drop us out of warp." He said and the helmsman slid the power bar down on the console. The screen before them showed the streaks of stars as the ship dropped down into the visible spectrum of lights. Then the lines slid down to the pinpoints that were distant stars. The enemy ship would appear as soon as they reacted to the change in speed. "Bring all weapons on line and fire." He ordered and the tension all across the ship grew as they readied their ordinance for combat and fired. They all watched as the icons flew away from the ship.

The spot they were heading to was empty now, but it would soon hopefully have the enemy craft occupying a piece of fiery hell.

The weapons officer was watching his targeting screen and a ghost image appeared on it. The dot hit hard and then faded away as it fled the area at high speed. The signature was similar to the stone ship, but with more mass on it. He shrugged his shoulders. "I guess the computer's playing games with me again." He said as the missiles updated and his attention was pulled back into the current fight.

*   *   *

Commander Zarg was bored and he was impatient to kill these troublesome humans and get back home to the glory that was rightfully his. He had almost boarded the enemy ship before they started this second foray through time. Who knew where these dumb creatures were going? He wanted a clean, documented kill. Then he would be rid of this prey and he would move on to the next one. He watched the useless numbers as they scrolled on his stony view. Then he jumped up and pointed as the enemy's metal box slowed down. This was it. They could use their spires soon. The enemy had stopped running. It had been a good chase. He had to admit at least that much to himself. It was all to cater to his own personal glory though.

"Slow us down!" He shouted at his crew and the great stone ship began to decelerate. He paced the command room. The metal box had dropped speed before them so it was now behind them a bit. He held up his arms and prepared for a battle cry. The crew watched him as the rage took him. The stone ship seemed to lurch to the side as it slowed. Something was wrong. The commander fell to the side as the crew held on.

"Sir, we have multiple impacts on us. The enemy is using their missiles again and they are somehow getting through our screen of repulsion," came the explanation. More explosions rocked the ship. The commander propped himself up. "Launch our spires. Destroy that metal box now!" He screamed and his crew jumped to comply with the order. The stone ship reformed a bit and large spears of stone broke off and launched at the human ship. The incoming missiles automatically tracked to the spires and blew them to fragments. The rest that were not engaged continued in to the stone ship. More explosions rocked pieces of it off and it slowed down even more.

For the first time, the commander feared for his life. This enemy had destroyed one ship out from under him and it looked like they would do it again. He would not have his brother to save him this time. He knew that something had to be done now. He pressed a button on the stone console before him. The reaction happened far below in the center of the ship. The massive drive system at the heart of it came alive with the thoughts of the engineers. The molten rock caught in the miniature black hole churned out unbelievable amounts of energy. The stone ship lurched forward and in seconds it was so far away from the metal box that the humans could not even track it. It had been an emergency escape maneuver. It would not help his story of glory much, but it had kept them alive for now. He turned to his bridge crew. "Fix this thing and get me back on the trail of this enemy. They need to pay and pay dearly for this outrage!" He shouted at them. The bustle of activity around him told him that he was being obeyed. He settled down for a few moments and then left for his own quarters. His madness was running deep. These humans deserved the worst death that he could dream up for them.

*   *   *

Once the enemy beat their hasty retreat, the *Cavalier* headed for Earth. They needed to find this wizard and return to save everything. Frank had told them that one particular king was ruler during this century sometime and that records were sketchy at best. They needed to head to Europe for this trip. The familiar blue green world scrolled into view as they adjusted course. They weren't too far out from it either. They could see Japan from here and the full continent of Asia beyond it. They veered into orbit and started an orderly descent towards the planet. They had not suffered any battle damage this time, so it was a lot smoother ride this time than last time. They didn't want to attract too much attention. The world was scarcely populated by their standards, but they could be seen in the sky from a long way off. They skirted the line of darkness that represented night on the globe below them. They followed the cover of darkness until they brought the ship down a few short miles from a castle looking structure on the British Isles. The ship nestled into a small canyon and thus was hidden from direct view. The landing gear took the brunt of the impact with the ground and the ship powered down.

Frank had managed to find his way to the bridge by now and he smiled at the Captain. "Sir, I think we should inquire with the locals as to who is in charge here." He suggested. Captain Glass still had his reservations. He also had very few options left to him.

"All right, dress appropriately for this era and send a small party to the closest structure to find our missing wizard." He said and Frank saluted him.

"Yes sir." He said boldly and left the bridge to assemble his small band of adventurers. They had costumes to don and a quick rundown on language used. They would still speak English, but it would not be the same here and now. There were records of some of what they needed, but the huge gaps in their knowledge included vital social integration and mannerisms. There were simply no records dating this far back. After all, the computer was not invented for centuries. It made Frank feel the weight of his background. He was a historian. He was charged with knowing what others had forgotten. It was normally a profession that got very little respect. The occasional battle scenario for a conference was usually the extent of a commander's interest in the past. Now the whole mission was being staged in a past that none of them were familiar with. Worse yet, the enemy was still somewhere nearby. The days and nights of nerve-wracking worry were far from over. This could still end badly from a single shot of the enemy's stone cannons. They chose garb that seemed appropriate. No one noticed that they all looked too new. The clothing was clean and in good repair. The small band of five men exited the craft and climbed the hill leading towards the nearest structure. Frank had chosen to carry a rapier on his side and the others initially thought it was a bad idea. It was on age-old adage that the sight of a sword draws men to fight. They didn't want any trouble. The whole idea of killing someone in the past and destroying a possible future was still a prominent consideration. These people had to remain unaffected by the presence of these adventurers from the future.

Bells began to ring in the distance. The sound was coming from the stone structure that the group was heading towards. Frank listened for a pattern and found the beauty of the tune in that sound. He had no idea what it meant, but he liked it anyway. They started off towards their goal in single file. This way their footprints would not give away their numbers. There was no one else around so they felt invigorated by the cool air and hoped for the best. There was not a man among them that did not want to get out of here with their quarry.

* * *

Father Scheel looked at his parchment. The light was waning now through the open-arched window and his candle would be insufficient for him to continue with the manuscript with his aged eyes. He carefully set down the quill and blew lightly on the page to hurry the ink up in drying. The Buildwas Abbey had always been a place of sanctity in this troubled area near the border of Wales. The Severn River was just south of the stonework that had been his home for over twelve years. The current Abbot, Henry of Derby, was having difficulties with some of the newer monks at the place. They weren't unruly exactly, it was just the influx of new ideas was having a disruptive influence on the normally peaceful lifestyle here at the Abbey. The fields of sheep were now fading into darkness and the handlers were herding them back to the stables even now. Years past, the monks had done this tending but now they had hired servants to take care of these menial tasks. It had been a pretty drastic departure from earlier sentiment. The page dried to his liking and he closed the tome. The pages were new so they still held that new parchment smell. Father Scheel liked that smell. He also knew that this book needed to be finished soon. It had been commissioned for a birthday gift and the date was approaching rapidly. He placed a mark in the source book and closed it as well to keep those much older yellow pages safe from the air and the light that could bring damage to those blessed pages. He straightened his back and felt the light popping sounds as it adjusted to the movement. He stood up and his feet felt tired. He wondered at that, but he had long ago refused to acknowledge the minor complaints of his body. The way of God did not allow for him to be held back by these distractions. He had to remain focused and do what was bid of him. The Abbot had asked him to do this work personally. He was gratified by that, but tried to avoid false pride. He knew that his position here was permanent. He had outlived others in this poor community. He had helped wherever he could. He had done his Christian duty and now he just wanted to rest up to start again tomorrow. He ruffled his robes a bit and then put his sandals on. The candle was nearly out but they were expensive so he extinguished it to save its time for later. The time candle had burnt down nine hours worth. No wonder his back was stiff. The manuscript would be finished in another week or two. He eagerly awaited the time when it was gifted and his work could be enjoyed. It was a little vanity, but he so enjoyed making others feel good. A sound from outside made him pause as he opened the large wooden door. He stepped back into the room and peered out the window. He tried to focus his tired eyes and saw movement out there. He had been looking at close objects all day and his depth vision had suffered for it. He knew not what was coming, but he did realize that something was. He headed to the bunkhouse to awaken his brothers. If this was some wayward traveler, then they should greet them accordingly. If this was some raiding party, then they should be ready to defend themselves. Unfortunately both possibilities existed here in this turbulent area.

He stepped into the room and the large door squeaked as he closed it again. There was stirring at the sound and he lifted his voice not quite into alarm, but definitely into 'pay attention' mode. "We must prepare for guests." He said and the four men in the room sat up and started donning their robes and sandals. The rough robes were plain and probably uncomfortable. They had never been a combat Abbey so they had no weapons to grab. Still, discipline and common sense were watchwords of the commune. They were in an area of civil unrest. They had brooms and rakes and other simple tools to use for weapons. Plus, since they weren't weapons by design, they would not offend the visitors if they were not hostile. Father Scheel led the way to the entrance of the Abbey and they got their first look at the newcomers. Whoever they were, they were not from around here. Their dress was something none of them had seen before. The vibrant colors and the outlandish cuts of cloth made them look like clowns or jesters. One of them stood like a warrior and none of them seemed to be in tune with god. They were standing proud before the house of the lord and they were not paying their respects to the symbol at the entrance. Still, for all of that, they had not made any menacing moves and they seemed happy to see the monks.

One of them came forward. He held his hands up in an inoffensive gesture of peace. His demeanor suggested that he knew more than his attire would suggest. This was no charlatan. This was a man of learning. This was something that the monks could pick up on. He spoke and the monks knew the words, but the accent was something they had trouble with.

Frank stepped up to the monk with the rake and smiled his most genial smile. These men had been awakened at the dusk and were now faced with men they couldn't possibly understand. "Who is in charge here?" He asked and they all looked at each other in surprise. He didn't get why at first, but when they spoke it became obvious to him.

"We are brothers of the Buildwas Abbey and Abbot Henry of Derby is keeper of this place." The lead man responded. His guard was still up, but an information exchange would do wonders for the drudgery of life they usually experienced at the Abbey. "Who might you be?" He asked timidly.

Frank looked up at the sky. "An Abbey?" He exclaimed. "That explains a lot." He said and father Scheel looked worried and confused. "We are seeking a man." Frank said to bring the conversation back to something understandable for the pensive man in robes. "As monks you must be record keepers?" He queried and the monks lowered their makeshift weapons.

"We are keepers of the word of God." Came the response from one of the men behind the father.

Frank made quick eye contact and then returned his gaze to the leader here. "Of course, please pardon our rudeness. We are not familiar with your customs or rights of travel. I ask for hospitality and possibly information concerning this man we are looking for." Said Frank and the monks set down their implements and slipped into host mode. They escorted the strange men into the Abbey and gave them rooms to house two men each inside. Then they left them for the night. The quarters were barren of all comforts. The straw mats on the floor were the only bedding and the bugs kept the men from lying down on those filthy mats. This was the perfect example of poverty. They had a roof over their heads, but nothing else. Most of them grumbled softly, but Frank found the whole thing exciting. This was a piece of history that he was being allowed to see and interact with. They did not know the exact year yet, and they did not know where the wizard was, but they had made contact with these men and avoided any ugliness in the first meeting. Things were looking up. As he nodded off to sleep, he realized that their clothes looked quite festive next to the dull robes of these monks. They had chosen their costumes poorly. He made a mental note to update the entries in the computer when they returned to the ship.

*   *   *

The abbot was a heavy sleeper so he was unaware that they had guests until he rose with the sun. He yawned and dressed and headed out for the morning exercises. He had to greet the day and there were prayers to be done. His responsibility as the guardian of the word of God in these parts was a serious obligation that he did not take lightly. He put on his sash of office and grabbed his bible. The worn leather cover had always brought him comfort and this morning was no exception. He felt the wave of warmth as the sun creeped around the columns and arches of the main foyer. He strolled purposefully to the main room. This particular Abbey did not have an altar, so they used a communion room to do their

133

praying and to speak to God. The sanctity of the place had been suspect during the plague years, but now it had been cleaned up and it regained its former glory. He knelt down before the shrine that was built before the north wall. He started his reading at a particularly good part of the bible that he had been thinking about the night before. The word was the word. He had dedicated his life to the principals in this magic book. It gave him confidence and strength. No one interrupted his reading until he looked up. Two of the monks were there. He felt a twinge of anger at the intrusion, but their eyes told him that something was happening. They were brother Layfield and Brother Stanton. They were younger men, but they were dedicated to the lord almost as much as he was so he felt comfortable around them.

"What is it brothers?" He asked when they missed the opportunity to speak.

"Abbot, we have had visitors this night." Stanton told him and his eyebrows rose.

"We are a house of the Lord. We give shelter to those in need as directed by the scriptures." He responded in an impatient tone and they knew that this would not be as easy as they wanted it to be.

"They are strangers from far away." Stanton continued unabated by the lashing. "Their mannerisms are strange to us and they portend to be after a man hereabouts." He finished and Henry looked back at him as if he had just spoken out of turn. Then he reined himself in and put on his smile again.

"Tell me then, where are these people from?" He asked and the two younger men looked at each other. It was obvious that neither one of them knew any more about the strangers.

"I am sorry, but I do not know." Stanton finally admitted. "They are in the west wing and we were instructed to allow them to sleep if that is what they are doing now." He said and the Abbot felt a twinge of concern.

"Who has ordered this directive?" He asked and the two men fell silent. "Come on then, out with it." The Abbot prompted. Layfield bowed his head. "It was Father Scheel that made the command." He said and it was just as obvious that he was simply responding and did not want to bring the ire of his abbot down upon himself.

"He must have had a good reason. We should meet these new guests." The Abbot said and both monks sighed in relief. They led the way to the west wing and in moments, the strangers were standing before the most powerful man in the community. They were still in those outlandish colorful clothes. The leader of them stepped up to the call.

"Good morning to you." He said and held out his hand to the Abbot. The idea of shaking hands with a commoner prevented the Abbot from moving at all as he looked these strangely garbed men up and down.

"The morning is a gift to us all from the Almighty." He replied in a starched voice that dripped of his arrogance. Frank felt the hit to his ego and made his best efforts not to retort. Instead, he turned to his companions.

"This man is the leader all right. No one can be that sure of himself in a place of inherent hostility." He said bluntly and then he turned back to the Abbot. "We need to find Zack." He said and the name meant nothing to the Abbot or the monks to either side of him.

"I do not know a Zack. What do you want this man for?" He asked, trying to make sure that these men were honorable and thus godlier,

"He is a wizard of vast power. He is to help us fight an enemy we have been unable to otherwise defeat." Frank said almost offhandedly and the monks cowered away from him.

"You speak of black magic and the devil!" Henry screamed at him. "You must leave us at once. You are not allowed on hallowed ground if you are consorting with the likes of witchcraft. You are evil, or at least have been corrupted by Lucifer. Get out!" He said and he threw a candle at the startled man from the future.

"Hold on a minute. We are not evil. We are being chased by beings you could not understand and we need this man to save us from them. Do you have records of births and such for this man?" He asked, still trying to reason with a man who was becoming more dangerous by the second.

"There will be no information for you here. You are blasphemers and you shall be cast out of the house of the Lord!" He said and he picked up a rake to swing at the men if they did not retreat. Frank noticed the change in demeanor and backed away slowly.

"Okay, okay, we are leaving. We will not bother you any further. We need this man to save our whole race and you are being an obstacle, but we will leave you alone to find what we need elsewhere." He said and he could see that the man was near panic. They had truly frightened him beyond reason. The other monks were just in shock. They watched as their leader exiled the men from the holy place.

Frank led his team out quickly after that. They would need to find someone a little more open-minded before they could find out if Zack was around or not. They still had not found out what year it was and so they couldn't even be sure if the right king was in place or not. The records were getting spottier as they traveled back in time. He had originally thought that this stumbling across a house of learning would be a good thing. Now he knew that it had been a mistake. They would have to make another trek to find out what they sought. It was hard to imagine a wizard living in these times though. The first seeds of doubt began to blossom in Frank's mind.

* * *

The monks watched in fear as the strangers walked away at a brisk pace from the Abbey. The thought of such heresy in a house of the lord brought much agitation and a sense of panic. They were supposed to be safe from that sort of thing here. The Abbot looked at the parchment before him and began to scribe a note to the King. These men in league with Lucifer must be stopped. Their outlandish clothes and their easy manner with things of the occult were grounds enough for their execution. He needed to send a courier with this note as soon as possible. He had the perfect monk in mind for the task. His hand shook a bit as he wrote the message in his fine script. It was not up to his standard, but maybe that too was important to the recipient. They needed help out here and quickly. He set down the quill and blew on the paper to allow the ink to dry. Then he rolled up the parchment and dripped the wax from his writing candle onto the seam. He pressed his ring into the wax to put his seal on it and then he put that into a leather carrier. The monk he had in mind had already been summoned and the man watched him carefully for the permission to enter the small room. Christopher Farber was his name and his past was somewhat sordid before his entry into the church and his life of repentance. His former life would serve him well now. He knew how to travel quickly and quietly. He did not need to keep to the roads and he knew how to remain unseen. The Abbot handed over the case and Brother Farber bowed deeply and then vanished, as was his skill. The ink was corked again and the Abbot made his own mental calculations. The messenger would get that letter off to the king and it would take him about three days to do it. Then the response would take three days to return and troops would take at least another week after that. So it was almost two weeks that they would have to hold the Abbey if this enemy attacked them. It was a long time and his morale was not good having come to that conclusion. He would brief his monks and they would ready their defenses. He set the quill in water to make sure that the ink did not dry inside it and then he placed it on a cloth to dry. It would do no good to have it rust up on him. Then he strolled out of the small writing room and into the main corridor to the Abbey. He would hold a meeting and tell his men what to expect. He only hoped that he was wrong about it. They were a sitting duck out here all alone.

* * *

Frank returned with his group to the ship and the Captain was not happy. They had not only come back empty-handed, but they had made some serious mistakes with the public relations from another time. The Captain had deployed his own information retrieval devices. A small satellite was orbiting in a geosynchronous orbit over the island to get them more information. After some local testing, he now had a good idea of the year as well from soil samples and basic population counts from the air. He stood over the scouting team and glared at their leader.

"You are supposed to study history, not become a part of it." He said in a gruff voice. He was obviously tired and his eyes showed the lines of more worry than one man usually had to bear. Still, his anger was justified. They had blown the mission pretty badly here. "You have contacted the monks from Buildwas Abbey and you have let them believe that you are servants of the devil." He said and he stopped pacing to sit down heavily in the conference room chair. "I have seen a monk leave the Abbey covertly with a message. You are being reported to the king. This can go either way for us now. You may have doomed the mission, or the added attention may help us find this wizard of yours." He said. His tone suddenly sounded less hostile and more tired. "Got any speculation on this situation now?" He asked and the team as a unit shook their heads. The Captain sighed. "I see." He said dejectedly.

Frank had his mind spinning in high gear. He knew that this was important somehow. He had to make the connections. The dots were there before him, he just couldn't make out the picture yet. "Sir, the monk that left, can he be intercepted?" He asked and Captain Glass looked up from his hands. He had dropped his face into them as he leaned on his elbows on the conference room table. He hadn't even realized that he had done it and he took his arms down when he noticed it.

"We could do it, he is good, but he cannot evade our eye in the sky." The captain responded and his tone asked for more details on the other man's thoughts. It was really an amazing ability to convey whole messages with a simple inflection, he had that gift.

"Well sir, if we stop the message from being delivered and return the monk to the Abbey, we may be able to minimize the damage to the timeline here. Second, we would need to convince the monks and the Abbot that we are not what he thinks we are. I don't know how we would do that, but I think the whole plan starts with taking the Abbey for ourselves and holding the monks hostage until we have found the information we need in their records." He suggested and the whole team looked at him as if he had just sprouted wings and horns. He looked around the table and noticed the shocked faces and then he chuckled. "We have no choice but to proceed with our mission here. We cannot convince them of what we are by sitting here in the ship just out of sight of their home. We will need to show them what we are and why it is so important for us to complete our mission. Then we can appeal to them intellectually. These are learned men, at least for the times and we can reason with them if we can just get them past this first assumption of theirs." He said, trying to sound reasonable but knowing that he was failing at that much at least.

The Captain looked around the room and he too found the reaction a bit amusing. "So what you are saying is that we try to win these men of God over by taking their home and locking them up?" He asked and it sounded ridiculous to everyone present when put that way. "We have a situation here; that much is certain. We also have an enemy out there somewhere that can kill us and this planet with us if they tried hard enough. We have to find this wizard and from what we have seen so far with our satellite, there is no magic here. There have been no unexplained occurrences so far. The population is down, very down. So we have determined that we have landed soon after the Black Death. The plague ravaged all of Europe in the 1400's so we know that we are around that. In fact, since no one is lying dead in the streets anymore, we are at least a couple of years after that. The soil samples and approximate census puts us at about 1463-ish, maybe as late as 1465. That means that King Edward the Fourth is the current ruler here and that is not the name of the king you specified in the original mission briefing. We are here at the wrong time again. So what I want from these monks is not whether or not this wizard lives around here, I need to know when he lived. We still need to go back."

The team all looked shocked. The Captain had really done his homework. Frank was most impressed. His mouth had fallen open as the information fell out before him. He now closed it with an audible click and the captain swung his gaze towards the historian at the table. "Sir, I did not know all of this and I apologize for my lack of details on this era. I shall endeavor to do better from here on out." He said and the captain nodded to him.

"Okay, so do we take the Abbey or do we try to use a more diplomatic approach?" He asked and the team seemed to jump on the diplomatic bandwagon. The Captain was pleased with that since it was the route he would have suggested and indeed ordered if they had not come around. "Then what we need to do is send a diplomat with you as you return to the monks and their decidedly paranoid leader." The Captain looked at them all again, he liked what he saw, they were all thinking about the mission and what they needed to do. It was a good start to the problem solving that needed to happen here. He waited for them to chew on what they had so far and then he prompted them for input.

"So, what are you going to do first?" He asked finally when no one came forward to suggest anything on their own.

Frank knew that it was his place to start this, so he stood up. All eyes swept to him as he did so. "What I see is that we need to address this Henry of Derby directly. The very first step is to stop his messenger as quickly as possible before he can tell anyone else about us. Then we need to show the Abbot that we have the power to prevent him from contacting the outside world. Then we will have his full attention and can explain further what we want and why. If we can put a religious angle on it, it may be a less bitter pill for him to swallow. I blew it the first time by mentioning the wizard and he translated that into witchcraft and the occult. We need to explain to him what we are looking for in terms that suggest a workable skill, not dealings with the underworld. It may also help if we show him images of the enemy. They are obviously not human and it may sway his mind that we are fighting for the side of good here against an evil that his mind can't comprehend. If he understands what we need, he may be able to help us search their archives for what we need. If he is unresponsive, we may have a long search ahead of us." He paused for a moment and held up his hand to forestall the Captain's objection. "I do understand that time is of the essence here. We need to avoid any potential delays. That is why I suggest that we spend a little precious time trying to convince this man that we need his help for good."

The Captain thought that over and he knew that it sounded right. He made the decision to go ahead for now. The Captain looked at Frank and smiled, and then he continued. "Good, so the first step is to stop that courier and bring him back here. Once the Abbey knows it is cut off from aid, they will be more likely to listen to what we have to say. As you have already discovered, faith can be a powerful motivator." The Captain at this point pressed a button on the console in front of him. "Please send in Mr. Fell." He said into the pick-up and the door slid aside almost immediately. The small man stepped into the room and all eyes were focused on him. He smiled genially and met each of their gazes with one of confidence and a happy-go-lucky manner that disarmed the potentially hostile crowd.

"Hello there. I am Chris Fell, and I am a communications specialist. I have been operating radio and FTL radio equipment for years. I have been involved with negotiations for large scale corporations and I have been involved with a treaty or two. I believe that I can be of help when dealing with these people and I am more than willing to help wherever I can." He said and the group did not know what to think. He continued on his trek around the room and he settled into a chair next to the Captain and pulled out a small case file. The ancient looking tan folder looked archaic. Of course when compared to the time outside the walls of the ship, it was high-tech indeed. He opened the file on the table and the rest of the people simply watched him. He pulled several sheets of bright white paper from it and spread them out in front of him like a poker hand. He pointed to the first sheet and smiled at his audience. "This is what we know so far." He said. He slid the paper to the center of the table where the reader was and the printing on the page was projected into the air above the table for all to see at once. It listed basically what the captain had said already. They knew the approximate year and what king was in power now. They knew a few small tidbits about the Abbey and they knew who was in charge of it. They did not have a complete file on him though. The records from this era were sketchy at best. It meant that finding an individual would be most difficult here. It also meant that they would have to look elsewhere or elsewhen for their miracle worker. The facts did not slow this small man down. He looked at the faces of his students until they had all taken in the data. Then he pulled the sheet back and placed the second one into the reader.

"This is what we need to know. You will notice that the identity of this wizard is not among the list. I don't believe that we will find this information here. We need a clue as to where to go next. That is all we really need here. But this must be determined from clues we find here. No one is going to come out and say we need to go five hundred or a thousand years back. We have to become sleuths here. We will be given generic information that will look unimportant on the surface and we will have to extrapolate what we need from it. At least this is what I have been told. My specialty is not sleuthing, or trying to figure it all out. No, I am a conversationalist. My job is to get to the clues that will lead others to where we must go next. So I will do most of the talking." He looked around the room to make sure that this one point was clear. "I will say things that you will think are odd. There is always a goal in mind and you must let it transpire as I dictate or we may never get what we need here and end up guessing the rest of the journey." He stopped for a moment. He looked at the Captain as if asking for permission to continue. The slight nod that was given was definitely the okay to do so.

"The next sheet we have is something of an oddity for this mission. "We have to determine what these people need. Yes we have things they need, just as they have things we need. A transaction rather than a theft will greatly help the local people's perception of us. They live in a minimalist style so it will be difficult to determine what they actually need. So this is where we must be extra cautious. If we offer something that is considered a luxury or extravagant item, we will alienate these simple people and lose any chance we have for getting at the information we need."

Finally, we need to know the strength of this Abbey. How many monks are there? How many servants do they employ? These people could pose a threat if they ganged up on one of us. We have to guard against an uprising. We need to maintain control of these people until we have what we need. The hard part is that we cannot look like we are doing it at all or they will resist us. In fact, they will definitely do so at least at first. The situation came to a head before any damage control could be done. We have a long way to go here, and as I understand it, not too much time to get it done. Therefore, I will have to take steps, sometimes drastic ones, to get us to the point we need. Negotiations are like a game of chess. There will be positioning and posturing and then it will shift to more of a poker atmosphere. They will try to get more out of us. We can afford to give a lot, but they don't need to know that. In fact, they should be under the impression that we are stretched to the limit and cannot offer much at all."

Frank interrupted the diplomatic man with a chuckle. "That shouldn't be too hard to pull off; we are stretched too thin for our resources." He said when everyone looked at him. He looked back and his shrugging shoulders said "What?" Then everyone turned back to the primary speaker here. Cris smiled at them and made an effort to look directly at Frank.

"You are right about that. We are nearly out of everything. If we cannot replace our stores with local supplies, then we will be rationing what we have left for the rest of the voyage." There were looks of scorn around the table at the very suggestion, but they knew that it was true. "We have a requisition list as well. He pulled the current paper and slid the last one into the reader. The list was huge. They needed so many things that this time period would not even offer. They would have to make the most of it from what they could find here. "We will do what we can but you all know that this list is impossible to fill here. We need to get going on this as soon as possible. So the ship will be taking off soon and we will pick up this messenger and return here to this location. When we approach with their man, the monks will be angry, but they will *have* to deal with us then."

He looked around the table as if to challenge them to ask him a question. No one spoke. The moment drug on for a few long seconds and the Captain broke it up for them. "Okay people, we have a plan now, let's get to it. Prepare for take-off and maybe we can nab this guy before it gets too dark out there." He ordered.

The group disbanded and the short look that the Captain shared with his diplomatic specialist would have sent shivers into the others if they had seen it. There was some hidden connection here. None of the others even suspected it. They left to get to their stations for lift off. The plan was sound and the order had been issued. The time for debate was officially over now. History would have to judge them on their actions from here on in. There were no second chances, no do-overs. It was for all the marbles and they could not fail now. It simply wasn't an option they could fathom.

* * *

The monks started their preparations for an eminent invasion. They barred the doors and they prepared for a physical assault. They were understaffed by no small margin, but they were determined that God would save the holy. They would hold this house and they would await the king and his cavalry to save them. It was all they had. There was no plan B.

* * *

Brother Farber kept to the shadows. The Abbot had been scared when he dispatched the younger monk to the king. The trip would not have been all that difficult except that the element of an enemy at the doors made the whole thing more urgent. He crossed a small river and scaled the far bank. He saw movement and darted to the ground in an effort to remain unseen. His own nerves were being tested and he knew that he was alone out here. There were no other monks. There were only citizens and they may be helpful or they may be evil. He didn't know which. His instructions had been explicit. He was to trust no one and he was to stop for nothing. This message was the most important thing he would ever do all of his life. He nodded his head and accepted the cause at the time. Now he was unhappy with his situation. He was trekking across the land, cautiously avoiding the roads and hoping to evade an unseen enemy that had somehow spooked his boss. The movement, or whatever had caused it, moved away and he relaxed a bit. It had been a wild boar trying to get to the river to drink. His own scent had scared the animal off. He would be more careful next time and he stood up and started running again. He followed the line of trees so as not to form a silhouette for others to see him in the distance. He remembered all the running of his youth and he felt the untamed elation of the chase. If he was unhappy about being sent here, he was more than happy with the actual trip. He had missed this in that stuffy old Abbey. The monks were friendly enough, but they had no fun. He wondered if he were allowed to hunt on this journey. He was not supposed to talk to anyone so purchasing a meal would be out of the question. His interpretation of the instructions gave him a go-ahead and he set his mind on finding a small game animal. It would be just like being a kid again. A smile crossed his face at the thought and he would have a fire too. It would be far enough away from anyone to avoid detection, but he would have fresh roasted game animal again. His mouth began to water at the thought of it. He would gather some roots too. It would be a feast. He heard a loud noise in the sky, he tried to look but his instincts had him diving to the ground and rolling into the underbrush to avoid detection. The sound was like nothing he had ever heard before. The twin turbine motors swung the ship around over the small copse of trees and settled it down in the open field just beyond them. The turbines wound down and the normally quiet countryside tried to return to normal. The exit ramp deployed and the colorful team of security personnel stepped down to the soil. They had their normal uniforms on and they wore needlers on their hips. The personal weapon could cut a man in half in less time than it took to fall to the ground. This was not the mission for them though. It was a mission to retrieve this messenger. They figured that he would resist, but were confident that he could not evade them and their technology. The lead man held aloft the sensor arm and the thermal imager showed him the hiding monk. He stepped directly towards the man and shouted to him.

"I can see you; you might as well come out and join us. It will all go easier for you this way." He promised and the security detail began to space themselves out in a net pattern. No one would get by them now. They held batons that would deal a nasty shock upon impact. The idea was to immobilize the target without causing permanent harm. "Come on out man, we don't want any harm to befall you." He shouted again and the monk popped his head up.

"You are demons from hell, I will not submit to you!" Brother Farber shouted back. He pulled his knife out. It was a keepsake from his youth. The Father had allowed him to keep it for sentimental purposes only. Now it looked like his only means of attack, and thus his defense. "The order will put a stop to you and your kind and the world will be saved!" He added. The full level of brainwashing was evident in that last statement. He believed in the church and somehow had bequeathed them special powers against evil. The only problem was that these men were not evil.

"We are both on a similar mission. We are trying to save the world as well, just not the here and now of it." The leader shouted cryptically. He was not authorized to tell this man the whole truth. That responsibility would fall to someone else, someone more suited to the task. "Now come out so we don't have to come in there and get you."

Brother Farber considered his options and he knew that he was trapped here. These people, whoever they were, were powerful. They had traveled in the sky to come for him. That meant that they had some sort of allegiance with spirits. He just didn't know if they were good or bad ones. The difference was crucial in his mind. These men looked like they were ready to take care of business too. Their easy and professional body language told him that they did not consider him a real threat. That worried him some and also gave him a spark of hope. He might be able to take one of them down if he caught them off guard like this. He pulled the knife back into his sleeve and put his hands together in the typical monk fashion. Then he strolled up out of the grass and bushes and out onto the field. The men were watching him warily and his hopes of escape plummeted. These men knew what they were doing. They were no imbeciles like he had dealt with as a child. He could have gotten away with just about anything back then. That is, until he started getting greedy. That was when he had been caught and the guard had treated him roughly. The magistrate had deposited him in the monastery instead of the jail only because he had begged for it. Now he was looking at imprisonment again. He knew this, but he also saw no way around it.

A few steps more and he was satisfied that they were not going to lower their guard for him. In fact, they had formed a semi-circle to enclose his escape routes. It was like a vice tightening around his freedom. He lowered his head and waited for them to take him. His time to strike would be later. At least he hoped it would be.

The lead man held the sensor arm up and it made a high pitched sound that was unpleasant to the monk's ears. The man in the strange clothes looked at brother Farber with a look of distaste. "I think I will take that knife now." He said and the look of surprise was genuine as the startled monk handed it over.

"How did you know?" He asked at last. By now he had been led into the flying machine and they were in motion. If felt strange to his stomach and they told him he would get used to it quickly. They had been right.

"The knife is metal and we searched you for metal as part of the protocols for incarcerating prisoners." The guard said, humoring the man behind the door. "Don't worry, if we had meant to harm you, you would be gone by now. Our mission is truly to save the world. No matter what you think of that, it is still the truth." The guard said and turned away again to monitor his console.

The monk looked dejected. He understood little of what the man said, but what he did get, surprised him. "So I am a prisoner then." He sighed and the guard laughed. His indignation flared and his anger swept across his face.

The guard looked at him almost quizzically. "You really think we need a prisoner here?" He asked, chuckling again. "There are many things aboard this ship that are inherently dangerous. You are here to keep you safe from them. We will be releasing you as soon as we reach the Abbey. So just sit tight, it will only be a few minutes more." The guard said and the monk was startled again.

"A few minutes; we were nearly a day from the Abbey." He said, almost choking from his surprise.

The guard did not laugh this time. He did find the situation laughable, but held himself in check. "We are not traveling on foot. You must understand that we have technology that allows us to travel much farther and faster than you would have been able to in this time." He said and he realized that he may have said too much. "Now just sit back and wait. It will not be long now." The guard ordered and brother Farber sat back and leaned against the wall. This metal box was like a small house that could fly around. It was pretty amazing and he wondered about its construction. Such a thing could haul supplies to a battle front or take the wounded back for treatment. Such a device could re-unite loved ones over great distances. Perhaps it could even take him to God. It was a wonderful thought and he wondered if it were so.

*   *   *

True to the guard's words, the sound of the ship changed again and they descended from the heavens above. This time they did not return to the small ravine near the river. This time they landed just outside the Abbey itself. The stone path shifted just a bit as the weight of the ship settled to the ground. Then the engines wound down and the ramp extended again.

Chris Fell stepped off of the ramp and onto the ground. His mannerisms suggested that he was in charge. For all intents and purposes, he was. This was his mission now. He was charged with finding out what they needed to know. Frank was behind him a short way and the original scouting party fell into step behind him. They started the short trek up to the Abbey doors.

*   *   *

A roaring sound like demons from the sky swept over the peaceful building as the monks inside cowered in fear. The sound grew louder and louder and then it shifted around to in front of the old buildings. A large object shone in the sunlight and settled down in the front courtyard of the Abbey and it opened to reveal many of those same people he had thrown out the day before. "So the heathens have returned." He mused aloud. Then he continued. "And they have some infernal contraption to give them power." Abbot Henry muttered to himself as he watched the display play out before him. He had the power of right under his command. He had the power of God behind him. He knew that it would protect his soul. He wondered what it would do for his body. The men came forward and he pulled his monks back. They could not resist this demonic horde. He knew this in his heart of hearts. They were outclassed here, but surrender was not on his mind either. He wanted a third option. He would smite these evil men down and then pray for their souls as he disposed of their bodies. It was definitely a dark thought, but he was trapped here. The messenger would take much longer to bring support to him and the enemy was at his door now. He had bows, but he wondered if they could really help against the servants of evil. He hoped that they would. The arrows were blessed and his men were at least somewhat trained. They were in place around the courtyard and they awaited his signal to fire.

The group stepped into the archway lined hall and as if on some unseen cue, arrows rained down upon them. Chris Fell dropped to his knees as the arrow took him in the shoulder. The look of surprise on his face would have been priceless if the situation were not so grave. The monks were fighting back. Frank cursed and drew his personal weapon. It was a compact version of the needler and he knew that killing any of these men could severely affect the timeline and this mission. So he drew into an alcove and checked for his shot. Cris was shouting something in the middle of the courtyard. He was asking for help. He had fallen over and he was writhing on the ground. One of the monks leaned forward for a better view and Frank aimed and fired his gun. The bow in his hands blew to splinters and the pieces snapped back at the archer. He went down in surprise. He was not harmed very much, simply bruised. It had been a masterful shot. The other members of the scouting party had taken refuge against the columns of the supporting archways. The monks were looking down from the roof, trying to find a target. Everyone ignored the screaming man on the floor. He was out of the fight.

Frank worked his way around and shot another bow as the archer drew back the string. He knew that he had been pressing his luck, but he also knew that this situation had to be defused before someone died. "Stop your attack and let us talk to you!" He shouted. "We don't want to kill anyone here. Killing is not a part of our mission to save the world!" He shouted and there was no response from the monks. They had defended this Abbey before and they weren't going to fall for any tricks like that. "Please stop before someone gets hurt too badly to be saved." He tried again and he caught a glimpse of another archer and he rolled out into the foyer to bring the shooter into his sights. He shot for the right arm. The needler would do a lot of damage, but the man would live. The archer loosed the arrow at the same time. The needles shattered the bow and the right arm of the monk. The arrow sailed true and creased a crimson line on Frank's shoulder. He felt the burn and he turned around to see another man aiming for his back. He wanted to fire, but saw no shot that was non-lethal. Instead he held up his hand palm forward and took the arrow through it. The pain was intense and he looked at the monk who had fired it. "You owe me your life. I could have killed you there. Now stop this and let us talk with your master." He said.

The monk made eye contact and the look of shock was priceless. He hollered out to cease fire. The arrows stopped coming. One of the scouting party members went over to Cris. He had stopped writhing and just started twitching. There was something wrong here. A quick scan told them the story.

"They are using poison!" He shouted and Frank looked down at his hand. He knew that his time was now limited. He could already feel the burn. He thought it had just been the pain.

"Get that antidote quickly. I am going to need it as well as he is." He said harshly. He put his pistol away and stared at his hand again. It looked really bad and only the fact that he was still in shock allowed him to think this clearly. The poison was no doubt coursing through his veins. He looked around and the monk that had shot him was standing before him. He made eye contact, but his eyes wouldn't focus. "We are not evil; we are here to save the world from an enemy you cannot understand. You must help us." He said and the monk knelt down and with a quick chopping motion knocked out Frank and he fell to the floor. The monk then snapped the arrow and carefully pulled the arrow out of the damaged hand and wrapped it with cloth to stop the bleeding. Then he lifted Frank and took him inside. The other monks helped with this and Cris was brought inside as well. The men were laid out and then the monks backed away. The Abbot looked on as the other strangers began to tend to their fallen comrades. He was an angry man, but there were wounded men here. His own oaths were in conflict and he wondered how people lived with themselves on great quests or holy wars.

"See that they are kept comfortable. Their honorable actions have earned them an audience. Beyond that I can promise nothing." He said and then he retired to his study to look up anything he could find to help him with this situation. He had infidels within his very walls. His initial inclination was to simply throw them out. His own personal code of honor prevented that now. He needed guidance and some way of dealing with this problem. If he could stall them long enough, maybe those reinforcements would arrive.

*　　*　　*

Frank felt a sense of vertigo as the fire swam through his veins. He felt the pull of consciousness and he shied away from it. He wound himself up in a comfortable feeling of bliss. This dream walking had proved to be considerably therapeutic for him and he loved the control he exercised in there. The images before him were rising unbidden in his mind and he watched them as if he were an outsider looking in on someone else's dream. He found that it gave him better clarity and he was then immune to fear and doubt inside this perfect world of thoughts and dreams. A lady in white robes hovered over a stream and her striking features caught his attention even more than her pointed ears did. She was beautiful and he felt, rather than saw, her in his mind. She was here. She was not a figment of his imagination. This was somehow different from all of the other dream images he had ever seen. This felt real. Not the kind of real that he was used to in dreams, no this was more concrete. She had somehow reached to him in the darkness and he yearned to reach back. He just didn't know how. She noticed him floating off in the distance and she twirled around to face him and her face was of joy. Her dazzling eyes seemed to peer through him as she approached his essence in the mist. He looked back at her confused. She got really close and he could smell her fragrance. It was of wildflowers and her fragile lean look complimented her features.

"You are still so far away." She said in a voice so melodic that he thought she had sung it. Perhaps she had. He couldn't be sure now. The dream time was so fleeting. "You have sought us and you are still very far away. You must come back to us. The world needs you. Tell the others you serve that you need to come farther back." She said and he looked startled.

"Who are you?" He asked and she smiled at him. "Where are you? I need to know where to find you." He said in his desperation.

She hovered very close now and she whispered to him. "I know not where you come from but I do know that you have traveled less than a third of the way to me. You must go farther if you are to succeed and that the prophecy may be fulfilled. You must hurry for time as we know it draws short. The chosen one trains hard and we shall help him to find you once you arrive. Beyond that, I can offer no additional intelligence." She said and she backed away. Her red lips looked as if they had something else to tell him, but she was losing her hold on this reality. Or maybe it was him who was losing hold. He felt a hand on his shoulder. There were voices around him and the image began to fade. He tried to reach out to her as she faded and his arm reached up in the real world. The people around him restrained him and he heard their calling.

"Wake up man, we need you here," came the command and Frank recognized that voice. It was the Captain. Captain Glass was at the Abbey?

The situation had definitely changed while he was away. He tried to move, but the many hands held him down. He flicked his eyes open and the scene was blurry and awash with movement. He could not focus on anything. He kept hearing the voices. "He is awake now, that's a good sign. Sir if you could just start that drip, we can get this flushed from his system." The words had no meaning to him as he tried to will his eyes to work. He was thankful that there was not a lot of light here. If it had been glaring at him it would have hurt. As it was, all of him hurt anyway. His left hand really hurt him. Then he remembered; he had been shot. An arrow had pierced his hand and he tried to look at it, but his argumentative eyes failed to respond to his demands. He tried to focus on that dream. The girl had been so real and he had never seen her before. She seemed to know who he was and what they were trying to do. At least she knew something about it. She had mentioned a prophecy as well. That meant that there was some form of records to find. Prophesies were written down. He was trying to figure out where to look first when his vision cleared. It was like snapping a filter off of a lens. It came into full clarity all at once. He saw the Captain over him, a look of concern written into his face as if chiseled there in some masterful stonework.

"That's it sir, his temperature just broke. It is going into remission now." The announcement came from just out of his vision. He thought he knew the voice, but it didn't matter just now. The news was good enough to override the need to know who gave it to him. He wasn't going to die. That was a good thing since he still had things to do here.

"Sir, I have been given a clue." He muttered and he was surprised at how thin his voice sounded. His voice had even cracked in that croaking attempt to talk. His throat hurt him as well. "I saw a woman in my dreams and she told me we need to go farther back." He said and the men laughed at him.

"Of course we need to go back farther. We told you this on board the ship. We just need clues here as to how far to go back." Cris said. Frank hadn't noticed him there before. His face had read concern as well, but now he had slipped his arrogance firmly back in place.

Frank tried to look at him, but his hurting throat would not let him lift his head properly. The Captain cautioned him to take it easy. "You were touch and go there for a while, you will need some serious rest before we can leave here. The Abbot has agreed to house you until we feel you are able to travel. They have helped in every way they possibly can. I must say, when you make an impression, you go all the way." He said and his smile seemed to disarm the worry that was growing inside.

"What happened?" Frank managed to choke out. A wooden cup of water was brought and he felt the cold water trickle down his throat. It was soothing. His tongue was swollen as well. He held his eyes on the Captain though. He figured that was the most likely source for any answers he sought.

"Well, what we had here was a firefight. You know about that already I'm sure." There was a slight pause. "That is since you did most of the shooting. The monks saw you disable two archers and then not shoot the third when you could see no way to avoid taking a life. That sort of thing speaks volumes to holy men. I did not see the actual battle, but the reports were pretty amazing. I would recommend you for field duty if we ever get back to a populated Fleet." He stopped himself short and cleared his throat. "Anyway, when they brought you inside, you were knocked out. It was the monk's way of relieving your pain. A little barbaric if you ask me, but he had already removed the poisoned arrow and wrapped your wound so it can't be all bad. We had to administer a general antibiotic to try to stabilize you and Mr. Fell until a proper remedy could be found. The monks provided us a sample of the poison and we were able to get to work to chemically counteract it. It took us almost a week to do this." He stopped again at the look of shock on Frank's face.

"Yes, you've been out for a week. In fact, the fact that you lived so long seems to have endeared you to the monks. The poison is supposed to kill a person or beast in less than an hour. While they were working on you, I had to come in to have an audience with the Abbot. He really is a stubborn man, but I can't fault him for being careful. I explained our mission and I explained how there can be no record of us ever coming here. We returned his messenger and he knew then that we were not a problem that was going away anytime soon for him. The mission was something that was simply beyond his grasp. He asked questions, and they were good ones too, but I could tell that he simply didn't understand the scope of the problem. Then he asked me what the enemy looked like. I had the images brought forth and he gasped. I was unaware of this, but lizard people are pictured in some of the ancient texts as servants of the devil. That was really what brought them around to our side. Apparently the whole situation we witnessed with the end of the world matches almost exactly something in the bible. The fact that it was destroyed by these servants merely made it all true for them. They immediately offered any help they can give." He paused as Frank worked on all of that for a moment. Then he continued on. "The library here is small. We have very little to work with here. But, what we did find as far as clues tells us that we need to go back to pre-English history. The rulers of this day would never match the king you had found in your research. There is a major piece of this puzzle missing and we are still looking for it now. We have a team in the archives tracing through everything two and three times looking for something obscure. The main idea here as that we need to go back before the Christ visit. That would put us off course by at least half." The Captain said glumly.

Frank managed to prop himself up on a pillow. "Actually, I have been told we are only a third of the way back." He said and the Captain looked at him in surprise. "I believe we are talking about three thousand years or more back. Maybe even more than that, I cannot be certain until I get some of the figures out of my head and into the computer. The woman was not precise, but I have a gut feeling that she will come again to help narrow down the search. I also believe that we are talking about a location in the center of the continent of Eurasia. I can't explain why just now, but I know that it is right. If you could give me someone to dictate to, I can get all of this down before it fades from memory." He asked and the Captain nodded.

"You say you want to take down figures from a dream? Well I guess this whole mission is based on little more than that, after all, a wizard? You are looking for a legend, or a fantasy figure. Science cannot support it at all, at least not that I know of." He said and the chuckle in his voice took away any of the sting of the comment. "Get well and remember all you can, we still have much to do to save our world." He said and he turned and walked to a couple of monks that were standing just outside of earshot to talk to him. Frank was left to his own thoughts for a while and he kept going over the scene in his mind. The beautiful girl and her message that he wanted so desperately to understand.

After a couple of hours, a monk scribe came over and sat down on the stone floor next to Frank. "If you will, sir I shall write what you say." He said and he laid the parchment out before himself and unstopped the ink bottle. His quill pen looked impossibly old but well cared for and he treated it like an instrument of God. He smiled at the fallen stranger and prepared to write.

Frank began to tell his story. He put in everything he could remember. He even put in what he felt or thought when things happened and when he was done, the monk looked at him in dismay.

"Sir; that is one dream vision that I am glad not to have witnessed. There were so many things in it that could be considered prophecy that it would take years to understand it all even if you had an oracle to consult." He said and he cleaned the pen and stopped up the bottle again. The parchment was long and he rolled it up now that it was sufficiently dry. He handed the roll to Frank, bowed, and left him to return to his own duties elsewhere.

All Frank could do now was wait for the next event. A meal perhaps, or a visit from another of the crew. No matter what it was, he had his new scroll and he wanted to get down to business determining what it all meant.

*   *   *

Brother Christopher Farber watched these strangers in their native environment. They were active aboard the portable house and then later he watched them at the Abbey once he had been returned. He was sorry to have been the instrument to break the Abbot. It was nothing he had any control over, but he still felt a twinge of guilt over it. He knew that his time with the monks was now limited. He wanted to know more about these strangers and more importantly, he wanted to become a part of this grand mission he kept hearing about. These people were on a quest of grand proportions and that was the sort of thing he felt that he was destined for. He yearned for that kind of action. His earlier days of adventure were the only outlet that he had found for it. He had heard tales of heroes and legends and that was what he wished for most. He wanted stories told about him and he wanted to be famous. He didn't know much else about the mission, except that it was to save the world. That was enough for him. He would do whatever it took to help these men finish what they had started. In fact, he had even seen a woman or two on that ship. He wondered at the logic of that, but he kept it to himself. If that was the only thing that seemed troubling, he would do just fine. Even now, he watched the fallen one. The man had lived against impossible odds. He had gotten aid of some sort but he still had to have amazing amounts of personal strength to still be here among the living. He stepped up to the man and knelt down next to him.

"How fare thee today?" He asked and the man opened his eyes. He smiled at the prone man and noticed that much of the color had returned to his face. He looked almost well. It was truly amazing. He expected an answer to his question, but there was not one quickly. The delay caused him some confusion. He decided to try again. "Are you feeling better?" He asked and the man on the mat focused his eyes on him now.

Frank looked up at the monk and smiled back. "I'm sorry, what are you saying?" He replied and the man sighed.

"You are feeling well then?" The monk asked, impatience beginning to tint his mood. "That poison was supposed to be lethal you know." He added.

Frank's eyebrows furrowed. "We cannot die before the quest is done. It is all that we are here for. The poison helped me to reach someone to help us though. I am trying to figure out what it all means now." Frank said and his mind was still fluttering through the images.

"I am Christopher, Christopher Farber." The monk informed him. "I can help you with that I think." He said looking thoughtful. "I have active dreams all the time and some of them even come true. Maybe I have seen something that will help you." He suggested and Frank propped himself up on an elbow.

"You really want to try?" He asked and Christopher nodded. His youthful energy was something that Frank lacked just now and that he wished he could regain. "Okay, help me to a table and we will examine it together." He offered and Brother Farber lifted the man almost easily. Frank updated his estimation of the man. The robes hid the fact that he was heavily muscled and probably quick of reflexes too.

"We can use the writing room. There is a table there and candles enough for our needs." Christopher said as they veered out of the main hall and into one of the many corridors. The construction was pretty much consistent throughout the dwelling. The age of the walls differed as different pieces of it were erected at different times, but the scheme and architecture was at least similar throughout. At least it was as far as Frank had seen. It was like walking through one of his history books. He felt as if it were not real, but it most assuredly was. They were here in the fifteenth century. They would travel back even farther. He felt the pains in his body begin to subside as the movement brought new circulation. He was still pretty weak, but he was motivated to get better. He was tired of lying around waiting to be served. He needed to be up and around again.

The writing room was off of the main corridor and it was on the south side of the complex. This allowed for at least some light all of the time through the windows on the south wall. The arc of the sun offered as much as they could have hoped for. The room was cold. Apparently no one had needed the fire for a few days. The monks had mostly been in the archives anyway. Brother Farber brought Frank to a high chair and propped him up on it as he pulled the chair and the man to the even higher table. The main candle was not currently lit, but it would be soon. Once in place, Frank waited at the desk as Chris lit a fire in the fireplace and then took one of the embers to light the candle on the desk. The smell of the fire reminded Frank of sleeping out in the woods. He had gone camping many times as a child. The smoke trailed up from the fireplace and collected in the vaulted ceiling where small holes let it out slowly. The high chair and desk kept him off of the cold floor. For that much, he was grateful. When all was done, Chris came back to the desk with a second chair and he watched as Frank carefully laid out his scroll. The lettering on the scroll looked rushed. It was not the standard that the monks were used to here. It was probably because the words were written as Frank spoke them. There was not time to be neat.

Christopher took in the entire scroll and Frank re-read what he had said. The words made sense to him only as shadows. The dream itself had begun to fade as he feared it would. Now the passages were like a puzzle to him that he just couldn't seem to find the key for. It was like his mind were locked from him and he could only see the shadows on the wall and not the figures dancing around inside. It was most frustrating. He was brought out of his musings as Christopher gasped.

"What? What is it that you have found?" Frank asked excitedly. "Tell me what you know." He prompted as Chris got over his momentary shock.

"You have begun a quest that I have dreamed about." Chris said. "I was in this place you described. The woman in white, I have seen her. She told me to leave home and come to the city where I was arrested and then sent here. I thought that she had set me up for the trouble that followed. I was angry at her for the longest time. It was only the Abbot that took me in and helped me understand that I wasn't mad at her, but at my former mischievous self that I started to let go of that hate." He said and he shook his head. "She was not trying to get me into trouble; she was trying to get me to you. I am meant to help you save the world." He said and the smile on his face told Frank that arguing about it would do no good. This man was now in for the duration of the mission.

"Okay, tell me what you know of this woman and what she told you about us." Frank prodded. His own experience with the strange woman was similar to what this wayward monk described. Perhaps there was more than fate involved here.

"Well, first of all, she is not a woman. She is an elf. I don't know what that means truly. We see elves in our fantasy writing, there are no records of them actually existing. I tried to identify her in the archive only to find that all references to elves are considered blasphemy and I had to desist in order to continue staying here with the other monks. I didn't want to be a disruptive force. If I had become a problem, then the authorities would have taken me to jail. People never come back from there." He paused, realizing that he had gone off topic. He apologized quickly and got his thoughts together to continue on.

"I listened to her talk for hours over many nights. She is amazingly smart and she knew much about things of the earth. I tried to tell her what I knew and she listened, but told me that there was so much more for me to know. I asked her to teach me and she said that it would not be possible until I got there." He stopped, and Frank looked startled.

"She told you that you would come to her?" He asked; he could not believe that he was asking the question for he wanted to meet her more than anything else in the world. If he could just lay eyes on her and her radiant beauty, he would give up everything else.

"Yes, she told me that she could teach me once I met her." He said and his smugness flittered away under Franks gaze. "She told me many things and that she was anxious to meet me someday." Chris looked content and Frank fell into line with him. If they both met this woman, it would be amazing. It would also mean that they had found their goal. If this monk could get visions from this elf woman, then maybe they could re-establish contact with her and ask her about the trip and when they needed to visit her. He sighed and realized that she probably couldn't tell them where and when she was; she could only influence their minds and hope the message is received. Finding this young monk was like finding a bread crumb on the trail. They were going to get closer to their goal. They just had to.

* * *

Commander Zarg felt the pull and strain as the stone ship tried to slow down again. They had taken a lot of damage from the humans and re-entered warp space without a true destination in mind. The streaks of light that were the stars formed as the ship neared the warp point and then they shortened into dots again. It was like a magical lights display that somehow failed to impress the impatient leader. His crews were busily reforming the ship and they would have to stop somewhere for additional rock to shore up the missing parts. Then there was the prey to get back to. They had made this chase interesting, but now they had sealed their own fate. It was no longer a commander following orders. He had been beaten by them twice now. His own personal honor was at stake here. He *had* to destroy them. He no longer had the luxury of killing them with his own claws. He needed to take them out no matter how he did it. His own family line would be severed if he failed this mission. The home world did not accept weakness and no one was allowed to live once they failed a mission. If they were lucky, his crew would survive to serve under another commander. No more than this was even considered. If they were found to be at fault for the failure of the commander, then they would be executed as well. It kept the crew motivated to make sure their commander succeeded.

He turned to his navigator. "Find out where we are and get us the supplies we need to return to combat effectiveness. In fact, get additional stone since we are going to use a lot of weapons on this prey." He said and his tone had iron in it. "They will not get away from us again." He vowed and the crew enjoyed his commitment. They needed him to be strong and decisive. They would follow him to death if need be. All of his glory would be theirs.

* * *

Captain Glass looked out over the vista. The river led out to the sea and he watched it peacefully as his crew worked in the archives of the Abbey a few miles behind him. The sun was nearing the horizon and he knew that he should be getting back. He had his own personal conveyance and it had made a bit of a commotion when he first unveiled it before the monks of the Abbey. It was like a motorcycle that could fly. It was a silver marlin airstream sail car and he had grown to love using it while on some pretty remote assignments. They were used for business as well. Survey teams often used the small and agile crafts in order to plot out colony locations and to research planetary assets. Others simply used them for the thrill of it like wave runners and snow mobiles. He was adept at making the thing do the most intricate and precise maneuvers. It was also the fastest thing on the planet just now. He sighed as the bottom edge of the sun touched the water's edge out there. He put on his gloves and primed the turbine. Then he flung a leg over the runner and settled back into the seat. He keyed in the startup sequence and the turbine came up to speed. This was a pretty remote spot and no one had come while he was here so he figured a direct take off would not be out of the question. He punched the throttle and the whole thing lifted gently off the ground. He felt the power beneath him as the computer made micro-adjustments to keep the craft hovering level. He tilted the controls forward and the thrust began to apply to the rear. He started moving forward. The edge of the coast was a rocky cliff here and he punched up the power as he sailed off of it. Without the land beneath him to push off of, he needed more thrust to maintain his position. He knew about this but he let the craft skim lower towards the water for the sheer thrill of it. He powered off the surface just above the water and the spray of saltwater swept out behind him. He could have crossed the country in less than an hour on this rig but he was enjoying the sensations at this much slower speed. He banked left and right to hear the spray behind him. Then he shot up into the air and swung around to return to the Abbey. As much fun as it was, he had responsibilities to tend to. He nosed the craft towards the distant buildings. The flight would be less than four minutes and he would beat the setting sun down to the ground.

The craft was flawless and he loved it so much. He did the maintenance on it himself as part of his own personal therapy. It made him feel better to tinker with the thing. He had outfitted it with a homing beacon and directional finders as well. It made the chances of getting lost drastically less. His ship could find the thing just about anywhere. He pulled back on the controls and the forward motion slowed somewhat. He let the throttle ease down as he descended towards his own ship. It looked grand from up here. He wanted so much to be on his way to the next place, but he didn't know where the new place was yet. He was frustrated at the waiting. The enemy was still out there somewhere and they had been outfoxed twice. They would not be so happy on the next meeting. He finally sighed and brought the small craft in and landed of top of the ship. There was a small platform there to receive it and he settled it down like a pro. Then he switched it off and pulled the lever to bring the platform back down into the ship. The crewmembers in the bay saluted and he waved them off. He started to get out of his flying gear and was just about to start the maintenance on the craft when the message came in.

A young ensign stepped up briskly and saluted the Captain. The return salute was fairly sharp because of the interest the unexpected approach raised. "Sir, we have a message from the archives." He said and handed over an old fashioned piece of paper. It was an elegantly scrawled piece of parchment from one of the monks at the Abbey. He thanked the man and sent him away so that he could read it in peace.

"Kind sir, defender of the world, we have found something that may be of interest and ultimately a key to your success." The first line read. Well, they definitely had his attention now. "The time you seek is long past. You need to go back to before you previously expected. According to scripture, we are talking the oldest writings recorded; you need to go back to before Noah and the Ark. The land before the flood is where you will find your wizard. We have made some calculations and your people have verified the early conclusions. The only one who seemed to be skeptical is your man Frank Muskerini. He is following a lead of his own about some beautiful witch from ages past. Our minimal research into his claims actually supports our theory of your needs. The witches would have been lost during the cleansing of the flood. The wizards would have fared no better. What we have been able to gather is an era for you to jump to. We will send the particulars of our findings with your crew. They are even now packing up to rejoin your ship. Thank you and your people for their diligence in your all-important mission. We hope that you enjoyed your stay here. There will be no records that you ever stopped by our humble Abbey." He read it and let out a long breath. He hadn't realized he was holding one. So they were closing in on an answer. They believe that they have actually found one. This was good news, very good news indeed. He turned the paper over and saw a PS on the back. "We have authorized for one monk to accompany you on your continued journey. Brother Christopher Farber has requested the honor and we had no reason to deny him. He is willing to do as you bid as we have freed him from his oaths here. May god be with you as you face the dangers ahead. Good luck." He glanced at the signature block. Henry of Derby, the Abbot of Buildwas Abbey and your host. It was a nice touch. The Captain put the paper in his pocket and headed for the bridge. They would get everything ready to move out once the personnel were all on board. They had been here too long for his liking already.

* * *

Back into the Void

Frank and Christopher had brought everything they needed. They had scrolls and tomes and whatever the monks could spare. They had his own dream sequence and they had experimented with the attunement as well. It was a root that one chewed as they concentrated on the focus. It was some form of hallucinogen and it would allow brothers to have a 'religious experience'. Both Christopher and Frank had tried this during their studies and Frank even managed to see the woman again. This time he noticed her ears and he asked her if she were truly an elf. She had nodded to him and her tone was quiet and dangerous.

"You must hurry, time is drawing short. If you are not underway now, it may be too late to save the world." She said and he felt a wave of fear as the realization sank in that she may be right. He had heard the warnings before but had figured that they were going to travel in time to return to the future and the conflict there. Now he realized that time was not the solid surface he had thought it was. If something disturbed the pond back here, then the future was re-written around the new ripples. He knew fear on a grave level for the first time. She tried to comfort him, but his shaking had continued and she made him wake up. He was still shaking when his eyes popped open. Christopher was hovering over him. It had been a frightening sight to watch the man curl up in terror at the spirit dream. That was not the sign of someone in control. It was the sign of subjugation. It was the sign that meant that someone could take him over. Brother Farber felt fear of his own over that. They both decided not to do that again until they had a more controlled environment. It would do no one any good to stumble onto something they couldn't handle by themselves.

* * *

The ship powered up and the turbines rolled and the *Lost Cavalier* jumped into the sky. The stars were the next stop and the monks of the Abbey watched as the grand vehicle pulled out of their sight. Their prayers were with the wayward warriors of god. None of them knew if they would succeed. They had no way of ever knowing. So it was for this reason that all writings about the visitation from the stars was burned and the ashes were swept away. After that, the faith of the monks started to crumble and the Abbey fell into disarray.

The gleaming ship of patched metal climbed ever higher and the sky fell behind them. The normal lights glittered on the various consoles around him and suddenly the Captain felt home again. According to the calculations, they needed to go back longer than they ever had before. They needed to go back twice as far as they had come so far. The course was already laid in from before and the order to continue was given. Everyone hoped this was the last time they would be going back. The future needed them. The sooner they got this out of the way, the sooner they could make the attempt to restore their race. The course plot line of the ship fell into place with the computer generated course and the speed began to pile on. They would use the same slingshot and bring the ship into warp. This time though, they would remain at warp for much longer.

* * *

The stone ship pulled fragments of asteroids into itself and the stone melded together to replace the lost mass. They continued to take on more until the limits had been reached. The ship would be a bit slower now, but the power source was practically infinite so they could just ask it for more. They began the trek back to the human home world. The crew was anxious to be back on the trail so they were all surprised when the search for technology turned up negative. There were no refined metals here. There were no advanced alloys to be found. The enemy was no longer here. Of course they had traveled farther back in time than the humans by at least a small amount. Maybe the prey had not come this far back. The trail would have to be found again. They had come too far to lose them now. They decided to continue to orbit the planet until the metal ship arrived. Then they could get a good trace on it. This elusive prey would not escape the clan. They would not avoid their own extinction. He had his brother and his crew and he would chase them for all time if need be. The longer it took, the bolder the legend they would become. He settled in to await the enemy.

It was about two weeks when the first signs of trouble appeared. The stone ship was orbiting on the far side of the planet from the conflict and that turned out to be all that saved them from the temporal flux. A wave of time distortion swept out since the stone ship was here twice at once. This was an unforeseen problem that needed rectifying. They needed to get out of here so as not to create a bigger problem, or worse, a temporal loop that would trap them for all eternity. The commander ordered the ship to sail clear of the danger zone and wait for long enough to allow the stone ship to warp back again. Then they could go in and get the human metal box.

The commander's memories haunted him about that particular incident. The humans had plotted exactly where the stone ship would drop out of warp and they had their weapons in place when it happened. It had been a risky move on their part since their munitions had no way to resupply without their supply chain. But it was also the move of a desperate and quick thinking commander. Zarg respected this human commander who had given him so much trouble. They had carved a ship apart trying to kill him and they had failed. They were tenacious and he wanted them all dead. His respect for them would allow them a death as warriors, not as a simple prey. Running was one thing, but this metal box was filled with humans of exceptional caliber. He felt pride in the fact that he had been sent after these people. He took away a sense of destiny from this mission. He would finish it all and then return home victorious. The human vermin would be eradicated and he would be a hero. His crew would all enjoy a loftier status for having served him in the greater service to the corps. He felt a twitch and something in his instincts told him that something was wrong. He looked around to see the source of the disturbance. A smaller male stood trembling in his presence and he spat at the upstart.

"What issss it that you need?" He asked in a biting tone. "I have humanssss to kill here, out with it before I tear you to shreds!" He ordered and the subordinate swallowed hard and then gave his report.

"Sssir, we have dissscovered that the humans have somehow damaged thissss ship deeper than we thought. The sssystem drivesss will not allow us to land on the planet. If we try to follow the humanss to the sssurface, we will not be able to take off again." He said and the commander looked furious.

"You are telling me that I can't follow my prey?" He asked dangerously. This would be one of the gravest insults in his culture. The underling knew that and he tried his best to shy away from answering. The commander would have none of it.

"Sssir, we have been disssabled by the enemy and we will need to regroup in order to take them down. They have reached the planet now, We have two optionsss. We can dessstroy the entire planet, or we can wait for them to leave the planet again." He said and the initial response to simply club the man was swept aside by the undeniable logic of the statement itself. But there were a few unanswered questions in this plan.

"What do we need to repair thisss ship?" He asked. His gaze was centered on this bearer of bad news. His feelings were that the entire bridge crew felt the pressure of his question though. That was the way he liked it to be. A good dose of fear would keep the rabble in line for him long enough for them to complete this accursed mission and return home.

"Sssir, we have been given orderss to persssue the enemy and we intend to do thisss. We need a few hoursss to set the ship right again though. The ssstone we have added hasss not been added into the power equation. If we land now, we may be ssstuck here forever."

"Take your few hoursss, we are going to follow thisss enemy and we are going to dessstroy it. Make my ship work and you will sssave your own life!" He screamed at the annoying crewman before him. "Now go and do thisss or I will gut you myssself." He said in that low dangerous tone that caused dread fear.

The cowering lizard man scrambled to leave the bridge. There would be time enough later to complain about his treatment. This was definitely not the right moment. In truth, the calculations had already been begun. He was just sent to stall the commander long enough to allow them to finish before he moved the ship into something they were unprepared for. This was turning into a much longer mission than he had signed up for. Sure it was great to be serving under someone with so much potential for glory, but it was also distracting being so far away from home for extended periods of time. He was ready to voice his opinions, but he did not know where to do so. There was no precedent for that sort of thing aboard a ship like this. He just knew that he was unhappy. He would have to bide his time and see what happened next. It was frustrating, but what else could he do?

* * *

163

The stone ship had orbited for three weeks when the metal box hurtled up into space again. They had not landed the stone ship and the crew breathed a collective sigh of relief as the enemy came towards them here in space. The commander was already passing orders to the crew as the enemy ship began to pour on speed again. The pattern was now familiar and the stone ship slid in behind it to make pace and align for a good shot up the kilt. The enemy ship would not be allowed to travel through time again. There was a general fear that they could disappear in time somewhere and that the stone ship would be unable to find them to bring them to their destiny. Gone were the thoughts of bringing these humans into close range and boarding the craft. They needed a kill and they needed it now. The weapons systems were brought to bear and when the order was given, a full three dozen spires launched from the great stone ship and hurtled towards the human metal box. "Let'sss sssee what they do with that!" The commander exclaimed.

*   *   *

On the bridge of the *Cavalier*, things were getting tense. "Sir, I have the bogey slipping back into our six o-lock position. They have matched speed and it looks like they are preparing to fire!" Came the strained voice.

Captain Glass looked at the plot and unfortunately he could not argue the conclusions of his scan tech. "They could just be trying to make us break off our run." He mused but the serious faces around him told him that they didn't believe it either. "We had better brace for impact. I believe they will send everything they have at us this time. We have proven ourselves too dangerous if they let us get into warp on them. Unless I miss my guess, that enemy captain over there has a personal score to settle with us on top of all that. The simple fact that he has orders to kill us only makes it convenient for him." He said. He watched and considered his options. "We will need to maneuver as we stay on course. I know that sounds like too different things, but really we might be able to pull it off. I want a spiral about two hundred meters wide around our current course. As soon as the enemy adjusts to the move, then we will pick a different pattern. Evasion this time is the key. We've got to keep those weapons off of us long enough to hit the slingshot corridor around the sun." He said and his knuckles were white on the arms of the chair. It was the only outward sign that he was nervous about this encounter.

The ship began to twist around the axis of their course and barrel roll around the point. It spread out from the line and started rotating around the new orbit it had created. Then the moment they all dreaded came. The stone ship launched its entire excess payload and some thirty-five or so spires shot forth trying to impale the ship. The range would put them in contact with the ship in about six minutes. Worse yet, they were smart and would track to the evading ship. Even now they were showing signs of matching the roll rate and they were still coming in. The rear batteries of lasers began to try to stab into the darkness at the offending stone spikes. They cut a few of them, but there were so many now. The Captain turned to the weapons officer as he exclaimed "Of course!" He started pressing buttons and down below decks crews scrambled to comply with the new orders. The Captain was up and over to the busy station as the thin man pressed buttons too fast to be understood.

"What are you doing son?" He asked just a bit impatiently, but also not wanting to stop the work. This man had pulled their fat out of the fire before; he was hoping that the genius could do it again. There was no immediate response except a quick glance. Then the speedy man entered a last set of codes and pressed the button that had just turned green on his board. The ship jolted as the launch to the rear was more than the rear launcher was designed for. The Captain was losing his battle with his own patience. "What have you done?" He screamed at his officer.

As if seeing him for the first time, the weapons officer blushed. "Well sir, I figured out that the spires trigger off of gravitic waves. They are steering them by pushing waves of gravity towards us. It was also how they sent our own missiles back at us before, that and disabling the electrical systems at the same time." He said hurriedly as he watched a new green dot fall behind them and the many red dots race up behind them at the same time.

"How in blazes do they do that?" He asked and the weapons officer shrugged his shoulders.

"I don't know that, but I do know that we can create a gravity wave as well. I have dropped a nuke behind us. It should detonate as the spires reach it. It should blow them off course and send them far enough from the gravity well to render them useless." He said and the look of triumph on his face did not last long.

"You deployed a nuke without authorization?" The Captain, not sure he believed what he was hearing at all. "I should have you up on charges before you could blink." He said and his wrath seemed destined to fall upon this hapless officer who had overstepped his bounds. Instead, his grimace turned into a smile. "I hope this works." He said softly. Then he strolled back to his own chair to watch the plots on the big screen in the front of the bridge. He turned to the navigator. "What's our distance to the weapon now?" He asked and there were a couple of quick calculations and then the answer came.

"Sir, we are one hundred and seventy five kilometers away and accelerating. We should hit about five hundred thousand when the spires reach the nuke."

The Captain nodded his thanks. "Well, that should be far enough away to make us safe from the initial blast. We will need to warp on schedule though. Straighten out our course. I want to be on an arrow when the shock wave pushes us forward and the enemy back." He ordered and the spiraling ship stopped its dancing and got back on line for the original course.

*   *   *

Commander Zarg watched as his spires crept up on the enemy. The enemy had started trying to evade the rock weapons, but the weapons were maneuverable and they tracked to the human ship's movements. That ship would soon be no more than wreckage floating in the void of space. It was only a few minutes away now. In fact, it was less than five human minutes. Then the enemy dropped something down behind them. It was small. Not a missile or anything active on their sensors. It was something dormant. Maybe it was an escape pod or something. They would make sure to blow it up when they finished with the ship. It fell behind the metal box and towards the weapons. Since it did not activate any warnings, they pretty much ignored it. It was more of a nuisance than anything else, a harmless distraction. They kept focused on the prize. It seemed odd that the enemy would give up their evasion techniques, but they stopped dancing around and went back to the course they had been on previously. In fact, they had never left it in the first place, only danced around it. They were up to something. Zarg ordered a scan sweep of the object, something did not add up. The weapons were almost to it now and they could get a feel about it from the spires. It was like having eyes out there in the darkness, looking at the curious thing in space. Then the device went active and warning alarms went off all over the stone ship.

Zarg stood up to yell at the helmsman, but he did not have time before the explosion happened right in front of them. A blast like a sun blew the spires away in an expanding circle of broken rock and the resulting shock wave slammed the front of the stone ship in less than three seconds. The whole crew was thrown around inside as the ship was knocked back and off course. The front third of it was melted by intense heat and friction. The rest was sent spiraling away from the enemy. Zarg felt the wall crush his shoulder as he hit it with a lung emptying thump. Many of his crewmates were in worse shape. He knew that. He also knew that the enemy was about to evade them again. The shame was terrible and made him act impulsively. He leapt and hit the accelerate control. The stone ship tried to figure out which way was up in this well of gravity that was a nuclear blast. The black hole began to destabilize and the emergency cut off was all that saved the ship from imploding on itself. It was true; they were going to need to repair the ship again. His own frustration was being mirrored by the crew he could see. He ordered a damage report and then he stomped off to sulk in his quarters. His brother watched him and the loathing for his brother and commander was beginning to grow. The man had lost his own ship and nearly lost this second one as well. There would be an inquiry if they ever got back from this mission.

*   *   *

Completing Training
on Multiple Fronts

During the next two years, I learned a lot about the elements. The isolation began to tell on me though. The other acolytes had no idea how I was doing and I had no idea how they were progressing. The only reassurance I had was that the master told me I was on an accelerated program. There was certainly enough work to do. My studies kept me up well into the night each night. The practice sessions were getting longer and the trips to the elemental room were now once a week. I had been developing in more ways than one. The physical demands of the casting had made me stronger. I was now toned and shaped by the efforts. I didn't notice this at first, but it hit me one day when I was dressing. The polished metal mirror surprised me with its image. I got embarrassed and dressed into my acolyte's robes and headed down to the elemental room. My next exam was coming up and I needed to be ready for it. I stepped up to the doors and stood on the correct spot to await entry. The room needed to be reset for each caster and this allowed the room to start that process. As I waited, the master came down the stairs to me. The hallway was intricately carved and I had spent quite a bit of time waiting here, so I knew every crevice and cranny of it. It was actually beautiful. There were cherubs carved along the top sill of the doorway and they were doing hand signals that represented the main protection spells. It was as if they were guarding the entrance to this powerful room. Perhaps they were. The master seemed to be in a foul mood and I kept silent as I waited. He stepped all the way up to me and then he nodded as if noticing me for the first time.

"You are here early." He said like he had done for every meeting. I was never late. "You will be pleased by the exam today I think." He said almost jovially. This was definitely unexpected by me. He never let slip any detail of an exam. His secrets were always closely guarded and I did not know what to say to the unusual comment. So instead I remained silent and he nodded again. Apparently that was the correct answer. There was a mechanical clicking sound from behind the doors and I readied to enter the room. The massive wooden doors swung into the room and I walked in with the master right behind me. When we were both through, the doors closed again. They locked with that same mechanical clicking sound and I knew that the exam had started. The same four stations of elemental material were there, but now there was a center post and a huge shiny ball on top. I had not seen this before and I was not going to get the chance to ask about it before having to deal with it, so I went through my normal set up chant. The energies around me started to coalesce and I could feel the tingle of heightened power around me. It was an invigorating feeling that I still long for today. The ball started buzzing and I stepped up to the examination location to start the testing. The hot coals were ready for use and the water was there. The dirt was right where it always was and the air around me seemed excited at the prospect of focus. None of them told me what was going to happen next. The buzzing grew louder and then it struck me, literally. Lightning shot out of it and hit me in the side. The force was amazing. I was thrown off of the mark and I slid across the floor for a bit. My side was burned by the hit and my robes were still smoking. The heat and shock of it all was totally unexpected. I pulled a wall of air in front of me to protect myself from another bolt. The lightning danced around and through it to strike me again. My knee felt the pain as the bolt caught it from the side. I screamed out and then pulled the energy to me again. This lightning attack was something that not even the scrolls had mentioned. The earth around me swept up at my calling and formed a ring around me and I pulled it over me like a blanket. The lightning stuck again. This time it hit the dirt and fizzled. A black mark on the dome was all the effect it had that time. I felt relieved at that. I hurt all over now from the initial two attacks. I needed to do something about that pole though. I could not hide from this thing forever. I opened a small hole in the protective covering and sent power through it. I sent the wind to knock the offending pole down. It didn't budge. I tried to encase the pole in the same protective barrier that was helping me now. It failed to complete. The pole somehow rejected the earthen power. Then I brought fire into the mix. If I could melt the pole, maybe I could bring it down. I pulled most of my remaining strength into the spell and sent a fiery blast that would have leveled a small village. The pole glistened and gleamed in that fiery light, but remained unchanged in height and attitude. It was somehow fireproof. I shrugged my shoulders and then brought my final element to the table. I pulled water out and formed a moat around the pole and then caused rain to drench the pole and the pole reacted violently. The lightning began to cover the pole as the water carried the power away from it. It took the energy and brought it to the ground below. It carried away the destructiveness and made it harmless in the dirt floor. I released my own protective spell and watched as the pole struck time after time, each time bleeding its own power away by the tap that I had set. It was a shame that I had not known this before. It could have save me the two wounds. I limped back to the spot as the pole died down to a dull gray. Then the room started to reset. The exam was over. The master stepped down from his gallery position and his smile was somehow evil.

"You handled the fifth element, I am impressed." He said and my look of confusion made him laugh aloud. "You did not know that there are other elements? That's quite normal for people do not see them as elements. The denizens of the dark powers have used the other elements for some time. They are considered evil because people do not understand the power behind them. Power is not evil, it only is. The energy is not evil, it only exists and what men do with it when they wield it determines the alignment of the action, not the power itself." He said. "You have just had your first run-in with lightning. I daresay it is not the last time you will see it. The other acolytes will not see this for at least another year. That is, the gifted ones won't. The others may never get their introduction. These advanced elements are not for the casual caster. There are four of them just like the primary elements. You must know that the thought of anyone knowing and controlling all eight elements frightens even the most gifted of the masters. That is why I have been forbidden from showing them all to you. I have chosen to show you lightning to let you know they exist. You must seek them out on your own. The room can show them to you, but without knowing what to ask for, it cannot help you much." He stepped closer, as if to whisper to me. I didn't think that was such a good idea if he was not supposed to tell me something. But I said nothing. "You will seek these answers and once you have found them, I will help you to overcome the difficulties. I have watched you as you tackle one spell or one particular element. You must learn to combine them for new and amazing effects. This you will find in the library as well. So I will let you go now." He started to step away, and then he reached back. "Oh, we need to keep your mind off of these wounds." He said and reached out and grabbed my side. The pain was intense and then it quickly faded. He was using a healing spell. I did not know that elementalists had any spells that could heal. I had seen the elf woman do it, but I did not know that others had the ability. It was definitely something that I would look up as well. I headed from the power room and out the doors and into the hallway. Several of the instructors were there. Somehow the gossip spread faster than the lightning I had just fought. They whispered among themselves as I passed them. I needed to get back to the library and start my studies. The thoughts of food were at least for now wiped from my mind.

*   *   *

The following bits were told to me by my good friend and long time companion, Maxillen. He is an elf of the old blood. He and his sister were on a quest similar to the one that I was destined for. In fact, it turned out to be the same one. None of us knew it at the time, but our lives were tangled together in a way that no one could have predicted. Well, at least only one person had predicted. The White Witch somehow knew it all. I hadn't thought about her for a long time. The thoughts of her beauty had distracted me at first and I had to let them go in order to train properly. But this part is not about me, it is about Maxillen and his sister Florena.

Max was sitting on the outcropping of rock above the tops of the top trees of the forest. He was looking out at the eagle in the distance. He was training to take his uncle's place as the animal handler for his village. He was in what they called first phase. I asked him what first phase was and he said 'observation'. How an animal thinks is reflected in how it moves. How it reacts to its environment can give great insight into the animal's motivations. The eagle in question was soaring high and circling over a small lake in the distance. Maxillen watched closely as it scanned the water's surface. The eagle's keen eyesight was looking for fish. It spotted something and circled tightly just once while ascertaining the possible hit. Then it shook its feathers and winged over into a quick dive. The mighty bird hit the water hard and flared its wings almost at the same time. The sharp talons swept forward and the splash concealed the actual grab. The bird took back to the air with the fish flopping around in its iron grip. It sailed up to the top of a tree and landed in some of the thicker branches and its sharp beak tore into the meal even as the unfortunate fish fought to get away. Maxillen watched the whole thing and he felt the power of those mighty wings and he felt the pain of the fish as it was devoured. He lowered his head and let the feeling pass. His link to the animal was complete. It was a good first try and his mentor was pleased. The two of them started climbing down since the show was over. The walk back was filled with descriptions. Max had to tell everything he saw and felt as they covered the ground effortlessly. The subtleties and the nuances of the eagle were exciting and the thrill of the kill was amazing. The counter point was the fear of the fish as it was pulled from its home. Then the helplessness as it thrashed in that unbreakable grip. Then there was the pain of being devoured alive. It was a struggle that went on all the time. Nature was a violent host. It was not the first lesson, but it was an important one. If caring were introduced into the system, then some of the weaker animals would survive. If they bred they could create more even weaker creatures and thin down the bloodlines. This was nature's way of keeping the species strong.

It was a truth that was repeated throughout the realm of nature. The stronger plants fought for the sunlight and the weaker ones shriveled and died in the shadows. Then some other types would take advantage of the dark like mushrooms. The conditions that killed other plants caused them to flourish. They didn't require the direct light to survive. In fact they died in it. With animals it was the same. If the environment changed slowly enough, the animals would adapt to the new situation and survive. The will to survive was strong in all life. It was just odd that all living things were on a borrowed clock. They would all die eventually. The mighty trees could live for centuries or maybe even millennia. The insects living inside of them rarely lasted more than a few days. The cycle of life was not one circle, but many circles linked into a chain of life and death that they all shared. It meant that all the creatures and plants were linked into the same system. The elves may not have been the first to understand this, but they were the ones who embraced this truth the most fully. Their society was one of coexistence with nature and all of its living things. They celebrated life and in return they lived long lives. Maxillen had taken his first steps into that understanding and his mind was beginning to hurt with the ramifications and permutations of the concept. Thinking was something he usually left for his sister to do. Still, the progress was good and he would never be the same again. He had killed today and he had died today. Those were big life-changing events. Later on, he would get the opportunity to witness more of the life cycle. It was too grand to experience all at once. His path was laid out before him and he realized that he was ready for it. So it was that he was not the same young man that had left the village. He had come back a man of nature. Like a right of passage he had risen to the challenge and embraced his own future.

*   *   *

Captain Milas took his men westward from the King's Field area. Now that they no longer wore the black armor of the king's calling, they were able to travel easier. They wanted to avoid contact with the citizens that they had abused in the king's name. These were, after all, honorable men. They headed out on a three day trek to the village of the ferrymen in order to book passage across the mighty Elder River. The Elder was one of the main tributaries leading all the way out to the Green Sea to the far south. It basically was the western border of the king's controlled lands. The general thought was that if they could escape there, then the king would have no control over them anymore. Their civilian clothing was pretty worn from their earlier ordeal and the military underclothes for their armor stood out too much. They also realized that they had no funds to replace their worn and tattered garments. This was not a major problem. They were strong men with disciplined minds and they could work for the clothes they needed, but it would take time. They wanted to escape now. The area to the west was simpler. There were only two main areas. One was the forest of the elves. Trespassers there rarely survived, so it was not their destination. The other was a vast uncharted forest with all kinds of things in it that would keep children and weaker adults away. They figured that the seclusion would protect them and they could set up a permanent camp and raise families far from the throngs of civilization that were still blossoming to the east. It would be a good, long and happy life without the rule of the king to get in the way.

That is, that was the plan before fate stepped in. They were heading westward still, and the ferryman village was just in sight. The smoke from fires was now high in the sky. They were under attack. The men had no armor now, but they still had their weapons. They began to run to the scene. As they approached, the attackers were sacking the western side of the village away from the ex-black squad. When they ran through the gates, it was obvious that the city militia, such as it was, was engaged on the far side. They dropped into formation like the trained professionals they were. They advanced through the streets and they finally saw the enemy. The beasts were standing upright using iron weapons and they looked brutish. They were like an experiment gone wrong. Hairy and stinking of filth, they were going through the village, slaughtering everything that moved. The livestock and the people were being cut down indiscriminately. They did not appear to be organized; they had the numbers to simply overrun everything. The Captain ordered a charge and they ploughed into the mass of attackers. Swords hacked away as the group cut through the surprised attacking force. It was more resistance than they had been dealing with so far. A cut here and a slash there and Milas' group soon found a patch of city defenders. They joined groups and the wounded and tired men seemed very happy for the support. Milas began to command them all. He drew his new miniature army up one of the streets and cleared it of enemies. The bodies of the fallen ones were on top of the villagers they had just slaughtered. It would all have to be sorted out later. They headed to cut off the invaders from the rest of the city. If the damage could be minimized, then many lives could be saved.

Iron and steel clashed as his men took up positions with their crossbows. He led the charge on the enemy line and he could hear the familiar sound of arrows whizzing by as he drew blood on his own. The front of the enemy line fell and the chaos of close combat continued. Milas was cut in a dozen places but his blade took down many of the attackers. He stepped forward against the pressure of the enemy drive and pushed his men farther and farther into the enemy lines. When they broke through, they started taking the group from the rear as well. More archers found the space to become effective and the tide of slaughter turned to the defenders. One of Milas' men was downed and one of the village militia stepped up to take the spot as if he had been trained as well. It was curious, but the situation did not afford them the time to ask questions. He commanded and the men followed him. They continued until there were no living enemy soldiers. The ones that were cut off were cut down. The hordes that had not been caught inside the village were fleeing. The attack had been successfully repelled. Milas watched as they ran and his sword felt suddenly heavy. He did not know if he was wounded, or just tired. He slumped to his knees in the dirt and two of the village militia picked him up and carried him away from the front lines. His men continued to fire arrows at the fleeing mass and a few more hits brought down some more of the enemy. He was deposited near the only physician in the village and the woman was definitely overworked. He would have offered to help, but he felt so heavy that death could take him and he would not resist. His sword fell to the ground beside him and the sound brought concern to the face of the older woman with all the herbs and salves.

"What have we here?" She asked and Milas tried to smile at her. He knew by her face that he had failed in his attempt. "You have been poisoned and cut so many times that I don't know if you'll make it." She told him as she leaned in close. "But if I fail to help you, then they'll kill me." She said. The look of shock did reach his face and she chuckled. "I saw how they brought you in. You are in the role of hero here. If I let you die, they'll hang me for my sins." She cackled and Milas couldn't tell if she were serious or not. He started to drift off and she shook him. "Don't you go dying on me now! I need at least a little time to make it all right with you." She admonished and he made eye contact with her. Her features were not clear to his fuzzy eyes but she did see into his soul through those eyes. "You are a bit of a mystery, you are." She said and she placed patches of cloth with leaves in them on many of his cuts. She tied them in place with twine to hold them in place. She whistled as she did this and her bony hands were somehow comforting. She had been a healer for a great many years and her technique was sterling. He felt the urge to talk and he opened his mouth to thank her, but no sound came out. She put her finger on his lips and told him to hush. "You haven't got the strength to waste on talking now. Just rest and let these patches draw out some of the poison. That'll keep you alive long enough to get some more fluids into you." She told him and then she went away to administer to someone else. With all that had gone on here, her methods and work ethics were firmly in place. She was not scared and she was not shaken by the blood and gore around her. She just patched or stitched things up and comforted where it was needed. The sounds of aftermath were still ringing off in the distance and Milas wished he knew more about what was going on. He trusted his men though. They would do whatever was necessary. He was as sure of that as he was of anything else in the whole world. They had worked together for so long that they were almost brothers.

He didn't recall it, but at some time Milas had fallen asleep. He looked around and it was mostly dark. There were some candles flickering over some of the bodies around him. The healer was probably still working on them, he thought to himself. He noticed that his sword was cleaned and wrapped in oilcloth and placed neatly by his side. He didn't know who had done that, but he was thankful for it. He looked around and his eyes caught a familiar face. One of his men, Jericho looked at him and the fact that he looked back brought a sigh of relief to the worried face.

"It is good to see you come back to us." He said in a joking manner. Both of them knew that there was no jest in the statement. It was his way of trying to lighten the mood of the fallen man.

"How goes the fight?" He asked; his voice was like a croaking sound. Since he couldn't talk before, it was an improvement. He looked at the man as Jericho's head dropped down in remembrance of the fallen.

"Sir, the enemy has been repelled from the village. There was help from the elves at the end. They came from the northern forest and caught the enemy as they fled. The enemy losses were total. The village is reporting that they lost a third of the population and most of the militia. There were about ten men left with us when the fighting stopped. Some of them fell like you did. According to the healer, the iron swords were dipped in poison and any cut would have accumulated the toxin in your system. You only survived because she was quick and knew what to do. Others weren't so lucky." The man said and then he started the grim news. We lost two of our own here today. We were all injured and needed medical attention, but the rest of us survived. I think you already know who they are. Boris fell while you were watching. Verlin fell later as they tried to counter attack our breakthrough. I think you were still around for that." He paused as he considered his next words. "Some of the militia here knew us. They fell into line and fought with the same precision. As it turns out there is a detachment here of former king's guards. I was unaware of any such but they say that they recognized you and were glad that you had gotten out of that horrible position that the king put you in." His tone said more than the words. He knew that the situation had been bad. He also knew that disobeying the orders had taken almost all of Milas' strength. He was a man of honor and dignity, his loyalty was important to him and to break it was a true sign of just how badly it had gone. Jericho was with him at the time. He knew how bad it had been. He was glad that others knew it too. They had reinforced that the decision that was made had been the right one.

Milas looked down at the sword. "Did you do this?" He asked, indicating the wrapped blade and Jericho shook his head.

"No, we have been taken care of by the elves. The administrations of the old woman were not enough and we were moved to the edge of the village just before nightfall. It appears that you were expected here and there is an audience scheduled for tomorrow morning if you are up to it." He said and Milas could not fathom why any of this was happening. Jericho signaled someone outside of Milas' view and a slender woman stepped around in front of him. Her long thin hands and her pointed ears basically told him that what Jericho said was true. The elf woman held a look of concern but she was already feeling better about the patient. The magic had brought him back from the brink and she was pleased whenever her arts could benefit others.

"You must rest if you are to see the witch tomorrow." She said in a lilting voice that sounded like sweet music. She waved her hand over Milas and he fell asleep instantly. Jericho sighed and then leaned back on the box he was sitting on. The elf woman looked at him. "Don't tell him too much. Something must be left for him to discover on his own. The prophecy is clear." She said and Jericho nodded to her. He knew more than he had told, but not nearly as much as this woman knew. He was about to ask her more when she waved her hand and he too fell asleep. She smiled and left the two soldiers to their dreams.

* * *

Milas awoke feeling more rested than he remembered ever being. His wounds had been healed and his outfit had been cleaned. It lay beside him and he dressed quickly. His friend and comrade Jericho was lying in a similar state and he nudged him to awaken him as well. He also dressed quickly and they started to look around. The sunlight was pouring in on them and they realized that they were no longer near the village they had been defending. An elf warrior stood not too far away and he was eyeing them carefully. The moment of tension passed when he laughed at them. It was obvious that he found their confusion humorous. He started walking over to them, and he held out his hand to shake Milas' hand. The Captain took the hand and shook it firmly. He was a little off balance here, but courtesy was still courtesy and he understood that.

"You are to see the witch now. Are you ready?" The warrior asked.

Milas nodded that he was and so did Jericho. The warrior held up his hand for the crossbowman. "This meeting is only for this man. You must wait here. Refreshments are being brought even as we speak and you will be reunited with your comrades in arms." He said gruffly. It sounded smoother than it should have because of the soft and silky elf voice. The emotions still came through though.

The warrior led the way. His white long straight hair fell halfway down his back and it fell over crossed short swords there. He had a longsword on his hip and the customary bow over a shoulder. He looked ready to pounce like a great cat and he walked with an effortless glide. Milas kept up well enough, though they went to an area in the trees that looked like a natural amphitheater. The vines and branches twisted together to make a protective netting over the main chamber and the tree roots made steps leading down into the vast bowl before the throne that was in the main viewing area. The woman in white robes sat atop the throne as if it were a part of her. She looked regal. Her long thin hands were stroking a squirrel that was seated in her lap. As the two men approached, she shooed it away and it left her begrudgingly.

"Ah, so this is the Captain of the Black Guard who has lost his rank and privileges in the service to the king for using his own mind and taking a stand for good and righteousness." She said and the words were not scathing. They were more of a list of accomplishments. Her voice held such melody that it could distract even the most stalwart man. Milas looked on, wondering where this was all going.

He stepped forward and bowed before the throne. "I must thank milady for the efforts on our behalf. The scourge had to be driven from the village and I am to understand that you and your people were instrumental in this task." He said formally and the witch smiled at him.

"Yes, we had a little something to do with that, but it was not our primary goal in this expedition. We came to find you." She said and the words brought a look of surprise to Milas' face. "We know of you and that you are important to a plan that is forming even now. There are things happening in different times and places and you are a piece of the overall picture of it." She said. "I can see that you are unaware of this. My people have authorized me to do whatever I see fit to ensure that my visions come true. It is in this light that I beseech you to come with us to the place of learning of a young acolyte. He is an important piece of this plan and he will need your protection." She said and Milas scratched his head.

"Am I to understand that I am somehow important?" He asked and the woman nodded. "I don't even know who you are." He responded and she stood up from the throne. Her guards tensed at the movement but she waved them down.

"You are right, that was rude of me. I am Solana, and I am a seer of legendary status. My people know me by reputation even before they meet me. My visions have seen many wonderful and terrible things. I need to make sure that this most important vision comes true for it concerns the entire world's survival." She said and Milas felt a wave of concern.

"I need to save the world?" He asked. "How can any one man do that?" He asked seriously.

Solana looked at him and her eyes looked sad. "No, you are not the one who saves the world, but the young acolyte is. You must protect him for I fear for his safety all the time now. Forces are working on more levels than I can control to bring about the world's destruction. In fact, in one of my visions, the world is already destroyed. So it is that we must prevent it from happening, not save it in the first place. I can tell you only two things about this mission. First is that you will be in danger almost constantly. I am sorry for this, but you are the only one that I have seen that can handle the mission. The second thing that I can tell you is that you will see things you will not understand. Do not be alarmed, I will tell you what I know when the time comes, but for now, that is all that I have for you. It is now time for you to decide if you can do this thing or not." She said and her tone meant 'right now'.

Milas thought about it for a long moment. The constant danger thing was not all that appealing, but he was used to that sort of thing as a king's guard. Saving the world was more than he thought he could handle, but to protect someone, that he understood. If the acolyte was that important to the survival of the world, how could he refuse? He looked around at the guards; they were all awaiting his response. He knelt down before the woman again. "Then I am the man you want. I will protect this acolyte with my life." He said and she nodded to him in acceptance.

"There is much we must discuss before we head out to this school. You will need new armor as well." She clapped her hands quickly twice and some of the guards disappeared. "Now come and walk with me while I tell you my visions." She said and the room around them reverted back to its natural form. The trees looked absolutely normal in a matter of minutes. He let it all slip by him as he listened only to her voice. "There is so much to tell…" She began.

*   *   *

The *Lost Cavalier* sped through space and time. This trip was longer than anyone had originally anticipated and there was nothing to do but wait as they raced along at unimaginable speed. The earliest calculations put the trip at a month. Now it was looking more like six weeks at warp before they would be close. The crew busied themselves with preparations for the first couple of weeks and then there was nothing to do but maintenance. The ship was humming along like a champion thoroughbred and there was little busy work to do. More than one crewmember realized that there was too much time to just think. In the idle time everyone's mind brought the memory of the fallen to the forefront of their mind and the reality of the situation set in. The Captain had become a hermit in his cabin. The crew could not lean on the man for the unity they needed now. Casey had trimmed down a few parts and was busily putting them together with meticulous detail. His ship would be in perfect order when they needed it to be. He found the work stimulating instead of just time-consuming. It was one of the reasons that he was so good at his job. He loved the work.

Below decks in the library, Frank and Chris, the monk, were trying to find out all they could to help the mission succeed. They had already gone over Frank's dream sequence and they both felt that the particular resource had been fully utilized and exhausted. It was helpful that Christopher was used to reading scripture. It had all the answers, but the effort to understand them was often beyond the reader. The dream sequences were similar in nature to that. They had also noted many of Chris' dreams as well. They had both seen the White Witch. Neither of them really knew who she was, but their shared experiences felt like a real connection.

Frank looked at the bottle again. It had held the vapors that caused the monks to have a 'spiritual journey'. They had tried to do this twice before with no success. It was like placing a phone call and the receiving end had been away from home. The link started to form but never completed. The lack of success made them worry that they may already be too late. They sat across from each other on straw mats on the floor. The mats were pieces of Chris' life and he had brought them rolled up on his back when he came on board. Frank hoped the link would help them establish contact. The bottle sent wisps of smoke up into the air and caused a fog around the two men as they concentrated on the vision of the beautiful woman. They chewed on the root as well to help stimulate the sensation. The grogginess of the drug began to overtake them and alter their perceptions as it had done each time. This time felt different. The air cleaner in the room had been disabled so that the fumes could hang around longer and perhaps prolong the event if it came to pass. There was a wash of sound and a flash of light and Frank found himself standing in a glade. The sun was shining and Chris was there too. They looked at each other in surprise and then they both turned as one to see the two individuals walking towards them. One of them was the White Witch. She looked as radiant as ever and the man with her was a human in fancy shining armor. His ears were normal and he did not move with her grace and style. He looked sturdy and strong though. The two men waited for the newcomers to reach them before speaking.

The White Witch smiled at them. "Ah, so you have arrived." She said to them. Frank smiled back to her like a schoolboy being noticed by his first crush. Chris managed to nod and reply "Yes Maam".

The woman laughed and her lilting laughter could have made the strongest man buckle his legs. The musical bliss of her happiness was like a solid living thing and when it died out, both men were sad that it was gone. "You are still coming right?" She asked them and they both nodded vigorously this time. "This is the protector that I have found to keep your wizard alive until you can arrive." She said indicating the strong man next to her.

The man beside her bowed to them both. "I am Milas, former Captain of the Guard to the king. I will defend the acolyte with my life." He pledged and Frank looked him squarely in the eye. This Captain's mannerisms were definitely professional. This was a seasoned warrior and slayer of men. He had scars over most of his visible body and Frank knew that he was being sized up as a warrior. He felt suddenly ashamed of himself.

"I am no warrior, as you can plainly see." He said and Milas gave a "humph" sound. "I am a keeper of knowledge and this man here, does the same." He said and Solana looked at Christopher.

"You are with them now?" She asked and Christopher nodded enthusiastically. "Good, that will make things better for the mission." She said and Frank felt a pang of jealousy. He shoved it down, not wanting it to color the event they were experiencing. The woman in white turned back to him as if that thought had been read. Perhaps it had been. "You are a warrior as well, a warrior for truth. You knew how difficult the mission would be and you charged into it anyway. It is the way of the hero. Forget this not, you are a champion. Truly you do not use a sword to achieve your goals, but you have fought and will do so again. The enemy follows you, although not as closely as before. The danger approaches and soon both of our times will be in peril. You must hurry so that we can work together to amend this atrocity." She reached up and touched Frank's cheek. "You are so close now I can almost feel your mind. It is closer than you have ever been. I'm glad." She said and she pulled back her hand slowly. She was so graceful that everything she did was like water flowing. "We shall prepare for your arrival. Good luck fine warriors and may the spirits guide your destinies and speed you along." She said and spread her arms wide. The flash and blast of sound shattered the dream and both awoke looking at each other in shock. They *HAD* established contact. The moment passed and they both felt tired all of a sudden. But the excitement carried through and made them jump up quickly.

Frank's face practically glowed. She had touched him and told him that she was happy that he was coming to meet her. It was more than he would have dreamed of. Chris had a similar feeling running through his mind. She was happy that he had tagged along on the mission. He was somehow important. At least he was important to her. That was all that mattered to him. Both men were hopelessly enamored with the woman and neither of them would admit it. Frank stopped short and his happiness flew away like a wisp of smoke from the bottle. "We did not ask her any questions. We are no closer to understanding when and where we need to be." He said heavily. Chris's elation died just as quickly as the realization hit him. It was true, they knew no more than when they started. It made him laugh that they had introduced themselves as keepers of knowledge and yet had failed to gain any new information at all. He vowed not to let the woman distract him so again. Frank took a similar vow and they started to reset the room to try again. They had succeeded after all; they could definitely do it again.

* * *

The king had recovered from his ordeal with that uppity Captain. The man had beaten him badly. His top advisor and his personal guard had been slain and the scar on his arm reminded him of the arrow that had taken away the dagger he would have plunged in retaliation for the man's sins against him. His new guard Captain stood there in all his glory. He had been a good fighter before, but now that he had status, his true mean streak began to surface. He was like the king and his ambition was only beginning to blossom. This was the kind of man the king needed. He would help to hold the power. He would serve him loyally as long as he felt the special protection of the king. The twins were still a threat. His rule would end by them he was sure of it. The advisor was gone, but the prediction was still there. It was a legacy that he meant to extinguish.

"You must go out among the people and seek out any twins born within my kingdom." He said directly and the Captain smiled an evil smile.

"Yes sire. I shall assemble a squad to enforce your decree." He replied and the metal of his armor made scraping sounds as he turned and marched out of the audience chamber. The king breathed a sigh of relief. He had brought this man up in status and he had worried about it at first. Now he looked to be the perfect man for the job. He would take credit for this work later. His public relations man would pay for his rejection of this candidate for the job. He waved for more wine and a small boy brought it quickly. Yes, he would remain king. His sorcerers were still working on his longevity spell and when they got it completed, he would have them all slain so that the secret would die with them. He would live forever and his reign would never die. He had the fear of the people on his side now. Soon, he would have his army rebuilt and the new troops would be blindly obedient and have the same longevity as he would. They would hold all of mankind in their hands and squeeze it until he was satisfied. The future would be glorious. There was only a pair of twins somewhere that could thwart his plans. His new Captain had better find them and eliminate them or he would have his head on a pike.

*　*　*

I dodged the massive beast and swung out my arms in a freezing spell that should have toppled it over. It roared in pain, but whirled around on me and I had to dive free to escape serious injury. The thing towered above me but I was armed with magic of five elements with more to follow. I sent a bolt of the new lightning into its chest and the charred flesh brought a nasty smell to my nostrils. The beast wailed in pain and stumbled back. I brought the wind up to force it still further back. Then it swirled around the monster and lifted it from the ground. With a large gesture on my part, the beast was hurtled through the air to strike the stone wall and I could clearly hear the cracking of bones in that impact. Blood spurted from its mouth as I readied my finishing move. The beast slumped forward, it's own life was ebbing away and I brought the fire down to finish it. A flaming ball danced above it and it knew that it was finished. The blast singed the fur and quieted the beast forever. I stood there, panting and the master reset the room again. He giggled a bit and looked me over.

"It is nice to see that you can still move and concentrate at the same time. That is the reason for this test. You have done well. Go and rest a bit and we shall try again." He instructed and I drug my weary self out of the room. There were several observers this time. It seems that more and more of the instructors were interested in the advancements of the 'special student' and I was paying the price in exhaustion. I had mentioned it once before only to be laughed at. It was a new concept to me that the magic took power from my very soul to enable the links to the elements. It was true that I was tired after a bunch of castings, but the power was so great and so addicting that I didn't mind. The gallery filed out by me as I waited for them to exit ahead of me. They each glanced at me with something of either respect or possibly jealousy as I stood there catching my breath. When the last one left, I was alone in the side room. I had to rest; I could feel the fatigue creeping into my marrow. The power demanded so much. The master had told me that this was normal. I would have been doing more exercises if I had not been in the accelerated class. Now I was ready to sleep. I didn't even feel up to a quick jaunt through the library. I had so far been unable to find any reference to the other three elements. I had suspicions of my own, but nothing documented anywhere as yet. It had been a most frustrating search so far.

I found the steps harder and harder as I progressed through the hallways to the room I was assigned to. The guards were there again. They were acolytes that were older than me and I could tell that they took this assignment as a punishment. They despised me for my new status. It looked like I was cheating to them. Perhaps it was true. The current exhaustion was a direct example of the difference in the training received. They allowed me in with a 'humph' sound and an evil stare and I paid them no attention at all. I was just too tired to care at this point. I should not have been so incautious. The room looked the same to me, but there was a shimmer that brought a flash of warning to me as the being teleported into the space with me. Reality took on a strange twist as the air around the being warped him into the place and threw off my equilibrium. He was on me in an instant and his blade was out. The man was dressed in all black. His dark brown eyes were determined and he moved like a cat. I felt a strike to the ribs as I tried to twist free. I had just fought a larger beast than this, but his reactions were much faster than mine. He adjusted and struck me again. I cried out and my door opened. The assassin looked at the newcomers and threw metal weapons at both of them. They clutched at the new wounds and fell to the floor. Whatever poison was on those blades worked too fast for them to raise any further alarm. It was distraction enough for me to get my bearings though. I brought forth a wave of fire to sweep the man back to the far wall. At least that was what I thought. But the fire did not answer my call. The man laughed at me and held up a vial.

"Your tricks will not work on me. Your silly elements have been neutralized around me." He almost spat at me. His short sword was out and the thin blade looked lethal. It was definitely an assassin's dagger. I pulled on the power of the lightning and felt the answer back. Then I knew that I could use it against this assailant. I just needed more time to accumulate it for the strike. I tried to talk with him to draw his attention away from the power I was amassing.

"My tricks are harmless to you? You must be a sorcerer of renowned ability to accomplish that." I said, daring him to explain his superiority to me. He stopped for an instant. Then he laughed again.

"Since you are about to die, I might as well tell you that I am no caster at all. I used a potion of elemental steal to stop your powers from building up. Therefore you are helpless before me now." He said as the energy began to crackle. I looked appropriately frightened.

"Please don't kill me. I will give you anything." I said playing the part I was expected to play. I cowered before the might of the would-be killer. The energy continued to draw and I would have to release it soon or burn with him upon the release.

"You little man, you are no great wizard. My employer has overestimated you badly. It is almost a mercy I give you now." He said and he stopped short when he saw my posture change to aggressive.

"Perhaps you could tell him that if you survive." I said and threw forth my hand, pointing at him as the lightning danced from the pointing finger to the man's chest. The blade glowed with the strike and then arced through the arm to his chest for a double strike. He dropped the weapon as soon as the bolt dissipated and his eyes grayed over. The heat of the power had fried them. His hair had stood on end as well. It did not look all that pretty. Then he fell backwards into the fireplace. If the fire had been lit, I could have finished him off then, but as it was I was able to call for help in the open hallway outside my room.

Moments later there were several men there. Teachers and students alike looked in on everyone in the room. The two acolytes were dead. They were cold already when I checked them. It was as if the life force had drained from them even before they fell. The assassin was not dead, but he was blind and his sword arm would never work again. The physician mentioned something about fried nerves. All I know is that after that, they moved my room periodically. Training did not even give me a break. In fact they increased it even more. There were no more guards on my door now. The acolytes refused to die for the upstart wizard. The schoolmasters did not force the issue. It was obvious that they were uncomfortable with my presence here as well. The danger seemed to follow me and I could not explain to them why. So, miserably, I continued the training in earnest.

* * *

A Reunion and New Friends

I received a summons after a considerably taxing round of training and I dragged myself up to respond to it. The acolyte that was leading me looked excited. It was the first time in a while that anyone looked anything other than scared or angry around me. I felt that this was a good sign. We reached one of the studies and the master was there. I had just left him so he had made good time to arrive ahead of me. There were visitors here and I saw the woman in white. The witch had returned. I stopped short and my mouth fell open. The acolyte slapped me on the back and pushed me forward. I clamped my mouth back shut again and stepped forward under the prompting.

"I see that you have grown a lot since last we met." She said in that melodic voice of tranquility and pleasure. She stood up and glided gracefully over to stand before me. She reached out and touched my arm. I had tensed for the contact and she felt the ripped muscles underneath the concealing wizard robes. She nodded to the master. "I see the training has been properly accelerated and that he is close to ready now." She said and I wondered how she knew whether or not I was ready. The master looked at me and smiled.

"We have been pushing him hard. Hard enough to break almost anyone, but he has held firm." He said and the pride in the statement was evident. I had no idea that the master was so supportive. He had told me that he was, but to hear him tell someone else meant that he truly meant what he said. I suddenly felt better and saw the truth of his words. I had been challenged every day. I had been exhausted beyond my own ability to remember it. I had survived an assassination attempt – twice. I had been given access to the library and exposure to a fifth element and all without the support of the rest of the students. I had to do all of this alone. It all became clear to me and the spark of life returned to my eyes. The witch noticed it. Of course she did. She noticed everything. Her seeking eyes never missed anything.

"He has come around nicely from that frightened boy that I can remember so well." She said to the master never taking her eyes off of me. Then she addressed me directly. "You were a dedicated young man, but you were not ready for the tasks ahead of you. Now you are at least closer to it. I am pleased with the results. I had considered taking you away to train you myself, but the decision to leave you here was the correct one. I can see that now." She admitted and the master practically beamed with pride. "The trouble is that the dark ones know of you and somehow they know that you are important. This latest attack proves this. I have brought you some help with your security." She said and she turned to indicate the other people that were with her. I had not even focused on them until now or I would have noticed that they were human and not elf like her. They were clad in ceremonial elfen armor though that had been tailored to their human frames. It looked grand. The men stood as well. They stood up as a unit. There were five men and they looked like each one knew what the other man was thinking at all times. They were definitely a team. The leader of them stepped forward. The feather in his helmet meant that he was not only the leader, but that he had the support of the government of the elves. He stepped up and the White Witch stepped aside easily. He held out his gauntleted hand and I shook it.

"I am Milas, former guard to the king and currently assigned to your personal survival as a personal favor to Solana and I pledge my sword to you." He said in formal tones. I did not know how to respond. This was happening so fast, as my whole career to this point had done.

"What does that mean?" I asked him, trying not to be rude.

He smirked at me. "Need it spelled out eh?" He asked and when he saw my confusion, he lowered his head. "My apologies sire, I thought everyone knew the code. I am personally pledging my life to you. I will defend you until I can no longer breathe. My men will also protect you unto their deaths. No harm shall befall you if there is strength left to us. It is imperative that you live and our oaths can only be released by you denouncing our service." He said and I felt a wave of shock. Of course I had no idea how to respond to that.

"Sir, your gallantry takes me by surprise. I do not know why this has come to pass, but the problems we have had here suggest that your services are indeed needed. I will try not to endanger you or myself unnecessarily and if you have instructions for me and my safety, I would be glad to hear them." I said trying to come up with the best thing I could to say. Apparently it was good enough.

"Sire, your speech suggests that you are wiser than your age might dictate. I am honored by your acceptance and my duties require me to inform you of potential threats as they arise. Your willingness to hear them will make my job considerably easier. For that I am somewhat relieved."

The White Witch, Solana he had called her, looked pleased as well. She had done this. She had brought these men here to protect me. She knew much more of what was going on than I did. She knew more than anyone I had ever seen. Yet there was no time to talk to her about it. Now that I had personal guards, she flittered away with the proper good-byes and thank you's. I was powerless to retain her for even the briefest of moments. The rest of the staff had precious little time as well. She had deposited her men and then she was off. I was left to wonder why I was so important. It still made no sense to me. Oh well, at least I would not have disgruntled acolytes at my door anymore. These people took their jobs seriously and no corridor was walked down without someone 'clearing it' first.

I found out that they had traveled with a sorcerer at one time so they understood that there were times that I needed to be alone. They took up their positions as close as possible without violating the meditation space. We had gone through the ritual of eating and studying and it was not long before Milas was impressed with my work ethic. I was so rushed and so busy that there was no time for mischievousness. He knew where I was supposed to be and when. The schedule was rigid and inflexible. That sort of predictability was perhaps a bad thing. It was pointed out to me that the enemy could easily read the patterns and know where I would be next. It also made the guards aware of where I should be and thus they would be alerted if I was not there. So I continued on unabated by the new security detachment. The school housed them in the adjacent room and they fed them regularly. They seemed to be relieved with these soldiers there. I must admit that the earlier attack had made me jumpy and I soon developed a healthy respect for the vigilance these men displayed. They took this job seriously all the time. So I made good time on my studies with the support of these men at arms.

* * *

The dark one looked at his shaman. The lizard man shaman was one of the most dangerous denizens of the world. His powers stretched beyond the living to the dead. They could reach beyond time and ask things of beings that were lost or ones that existed only in the future. Their bodies were smelly and half-rotten due to their life-force well that allowed them to amass their power. They were half-dead. In truth, the leader feared them at least partially. His command of them allowed him to use their advanced powers without being dead himself. That was the limit of their value to him. If they lost that ability, he would have them all slain. For now, though, they were a valuable asset and he needed to know what they knew. He leaned forward as the shaman rasped out his greeting. The typical slurred speech of the lizard man was accentuated by the half dead being before him.

"Sssir, we have found our brothersss from the future and they are coming to the now. They ssseek to eliminate the humansss and we need to be ready when they come ssso that we may follow them to the future. The world will be oursss." The shaman said. He bowed low when he finished and the leader held his hand aloft to allow him to rise again.

"What mussst we do to make ready?" He asked and the shaman smiled a nasty grin that showed decayed teeth in a decayed mouth.

"Sssire, we mussst kill the human wizard. He has survived the assassin you sssent and his sssurvival marksss the end of our people. We mussst take action directly against thisss man and bring him down." The shaman hissed and the leader looked at him knowingly. The shaman had great power, but he was also a slave to the powers from the other side. His current words were that of the demon that possessed him. Still, if the assassin had failed, it was possible that the human was actually as dangerous as the shaman had predicted. It was too big of a chance to take. He needed to have everything ready when his brethren arrived from the future. He did not understand how they could be coming to the past like this, but he did not make the mistake of rejecting the prophecy simply because he did not understand it. He wanted to be a hero to his people and help to destroy the human infestation that was overwhelming the world.

"We shall sssend a detachment to the magic place and burn it down. The human will die inside as the fire consssumesss him. Then we shall be victorious when our brothers from another time arrive. The coming is at hand and we, the vigilant mussst be ready for it."

The shaman bowed and left. The guards around the chamber did not flinch or move. The leader looked out at them. They were like furniture, they were always there. He did not like them; in fact he hated everything and everyone. His ascension to the throne had been violent and demanding.

He was in charge because he had killed everyone who could stop him. This new mission was very similar to that. There was one block to his plans and he would pluck it out of the picture and grind it to dust. He grabbed his spear and stood up. The wicked-looking bladed weapon was long and black. The barbed blade was twenty inches long and when used made the victim bleed even while it stayed in the wound. It was also enchanted and it stole life from whoever it touched. He wore a special glove in order to wield the thing in the first place. His smile was a row of uneven sharp teeth and it made him look even more evil than he was. "We need to kill thisss human now and then witnesss our victory!" He shouted in the chamber and his own voice echoed back to him. His orderlies left to gather a hunting party and he felt the fire in his blood build. The rage would take him and he would cleanse himself in the blood of his enemies. The thought gave him a moment of rapture and he knew that he would fulfill it. He bowed to the idol carved above his own throne and then he stomped purposefully out of the chamber to make ready for travel. It was time for evil to take a direct action in this twisted struggle with good. He would end this wizard and the hope that rides with him. Then the humans would fall. His moment of glory was coming and he held the spear aggressively as he prepared to leave. "Thisss will be a great day." He said to himself as he strapped on his gear. "The enemy doesn't even know that I am coming." He said and then let out a belly laugh that would have frightened the townsfolk of neighboring areas. The fire was with him fully when he left his fortress and headed out with a team of warriors. This one puny human had little or no chance against them.

*   *   *

Commander Zurg tossed and turned on his mat. The night was filled with visions and he was troubled by it every night now. They were dark things. The images made him shake and quiver like a youngling and he hated them. Upon waking, he remembered none of it. His temperature was elevated and his fists were clenched as he tried to calm down. He got up and stepped into the shower. The water usually brought him back up to temperature and now it did the reverse. It cooled him back down to normal. In the past he had always directed this aggressive energy at his enemies. It was a tact that had served him well and now he was even more frustrated at this elusive enemy. The chase he was on was now of legendary status. They followed the human metal box through time to the beginnings of their race. It seemed somehow fitting that he was going back to a time where his people co-existed with the humans. There was a spark of anger over their extinction on this planet. The history of the lizardmen was violent and tumultuous. In fact, they had been a war-like people for as long as anyone remembered.

He cooled down substantially and the water ran dry. He blotted his green scaly skin and stepped out to dress. The room was utilitarian and lacked any softness. He despised softness and comfort. It was not the way of a true commander. His brother had held these quarters before he had transferred command and he had been impressed with the sparseness of the quarters. It meant that his brother felt the same way about it. He would make a good commander in his own right when they returned to their people in the future. The glory was going to be big enough to share. The whole crew would benefit as the story circulated throughout the Fleet. His name would be synonymous with the story characters he had heard as a youngling. He looked forward to that recognition. It was the reason that he was where he was today. It was the dream of every warrior to be revered by the people he protected.

He finished donning his uniform and grabbed all of his personal weapons to head out to his duty station. He tried to hide the fact that his exhaustion was getting critical. He needed to be strong in order to keep the crew in line. He would not fail them and he would not relinquish this command. It was a heavy bill for his body to pay, but he was willing and able to do so.

"Ssstatusss report." He bellowed at the officer on duty when he entered the bridge. His harsh attitude had taken more than one such officer by surprise. This time, though, it did not.

"SSSir, we have relocated the humansss trail. They are ssstill heading back in time and we are following at a dissscrete dissstance to avoid detection. We should appear just after them at whatever time they ssstop on. The data sssuggestsss that they will be ssstopping sssoon. We will be ready to pounce when they do." He completed smugly and the commander wanted very much to strike this insubordinate man down. But the truth is, he had followed his orders as well as could have been expected. He knew what was going on and had reported the status just as he had been ordered. So, he bit back on his anger and dismissed the man to take his rightful spot in the big chair.

He pressed a button on the chair and a connection to the engineering section of his stone ship responded respectfully. "I want our weaponsss ready when we enter normal ssspace." He ordered and the affirmative reply he received was good enough for him. He closed the connection and then went over the tracking data of the enemy. They had not even altered their course for weeks now. It had been a boring chase and he longed so desperately for it to be over. He wanted badly to sink his claws and teeth into the human's soft flesh. He would bathe in their blood and shout at the gods themselves to announce his victory. The images in his mind overran the dull screens and panels around him. He was the star of his own personal movie in his head. His ego would keep feeding him endless footage of his victory and using that, the time would pass. He shook himself and looked at his crew. "Keep sharp, I want that enemy ship as soon as it slows down." He demanded. There were no negative responses.

* * *

The commander's counterpart in the ancient world was rapidly gaining ground. The small attachment of lizardmen was heading to the school and the small villages along the way were only the warm-up for his men. They killed and slaughtered as they crossed the countryside. He had wet his claws more than once and it drove him ever farther into the frenzy of bloodlust. He could feel the time closing in. He could sense the fear of the people he killed and he let it roll over him like a waterfall of emotions cascading onto him and bringing him closer to rapture. His eyes were blood red from the lust and he reveled in the shivering and quaking of his victims. He had met with some resistance and he had treated those defenders harshly when he towered over them in victory. He had dismembered two of them while the survivors watched. Then he had killed the survivors and moved on. Nothing would remain alive while he was on the warpath. Even the buildings were razed before his team headed out of a fight zone. Since they left no one alive, there were no warnings for the next town. The warriors would simply rush in and kill indiscriminately. Spears and bows were broken in the fight and were replaced from the bodies of the fallen. The team could just continue on this way until they reached the ultimate goal. The school was not far away now and they would build up a decent frenzy by the time they reached it. It would not be long now.

* * *

The academy was heavily fortified and the guards were relatively sharp. There had been no deliveries from the local townsfolk and that meant that something was wrong. They did not have the means to become self-sufficient in this old keep. They needed supplies from the outside regularly in order to maintain themselves and continue the training of the recruits and acolytes alike. The distant fires on the horizon were the first warning that something was seriously wrong. The master was brought to witness the view and he had done a small spell to allow him to see farther than normally permitted by his aged eyes. He clearly saw the lizardmen killing and torturing the citizens of the outlying village and he ordered the doors barred and the school sealed.

"We have to mount our defenses as the enemy is coming here. I know this to be true. I have foreseen this and we need to do as I say in order to hold the school against this destructive force. The lizardmen are approaching and razing the towns as they go. Our supplies and support are already gone and soon they will be at the gates. We will need for the acolytes to take their places on the wall and if the gods are with us, we may yet prevail here." He told the assemblage before him. He had the instructors usher the acolytes out and they were all assigned to their posts.

I was assigned to a tower. I guess he knew that they were after me. I would work on my spells and if they somehow got through to me, I would give them a taste of nothing they had ever seen before. I wish that I had figured out what the other three elements were, but as yet, I had not. I had the five at my disposal and they would have to serve. My guards were with me and two of them were in the stairwell to this tower. They would hold off whatever came that far and give warning to the rest above. Milas had a different idea. He had two crossbowmen pointing out the windows and he hoped that if the enemy got close enough, they would reduce the numbers from the safety of this dizzying height. His eyes were grim as he made contact with me. We were both as ready as we could be and the rest of it was just waiting. If only the witch had been here, then she could defeat these creatures without us. But we were the defenses and we would do our duty as best as we could.

The lizardmen started across the fields that surrounded the school. The ancient building was actually well protected against this kind of assault, but these creatures did not seem to be worried about it. I could not see them clearly but the word was passed that some of them were part dead. That was not a good sign. It meant that they had some form of magical support. Disease and death usually followed fights with the dead. The acolytes and instructors held their spells until the enemy was almost close enough for the archers to hit. Then they released as one. The four elements and their associated elementals were busy this day. The ground heaved and the air whipped and fire erupted from the sky. Waterspouts formed from out of nowhere and the enemy suddenly stopped. They had somehow known just how far they could go. The spells did some fringe damage, but were otherwise deflected by some form of shield the lizardmen had before them. In fact, it absorbed some of the expended energy and became stronger. One of the crossbowmen loosed his shaft and it sailed down that long distance to strike one of the lizardmen in the leg. The warrior continued to march forward as if he had not been hit. Milas cursed and then both of the crossbows were firing and reloading at an impressive rate.

Milas looked at me with a serious tone. "They are already in the blood frenzy. There will be no reasoning with them and all we can do is kill all of them before they get here." He said and the sigh hidden behind his statement told me volumes about his capacity for good. He was actually upset at the prospect of wiping them all out.

The enemy charged forward. The losses they took so far made them look patchy. They made up for their small numbers with pure ferocity. The acolytes sent another wave of power at them and the shaman behind the group captured the elemental force and redirected it back at the defenders. The walls shook with the applied forces and many of the acolytes were knocked off of the wall. Without the protection they knew they had, they fell quickly to the advancing lizardmen. The scene was terrible and I had trouble watching it. The crossbows were firing at an impressive rate for only two firers. The enemy continued to the gates unabated. They looked somewhat like pin cushions with all the bolts sticking out of them. The last stand was going to be inside the keep. The massive doors were flung out and splintered as the shaman made the wood age a millennia before the warriors struck it. It gave easily and they were inside hacking down students and faculty alike. The spells seemed useless now and it came down to anyone who could hold a weapon lived for a little longer. Milas watched in professional detachment as I gawked in horror. He pulled his crossbowmen back and they drew swords and picked up their shields. They were readying for the final assault. I knew that there was something I could do. I just didn't know what it was. I had already thought of the lightning and I could see no way for it to help the defense. If I struck out in the courtyard, I might hit friend as well as foe. Maybe when they were in the corridors, I could use it to hold them back. By the time they cleared the courtyard, six of the warriors and the shaman came up to the entrance to the tower. They knew where I was. Maybe they could sense my power. I don't really know. I do know that I was scared; more scared than I had ever been. These monsters wanted me dead.

The enemy had lit the buildings and support structures. Most of the building was ablaze. Milas cursed at the logic of it. "They are going to burn us out." He almost spat it out. "We will have to advance to them and not hold a last stand in the stairwell." He announced and his men shook their heads. They were ready though. There was no doubting their dedication. These men would follow Milas anywhere, and into any situation seemingly without question. They started down the stairs in columns of two and I was in the middle of it all, being pulled along. I kept the words of the spells in my head and I was ready to point at anything that presented a threat. Milas was ready to kill anything that blocked our path as well. When the moment came, we were ready.

The six came around the corner as one and they were already charging towards us. Milas leaped forward and started running to meet their charge with half of his men right there with him. The shaman and I made eye contact and he smiled. It was a frightening sight and I threw my first spell in haste because of it. The lightning bolt arced over the human warriors to the lizardmen and struck the wall next to the shaman. Fragments of stone showered the old one and he was cut in a few places but otherwise he ignored the attack. He started chanting and I could feel my life slipping away. He was trying to steal my life force from a distance. I hurried through the next set of arcane words and the stone sphere sheltered me and the remaining warriors with a barrier of stone. I could still feel the drain. It was not a sufficient barrier and I would die soon if nothing changed. The warriors looked at me in shock. I dropped the shield and took off running at the shaman. They followed with their lethal steel waving in the air. A war cry came forth from my very soul and it held power that I was unaware of. The wave of sound crashed forth and swept all of the combatants down including the shaman who was properly as startled as I was. I had discovered another element. I wish I could say how I did it, but at this point, survival was more important than study so I began to cast again as I ran forth. The men with me saw the opportunity and began attacking the fallen lizardmen. The warrior lizardmen died quickly under the ruthless assault. Milas regained his footing and charged the shaman. The wily old half-dead shaman spun around and brought up a staff to bear and Milas flew backwards from a blast of cold. I originally thought that it was a blast of water, but there was no water in it. It was just a wave of cold. Milas shook on the floor and the frost on his armor was evidence of the discomfort he was experiencing. He was out of the fight. I had no sword of my own, but there were a couple of weapons on the floor near the fallen warriors. I swept one up on my way in and I began another bellow of a battle cry. With the heavy axe in hand, I carried the strength of five men as I struck the shaman with the axe. It dug in deeper than I would have imagined and the right shoulder and arm separated from the creature as I fell to the side from the impact. The shaman dropped in place and just twitched as I threw up from the gore. The warriors finished off the rest of the fallen lizardmen.

It was time to put out the fires. The fight was over. Many had died this day and somehow I had survived. Milas needed warming up fast and I brought fire delicately to him to bring his temperature up. When he started sweating again, I backed it off and his men took him back to be checked out. We retreated back to the tower as others administered to the fallen in the courtyard. I will never forget the actions of this day and I will never be the same again. My view of the world had changed forever. I had also seen two new elements. There was sound, and cold. Now that I knew what I was looking for, I was in a hurry to get back to the library. I would learn all that I could in order to survive the next attack. I was not delusional enough to believe that it was all over. I was now more dedicated to surviving than any other man I had ever known. I began to believe that I was meant for something more. I did not know what, but I knew there was some higher calling. Milas said it was to save the world. I know that sounds too much for one man, but I began to believe the story and I wanted to be ready. I did not want to disappoint and I owed it to so many good people that had died around me. For them I would do everything I could to make it all work out. There was nothing else that I could do. So it was with this new dedication that I dove into the archives and studied for all I was worth.

* * *

The failure of the lizardmen to kill the wizard child was not taken well among the leaders of their kind. The buildings were razed, but the people had survived. The shaman had been lost and some good warriors had given their lives for failure. This was unacceptable. They were supposed to be elite. They were supposed to be unstoppable. The council met to discuss the next move. The situation had changed. There was no point in remaining in hiding any longer. The humans knew that the lizardmen wanted this boy dead and now that they had tried twice, the task seemed to be out of reach. They gathered and talked and postured about their own strengths and the weakness of the fallen. By the end of the heated discussion, they were ready for all out war. The prophecy was still the prophecy and this human had to die in order for their future brethren to be successful. The outcome would be glorious and they would earn the respect of their future brothers. This was a common goal among them and the options were thinning out on what they could do about it. Between them, they represented four nations of lizardmen. They could sack and take the school easily enough, but would the wizard be there anymore? They needed more information to be sure. The planets were aligning quickly and the prophecy was almost upon them. The time to move was now. If a clear leader had been defined, the whole plan could have moved forward and this discussion would be moot. Unfortunately, the high seat had been vacant since the death of the previous leader. Now they were disorganized and the bickering and squabbling stagnated the council and kept the people immobilized. It was a situation that had no answer for the lost folk. Frustration mounted and if nothing was done, the council members themselves would begin fighting. They each had the bloodlust potential in them. One could not achieve elevated status without at least some of the berserker rage. It was a sign of greatness among them. A few of the bolder ones had tried and been brought down by the others in a fit of jealousy. The basic problem was a lack of direction. They had no focus and no plan. This was the worst condition they had ever seen. The current speaker tried to tell them what was needed. His ceremonial garb held the bones of his slain enemies in it like buttons on a shirt. He stomped his feet and slapped his tail on the ground.

"Delegatesss pleasssse, a moment of your time." He said raising his voice to be heard over the clamber. "We mussst not fight amongsssst ourssselvesss. We have an enemy to fight. It isss an enemy that has already defeated sssome of usss before. Thisss makes it a matter of honor to avenge our dead. No matter what we may think of them persssonally. We have an obligation to find thossse ressssponsssible and desssstroy them. There isss much to be done and little time to do it. Can we not make a plan to rid oursssselvesss of this human child and be done with it all?" He asked the assembly and the general feeling was consent, but the idea of a plan was so far removed that none of them would agree to anything that had been presented. The thoughts of how to proceed had eroded down to posturing and political intrigue. The speaker was not ready to relinquish the floor. He slammed his tail down on the wooden surface and the slam echoed across the chamber and the assemblage fell silent. He nodded his thanks to them and continued.

"You have ssseen what we are up againssst. You have ssseen what we mussst do. You know that the prophesssy isss about to be fulfilled, and yet you do nothing!" He spat the words at them as if they had become some vile parasite to be cut free and swept away. "We mussst act now! There isss no other time. Thisss human mussst die even if we expend all of our forcesss to do it. Can't you sssee thisss?" He asked them and there were nods among the assembly, but not very many of them. The positions were just so entrenched that no one would budge. The speaker sighed and lowered his head for a moment. When he lifted it again, his eyes were different, focused and dangerous. "Then you leave me no choice. I will lead my people into war againssst this human sssettlement and bring it to the ground. I can no longer wait for you to sssee what needsss to be done. I will have to do it myssself. May the godsss sssee your cowardice and punish you accordingly. If you had any of the bloodlusssst, you would join me now and we would achieve blood and glory together." He challenged and many of the delegates looked on in shame. They were supposed to be leaders and warriors as well. This one man had just shamed them all. Several of them held up banners to proclaim their loyalty to the speaker. Before long, an infectious feeling of ascent began to sweep the room. Chanting started and in moments they reached a frenzied crescendo and the whole chamber rocked with stomping feet and tails. The howls and shouts of the group continued on for quite a while, even after the speaker left the chamber to begin his preparations. He now had the support of the council and the banners of about seven of the holy houses. That would mean that he would march with over a thousand warriors. Surely no human settlement could withstand that. He felt relieved at the prospect of freeing himself from the council and actually entering a battlefield. It was more his style and he could not wait for that battle to be joined. His personal glory was almost assured.

*　　*　　*

Solana returned to the elf village in the tops of the lofty ancient trees. She felt most at home there and she had business to attend to here. The twins had each been going through their training and she was anxious for them to mature in time for the quest that they must embark on. They were a part of the plans and schemes to save the world. She knew this but had yet to tell them of it. She needed to move the pieces soon in order for the game to be played. It was like an elaborate chess board across the world and the forces of darkness were already well in place. She knew that time was drawing short and that if she moved too late no one would survive in any time. All of her hopes rode with that group of adventurers from the future and the wizard who had been training now in earnest for two years. The whole of the world and the human race hung by a tenuous thread and there was already a force there to cut it. The situation could not be more perilous. The fact that these adventurers were even trying was a testament to the survival instincts of the human animal and the main reason that she had been working so hard to help them. Her movements were slower than they used to be. She had expended her life energy in spells across time and dream walking to nudge those she needed in place. It had been a nearly impossible task, and yet she was doing it. With such an effort, how could they fail?

The village elders had greeted her warmly and instantly saw her exhaustion. They offered her comforts that she refused and they kept the masses from her to not tax what little she had left too much. She greeted everyone warmly and she smiled at them. Inside she was worried. Inside she was in turmoil and fear of the future and the ultimate demise of the entire world kept her mind from reaching the proper focus. Her resolve had been tested on more than one occasion and her belief of right and wrong had carried her through each of those events. She was a strong woman and her will could move mountains. The tribal healer had offered her some herbs to help her regain her strength. She took them from him with a nod of thanks. She put the colored leaf on her tongue and instantly felt the wash of energy as her aura started to right itself. She had not believed that it had been so wrong, but the results spoke for themselves. Her cheeks began to regain their color and everyone around her breathed a sigh of relief. After she was more rested, they came to her to find out what she needed. The chief and two of his aids were at the meeting.

She sat in the cozy room inside the tree that had been grown for her home. The woven blanket she had draped over her was comforting as well as warm and she practically glowed in the contentment it brought her. The chief had entered first and his aides had followed him into the small space. It was now crowded and the feeling of coziness evaporated in the confined place. She tossed the blanket aside and moved to a chair to accept her guests. They similarly took seats and awaited her words of greeting. She looked at them as if from far away. Her mind was on other things, and other times. She could feel the tickle in her mind that meant that Frank was trying to contact her. If she could manage the power, she would respond after this meeting. If not, he would simply have to wait. She was a bit uncomfortable with his affections. She understood them and indeed was using them to help convince him to stay on his course and complete the mission. Everything depended on that. A pang of guilt struck her as she regretted using his emotions in this manipulative manner. Still, she had done worse things to make this plan work. She just hoped it was all for something worthwhile.

She had not spoken to the chief yet so he cleared his throat to get her attention. She snapped back to the here and now and he was relieved at the quick change. "I am sorry, do you need something?" She said to him and he chuckled.

"Actually, that was my question." He replied to her and they both chuckled at the irony of it all. "Seriously, you come here so infrequently that we miss you and need you. Still, your mission, whatever it is, is all consuming and we understand it to be a part of what makes you what you are. The power has many demands and you are paying them."

She looked at him and her eyebrows rose. It might have looked threatening to some, but he knew her better than anyone else did. It was a sign of offense. He held up his hand in defense.

"We do not mean to say that you have been negligent in your duties or any other such thing. It is simply that we have not seen you around for a while. When last you were in the village, you dealt with the young man, Maxillen. Then you left without a word to the council or to me as chief. That sort of thing shakes the people's belief in you and undermines my authority based on your slight to me." He said. The politics of it all made her head hurt. She had bigger things to worry about than this. It was so unfair.

"I have been on a mission; that much is true. Maxillen and his sister are a part of it somehow. I do not yet know their connection, but they are important to the future survival of the humans." She said and the chief shrugged his shoulders.

"What do we care if the humans survive or not? They are not a part of our society and they shun us or worse whenever we meet up with them. I believe in your visions, I always have. That has not changed. It is possible that it is your judgment that has been manipulated here." He said and he knew when he said it that it was dangerous ground upon which he tread.

She looked at him with fire in her eyes. He hoped that she would not pull it from the sky to fry him in place. "You pompous old man!" she yelled at him. "You think only of yourself when the fate of this world hangs in the balance?" She asked and her tone suggested that she wasn't going to wait for an answer. "I have been trying to save the human race in the distant future. There is a time when we will be no more and this planet will belong solely to them. This is the future that had been destroyed and they need help from our time to restore what has been lost. If you think that it is not important, then maybe you don't understand this world as much as I do. We are a dying breed. We live a long time, but we do not have the ability to procreate as frequently as the hardy humans do. This will cripple our ability to survive in the long run. You must accept that this is a truth, not a vision from my head. The facts are before you already. The humans will rule this world and then they will be destroyed by another force that is sinister and relentless. There is a group of these future humans coming here to find a wizard that can help them defeat this enemy in the future. If this succeeds, then they may be able to prevent the destruction of this world. Yes, this world of trees and rivers will cease to exist and they are the only ones with the power to reverse that outcome." She said and her steam had died down somewhat. The chief had not known anything about her plans until now. He had nothing to say to the magnitude of her beliefs. He did have more to say though.

"You are a protector of us in much the same way that I am the chief. You have been charged with much responsibility and I think you need to remain focused on our well-being. This mercy mission of yours to the humans of the future seems so distant now that it sounds a bit ridiculous. You need to help the harvest this year and then the animals will need tending to over the winter. There is much to do here." He said and her face started to turn red.

"Have you not listened to what I have said? I am trying to save the world!" She screamed at him. The two aides leaned back from the force of her will. "The mission is more important than all of our lives here. We have no choice but to see it through. If it all happens before the harvest is over, then I can help with that. If not, then a lesser harvest will simply mean that we ration our food this winter a little better. Now leave me to take care of the people. I must consult with the human from the future. He summons me even now as we speak." She said and he looked at her surprised.

"You mean they can contact you?" He said in disbelief.

"Yes, they are quite resourceful and have found a way to talk through the ether. We will not speak on this again until after I have completed this mission. Then I will tell you everything. You must trust me until then. I need your support and your prayers that this all works out. The forces of darkness are already in motion and I need to make sure the twins are ready to answer when they get the call." She said plainly. There was a hint of begging in her tone. It sounded quite wrong to their sensitive ears. This was obviously more important than anything they had spoken of before.

He stood up and bowed to her. "We shall leave you to your important work then." He said and backed out of the small space. His two aides followed him humbly away from the dangerous woman and her precious mission. Once outside he turned to them. "You see what I have seen. She is no longer a servant of the people. She has taken on a mission for the humans. We must act soon or lose her forever. I will need your recommendations as soon as you have them." He told them both and they nodded gravely. He would put an end to this nonsense once and for all.

* * *

The *Lost Cavalier* had been traveling now for more than three weeks and the daily practice of trying to contact the White Witch had been only marginally successful. The two men were spent and their concentration wavered with the fatigue. The ship was getting closer to the point and they could both feel it. They were most worried about overshooting the mark. That could be catastrophic. Frank held onto his imager. He had taken pictures from the experience using some of the latest dream scanning equipment. It had severed the connection when the witch found out about it. Such things were the work of evil. She had told them as she slapped them with her power and broke the link. They had not reached her again. The mission was still the mission; they seemed to no longer have someone on their side in the past. According to the latest set of figures, they would drop out of warp in about two days and they wanted to be as ready as they could be. That's what made this disconnection so frustrating. Try as they might, the woman did not answer them and now they had nothing left to do but wait. One of the changes from the last foray into the past, they would not wear costumes this time to try and blend in. They would go out in uniform. The last batch of costumes had been so off that it was worse than their normal clothing. No one knew what was worn this far back anyway. These people certainly wouldn't have modern materials like polyester and even the refined cotton thread would be rare. Animal hides were non-existent on the ship so that option was out as well. They would have to go as themselves and not waste any time or energy on trying to convince people that they belonged here. It was obvious to just about everyone that they didn't.

Outside the ship, the darkness of void swallowed them up. The loss of the stars was unsettling for anyone who could see outside. Most people stayed away from the windows entirely to avoid the uneasiness the absolute darkness brought. The Captain sat in a lounge chair. He had been working on his duty logs. They had been a bit back-logged since the encounter with the Abbey and this break in the action was just the excuse to get things caught up. His paperwork was almost all in line already and it was just these verbal logs that remained. He had written letters to families that no longer existed about lost crewmembers. He had processed supply request forms for the Fleet in case they ever returned. He had kept himself so busy that nothing seemed trivial anymore. He was amazed that their food supply was still holding up. They had added some local food on the first two stops, but still, they were in the process of a month long journey where no stops were possible. They were stocked accordingly. It was something that he would not have worried about if the time had been tight. Now he was pleased that his requisitions officer had been so good at his job. Rationing was not yet a requirement. The retrieval team was prepping their gear on the lower decks and he knew just what it would look like if he went down there. They were cleaning weapons and gear. They were practicing all sorts of maneuvers and testing communications equipment and other mission essential gear. It was just as busy as he was but in a more physical way. He somewhat envied them for it. He wished he had something more to do with his hands. Still, he had worked his way through three weeks of projects so far; he could continue a couple of days without too much trouble. So really, with his lofty position and all, his situation was exactly the same as Frank's. He could only wait and see what came next.

* * *

As impatient as the humans seemed to be in their long flight, the lizardmen took the inactivity worse. Fights had broken out over simple things and everyone was cranky. They were warriors, being trapped in their stone ship without the comfort of the stars and the enemy in their grips was maddening. The medical facility was almost full now and Commander Zarg was fuming and fit to be tied. He wanted to kill something. His blood was in rage almost all the time with no outlet. He wanted so much to take out these humans and return home. He wanted more than anything for his name to be shouted on the home world by millions of impressed citizens when his story was told. He knew that his warriors could still fight. The injuries were not all that serious. It was just their own release for the same frustration that he felt. He tried hard not to take it out on the bridge crew. His brother would have stepped in if he had gone too far. So far he had done an admirable job of controlling himself. He watched the display. They had been following the trail of the human metal box for a long time now. How long could they continue to run like this? Surely they were having disciplinary problems too. They were not warriors after all. They were not tied to a blood oath to fight or die for their commander. They were just sheep to be slaughtered for the greater glory of those in charge. This chase would end. They always did end. It was just a matter of how long until it ended. He hoped that the enemy still had fuel when they slowed down. It would be no sport at all to take a stalled ship from space. This wonderful and frustrating chase through time would be the talk of legend. He only hoped and prayed that it would be over soon so that he could get on with the ruling of this place. He would control this sector of space and thus the ruins of earth would be his playground. He had so many plans for the little green globe. Of course it was destroyed in the future, but here it was ripe for the taking. This idea of vanquishing a people throughout their history appealed to him. There would always be another battle, another conquest to be had. All his people would rejoice when they found out. His place in history would be assured. He wanted so much for that to happen he could almost see it in the eyes of the woman before him. Then he realized that he should not be seeing a woman at all. There were no women aboard his ship and certainly none of the fair skinned human types. This woman was leaner than most humans and her pointed ears made him worry. He tried to blink his eyes to make her disappear, thinking that she was a figment of his imagination. She looked back at him from the display. He glanced around to see if anyone else saw her. They were going about their business as if nothing was wrong. He stood up and her face followed him. She kept eye contact and he stomped from the bridge and left for his quarters. She stepped from the display onto the bridge and still no one paid her any attention. She followed the commander and he looked back over his shoulder with fear in his eyes.

He saw her pass through a closed stone door and he knew that he was dealing with a spirit or ghost. It was something he thought parents told their children to frighten them into being good. He never thought he'd actually see one. "Stay away from me!" He shouted as he began to run to his quarters. The woman followed behind in a graceful flowing way. Her white robes swept as if by some non-existent wind and she radiated beauty. He was not amused. He dove into his room and sealed the door. The stone congealed and solidified across the former opening. Solana swept through the solid wall and stopped before the shaking lizardman. "What do you want of me?" He asked almost in a panic.

"You are the leader of this hunt and you are the only one who can stop it before it is too late." She told him in a reasonable tone that tried to diffuse his fear. It didn't work. "Your men have earned their place of respect and you should get home before the Fleet forgets about you." She said, still in that reasonable tone. "The Fleet is moving on now that the humans are gone. You are alone in the hunt and they think that you are lost. Your houses grieve for you and your names are fading from memory. Can you let this happen when there is something that can be done?" She asked him.

"You know of my people?" He asked, trying to make sense of it all. She nodded to him. Her smile made him nervous. He felt that she knew more than she was telling him. All this and the fact that she could not really be here made him second guess his sanity. "You cannot think that I would abandon a hunt incomplete." He told her matter-of-factly. "My people would never allow me to return home empty handed.

The woman in white hovered softly towards him. "You have a trophy already. You were a member of the Fleet that destroyed the human home world. You can simply report that you destroyed the human ship and that your hunt was successful. They will not come back here to verify your claim and the glory could still be yours." She offered and he did smile at the thought.

Then he shook his scaly head. "No, it would not work. I would know and my crew would know. We need to kill the humans in order for this hunt to end. Our honor code is specific and no one would dare to bring down the wrath of my people if the truth ever got out. So we need to finish this hunt no matter how long it takes." He told the apparition before him.

Solana lowered her head. "I thought that you would feel that way. I have taken great steps to prepare for your arrival and now I am taking the final step to make sure you have no chance of completing your hunt." She told him and her tone was now icy and calculated. She reached forward and the commander was surprised that she could touch him. His forehead burned and he faded from consciousness. He slumped to the stone floor and remained still. The woman in white shook her head and vanished as the spell completed. He lay there like that for several days before any of the crew mustered up the courage to enter the chamber without the required permission. They rushed him to their medical facility as he was dehydrated and hungry beyond normal measure. He was incapacitated for command and his brother took charge. The ship was still on course for the human ship and they would monitor it closely for when to drop out of warp. This time, however, they would hold a little longer so that the humans could not ambush them again. He watched the display as the metal box decelerated and dropped out of warp. He counted to five and then ordered his ship to slow down. The crew complied with the order, but nothing happened. The stone ship stayed at warp. Everyone started rushing here and there looking for the fault. The stone ship kept running backwards through time and when it finally slowed down, they had overshot the mark by over one hundred and ninety years. They would have to wait for the humans to come before they could continue the hunt. This was bad news and the crew felt the crushing weight of disappointment as they prepared to land on the planet below. The great stone ship came down on the far eastern edge of the only continent on the green and blue world below them. The ship came in over a beach and the sparkling water. They knew that temperatures were the enemy so they stayed south as they veered inland. The open desert to the south was too hot and the ice to the north would kill them. They were going to be here for a long time. They brought the ship down and set it just on the edge of the beach. They shut down the systems and the stone was melded with the existing crust of the planet to form an unbreakable foundation. The stone ship became a fortress. It was going to be the home of the lizardmen for some time to come. They settled down to make a new life for themselves until the day that they could complete their quest and rid this world of the dreaded human infestation once and for all.

* * *

An Ending and a Beginning

Solana wiped the sweat from her brow. The casting always took something out of her and over time and great distances it was worse. She felt the pang of death about her like exhaustion greater than any other. She knew that she had overtaxed herself to give the *Lost Cavalier* a fighting chance to succeed. It was the last thing she would do. She laid down upon the soft fronds that was her bed and she looked up at the tops of the trees. She had done everything to save this world and she had done it at the cost of her own life. Even so, she held no regrets save one. She would now never meet those brave travelers heading her way. It gave her a twinge of sadness that she assumed they would feel as well. It was the only down side to her many castings and her manipulations of people across time and space. Her people would recover from their loss. They were already considering her a traitor. Her abilities could have stopped that before it began, but it would help them to let her go. The flowers around her began to wilt as they too felt the sorrow of the departing spirit. Her head tilted just a bit as the muscles relaxed for the last time and she let out her final breath. Her mind and spirit were at peace.

Mere moments later Florena stepped up to find the expired witch and she broke into sobs as she called out for help. It was not long before the whole village gathered and took the body away for an honorable disposal. The twins drew to each other for support and they gathered their things. Solana had told them that they were supposed to go to the humans upon her death. She had made them swear to her that it would be done. Neither of them thought that it would be so soon, but that is the way of things and they were honorable and just. They left the following morning with no one even noting their departure. The three days of mourning made the village quiet as the two young adults changed their lives from villagers to adventurers. It was a change that neither of them could foresee and that neither of them was probably ready for. Still, they were walking the long road and their fates were tied to others that they had yet to meet. I awaited them, although at the time, even I did not know it.

*   *   *

The school was rebuilding and many of the younger students had survived. They had been hidden away when the fighting began. Now they were the menial labor used to repair the stone and sweep the debris away. A new master had taken over for the fallen mentor that had taken me under his wing. I was being shooed away as soon as they felt that it would be safe to do so. The trouble I brought down upon them had been inexcusable. Of course I had no idea how it kept happening. I did not know why I was so important. It just seemed so impossible. I understood now that there were forces at work that I had no control over. I had buried myself into the studies again now that I had a clue as to the other elements. It turned out that once I knew what to look for, there was a ton of information on the other powers. The only set back was that each of the new additions to my skills came with warnings about using too much power and consuming too much of the caster. These secondary elements were powerful, but they were also dangerous. I spent a lot of time in the elemental room and my guards seemed impressed at the new abilities. I could freeze things in place and then thaw them out again with the fire. I could throw flaming balls of earth at the targets. The mixing of the elements brought countless new spells and skills. It was truly an age of discovery for me and I felt the energy flowing more freely to me when I called for it. The elementals that had attacked me before had somehow realized my potential and they were actually excited to come when beckoned. They knew that something was going to happen and I did not care what motivated them. I knew that the training was going well. Most of the instructors that remained refused to train me. There were many grumblings about too much power for one man to handle. I felt confidence rising within me and I worried that it was conceit. I felt the power and I worried that it was going to control me instead of the other way around. Milas had tried to convince me that I was a good person and so could not be ruled by the forces I commanded. I was unconvinced and I kept my guard up all the time against that possible fate. For if I managed to master all of the elements and was then subjugated, it would mean a very powerful tool for evil will have been forged. I could not allow that to happen. The struggle within for more and more skills was the first sign of power madness. I had to back away for a bit and just manipulate what I had learned and not gather more and more without reason. It was a fight that could not be won for me by others. I had to fight it on my own. I was working away at a particularly tough sigil when the whole of magic came to me as if in one glorious piece. The elements were all one. They were not distinct things anymore. They were the embodiment of the power and they were what made the world. Everything from the mighty trees to the tiniest snail was all wrapped up in these elements and I was now privy to everything that connected to them and connected them together. It was an amazing feeling. It was an epiphany of massive proportions. I looked out at the world with new eyes. The power wrapped around each thing and I saw it as if I had been born to do so. When I stood up and looked around, I could see everything about the man who was my guard. I knew what he had done his whole life and what he was going to do. I saw his child and his wife that had been slain so long ago. He looked at me and the connection was realized on both ends. We shared thoughts and emotions for a brief moment and he looked at me with new light.

"Sir, you have done something amazing. You will be the savior of the world." He blurted out. I did not know what he meant, but apparently he could see things inside of me that I had not. I wondered if I could see more in him than he knew. Perhaps it was so. He stepped forward, his professional demeanor dropped for a moment. "Sir, you are the one we were sent to protect and now I understand why. I personally vow to protect you in any way that I can in order to help you attain the future that I see within you." He said solemnly and I blushed.

"You see things that I do not. Perhaps you should tell me what they are so that I can know them when they come." I suggested and he shook his head.

"If they are inside of you, then you will know them when it is time. Foreknowledge could affect the way you react to a given situation and I will not risk the world on my interpretations of what you will do someday." He said in the most reasonable tone I have ever heard. I had to admit to myself that he had a point. Some things weren't meant to be known. I knew now that there was no mistaking my own destiny. I was meant to do something big. I was supposed to be strong and powerful. I was supposed to save everything. No matter what the case, I now had convinced this man that I was important and he had vowed to keep me alive to do whatever he had seen. There was nothing more that I could say to that. I thanked him and sat back down. The connections were everywhere and I needed to understand as many of them as I could. They were like tendrils of emotions stemming from out of everybody. The links were all different too. Some were thick and tough. Others were frail and light. This new information would require a lot of work on my part. I sighed out loud. The guard smiled back at me. He had seen something more of me than perhaps I realized, for now he got my internal jokes as well. It was an unsettling thought. Well, hard work was nothing new to me and there was no time like the present to get it done. So I moved back down to the archives to see just what else I could learn. I took some bread and cheese with me and left with my personal guards checking the halls as I went as usual. It was to the point that they did not disturb me at all. They were evident when they needed to be but blended into the walls and furniture when they were not. It was most impressive.

* * *

The loss of the White Witch was felt all across the kingdom. The land wept as rain broke out over the woodlands and made travel miserable. The denizens of darkness moved with added haste at the event. They did not know the cause, but they could feel a shift in the balance of power as good had lost a powerful agent. They were ready to do something subtle to tip the balance even further in their favor. With luck, they might even do something that can't be detected or reversed. That was the goal of every worker of the dark arts. The loss of the light would be the legacy that they would leave behind.

The shaman of the lizardmen looked at his people. They had worked hard to get where they were. They had done things that would have brought down entire nations upon them if it had been discovered. They had done all of this to stop humans from doing something in this time. The wizard that seemed to be the focus of this plot was still alive and that stuck in his craw. He had sent an assassin and he had sent agents out to take care of this problem. They had even lost a fellow shaman. The battle had been a weary one and the distance had been so far that they had been simply stretched too thin to accomplish the directives. The council had debated until they turned blue about a possible follow-up mission. The attack they had planned now was over a thousand warriors strong and now they were all bogged down in mud. He felt their distaste for the traveling conditions but he expected them to do their duty. None of them wanted to face his wrath if they failed. He needed to destroy this wizard even if he had to level every human settlement he could find. The signs all told him that the brothers from the future would come and attempt their mission. He had been raised to believe this and he wanted to finish this mission and thus save his brothers some time and effort. That is, if they proved his faith to be accurate by actually existing. Faith was a strange thing and he knew that the legend could have been written by someone who just needed something done. Either way, he had worked hard to get where he was and to reach this appointed time and place. This war was the only way they could succeed before the proposed landing time mentioned in the scriptures of legend. Glory or not, he had put his whole life on the line for the next few days. It was all coming to this and he felt the jitters of such an important event approaching. It made him even more careful and it drove him almost into the bloodlust of his people. He pushed it aside again. The bloodlust would not help him with his magic. It would not help him to unravel the secrets of the old writings and it would not help him command his men properly. The mucky terrain was sending many of his warriors close to the edge. He may have to quell them soon if this continues.

*   *   *

The *Lost Cavalier* dropped out of warp and the streaks of light appeared and pulled back to the dots of light that represented stars. They were in orbit of Earth, but it did not look the same. There was only one landmass and it did not at all look like the Pangaea the scientists had projected. It was like a vertical band from pole to pole down one side of the planet. The water looked endless on the other side and even though it was unexpected, it was a welcome sign. They would not have to guess which continent held the people they needed to find. The southern region was separated from the northern by a vast desert at the equator and a full scan showed only wildlife below that point. It was abundant, but there were no signs of civilization at all. The northern port was a different story. There were rough roads and stone structures. There were masses of people down there. The first thought Frank had as he looked over the shoulder of the scanner tech was that the theories of the distant past had been wrong. They would need to get a sample of the rock down on the surface to date the planet now, but the emissions were zero. The pollution was also near zero. There was nothing more hazardous than a wood fire down there. No coal or fossil fuels were in use down there. There were no dinosaurs either. They would have been extinct long before this time most probably. Of course it was all just conjecture at this point. They really needed to get down there and see just what was going on. The excitement of the unfamiliar home world was spreading around the crew and when the Captain ordered the ship to descend, there was almost a cheer on the bridge.

He looked around at his people and he felt the same excitement they felt. The burden of command was heavier now more than ever. They *felt* close. They had done what seemed to be impossible. They had traveled back to before recorded history in order to find a needle in a human haystack. Of course, the idea of finding a single person here seemed somewhat ludicrous, but here they were and the scanners did not lie. There were people down there. Were they like his crew? Only time and first contact would tell that. He tried to settle down. He saw his hand trembling and he hid it along the side of his thigh as he sat in the command chair watching the screen. The air was clean and the clouds that had been covering most of the upper half of the one continent parted as the ship sped through it. It left a streak of blue in its wake and as it lost altitude, it carried some of the light from the sky above with it. It looked like a falling star bringing golden warmth to the world as it came down. In moments, the basic outline of the tiny kingdom laid out before the captain with one question on the helmsman's mind. "Where do we land?" He rubbed his chin and then called Frank over to look at the diagram. Frank made little sense of it at first and then it clicked. He smiled and then conferred with Christopher. The monk pointed to the northern area of the display and smiled. Frank nodded and then they both looked at the Captain.

"That is where the school is, we need to go there." They said as one. The feeling was a bit creepy, but the Captain nodded to them and targeted the spot they had indicated with his stylus and hit the send key on the display. The ship altered course as the new heading was entered and it was not long before the ship began to descend into the front courtyard of the massive building that set both the historian and his friend into a fit of excitement. The school looked just the way it had in the dream sequence that they had shared. The turbine thrusters spun up and the metal ship set down gracefully on that front lawn and acolytes began to pour out of the damaged building alarmed. They began to assemble with their spells ready and nothing happened from inside the ship. They did not know what it was so the general feeling was that evil had come up with something new here. Milas looked out of the higher window and froze. The metal thing in the courtyard was large. It was too large to be the work of any of the people that he had ever known. The flying mechanism appeared to use brute force instead of magic to propel itself. It was the work of someone with an industrialized mind. He knew tinkers and men who were good with their hands. This took more than even that would suggest. The story from the witch was that people were coming from the future. If they had metal works like this in the future, then this had to be what they were waiting for. His skeptical side kept nagging at him to defend the wizard. This was, after all, his primary job now. All that he really knew was that the acolytes and instructors alike were scared. They seemed to be readying for a charge and he knew that it would be pointless against whatever had come in that machine.

The assemblage that was forming outside represented a security risk to the ship so the few crew by the airlock were waiting for the professionals to figure out how to handle this delicate situation. They needed to make contact without an incident or violence of any kind. They did not know what this wizard would look like and if they killed him in a scuffle, the entire mission would fail just when they were so close.

Frank descended the ladder leading to the appropriate deck and he met up with Casey the engineer. The two of them had a plan for a quick high-tech defense for the initial confrontation. It required a little tweaking of the sensor array and channeling energy into it. Then they could project an invisible force field that would stop almost anything from hitting the men as they came down the ramp. To these people it would seem like magic. Since Frank was one of those scheduled to be on that ramp, he definitely wanted that added insurance. He had already been wounded to win over the monks. He did not want to go through that again. He almost hadn't lived through it last time. He was glad to have gotten here and he was prepared to meet with the witch. He had dreamed about her a few more times in their travels here and always she seemed saddened by him. He did not know why. Casey popped open the circuit box and started connecting things. Frank stayed out of his way since he had no knowledge that would help this situation. He had tried to think of what to say and nothing seemed right. He would just have to wing it out there. There was no other way. These people were from such a different time that they had practically nothing in common. It would take a lot to manage this contact. He watched as Casey's hands moved quickly and surely in that bird's nest of wires. It still amazed him how the man's mind worked. The status light at the top of the panel turned amber and then green. The energy feeds lit up and the power was now being routed into the array. All they needed to do was trigger it and the field would be in place about fifty paces beyond the ramp. That should allow for him to talk to them on their own terms a bit. The Captain wanted to go with as well, but his security officer had strictly forbidden it. He was simply too important for the mission to risk on a first contact scenario. The team from the last encounter was present plus Christopher the monk and Cris Fell. Cris's blundering at the last encounter had made him rethink his technique and now he was ready and anxious to redeem himself. They all stood at the ready inside the closed hatch as the controls were hit to extend the ramp. The hatch would open soon and they would need to look composed as they marched down the ramp and out into the courtyard before the on-looking throng outside.

*   *   *

Milas watched intently as the gathered students backed away from the new sound. A metal plank seemed to be sticking out of the metal airship. A humming sound accompanied the movement and made everyone nervous. Spell chants were uttered under breaths and everyone prepared for the worst. The plank came out all the way to the ground and its top was covered with a pattern of some darker material that none of them knew of. Then a light shone at the top of the plank and men were seen silhouetted in it. It was a gangway to exit the chariot. There were six of them, they looked human enough and they were not moving in a menacing manner. The moment was tense and it seemed to drag on as the newcomers walked purposefully down the plank. They looked like soldiers without armor. They carried no visible weapons so perhaps they were casters. They held no charms or wands either. They did not wear robes that could hide all of their spell components. They walked to the end of the metal ramp and then stepped out onto the grass. The man in front of them held up his hand and the rest of them stopped in place. He smiled at the assemblage and spoke some words that could not be recognized. His mannerisms looked friendly enough. Everyone decided to wait and see what these people wanted. There was no point in trying to kill someone with so many unknowns around them. The new master of the school stepped forward to meet this leader and the two men stood a few paces from each other.

Frank watched as the leader of this assembly stepped forward. He had to admit that the man had guts. The whole idea of a ship landing on your front door could not have been all that calming. The man seemed to be actually approaching enough to make physical contact. Frank did not want him to bump into the force field so he held up his hand in a motion of stopping. The man did stop and his face showed that he was curious as to why. Frank nodded to the ship and the force field was dropped to allow him to advance and Frank motioned for him to do so. The leader stepped all the way up and Frank held out his hand in friendship. The master did not know what to make of it so Frank took his hand and shook it in greeting. The man seemed to understand the purpose and he smiled back as this first step was realized.

"How do you do? I am Frank Muskerini and I am here to see if you have a certain wizard that we are looking for." He said as amiably as possible. The leader looked at him in question. It was obvious that he had not understood the words. This was something that Frank should have foreseen, but the White Witch had been able to understand English, so he assumed that everything was going to work out. Frank held up his hand, again it was the gesture to wait a moment. He keyed his communicator mike and asked for a linguist to come out if they had one. There was a pause as the ship's records were queried. The answer back was something of a personal tragedy. "You are the most qualified person on board." Came the response.

The tiny electronic voice made the leader start and he held up his hands in a threatening manner. Frank stepped back quickly and Casey threw the switch to activate the force field. The spell was one of fire and the ball of flame danced from his hands and flew towards the six men before him. They were obviously working with demons to have detached voices in their heads. The fire darted out and seemed to hit something solid between him and the intruders.

Frank could not believe what he was seeing. The man had conjured fire and thrown it purposefully at him. It was the most exciting moment of his life to date and at the same time the most frightening. The force field held against the attack and the fire dissipated away harmlessly. Frank stepped to the edge of the field and tapped on it. The sound of static electricity told him that the field was still up after the attack and also told the leader that his attacks would be useless now. He tried to speak French to the leader and there was no response. He tried German and there was no response either. He tried Russian and the man now knew what he was trying to do, but still failed to understand a syllable of it. Christopher tapped Frank on the shoulder and stepped up to take his place.

"Do you understand me at all?" He asked in Latin. His time as a monk had afforded him the chance to learn a bit about the language. There was a twinge of recognition, as if the words were similar but not a match. The leader sent for something or someone and everyone waited as both sides eyed one another. In moments a younger acolyte came up carrying something fairly heavy. It was a stone bowl. The acolyte set it on the ground carefully and then pulled a bladder that he poured water into the bowl from. Then he bowed and backed away. Frank knelt down before the bowl. It was carved from a single block of the stone and the water inside of it kept reflecting shiny bits in the grain of the rock. He and Christopher kept watch as the leader began to chant and wave his hands over the bowl. Much to the visitor's amazement, an image formed in the bowl and as they looked down into it, the beautiful woman they knew appeared. It was the White Witch. Both men looked excited at this small bit of recognition. She really did exist. They were in the right place! The mission was back on schedule and they had done the impossible to get here already. Of course the mission was still far from over, but the moment made them both grin widely. The leader mage seemed to be sharing the moment of happiness. His tense shoulders relaxed considerably and he waved his hand over the bowl to dispel the image. He beckoned for the newcomers to follow him and they all marched up to and into the school. The once grand and proud school was currently in a state of disrepair. There were signs of a recent attack and the tools and stones were lying all around waiting to be installed in the walls. Half-burnt tapestries adorned the walls and the smell of smoke was still present in the bigger rooms. The leader took them to a reading room just off of the library and bade them to sit and wait.

* * *

Milas had watched the exchange in the courtyard. When the strangers were brought in, he knew that the master was coming here. He hoped that the man had enough sense to put them into a neutral spot and not bring them up to the quarters. He gave orders to the guards and crossbows were stowed away and swords were drawn. There was no excuse for letting one's guard down.

I waited anxiously in one of the chairs. The tome I had been reading in had failed to hold my attention for long. The moment of my destiny was here and I was being kept from it for my own good. It would still come, but in an orderly and safe way. For that I was grateful. Milas had told me that the newcomers spoke words that no one could understand. I had not heard any of it yet, but the delays outside had to be a sign that he was right. Most of the afternoon had gone by while this or that was being addressed. The ship in the courtyard looked so unusual. Of course I had never seen anything like it. The metal was in layers of some kind. Extra pieces appeared to be attached all over the thing. Its metal feet had sunk into the ground pretty far so it was heavy too. Yet for all of its massive weight, it could fly. It was a concept that struck me as odd at the time. Perhaps these people had magic enough to help me save the world. I wished the witch were here with me so that she could guide me through this. But alas, she was not. In fact, I had not heard from her for a bit and a sudden pang of worry struck me. So did the certainty that she was dead strike me to the quick. I don't even know how I had come to that conclusion, but it felt locked into my mind. She was dead and I would not ever see her again. It saddened me even as the master talked to the guards outside the room. He explained what had happened at the scrying dish and he felt that it was now safe for me to meet them. Milas seemed more worried about it than I was, but paranoia was a part of his very nature. We went down as a group to see the strangers. We entered the reading room and they all stood up. It caused a flash of tension in Milas and his crew but they did not draw their steel. They only put hand to hilt in readiness. The strangers sat back down in reaction. It seems that they did not want a confrontation either. As I approached, they looked directly at me. One of them said "Is that him?" I understood what he had said! I don't know why I did, but it was clear as a bell to me.

I decided to answer him directly. "Yes, I am the wizard you seek." I said. All of the strangers' eyes went wide as they realized that they understood what I had said. "I have been training in order to help you save the world. Since I did not know what would be required, I tried to learn all that I could. Hopefully it will be enough." I said to rush them over their initial shock. Apparently I was speaking their language because the master looked at me in shock as well.

A man stood up and smiled at me. He held out his hand and I reached instinctively out to grasp it. "It is a great pleasure to meet you at last. I am Frank Muskerini and this is Christopher Farber from the order of Buildwas Abbey. We have come a long way to find you and all of our hopes ride with you on this grand mission." He said. I did not know what his background was, but his speech pattern was almost grand. I nodded to him and then looked at the other members of the group. They each introduced themselves and when it was all finished, I asked the master to leave us to discuss this mission. I kept my guards in the room though. Milas wouldn't have let me do otherwise anyway. He still did not trust these people and I had to admit that they were both exciting and dangerous. We discussed the mission as they saw it from their first contact with the aliens and then their subsequent race through time to reach here. It was a grand tale and it seemed that the aliens were also here in this time somewhere. That complicated things a bit since they had the power to destroy the world back here. I would have to figure out something to do about that before we could move forward to do this grand thing. The discussions went long into the night and candles flickered by as the hours passed.

* * *

Maxillen had taken his vows seriously to head for the school and he had his sister with him. They made excellent time through the woodlands. It was their natural habitat after all. They had to hide here and there for the lizardmen were moving in force. It gave them a sense of urgency. It did not appear to be a coincidence that they were heading the same way as the army. They passed group after group using the natural stealth of their race and the knowledge and tricks of the woods. They somehow managed to get ahead of the column and they ran until exhausted more than once to get here. He was a good shot with his bow, but how many could he possibly take down before they were overwhelmed? It was much better to bring the word and hope for reinforcements. Fear made their steps even lighter and the day and night traveling brought them to the gates of the school at least two days ahead of the lizardman force. The gate sentries were acolytes and they held the two elves as they heaved and puffed air. They had run until they could run no more. They could not yet speak.

When he did speak the message was grim. "A … large force … of lizardmen … are coming … got to warn … the wizard." They stammered out and the acolytes led them to the master. He had them set before him and he fed them jerked meat and bread. They ate hungrily and then they both stopped at once. They looked ashamed of themselves. "Sir, we need to warn the wizard that the lizardman army is coming." They said as one voice. The master looked at them carefully. He was a good judge of character and he studied them for the telltale signs of a lie. He didn't see any. This worried him because the school had lost so many of their staff and students already to a scouting size force and now an army was approaching. The repairs to the walls were not even completed as yet. Their defenses were depleted and the number of skilled casters was notably limited. This was not good news. The master left them to the remainder of the meal and summoned one of my guards. This was a bit of news that I needed to factor into my plans. In truth I had no real plans. I was hoping these travelers told me what I needed to do. The future, as I saw it, was full of utter mystery. There would be no easy way out for me now that they had arrived. It was several moments later when the guard came in and quietly reported to Milas. His mood turned dark as the man spoke to him. I braced myself for the bad news.

Milas acknowledged the report and the guard was ushered away to resume his duties. He looked at the group and his face had turned from grim to emotionless. That was when I got really worried. He looked at me because he knew that the others could not understand him. "There is an army heading this way. The lizardmen are going to make another attempt on your life. There were no numbers given but the report says that two elves brought this intelligence to us at the risk of their own lives. I will question them momentarily and hopefully they will have some of the tactical information we need. I suggest that we wrap this up and get our defenses in order. If this force is more than a hundred then I don't see how we can defend against it." He finished and I swallowed hard. I repeated what he had said for the others to hear and they all looked disturbed. As I watched them they grew agitated. The word lizardman seemed to make them almost panic. We broke up the meeting and they started talking to themselves as I set up my spell components. I would need a lot of elements to repel that many attackers.

Frank came to me and his face was set just as emotionless as Milas' had been. "We have told the ship to rake the army a few times from the air. It won't take them all down but maybe we can reduce their numbers before they reach the school." He said. I heard that same loud noise as before. It sounded even louder now. The metal box outside rose off the ground and turned around towards the enemy. Apparently they were going to take the battle to the enemy. As grateful as I was for the help, I didn't understand what they could do in that box like that. I let it go for I needed to get things ready. I had two guards with me. Milas had gone to make preparations of his own. The two elves had been sent to my location upon their request. The master had granted them the opportunity since they had risked everything to come and warn us. I was just putting some notes in my pocket as they entered. They were not so tall as the witch had been. They had the same slender build though and they were dressed in clothes that looked out of place here. They were obviously meant for the woodland areas of the world. If they had stood still out there, I would not have even seen them. One had a longbow across his back and he looked like he knew how to use it. They had a strong resemblance to each other. I guessed that they were brother and sister. They both knelt before me and I felt uncomfortable.

"Milord we are sent to help you with your mission." The male said. I did not know his name at that time but we were to become close friends indeed. I had the same feeling that I had when the good Captain made his vow to me. It was exciting and frightening to be in charge of someone else's well-being. These vows amounted to the same thing.

"I would know your names." I replied in my most regal tone. I knew that my younger age would take away the sincerity I tried to project. They smiled at me to prove that they saw the fear in my eyes.

"I am Maxillen and this is my sister Florena. We are sent by Solana, the White Witch, to aid you in saving the world." Max said and I sat down, flabbergasted by the boldness of the statement.

"You were sent by that vision of beauty?" I blurted out. "Where is she? I hoped that she would be here when these travelers arrived, but she was not. I have been simply going about business guessing at everything. Her council would be invaluable now." I pleaded and they both suddenly looked sad. Their reaction made my heart drop. "Oh my god." I exclaimed.

Max said in low tones, "She has died. Her last wish was for us to join you. She said that she had been training us for this day. We will do whatever you ask to help with this for it is our oath to honor her wishes." He said. His convictions were unshaken. I instantly felt that I could trust this man, this elf, before me. He looked pretty young too; it made things seem just a little more balanced somehow.

"I grieve for your loss." I replied in an automatic manner. My thoughts of her were shattered. She had died and I would not see her again. I hadn't realized that she was such an important thing in my life. It was true though. I had somehow felt the loss before this moment. I had simply passed it off as something else, indigestion or some other such. "I, I don't really know what to say." I said honestly. "I know that we need to fight soon, can you help with that?" I asked and they both stood up strong.

"Yes milord we can fight." They responded as if of one voice. They seemed to do that a lot as I recall thinking back now. Still, they were instrumental for the upcoming events and I would not do them the disservice of neglecting that in these notes.

"I will have fighters around us to help shield us from direct assault. This will afford us the opportunity to do some ranged attacks. I see your bow and I have no doubt that you can use it. I don't yet know what you can do young lady but I am certain that if you were trained to be here now then it will be relevant somehow." I said. I was no longer thinking. I was working on instinct as I did when I was casting. It had always served me in the past. It had even discovered me two of the elements that had so eluded me before. They both nodded and we went to the wall to see how far away the enemy was. If we had any luck at all, then they would not be close enough to see yet. It would give us time to set up who would defend where. The professional soldiers did this without discussion. They pointed and directed without a word and then set up their posts to monitor their area of responsibility. It was truly amazing to me.

When we reached the top of the wall, the enemy was not in sight. The two elves looked out as if on a line to the direction they fully expected the enemy to come from. They had seen the enemy after all. I asked them if this was the correct heading and they nodded that it was. "Milord, they are vast in number and we will have difficulty defending this stone structure. We would be happier stealing you away into the woods and hiding you from harm." Florena suggested and I shook my head.

"I understand that, but I have been practically raised here. I cannot abandon them now in their hour of need. We must repel these invaders and then it seems we must take flight in the metal box and save the world in another time. It sounds so crazy but that is what they told me." I said and they took it all in stride and simply nodded.

They noticed my expression and both chuckled. "We have known about you and your mission almost since birth. Solana told us often about how you would be brave and bold and clueless at the same time. In truth, it is quite funny. I am so glad that you are who you are and that we are here to help you. It means that all that she told us was accurate and that we will get to save the world as she promised." Max said as he strung his bow. The workmanship on the bow was flawless. I had never seen such a thing before and the arrows were equally good. The fletching was aligned so that the arrow would spin as it passed through the air for more accuracy over a greater distance. I had never seen this type of thing before either.

We had gone over who would do what and where when the distant sound of the metal box came to us. They were flying low this time. Lights danced around the ground beneath them as they used weapons that I could not understand on the invading army. Great scars were cut into the grass and Earth as the beams of light sliced enemies and ground alike indiscriminately. It was a slaughter from above. The leading edge of the enemy was broken and disorganized. They were not truly advancing on us, they were running in fear. The box was running them into our arrows. Even so, there were hundreds of lizardmen in that field as the box harried them right up to the gates. Volleys of spells cast out and cut down more of the beasts. When the range was right, the crossbows around us fired and even more of the beasts were injured. Their blood rage was in full swing and it took a lot to kill one of them. I felt the winds build up as I pulled the elements to me. They lifted me up from the top of the wall and I shot out over the battle. The winds whipped up into a frenzy and everyone watched in amazement as I combined my new skills into something they had never seen before. The cold was introduced into the wind and the then clouds came and rain poured down upon the freezing air. In seconds the leading edge of the lizardmen were encased in ice and their metabolisms were slowed down to a hibernating status. The front edge was now in the way of the rest of their forces. The crossbows and arrows continued to rain down upon them and I willed the winds to take me back to the top of the wall. I stepped onto the flagstones and both elves looked at me in shock.

I shrugged my shoulders. "We needed a wall, and the stone one was not repaired yet." I said and then we turned our attention back to the fight outside. I pulled the lightning and sent it dancing out into the throng of enemies even as they pushed over their frozen fellows to gain access to the wall. They were even hacking them down to make way for the rest of the force. It was gruesome and nasty. I saw Milas charge the ones that came through the gate. He had a pole in his hand and it drove through two of them at once and then he swung the sword with practiced lethality. His men formed on him and they were cutting a wedge down before them. Florena held out her hands and spoke words of power. The grass in front of the gate suddenly sprang up to form a copse of gnarled and twisted vines. It would not stop the lizard steel long, but it offered a brief respite for the tired warriors inside. The last of the lizardmen inside were cut down without the support of their fellows and Florena grew another and another wall of plants before the gate. The enemy began to climb the vines and she realized her mistake. She had accidentally supplied them a natural ladder to the top of the wall. A new pitched battle broke out in the lookout areas of the wall and the clattering of steel was mixed with the sounds of pain and death. The metal box came in low and the force of wind from the bottom of it sent several of the enemy and friends alike off of the wall and out into the masses outside. People were dying and I needed to act fast to stop this. I called upon the winds again and soon I was out over the mess again. Several crude arrows sailed past me but a moving target is much harder to hit. I called forth fire and sent it rocketing straight down at the ground and the twisting and turning mass of bodies down there. It hit the ground and roiled out in a circle from the impact point and the smell of burnt flesh added to the gore as many of the lizards were fried alive. They fell in large groups and the heat melted them together. They would be reduced to skeletons before the spell ended. It also burnt the vines away and the ones climbing them died with horrible screams of panic and pain. The gate was revealed again and it was now last stand time. There had to be at least a couple hundred of them left and I was running out of ideas. A lucky shot grazed my leg and my concentration slipped with the pain. The winds no longer held me and I plummeted towards the ground. I was falling directly into the enemy and I tried to regain my focus as my brain panicked. The ground rushed up fast and a giant lily pad formed below me as I hit the ground. The spongy green pad must have been twenty feet wide and at least a foot thick. It took much of the force of my landing away and I laid there dazed as the enemy tried to find a way over the green stuff to get to me. I was the reason they were here. I was the focus of their attack. It must have seemed unbelievably close to them right then.

Arrows from the wall mixed with bolts to cut the close enemies off of the lily pad and Milas was leading a charge out into the mass cutting his way to me from the gate. He had a look of fear mixed with determination on his face. I flipped my head from side to side to try and shake it back to normal. I could sense the shifting and pulling of the pad and I could hear the grunts and hollers of the enemy as the lizardmen tried to get to me. I also heard the arrows and bolts whiz past as they struck unerringly into the most dangerous foes. Then my vision cleared and I stood up with difficulty. As I watched, the brave captain took many wounds. He had given up defense entirely to cut a path to me. I needed to act fast before they cut him down. His men were hacking and slashing around him trying to fend off the many attacks but they were still getting through. I felt sheer terror as I watched the carnage. The snarling beasts wanted me dead and they were bent on destroying anything that got in their way. I watched as Milas took hit after hit and I knew that even his strength could not last forever. My mind raced for something to throw that would help, but nothing came to mind. Milas kept coming forward even with a spear running through his thigh. His men had fallen too and he was now alone and cut off in the mass of moving bodies and killing blood frenzy. My panic reached the point of insanity and I pulled power without thought. I pulled from all eight elements at once and I doubled over with the effort. I could feel the elementals' surprise as they collided and joined with each other. They continued to pour in and the demand on my body was immense. I kept pulling, not realizing what it was costing me. Then the moment came when I had no more to pull. My rage took me and I released it all at once. It was like a wave of force stronger than anything I had ever thought of before. Bodies flew away from me like petals from a flower. They flew in all directions and they did not stop until they were quite a distance from me. They hit the ground lifeless and the elements kept burning and freezing them as the winds spread. The lightning brought loud noises and shock to everything and when all was said and done, I was lying in a crater of destruction. My body did not want to move. It was as if I had given all of my strength for this casting and there was no way that I could even try to stand. The soldiers were lying on the bloody plain and the acolytes came out to rescue them. I was brought back inside and from what I saw as I was being carried, the lizardman army was no more. The master had survived this encounter since most of it had been carried to the enemy instead of letting it come into the school itself. We still had casualties, but they were much lighter than last time. He came to me as I lay in recovery. It would be some time before I was ready to travel. Milas had been rescued as well. He would not even accept help until he was told that I still lived. I could not fault his sense of duty, but I worried for him so.

*   *   *

Commander Zarg looked on as the battlefield erupted in flame. He and his small group had watched the entire engagement from a safe distance. They had watched the human's metal box render many of the warriors helpless and then he had personally watched the wizard bring forth what appeared to be a small nuke from his own body. It was most impressive. Such a warrior would have gone far in the Fleet. Still, he was the one that the humans had come for and now they were already together. His planning and scheming and manipulating the resident population of his brothers had failed. They had not eliminated the boy before the future humans arrived. He spat on the ground and the fire in his blood was still there. He was now older than any of his kind had ever been reported. His brother had to be put in suspended animation awaiting this event and now he was still young and fresh. It was a cruel twist of irony that had brought them to this place and not able to fight the prey. He felt the cheating of fate like a knife thrust to the heart. He wanted so terribly to kill those that had taken his glory from him. He would die in this older time and his people would never know of his exploits. He had long ago given up the notion of returning victorious. They had lost. All that was left now was revenge. The past one hundred and ninety years had bent him and made his body frail. He no longer had any teeth and his weary bones were dry and brittle. Even with all of that behind him, he was still dangerous. He had been working on his plans for so long now that many of his kind did not even know that they had been manipulated. His stone ship had been broken down to make his fortress and now the last bits of his technology had been used to fabricate a weapon. He lowered his hand to signal for his troops to load and prep the weapon. The coils on the top of it looked like something from an old sci-fi movie and the main base looked like the turret on an old naval battleship. It was a disruptor of sorts. It was designed to crumble walls and topple buildings. It created seismic activity beneath the structure and broke down the elements of stone. He stepped aside slowly and the group went into fevered activity to comply with his orders. In moments, they were primed and ready. The massive device stood out from the hillside where it had been drawn by a giant lizard and the barrel was pointed at the front wall of the school. The dead still littered the countryside and some of the younger of the humans were out and about seeing what they could take from the fallen. The whole scene disgusted Zarg and his blood rage began to boil as the weapon cycled up. The modulated rumblings below them were only the beginning and a nasty smile crossed his aged face. The weapon built up over the next five minutes and then it sent a pulse into the ground at the base of the wall. The center area of the wall crumbled at the base and then fell in on itself; taking the gate with it. The surrounding walls fell in on top of the rubble and a vast cloud of dust and debris rose to obscure all vision of the damage. The acolytes outside of the wall turned as one as the whole thing came crashing down. The defenses were now down. The weapon began to cycle back up again for another shot. It was like kicking an anthill, the scurrying of frightened humans was like heaven to the gnarled old commander. He would kill them all. The dust had just begun to reveal the fallen wall when the second blast came. A supply building dropped into its own foundation as the power ripped through it without resistance. Zarg laughed hideously as the machine cycled up again. This was the day he had been waiting on for over one hundred and ninety years. He would savor every moment.

* * *

There was a loud rumbling outside and a crashing that seemed to go on forever. Then someone shouted that the wall was breeched. I could not move yet and the acolytes around me left to see what was going on. Frank had come to my side and he told me that they could possibly help me better on the ship. I didn't want to leave the school under attack, but I knew that just now I was useless to them. I couldn't even nod back to him. I blinked my eyes twice and he scooped me up and carried me away. I couldn't even wipe the tear that streaked down my cheek as I heard a second blast shake the very foundations of the school. As Frank carried me to the rear of the school, presumably where the ship had landed and was waiting for us, the elf siblings met up with us and fell into step with him. Milas had even stepped up. He had bandages all over him and they were stained red. He moved slowly, but he was not going to be held back. A third blast hit the school and it felt like the end of the world. I would have mentioned it if speech was coming more easily. Instead I just bobbed with the rhythm of Frank's gait and hoped that we would escape in time. As it turned out, it was a close thing. The main building crumbled in on itself as we reached the entrance ramp to the ship. The debris was coming as the hatch closed and cut us off from the scene. Frank yelled "Now!" and the ship lurched up into the air. The source of the attack was readily apparent from the air. A small group of lizardmen was operating a strange piece of equipment and a blast from something called a laser cannon stopped the weapon from firing again. One pass over the area told me that the school was gone. There weren't even any support buildings anymore. It was so sad.

I was brought to a room with white lights and tables in it with white parchment on top. They laid me on one of them and started checking things around me. Someone held my wrist and looked at their own wrist at the same time. Someone else put a thing on my arm that tightened until it was painful and then loosened up again. They were all moving quickly and efficiently and I could do nothing but watch them. They stuck something sharp in my arm and fastened a tube there. There was a bag hanging above it and they told me that it would help to make me stronger again. I didn't know how a bag could do that, but I certainly felt weak enough to try anything.

Maxillen and Florena were ushered into a small room and told to strap into the seats. It was their first time on board a ship as well and everything was so unlike their forest. There was metal everywhere. The air smelled wrong somehow. The feeling of grass was a distant memory now. They had their duty and they would stay, but they didn't have to like it. Fear nagged at the back of their minds as they braced for something they could not understand. It was most unnerving.

The ship continued its ascent. It left the confines of the world that I only understood a tiny part of and left for the stars. These were things that I knew practically nothing of. So as I lie on a table inside the metal box of a ship, the ship began to race towards the sun. The speed kept building up and when they slingshot around the sun, then the ship ceased to exist in the time that I knew and we were on our way to destiny, whatever that was.

*   *   *

FULFILLING A PROPHECY

The loss of the weapon on the hillside began to drive Commander Zarg insane. He no longer had the parts to make another one. He called upon his brothers in the various lizardman clans and his focus was on the human civilization. He figured that if he destroyed them all now, then they could not have birthed the crew that had come back to retrieve the wizard. If they never existed, then the whole mission would never have happened. They did not know who was important to remove. They only knew that all humans were now targeted for extinction. Zarg appointed his brother as general and together they plotted the end of the human race. The recent battles told him that his people were not ready to face the vast numbers of the human menace, so he crafted his plan to take his people back out into space. They would work hard and build their empire. They would make great stone ships and come back to this puny world and destroy it. The glory that he had thought so far gone was now in his mind again. His aged body could not follow through, but he would leave a legacy behind. His name would not be forgotten and the humans would still pay. The elf woman had come to him in his ship and foiled his plans and for that they would all pay. Before they could leave, he needed to remove the elder races from the world so that they could not help the humans prepare for his people's arrival. His blood rage needed satiating and the rubble below would provide him some small amount of slaughter. So, with his creaky bones and all, he started limping down the hill with his people in tow. They lifted their weapons and shouted the battle cry that he no longer had wind for. He barreled into the carnage he had caused and the rage took him completely. The defenders were sparse and his rage flamed on at the lack of victims. He went from area to area looking for more. He met up with a human that looked at him with disgust. He lunged forward only to strike a solid block of nothing. His rage made him even crazier and he slammed against the unseen force again and again. His frail body was breaking and he knew deep inside that this would be his last fight. The shaft took him squarely in the chest and his blood rage died out in those final moments and he received total clarity. He looked down at the spear. It was one of his people's spears. It had been lost in the earlier fighting and now was being used to end his life. The irony struck him as funny and as he fell to his knees which broke on impact with the stone floor, he laughed, low and guttural. The spear twisted and tore his insides and as it pulled free, his guts spilled out onto that stone floor and he watched it in fascination as he wavered back and forth. Then he fell forward dead. One last twitch and then Commander Zarg was no more.

That did not end the total fight though. The lizardmen were fueled by their rage and they were not all as aged and fragile as their leader had been. They slaughtered the humans at the former school to the last individual and then they searched the surrounding countryside for more. There were blood parties and feasts after that and the pitch fires burned into the night as they camped upon the wreckage of their victory. Zarg's brother knew that the commander was dead. They were twins and the link had been severed during the fighting. He knew that his mentor in Fleet and his sibling had died with honor. It was a true warrior's death and he only hoped that he met oblivion with as much conviction. He sighed heavily as he considered the future. The hunt was now lost. The prey had eluded them permanently and now they needed to decide what to do next. Zarg had mumbled something about heading back to space. The thought actually deserved consideration. The technology and stone bending could still be used and they could train these lizardmen here to do it easily enough. If they could colonize someplace else, they could come back and destroy this planet and stop the future from happening once and for all. He made the final decision to attempt this plan. He would need help, and lots of it, but he had all the time in the world to do it. There had been some other talk about elves, but he was no longer interested in that. He would take his new people out into space and they would prepare. It was the way of the warrior. Training was the most important thing. He felt the warmth of a good plan reaching fruition and he started thinking about how to pitch it to the locals so that they could pull off this massive task. He was pretty sure that none of them could stand before one of his arguments but you always prepared for resistance and then crushed it to accomplish your goals. It was also their way and he knew more than most what would happen if they faltered now. He had lost his brother and he had lost his ship and his family in the future. They had come back here on this fool's errand and now they were stuck. Time travel forward was trickier than back and he wasn't even sure they could do it. He was not versed in the theory of it all anyway. In fact, no one alive was. He closed the door on that line of thinking. He had to live in the now and make of it what he could. His resolve was solidified in that comforting thought and he actually smiled at the others as they celebrated by the massive fires. It was rustic and good to be among his own people in their natural state. The years in Fleet had not dulled his battle frenzy and now he felt the celebration around him as a cleansing thing. He would take these people to the stars and he would make them ready to face these humans again. He vowed to his brother's corpse as he grabbed a tankard and drank the blood of the victims that was passing around the rowdy group. "Today we celebrate, tomorrow we train!" He shouted and the tankards all rose to him as the warriors shouted in unison. "We train!" It was almost a religious experience for him and he bathed himself in the camaraderie and prepared his mind for the trouble to come.

*　*　*

When word finally reached King's Field about the loss of the school, the people rose up and demanded action from the king. He had done nothing to defend them even after the earlier reports that something was wrong there. This was even after his failure to respond to the goblin threat at the ferryman village and the people had seen enough. They stormed the castle and took him bodily out and hung him before the masses. He swung in the breeze in death as the onlookers spat at him. The seers all bowed their heads. They did not know how, but twins had taken away his rule. The prophecy had been fulfilled even though none of them knew it. They just put it up to mystery and continued on with their lives. The humans spread and multiplied until the lands were fully populated and then they branched out into other landmasses. The Fleets of sailing ships allowed people to spread and become more diverse. Languages were developed apart from each other and cultures were born. A shining era of mankind was birthed and they were blissfully unaware of the enemies that had taken to the stars to await them.

*　*　*

DECIDING ON A PLAN

The *Lost Cavalier* moved through time as the occupants discussed and argued about just where they should go. I had made a full recovery and Milas was mending better than anyone had expected. His wounds would have killed a lesser man. I had not underestimated him this time. I knew that he would not give up. At least he would not if he knew that I still needed protecting. There were many questions for the elf twins and they were otherwise treated like royal guests on board the metal ship. The argument had become more and more heated as the two sides solidified their positions. I watched as an outsider. This seemed strange to me since they had come to get me and have me help them. Now they were too interested in themselves to receive that help.

The viewpoints were pretty straightforward. One group wanted to go back to the point in time where the Fleet first met the lizardman force and direct them away from the threat and thus prevent the war that ensued and destroyed almost the entire race. This seemed like a pretty good plan to me if they knew exactly where and when the human ships first contacted the Lizzies. I doubted very much that the first contacts ever survived to report it so that simple fact was in doubt. The other viewpoint was a bit more complex. They wanted to take the ship back to when the Fleet was being first built and introduce new weaponry and stealth systems to allow the human Fleet to fight off the aggressors when they did eventually meet up with them. Of course that particular route required nothing of me so I am not sure why they had come back at all to get me if that was what they had planned to do. There was a third option that none of them was taking seriously. It had been proposed by Frank. He wanted to go to that first known colony destruction and attack and destroy the lizardman ships before it had been completed. That would save the most lives in our initial action. We would then be able to rejoin an almost intact Fleet and thus lead the fight personally to hopefully stop the eventual destruction of the world.

Oh, I also noticed that they call the world Earth. It was not a term that I had heard before, but there you have it. Languages being what they are, it was truly amazing that anyone could speak to each other. The current speaker was going on about how the Fleet could still be defeated even if we try to help them. If we were destroyed in one of these battles, then the whole plan would still fail. It was just not sure enough. To some extent I agreed with him. I sat back and watched this process, growing a little bit impatient as the same points were brought up over and over again. Really both plans were flawed. I could see holes in them as if they had not been thought through. I hadn't realized that all of the plans had so far been aimed at retrieving me. Now that this part of the plan had succeeded, they were unsure where to go from there. I noticed right off that all of the plans were military in nature. Perhaps they could not think of anything but war. I would make my suggestion when they used up all their steam. It was interesting to me how each of these people had the same goal and no one agreed on how to go about it. The other quiet person in the room was Captain Glass. He sat back and watched as the debate raged on. His inactivity confused me. I wanted to ask him why it was so but I felt that questioning the man who had come for me was not such a good idea. The talking went on for quite a while and new points stopped emerging. They were just rehashing old ones now. Somehow the Captain had also recognized this and he stood up, silencing the room.

"Okay people, I had opened up the floor to debate to get new views of the same problem we have been facing since this mission began. The arguments were the same ones I have been fighting in my head since the beginning." All of the previous speakers sat down and gave their attention to the leader of this ship. They at least showed that much respect. "What we have seen here is that we are still just one small ship. Yes we could possibly change the outcome of the war by helping Fleet prepare for the anti-electronic warfare required to defeat the stone ships. It is also possible that the Lizzies could react to it and still destroy the world. Therefore, that plan is not sure enough to take our one chance on." He said and the silent room felt the tension of the moment. When the Captain spoke again, his exhaustion was evident in his tone. "Furthermore, the plan to stop the first contact from happening is fraught with peril. Even if we succeed in finding the exact time and place that the first ships were attacked and steer them away from their projected course, who's to say that humanity wouldn't stumble across the enemy in some other location and then history would repeat itself to the same catastrophic conclusion." He sat down. The weight of the choices had been weighing heavily upon him for some time now and he was at least partially relieved to have an audience to share it with. "Finally, the plan to stop the first colony from being destroyed has a couple of flaws in it as well. What happens if the force that does the deed overwhelms us as we are only one small ship? If we tried to get some of the other members of Fleet to follow us to defend a base that had not been attacked yet, they would wonder how we knew it was going to be attacked. We would be considered suspects in one of the most heinous crimes in Fleet. We would be incarcerated and of no use when the attack came and destroyed the colony. Then history would humbly repeat itself again. No, these plans will not work. They are at least uncertain and at worst ineffective. We have gone to a lot of trouble to bring this individual here and I think we need to find a way to utilize his unique skills to accomplish our goal." He said indicating me. I stood up and leaned on the massive table that was the centerpiece of the room.

"You all know better than I what problem you face. I have not seen what happened and I know that my background would prevent me from understanding completely what was lost if I did see it." I said and they all nodded or fidgeted one way or another. "Still, what I see is a bunch of soldiers trying to solve a problem that a politician should be addressing." I said and eyebrows rose around the table. "You seem to have decided that a military response is all that will work. Have you tried talking to these lizardmen from your time? I know a little about them from my time. They are warlike and determined. Once they are in the blood rage they will fight until they are killed. I have witnessed this myself and I actually struck one down once personally. It was one of the most terrifying things that I have ever done." The group seemed to appreciate that last statement as well as I'd hoped. "What I see is that we need to contact them before this war happens and negotiate a peace before the war breaks out. My skills may not be the best thing for you here, but at least it has the highest chance of success that I can see." I said, hoping that no one would find holes in the plan. I couldn't see any, but that meant nothing. My plan was more driven by hope than actual thought and evaluations. It was obvious around the room that it had never been considered. Perhaps they did not understand their enemy as much as they thought they did.

The Captain looked ahead as if he was calculating something and his eyes were unfocused. The rest of the people were taking notes and thinking about possibilities. I was glad that they even considered my approach. We were still moving forward through time so a decision needed to be made before too long. There would be other calculations to make and I understood none of the math involved. I would have to trust the people that did on that count. The quiet around the room seemed like a good sign to me. At least they were working on the same plan instead of fighting over several. The Captain returned to the room mentally and he smiled.

"I think you may have something there." He said to me and the others around the table looked up from their notepads. "What I see from this new angle is a good chance to prevent most of the major catastrophes and maybe, just maybe a way to survive all of this to return home." He said and he drummed his fingers on the table. In the quiet room, it sounded really pronounced. "We need to start researching first contact and then find a target time to emerge in. We have a running clock on the bridge that gives us our best guess on our current time outside. It is the result of a brilliant computer projection from our trip back. Still, we have much to do. I want our best minds working on what we need to say and do and who we need to talk to. We will find the Lizzies before the war and we shall beseech them to sue for peace with us." He said with finality. When he stood up again his step had a bounce to it. The weight of authority was not pulling him down so badly. He had purpose again. He smiled at me in a way that told me he was pleased. I sat back down and watched as the people filed out of the room. They were presumably heading out to get to work on the problem. It was the first forward thing that I had seen since coming on board this ship. I was glad that Milas had not been in here during all of this discussion. He would have cuffed at least one of them and shouted a lot. He did not have the patience for that sort of thing. He was a man of action. In some ways I envied him. He was never uncertain about what to do next. He was steadfast in his honor and resolve. He was a pillar of strength and you could rely on him totally. In fact I already had more than once. I saw some of the same features in this Frank from the future. He had the same sense of honor and I could see that his strength of will was as strong as Milas' physical strength. I wondered briefly if he even knew his own potential. Most people never realized their own strengths until they were tested.

The Captain was still standing there. The others had gone and now he looked at me. "You really helped us get out of that there." He said truthfully. I already knew that of course but it was nice to be recognized for it. "We have a long way to go to save our homes and families. I will need you to stay focused on this problem and this problem alone. Once this is over and we have saved the world and the race, then we can deposit you to any time and place you want to be." He said, offering me something I could not truly understand.

"I do not know about other times and places. I was a student of elemental magic. My place is with humanity on the world I was born to. I must serve in order to justify my skills and studies. The price of power is always responsibility. I have already failed to save the school that gave me these skills. I must not fail here or all is lost. Beyond that, I can see no future. Everything is now. Everything is here. All else is a fabrication or a dream. Once here and now have been fixed, then we can explore what comes next." I said and I really felt it in my heart. It was as if I was explaining my soul to myself with him in earshot. It felt good to finally understand it all and he seemed surprised and impressed with my thoughts. We had a plan and now we were moving towards it. The next few weeks would determine the fate of more people than I could even imagine.

* * *

Grand Commander Phylus had spent years of his life building and growing the lizardman community in the stars. He held the focus of his people on war and survival. The humans that had forced them to leave would eventually pay. They would eventually reach the faithful warriors and his people would be ready to take them all out. The roles would be reversed and the true power would fall to the lizardmen that commanded the Fleet. Vast stone ships were constructed and amassed. His original intentions had been to raise this Fleet and return to Earth and destroy the humans there. He had long ago given up that dream. Instead he awaited their intrusion into space. He would crush them on his turf. They would not even know what had hit them. He sat atop his throne and he held up an aged hand. His scales were dry and his muscles shook. He was nearing his end and he was holding on simply to see the final battle begin. He had directed his people from that first ship and now they were colonizing worlds in many systems. The great stone ships were not bothered by distances. They could continue moving forth forever if the warriors inside continued to flourish and multiply. Then a new colony would be born when they arrived on a suitable planet. He had left books of rules and words of wisdom for his people. He was trying to protect them from the human infestation. The only problem was that his own faculties were pretty much gone by the time he decided to document things. It was really just a bunch of nonsense and nobody had the gumption to openly tell him that he was in error. Instead, a religion was based upon it and the rituals he had written down became rites of passage and tests of valor. The funny thing about it was that his legacy was the very violent people that had caused him to come back in time in the first place. His brother would have been proud by just how far he had managed to produce the society that they had both dreamed of. His brother had died in the past. He had to live as long as he could to see as much of the future as he could. The years were too much for him though. He could never again see the life that he had once known in the Fleet. He was in control of it but his body was old and frail now. He was no longer the warrior he once was. The race tolerated him for his expertise. He scoffed at that. He had no extra knowledge anymore. He had given all that he knew back to his people. The manipulation of stone and the secrets of the black hole were now common knowledge among his people. He had brought this information from that distant future. Now he had given his people a chance to make that other reality theirs. It was the greatest gift he could give. The religion was spreading and the symbols were being painted and carved in every corner of their new space-bound society. His power was fleeing him as his own life force began to fade. He had left a legacy that no one else could touch. His path in history was assured and now his people would become strong and rule the galaxy. He died upon his throne with a smile on his face. His life's work was completed.

The people held vigils and sermons for him and his passing. The names of the crew of that original ship from the future were now hailed as heroes. They were the god-like warriors that had seeded this culture and allowed the people to leave the hostile world and start anew. Shrines were erected and branches of the religion spread throughout the colonies. The scriptures of nonsensical writing were interpreted and reinterpreted and before anyone knew what was happening, the entire race became a massive cult. The bloodlust would serve the people well as they swept across the galaxy destroying the weak and taking what they wanted from the fallen prey. An era of terror began. Each conquest fueled the war machine further and built up the forces. The Fleet of stone ships was now numbered in the hundreds and the command structure allowed for the expansion of the people. The society was still linked to the guiding principals from the religious upbringing of each member. The bloodlust became the call sign of the faithful. The search for conquest and glory became the main driving force behind the entire species. Thousands of years passed and the faithful blanketed most of the cosmos with blood. It was this point in time that the *Lost Cavalier* returned to normal space.

* * *

Captain Glass sat in the command chair. He was worried about the selections that his experts had come up with. Of course they really had no choice now. They were fully committed to this plan. The tiny ship careened through the cosmos as it sped away from the unsuspecting Earth. The enemy was out there. The best calculations told them that the enemy was out there in at least some measure of force. The first colony destruction would occur in about three years' time. That meant that the human expansionism had placed them at least close to the enemy borders. So it was to this farthest reach of humanity that they were headed. They wanted to make contact in a non-violent manner and then be brought to the leadership of the enemy force. It was a long shot they all admitted. The tension on the bridge held a twinge of hope to it. They needed that little spark of a chance. The whole situation seemed hopeless without it. He eyed the read-outs and they all looked green. The ship was doing well considering what it had been through. If they succeeded, it would probably be decommissioned. It was way beyond typical repair. He pushed that thought away. The loss of a ship was a personal thing to any captain. Frank had a front row seat on the bridge. This had been his mission from the beginning. Christopher had somehow been added to the crew and now he was seated in the station next to Frank. It was an observational role only. Neither of the two men had the skills to warrant being on the bridge. Their specialties were a bit off-center for the day to day operations of this small ship. Still, they were important to the current plan and the final add on to the bridge was me. I stood next to the lift where I was told to go when the trouble started. I hoped that we would not need such precautions, but the whole mission was decidedly dangerous. We were going to head directly into the path of trouble. If they shot on sight, we may not survive the next few days. We would be reaching the frontier in about two days time and beyond that no one could guess what our life expectancy was. The sigh the captain let out pretty much summed up the whole feeling on board the ship. They had come so far to be in this situation. Everyone had been so high-strung for so long they were all exhausted. I felt the weight of the situation upon my shoulders. Their hopes all seemed to ride with me. The burden was immense and I was not all that sure that I could even help. I wanted to help, but how much can a young man do against an army of lizardmen with advanced technology? I only hoped that we would succeed and save the world that I wanted to get back to. Nothing else really mattered.

A voice cut through the tension and silence that had fallen like a blanket over the bridge crew. "Sir, we have a radar contact." The tactical officer said clearly and the lack of tension in that professional voice seemed to calm the rest of the crew. The Captain looked at his board and noted the red dot that highlighted on the very edge of it. The ship was sailing in a straight line towards destiny and now this contact seemed to be pulling to the side a bit. It was a pretty sure bet that they could see us. We waited a few more seconds as the captain thought about the possibilities. Then he surprised us all.

"Cut the power down a third and bring us on heading to meet with them." He said. The crimson icon seemed to hold everyone's attention as we sailed in closer and closer to the enemy ship. As we got closer, more information was coming in from our sensors on just what we were seeing here. It was one of the stone ships. There was no power signature that we could see. There was a huge gravity pulse in the center of it and we slowed down even more as it came for us at a normal pace. We were not showing signs of panic and it obviously confused the other commander. Whoever it was came in for a closer look at us. We were left with nothing but our thoughts as the two ships closed for the next thirty minutes.

* * *

The battleship Procion cruised in its normal patrol pattern when a disturbance in its sensor grid brought the attention of the faithful to the intruding pit on the stone display. The sensor grid was like a spider's web centered on the patrol coordinates and spreading out in all directions. Its commander looked at the new dot as an opportunity for glory. It was the common orders from the grand leader and his own sect of the faithful. He watched closely as the prey slowed down and veered towards him. It was the most unusual behavior for a doomed enemy that he had ever seen. The whole idea of something new intrigued him and he maintained his speed and adjusted course for an intercept. If they wanted to play games, he would play and see what this game was about. He had his crew ready to launch though. He would not be caught unawares. His crew watched him for the signs. The bloodlust was held in check but only barely so. It was a near enough thing for him and it was exactly what they were looking for. He checked his own emotions for a moment and checked the records for this metal box before him. It was somehow familiar. He had seen it before. He wracked his brain for the reference. He was still working on it when he heard a gasp from a member of his crew. He looked down at them and he saw a warrior clutching his chest. His eyes were open wide and disbelief seemed to be written plainly on his face.

He snapped back to attention. "Sssorry commander, but that ship, I've seen it before." He said and the commander looked at him closely. "Sssir it is the human ship from the writings." He said and commander Grawl started. Could it be? The ship of prophecy was here? It was supposed to have traveled through time to the distant past. It was the reason they were out here in space. This ship had changed their barbaric race into the faithful they were now. He wasn't sure what to do about it now. He could blow it out of the sky and be rid of it, but he wanted to know more. There were so many questions in the faith. There were so many cryptic lines that made no sense. The humans aboard that metal box could be the ones spoken of in the writings and if so they would have valuable answers for the faithful. The prospect was awfully enticing. They needed to take this metal box for their own and learn its secrets. With the answers to who they were and why there were here, he could return to the Fleet victorious on a front other than was the norm. He could become an icon himself. If they could capture this ship, then maybe he could take his rightful position among the elite of the lizardman society. His family would be taken care of forever and his name would appear on schools and statues throughout the colonies. The banners and ticker tape parades passed before his eyes as he tried to picture it all. The feeling of warmth caressed him and he realized that in order to realize that lofty goal, he needed to act now.

"We need to take thisss ship for our own. The humansss on board mussst be captured alive." He said in an uncharacteristic statement that took the crew by surprise. "If thisss truly isss the ship from ssscripture, then we need to proceed very carefully. They may have answersss that we need. Control yoursssselves now and we shall reap the glory of disssscovery for all of our kind." He said and with that one statement, all of his people were on board with the new concept, for glory was the goal of every warrior since time began. "Bring usss up next to them. I believe that their intentions are not hossstile or they would be readying weapons for us. We show no sssuch activity. They will want to meet with usss. I do not know how I know thisss, but I do. I will have my sssecond with me and we shall take the ship for the glory of our sssect. Thisss will be a great day for usss and it will change the courssse of history for both of our peoplesss." He proclaimed and he stood up at the last statement to change into his best armor. The ceremonial garb of the true warrior was just as effective as its menial counterpart, but much more ornate. He would look the professional warrior when he met these travelers from both past and future. The rendezvous would take a few more minutes. He opened the stone hatch and looked out at the metal box still quite a ways off. It would not be long now, his destiny waits.

*　*　*

The stone ship slowed as the *Cavalier* slowed. It looked exactly like what they wanted. The ship was slowing for a meeting. They would end up side by side on their current courses and rates of deceleration. The crew could not believe their luck. They had no contact with these people and yet no shots were being fired. This was the first really good sign that there was a chance for success that they had seen. If these people were reasonable, then maybe the whole mission would save the human race and the Earth would not have to be demolished. Frank had already gone below to get his team ready for first contact. I was with him and so was Christopher. We had no skills in the vacuum of space. I had not known that such a thing even existed. The ultimate cold and darkness sounded like a version of hell to me. The lack of air simply sealed the image for me. The fact that humans had progressed far enough to venture out into the stars still had me amazed. Yet, the proof was right before me. We were out among the stars now. They were not a curtain covering our world as I had been told. They were actually so far away that I would never see one close up. Casey had told me that I would have died if I had gotten anywhere close to one of those stars. They were not diamonds as I had known. They were something called hydrogen gas. They were actually on fire. The fires of perdition I imagined. It all seemed so fantastic to me. Now though, the focus was not on those celestial bodies. It was on the stone ship that had nestled up against the *Lost Cavalier*. We were all geared up and when the hatch opened, we could see the lizardman warrior on the far side. He had stood before an open door with no special suit. I do not know how he was breathing. He leaped forward and his course sent him straight at us. I stood back as Casey operated a long stick to hook the warrior and bring him into the hatch. A second warrior, not so grandly dressed, took the leap as well. We finished bringing in the first visitor and then snagged the second one. Once they were securely in, we closed the hatch and the automatic system brought the air pressure up to normal for this compartment. When the telltale lights turned green, Casey hit the button that opened the inner hatch. Once inside, we took off the helmets and I watched as the two warriors seemed to size us up. It was not the most comfortable of situations and it did not last. Frank bowed his head to the lead warrior and thanked them for coming over and asked what it is they wanted. There was a long pause. We were not sure why. The silence spread out for even longer as we wondered if we were understood. Then the warrior spoke to us.

"I am the commander of the great vessel over there. I have come to your metal box to find out who you are and why you are in our ssspace." He said clearly enough for lizardman talk. Frank was about to respond when I pulled on his shoulder. He backed away and fell silent.

"I am the last wizard of Earth. We have come a long way to find you and your people. We must ask you not to fight our kind. We are not the enemy of your kind. We are important to the survival of both of our species." I said, laying it on just a bit thick perhaps, but he had not attacked us so far. I was willing to run with that as a good sign.

"You asssk for peace?" He asked; the concept seemed a bit strange. "What kind of warrior ssseeks anything other than conquessst?" He asked, I could tell that he was getting disturbed by this conversation.

"I seek peace; that is true. But I do not seek peace out of weakness. I seek peace out of honor for you and your kind. We both will fight and die for a disturbance that we do not even understand. If we unite, there are no problems that we cannot overcome. It is a stronger alliance that we seek." I added. I hoped that he understood this concept as well. All of my dealings with them told me that he wouldn't. They were a clan oriented people, but they did not unite or they would have been more dangerous even way back then.

He seemed to think about the concept rather than just dismiss it out of hand. I again took it as a good sign. What he said next worried me though. "Ssso what do you offer to this alliance?" He asked. "We offer the force of will and ssstrength of courage to the union." I could tell that he wanted me to boast of something, but I could not think of anything right off the bat. Christopher stepped up in my moment of need.

"We offer knowledge of faith." He blurted out and the commander looked at him in surprise. He was obviously agitated, but he held his bloodlust in check. It was the first time I had ever seen a lizardman do so.

"We are the faithful. We have the knowledge of will and power from the old writingsss. You are in our writingsss and it is thisss that has sssaved

241

your puny lives ssso far. If you have any real knowledge of our beginnings, then we can dissscusss our plans for alliance. If you are being falssse, then I shall rend you limb from limb myssself." He said and there was no sign of humor in his tone.

Christopher drew back reflexively. I took the lead on the conversation so that we did not show too much weakness. "We offer faith of a different kind. We offer a recounting of history and we offer our beliefs unto you." I said, hoping it would be enough. It wasn't.

The commander drew in a huge breath. He was trying to calm himself. He had something else he wanted to discuss. "We need the knowledge of our own beginningsss. Do you have thisss information?" He asked directly. I began to draw the elementals of the air to me. I also pulled in some of the shock ones as well for good measure. The spell was in my mind and the power accumulated quickly.

"I don't know if we have what you are looking for specifically. We do have a bit of information about how some of you followed this ship back through time. Much more than that, I'm not sure what we can offer you." I said and the commander gave in to his blood frenzy. He growled and then shouted a battle cry that raised the hairs on my neck as he dove forward. I released the energy and the air between us solidified. He hit it like a wall and bounced backward off balance. I swept my arms forward and pulled the shocking power of lightning into the wave that swept over him and his metal armor. It had a secondary effect that I was unaware of. The power in the ship died and the lights went out. We were plunged into absolute darkness and a scuffle ensued. There were cries of pain and clanking metal. I kept the wall before me and waited for the power to be restored. The lights flickered and then came on again. The commander and his second were dead. A crewman had been impaled by a long metal spike that pinned him to the wall. He was dead as well. Christopher looked at me. He was bleeding on the shoulder but it was certain that he had killed both of the lizardmen. My opinion of him raised a few notches. He had learned blind fighting and he had killed two overpowering foes. It also meant that the situation outside was going to get more complicated. We had a powerful warship outside our closed hatch and two dead lizardmen in our corridor. I needed to do some serious damage control and fast.

I ran up to the bridge. We needed to tell the ship that two of their warriors were down. It was not going to be easy. I was out of breath when I darted through the hatch and onto the bridge. My quick entry made everyone turn to me and the Captain looked at me with horror on his face. "What have you done?" He asked in shock and amazement.

"The boarders are dead. They attacked us after a short amount of parlay and we need to inform the ship out there of their demise." I said and I tried to look confident even though inside I was shaking like a leaf. "Let me talk to them if you have the means." I beseeched him. He thought about it for a moment or two and then he sighed. They had come this far, might as well go all the way.

"Open a channel to the enemy ship and see if he can salvage this disaster." He said wearily. I could tell that there would be a lot of discussion over this mission when the crisis got over. That is, if the crisis got over.

The channel opened and the image of the stone ship outside changed to a group of lizardmen at various stone stations on their sparse bridge. The one sitting in the command chair spot was nervous and his people around him looked like a lynch mob. He would not be in charge for long. I looked at him and gave him a nod. He stood up and hissed at me. I held up a hand to forestall whatever he was about to say. "You are now in command of that vessel permanently." I said without preamble. "Your previous commander is dead and so is the other that was with him. He attacked us on board and was neutralized." I said, trying to hold a stone face as the lizardman seemed to shake in terror before me. He shrunk a bit in the eyes of his peers. I knew that he would not last a day in that chair. "We grieve for your loss. However, they died like warriors. They were simply overmatched." I said and there were grunts of satisfaction just out of camera. I heard them none the less. "I suggest that we meet in a more neutral place to discuss an end to the hostilities of our peoples. I know from your last commander that you understand the special nature of our ship and crew. I would therefore advise that you harm none of us. The consequences to your own existence would be severe. I am the last wizard of Earth. I will not tolerate disrespect or disobedience." I said. I hoped that it wasn't laying it on too thick. The response from the other ship was promising though. I did notice that the captain remained completely silent throughout the exchange. "What place would you like to meet?" I asked, placing the burden of location solely on this quivering mass that should not be called a warrior. I felt more composed than he looked, and that was not saying very much.

"You can meet with usss on the groundsss of our forefathersss." He replied and his crew all turned to see what he was up to. He was smiling at them. He knew something that I didn't. It made me nervous. I tried my best not to let it show. I didn't want him to get all devious on me. I wanted to maintain the upper hand. He had lost his chain of command and was obviously out of his league in communications with aliens.

"Very well, lead the way and you must ensure us that we will not be attacked en-route to these grounds of your forefathers." I said trying to placate the Captain and hopefully show that we were willing to follow them if assured. It was a leap of faith perhaps, but not so much of one that we couldn't turn tail and run if we had to.

The new commander looked even more worried now. Perhaps he had planned some sort of ambush for us. It was difficult to tell. "I – I promissse you that we will not attack you during your travelsss." He said a little too carefully. I was unconvinced.

"That is not what I asked you for. I told you we need your word that we will not be attacked. You must keep other ships from attacking us as well to make this promise." I prompted and he fidgeted even more. I knew for a fact that he was up to something now. His crew was looking more agitated too. I didn't know if it was with him or with me. Either way, I no longer trusted them enough to follow this ship anywhere. "Okay what I am seeing here is that you are unable or unwilling to commit to our safety, so I will not recommend that we follow you. You must meet here or not at all." I said keeping a firm stance. The moment was a dangerous one and I hoped it would end alright. I tried to push just a little bit more. "You will meet with us here and now and we will discuss the situation. I understand that you seek answers to questions that we may have a chance of answering. I am willing to hear those questions when we meet. You will kindly meet us here on this ship. I will make arrangements to see that you are kept comfortable and protected. No harm shall befall you here if you behave. It is the same offer we gave to your commander but he had to attack us.

There was a scoff on the other end of the line. The commander's grip on his crew was loosening. He was about to lose control and then I would have to start again with another warrior who just might not listen. I had to keep him talking. I just didn't want to look desperate as I did it. "You must tell me that this is acceptable or I will terminate communications with you now and this ship will destroy your vessel." I said in a brash and militaristic tone. It was something that I found difficult, but I managed to sound at least partially convincing since there was now a gasp on our bridge. I ignored it but the lizardman caught it. He looked decidedly nervous.

"You mussst not desssstroy usss. We are membersss of the great Fleet of the faithful. Our membership in the grand sector isss only a sssmall sssign of our importance. We would be avenged if we were attacked." He replied shakily. I could not tell if it was a bluff or not, but I had more than a suspicion that it was. It was probably more truthful that he was not liked among his own Fleet and that there were commanders out there that would pay to see his demise at my hands. I hoped to scare him into complying, not to actually destroy that ship. It was quite possible that the *Cavalier* was not up to it anyway. I had powers out here, I didn't know how many or how strong, but I knew that I had them. I could feel the elementals just out of sight waiting for a brief chance to reveal themselves to me. They wanted to be used. This was something new to me and I was not sure how to handle it. I stayed with the straight and narrow path and hoped for the best. "I will show you that we mean business. I will send your ship away but you will not be harmed this time." I said and I pulled my arms up to control the elementals around the enemy ship. They had been summoned and now they were ready to do my bidding. The center of the enemy ship was a huge amount of graviton elementals. I caused them to push the stone away from the *Cavalier*. The force was small at first as the elementals tested their strength. But as I watched, they accelerated away and soon they could not be seen. The stone ship was moving away at high speed and the connection broke off as the range increased even further. The threat from them was no longer immediate.

*   *   *

Aboard the lizard ship, the new commander looked around as the stars spun by on his viewer. They were moving, everyone on board could feel that. The human had somehow caused the whole ship to move. It was some form of magic that they did not understand. In fact, they knew some of it. Their own technology was based on manipulating parts of nature. The black hole at the center of their ship was an attest to that control. This was part of their nature and thus this spell seemed so much more powerful to them. The ship did not answer the call of the navigators at it should until they were sufficiently away to allow the influence of the one human to fade. This human ship had to be the one from the scriptures. This human wizard must be the one in the oldest writings. It was an amazing thing to find this ship after so many years. The crew that had been about to revolt forgot their struggles and all feared this new wizard. The black hole in the center of their ship finally started responding to their commands. The ship was spiraling away from the metal box and they needed to get back in order to have the meeting this wizard had commanded.

"Concentrate you Worthless Scum!" The commander shouted. The ship did operate on thought waves after all. "We need to get back before he dessstroysss usss all." He cried out and his crew agreed with his assessment of the human's power. They all settled down and began to wrest control of their ship back from my spell. They managed to stop its acceleration and started it slowing down. The power returned to them slowly and they headed around and back the way they had come. There was more than one sigh of relief to finally see that the human's metal box was still there waiting for them when they got back.

I was still standing on the bridge with the communications line open. When they returned to range, the image of an overtaxed crew met my eyes. They were still fighting the spell. I held up my hands. "The spell is lifted." I said and the pull on the ship ended. "Bring it back alongside us and we will have that talk. I will hear no more of your unrest within your crew. You must command them or you are not worthy of my time. Hurry up and get over here before I lose my patience." I commanded and then I signaled for the operator to cut the line. The screen went back to the view outside the ship. The stone ship was farther away now than it was before but still closing. I let my shoulders slump down and released a heavy sigh.

The captain looked at me with daggers. "What do you think you are doing?" He asked in a voice that cracked with tension. "You threaten and posture to a group of people that can destroy all of our settlements and Fleets? Are you insane?" He bellowed at me. I held up a hand to try to stop his rant. It failed miserably. He was not going to be put off now that he had gotten started. "You are a guest on my ship! We spent a lot of time and trouble finding you and you engage the enemy with rhetoric and threats." His face began to turn red. The bridge crew was startled as well. Something did not seem right here.

"Why don't we take this conversation to a quieter room?" I asked reasonably. He stood up quickly, like a tiger about to strike. Then he stomped off and I hurried to keep up. His hands were balled into fists as he strode purposefully down the corridor to that same briefing room. Once the door sealed behind us, he let it all loose.

"You have violated so many protocols that I could have you killed for treason against the whole species. You know what we are up against. You know what they can do and yet you provoke them and bait them into the kind of slaughter we are trying so desperately to avoid. Need I remind you we only have one shot at this?" He could have gone longer, but I made eye contact and the temperature in the room elevated quickly to uncomfortable levels. He was much older than me and supposedly wiser, but now he had angered me as well. The only difference was that power answered my will.

"You will sit down and listen to me. The situation is more complex than your original plan allowed for. The lizardman army you are fighting, or were fighting in the future, whatever, are the descendants of the one that I grew up knowing. I can see now that they are actually the descendants of the ones that followed you back through time. That is how they left for the stars when the world did not know about such things yet. Furthermore, the tales of this ship and probably me have been passed on from generation to generation and has become some sort of religion for them. In essence we are the reason that they are out in space. We are the cause of their aggression against all humans. This ship created the history it was trying to avoid." I realized just what I was saying and even so it sounded right. I stopped talking with that realization. I could tell by the look on Captain Glass's face that he was just as stunned as I was. The first and foremost feeling that I got was that in order for the problem to have existed in the future, they had to have come back to the past. Now that we were in a different time altogether, we had to somehow break the loop that they had started. The concept was beyond my simple reasoning. At least, I hoped it was. The responsibility that comes with that much knowledge is tremendous. I sat down and stared at the man as his mind turned over the problem.

He seemed ready to speak and he swallowed and paused again. He seemed to be more troubled than confused. He looked at me again. "I will have to think about this some more." He said and his normally drumming fingers were uncharacteristically still. "I see no flaws in your logic. I see no loopholes that can save us. I am at a loss just now." He looked like he had the weight of the universe on his shoulders. "Could I really have caused this whole thing?"

I looked him straight in the eye and he started to squirm. "No, not by yourself." I replied simply. He looked away, off into the distance. His mind was probably floating back to that first meeting with Frank. The whole plan had seemed so far fetched and he was desperate for an answer, any answer.

"I, I didn't know that this would be the result." He stammered out. I could tell he wanted me to tell him it wasn't his fault. I was unsure if I could. "I mean, it wasn't my idea but I did authorize it. It seemed to be the only way." He said.

That was something I could respond to. "From where and when you came, it was the only solution. Don't you see that we are here for a reason? This is a race of warriors. Strength is all that they understand. We are in a unique position as some sort of religious icon to influence them and abort this war and stop this loop. This is our one chance. What we do now changes everything, for all time." I said, trying to bolster him up to the difficult tasks ahead of us. I only hoped that I was strong enough for what had to be done. If not, this would all come crashing down on us. I stood up again. I needed to be available for this next meeting. Every contact with these people was now crucial. "I need to get ready for the meeting. I suggest you pull yourself together and try to think of some way to help me. If we show any sign of weakness, they will destroy us and the world will end." I walked towards the door and pushed the button to open it. "Hurry up though, we haven't much time." I left him there to his own thoughts.

*   *   *

The stone ship had come alongside as was commanded and their boarding party was only four members. It was the new commander and three lesser officers. They would not risk first and second in command anymore. At least they were thinking now, it was a good sign. I stood in the hallway with a warm smile on my face. Since I was so much younger than those around me, I had to project an air of confidence that I didn't really feel. I did my best though. The small display of power did wonders to make sure they remained properly wary. Frank was at my side and Christopher seemed inseparable from Frank. I was glad enough to have them there. They were each more disciplined than I was and together we held a pretty good front. Frank had mentioned something called poker and he had said that he hoped that I never learned to play it. It was all confusing to me so I put the thought aside. We had two security personnel behind us in the background in case it did hit the fan again. If that happened, we would fail. This needed to go perfectly in order for us to move on to the next phase of the plan that I was making up as I went.

The new commander, I had not heard his name yet, eyed me carefully before he approached. I knew that I looked insignificant to him. I was only a young man and much smaller than the others. However, I was the one in charge here. I had my weight evenly distributed and I was ready to move in a flash. It would not be to run either; I was projecting power and force. I would be the aggressor if it came down to that. I just hoped that it wouldn't. The memory of killing the one lizardman that I had was horrible enough. I could sense that Christopher was ready too. He looked normal outwardly, but his eyes missed nothing. I decided to ask him later about his training. Finally though, the commander stepped up.

"You sssee that I am complying with your demandsss. There is no need to endanger my ship any further." He said with a slight tilt to his head. His party tensed thinking that the comment was a possible offense to me.

I looked up to stare him straight in the eyes; he was quite a bit taller than I was. It really felt as awkward as it must have looked. "I have not endangered your ship at all. I told you when I moved it that you would come to no harm." I replied with an even tone. There was no humor on either side of this bargaining table. "I need some assurances from you that you will behave here. This is a civilized ship and we will not allow barbarism to rule here. This of course applies to both sides of this discussion. We will not attack you unprovoked and we demand the same from you." I told him. I could feel a slight shake of my knee and I stepped a little bit forward to hide it from the towering warrior in front of me.

"Your proposssal isss acceptable. I, nor any of my people here, will attack you without provocation and we asssk the sssame from your kind." He said to make sure that we were going to hold up to our end of the bargain. It was a little repetitious, but I understood it completely. They had lost their former commander to an earlier skirmish aboard this ship.

"Then it is agreed." I stated flatly and I smiled at him. It was probably the most disarming act that he had ever experienced. The commander's shoulders sagged with a small show of relaxation. "My name is Zack." I said to him and he looked at me oddly.

"I am commander Bruul and I am not happy to be ssstanding before you." He said honestly. "I was told that we were going to take thisss ship from you to learn itsss sssecretsss. Now I find mysssself in the posssition to asssk for what we need to know. Thisss isss not the way of the warrior. We usually take what we want or need. For thisss change, you mussst give usss a little time to adjussst." He said, bowing his head slightly at the request for leniency.

I looked at him carefully. I was trying to see if he was telling the truth. He seemed to be. He looked sincere. It was an admission that I didn't expect. I tried to turn it to a positive angle. "You have already come so far since I last saw your kind. You are among the stars now. You have seen and done so much already. The earlier people that I knew labeled you as savages. I knew that they did not understand your potential. I had hoped for so much more out of you. Now I can see that I was right. You have the capacity for cruelty and domination, but it is not the only thing you are capable of. You can work together with others for the greater good as well. Conquest is not the only path to glory." I paused for a moment because I saw his eyes light up at the word glory. I had struck a cord with that one. "Do you understand what I mean?" I asked after the short delay.

"I underssstand that you sssee more than combat to life. I do not sssee how you can gain glory from it though." He admitted.

I nodded to him and held up an arm to direct them to the galley of the ship. There were tables and benches there. They would have had trouble sitting in chairs meant for humans. We humans did not have that pesky tail sticking out our rumps. "Perhaps we can discuss that in here. It is a place where we can be seated and relax a bit. Concepts like this could take some time." I suggested and everyone filed into the galley. We all sat around a long table with a speckled gray laminate top and folding legs for when it was in storage. The whole group looked odd to be sure. When all the members were seated and in place I continued my speech. "You see the glory of combat as do we. There have been heroes and legends among our people as well. Not everyone is made to be a warrior though. There are great thinkers and there are dreamers as well. The idea of taking both of our peoples to the stars is the result of just such thinkers and dreamers. A warrior would still be fighting with sticks and stones on a single world's surface. It took something more to arrange this meeting. Your people surely have developed other skills than killing haven't you?" I asked and Druul nodded vigorously.

"Yesss we have engineersss that control the shipsss in ssspace. They think what the ship should do and then it doesss it. They do not fight." He said and the others with him nodded their agreement. It was the first thing in common between the two peoples. It was a good start.

"Good, that is important. Do these engineers get a piece of the glory when the ship succeeds in a particular campaign?" I asked and he looked uneasy.

"No, they do not share in the glory. The ssspoilsss certainly, but no glory. They have spilled no blood." He said adamantly.

"That seems odd to me. If this engineer did not do their job, then the warriors could not have gotten to the fight. Don't you think they deserve at least some respect or glory from the warriors at least for allowing them to reach their goals?" I asked and he now looked uncomfortable.

"I had not consssidered thisss." He said simply. At least he was thinking forward thoughts now. He was open to this discussion. It was more than I thought I could have gotten from him on a first meeting.

"There is more than fighting too. Do you know how much harder it is to get to know someone than it is to blindly kill them? Differences and fear can make it more challenging that you might imagine. We have spent this time with you and it is more difficult than I could have hoped for after your first two men attacked us. It took a show of power to arrange this. I admit it. But notice that I gave it to you without hurting anyone. That is the true challenge here." I said. Frank put his hand on my shoulder. He was just showing his support. I think he was seeing where I was going with this. I hoped he did for I was not sure yet. "You have the ability to do the same. Your engineers have great power as I do. They have just not been asked to learn it. If you share your glory with them you may find them more willing to help you do things. Everyone wants to feel needed. Everyone wants to be a part of something bigger than themselves. This is one of the great truths you are asking me for." I said, trying to end on a high note. I needed a couple of minutes to come up with my next argument for peace.

The mention of their questions brought all of them to attention. It took them a moment to calm down again. "You have told usss that peace isss harder than war." He shook his head. "I do not know if thisss is ssso , but I will think on it carefully. You have told usss that everyone isss important or meaningful. To usss thisss isss a new idea. I will have to talk with othersss to sssee if they agree with it." He said and I shook my head slightly.

"No you don't. I have told you and you should accept it as truth. I will not lie to you about something so important as that. You have been doing the same thing for centuries now. Did you not think that something should change? Growth is change. You have great potential, that much is true, but you have not grown for all of this time. That is why I am here to give you a push in the right direction. Can't you see that I am trying to help you?" I said, pushing my weak poker hand to the limit as Frank would have put it. For all of the tension in the room, my party did not tip my hand at all. They were supportive and did not flinch away from my words. It made the whole speech even that much more believable.

The commander did not seem convinced yet. He was shackled by his upbringing. He was trying really hard to understand, but there was a mental block in his way. "Ssso what you are sssaying is that challengesss to be overcome allow usss a path to glory?" He asked, trying to find a handle on it.

Frank spoke up then. "Yes, that is at least a part of what he is saying." He pulled a small cube from his pocket. He handed it to the commander and smiled at him. "This is a puzzle cube. It has many combinations in the way it can be moved, but there is only one solution. There are some people that can look at it and solve it right away and toss it aside as a minor distraction. Others struggle with it and when they finally get it they gain happiness from the effort. Still others will never divine its secrets and will walk away angry from their failure to complete it. Challenge is a measure for how much you will enjoy the outcome. In the past, you have gone to combat harder and harder foes in an attempt to find more glory. The enjoyment for you is that glory and the difficulty of the enemy is the challenge. It is the same thing." He said and I nodded my approval as he backed away again. The commander looked at the cube. It looked impossible. Its many colored sides would not align for him, he was sure of it.

"Ssso inssstead of fighting, we should do puzzle cubesss?" He said skeptically.

Frank held up his hands. "No, this was just one example. You must find your own challenges. They must be hard enough that you will have to grow to complete them yet not be too hard as to make you give up." He said. Some of it was starting to sink in. I could see the spark of the idea spreading through each of them.

"Well, this is a good start to our talks. Do you have any questions about this first truth?" I asked and I hoped that they didn't.

"We mussst return to our ship to disscuss this with the crew. If they do not undersssstand thisss, then the ressst of us will be even harder to sssway." He said and it all sounded logical to me.

"Of course, I will walk you to the airlock then." I said and I led the whole party back out into the corridor and down to the airlock. A line was shot over to the stone ship and they were soon all back aboard their own ship. I had told them to contact me when they were ready for the next talk. I needed some help for that as well. We still had so far to go. But I felt some satisfaction at how well that had gone. There was just a slight worry about how his crew would react.

* * *

Druul stepped back aboard his ship and the looks on the faces of his crew were a mix of curiosity and fear. Perhaps for the first time he had their attention without their scorn. He had gone over to the enemy ship and he had returned. He hadn't taken it over, but he had returned unharmed with his party. He stepped through into the main portion of the ship and the stone hatch sealed behind him and his small group. He stretched as if bored and then he smiled at them.

"That isss the ship from the ssscripturesss." He announced and there were cheers across the ship. He let it all die down again before he continued. More of his people were coming to the main room even as he spoke. "They have knowledge for usss. They have great power that they will share with usss." He said and there were more outbursts from the crowd. He stood taller as he felt the welcome wave of acceptance among his crew. He had become their leader now truly, not just in name and rank. He let them bellow and shout for a while. This was a form of glory that he was soaking up. The earlier lesson of the day started to ring home for him. He now had this new glory and position without bloodshed. It was something new to be sure. He hadn't really believed it until now. "We have much to learn from thisss ship and I will take the lessonsss from them directly to you." He announced and the chatter erupted again. They were asking many things all at once. He couldn't make them all out but most of it was like "Who are they? What do they know? Can they make us stronger?" and the most wanted question of all, "Why are we here?" He knew that he couldn't answer these questions yet. He simply hadn't learned enough yet. He held up his hands to silence the crowd and forestall any further questions.

"I know that you want to know thingsss. I need to know them too. I can tell you what I learn each time I return. There isss one thing you mussst learn now, and it will be difficult to undersssstand. It wasss difficult for me to undersssstand." He paused as the people that had been cheering suddenly took on a serious look. The statement had carried so much weight with his newly defined influence. He was proud to be the leader now. It was no longer a burden to him; but a responsibility that he would try to excel at. He nodded to them as a group. "We must find our glory in new ways." He said and there were looks of confusion all around him. He watched carefully as the words bounced around inside the brains of his crew. He had warned them that it would be difficult. He stepped up to the display area of his console. The stone shifted in color and displayed a map of the local stars. He pointed to one of the spots on the rock face display.

"What does thisss ssstar have?" He asked and many of his people craned to see where he was pointing. "It is jussst a ssspot on our disssplay and yet it representsss ssso much more. What do we really know about it?" He asked. One of his people blurted out a response.

"We know not to fly there, it would melt our ship." He answered and Druul, the leader of these folk, laughed aloud. The sound startled his men.

"Yesss, we know that much. Isss that all?" He asked of the whole group. There were many stares and scratching of heads as they wondered where he was going with this.

One of his boldest warriors finally stepped forward. "We know that it hasss no life on it, ssso it is unimportant." He replied as if he had found the only right answer that meant anything. It was his warrior's arrogance that was bringing him to this pass.

"No, we do not know that. We know that there will be no life there for usss to fight. If there isss life down there, we have not sssseen anything like it before. We know that no humansss live there, they are too weak to sssurvive on the sssurface of a ssstar. Isss that the only thing we can tell about this dot?"

There were no more answers and the warrior backed away from the line. Druul stepped away from the console. "We could learn ssso much more about that dot than what we care about now. We have learned to classify everything in a military way. Can we kill it? Or can it kill usss? That is all that we know. We are missing the big picture here. What if that ssstar has a planet around it that we could plant a colony on? What if it had metalsss that we could use or a new kind of stone that would allow greater manipulation by our engineersss? Our shipsss are the same as they have alwaysss been. They have not gotten any better since anyone can remember. Should thisss not be a source of worry for usss? If we do not change, can we be any ssstronger?" He asked them all seriously. He had their attention fully and he knew where he wanted to go with this, he only hoped they could bridge the gap from what they knew was true to what could be true.

"We need to grow and adapt to changesss around usss. We were not put out here to just kill and kill until there isss nothing left out here but usss." Many eyes looked at him sternly. It was their goal in life to spread the church and prepare for the humans infestation. They had done nothing else for many generations. "Our sssect hasss become powerful among our people and we have dealt many a blow in the name of our cause. I am ssseeing now that we could have done more than thisss all along." He paused again as the emotions of his crew rippled with surprise. "If we had taught othersss our beliefsss then they may have joined usss. Our numbersss could have doubled or tripled over thisss long campaign. Inssstead we are alone out here except for the ship of prophesssy. Do any of you think that thisss is a missstake, or random chance?" He asked them and there were vigorous shakes of heads around the vast room. "We have been chosen to passs the knowledge to the ressst of our people and to carry our people into the future ssstronger and better than we are now." He said with finality. He had finished his argument and all that was left was to watch to see if the seed he had planted in their minds would sprout. If so, it meant that their future was brightening already. He left them all there, he retreated to his own quarters and once inside there, he collapsed onto his bunk. He had done what Zack had told him to do. He had been nervous about it. He had been worried that his newfound respect would be lost. Instead he had held firm to his new convictions and made himself stronger than he had been before. He even noted to himself that he had done this without violence. It was the second time since returning to the ship that the human wizard's words had been proven true. He wondered how much more that young human knew. It seemed amazing, even laughable that he knew so much that the people needed to know. He started thinking about what he would ask the next time they met. He wanted to succeed now. He would gain more glory this way than he had ever gotten all his life as a warrior.

*　*　*

After some needed rest, the small group assembled in the conference room. A lot had happened and they all wanted to know what I had in store for them next. I only wish that I had thought it all through. At this point, I really hadn't. I had viewed all of the recordings of the final battle and it frightened me beyond my understanding of the word. Such a power existed and it had been used to disastrous results. I did not know how to combat such a thing as that. The only saving grace was that the particular event would not happen for another fifteen hundred to two thousand years from the current time. That meant that we still had a chance to avoid it. This was our primary goal. It was the reason that the *Lost Cavalier* had come back in time to find me. It was the reason that I had pressed this confrontation so hard. I had to appeal to this smaller crew and the lessons had to sink in or an attempt at higher levels would fail. I wish that I could see what was going on over there in the other ship, but I could not. The beginning had been laid in place and I hoped that it was a solid foundation.

We needed to shift the primary thoughts of conquest onto something far more constructive. Who knows, if we play this right the human race could even benefit from these lost brothers. The animosity had run for millennia already, we would have to work hard to put an end to it. Frank looked happy. It was a stark change from his normal busied and bothered look. He was genuinely happy about something. I held just a glimmer of hope for a possible suggestion from him as the meeting opened. The chair was not open to him just now though. The Captain held all eyes as he opened this get-together.

"Okay people, we are all up to speed on what has happened so far right?" He asked and there were nods all around the table. Satisfied, he continued. "We are in what I have to describe as treaty negotiations. That is a cut-and-dried way of putting this situation into by-the-book parameters. I know it falls short of that description, but that is how I put it in the log. Zack here has planted a seed among the Lizzies and we can only hope that it works. These negotiations have all of our hopes riding on them and we must tread carefully from here on in." He said and everyone seemed to be in agreement again. Then he turned to me directly and his face seemed to change. "Just what did you do to send their ship away for a time?" He asked bluntly. I had wondered when that subject would come up.

"Well, the center of their ship is a strong graviton force." I said and Casey's eyes lit up. The rest of them looked confused. I gestured to Casey to explain it to them.

"Well, what he is saying is that the middle of their ship is a high center of gravity, like a miniature black hole. They manipulate the gravity to make the ship move without an external propulsion system." He told them in rapid fire sentences. Then he turned to me. "You can sense that?" He asked and I nodded.

Then I pulled the conversation back to target. "I used the graviton elementals to command their ship to fly away. The forces are the same as they are for a world or a moon. They are just more focused in the lizardman ships. I don't know how they put such a thing inside those great stone ships, but it is a powerful force that can be used by anyone who understands the elementals behind them. It is one of the eight elements of power." I said and then the Captain sat back, he was obviously thinking about something else. Whatever the case, he said nothing more. I held the chair then and I gestured to Frank. "I think you have something for us today?" I asked.

He grinned at me. His happiness was becoming infectious. Honestly, it was a good thing to see. "Yes, I have a few things to bring up here." He said in a flush." He had a pad in front of him that he had taken notes on. He thumbed the button to make the screen scroll down a page or so. "First of all, we have hit with some luck here with this first encounter. As sad and dangerous as it was to kill the first commander, it established our strength before the enemy. These are warriors as you know and strength is all that they respect. Secondly, Zack showed them that he had power over their ship and proved the effectiveness of our strength." These events set up the correct situation for them to be responsive to our lessons. It was primarily fear that has kept them in line so far. If this remains, then the negotiations will fail. We need to prove to them that we can be trusted and that we trust them." There were scoffs around the table, not everyone, but quite a few. "No listen to me. If they think we can destroy them they will try to become stronger, or they will look for a weakness that they can exploit to try and take us down to eliminate that threat. It is the way of the warrior. Sooner or later they will succeed and all will be for naught. We need to establish a real treaty of equals. Their religion seems to credit us with the generation of their race. We all know that is not true, but it did send them out into space. The difference may be subtle enough to exploit, but how we do so will determine their overall reaction. If we are going to stop the future we all know already happened, then we need to change the now. We need to get the humans and the lizardmen talking on governmental levels. This one ship cannot do this alone, but we can do a lot to prepare Earth for an encounter and prepare these people for our own prejudices. It would go a long way towards smoothing out relations between our peoples and preventing the war that we have already lost." He stopped, having run out of steam, but his point was well taken. No one had considered the lizard people as equals. Now they were forced to consider this new idea and to embrace it or fail.

I breathed a heavy sigh. He had made all valid points and I could not see any holes in his logic. The problem with it was that it meant that we needed to get in touch with human commanders and then bring them together with the leaders of the lizard population. This was going to be complicated at best. I shook that negative thought out of my head and looked up again. I had all eyes on me again. They were waiting for a reaction I think. "It sounds good to me, I don't know how to get all of those pieces to the same table, but the puzzle is laid out before us." I said, trying to keep it a bit more cryptic than normal so they would not have questions for me now. I needed to think. What we had for a situation was that we were being worshipped as creators and we had to convince these savages that they were equal with us and thus should not attack us. We needed to open lines of communication and we needed to do it all before the few lizardmen we impressed got wind of our inherent weaknesses. We were only one ship in the cosmos and they were a Fleet of aggressors. It was not good odds no matter how you added them up. The thing they needed from us now was information. It was at the heart of their commitment to us. The balance of power was held precariously in place by this one truth. We knew things they didn't. What could we teach them next? What should we teach them to maintain this balance? It was all so difficult to guess. Surely another preaching of peace would not be effective. I would have to give them more somehow. These were the things I needed from this group and they were content to let me figure it all out myself. I sighed and stood up. "So unless you have something more for me, then I will adjourn to my quarters and think on it all for a bit." I said wearily.

The captain looked at me and he knew what I was going through. His shoulders had felt the burden for so long and now that weight was on me. I could see in his eyes that he knew it. He smiled at me but there was no menace to it. He was honestly sorry for the burden that I bore. He was relieved that it was not his, but he did not wish it upon me either. "Go ahead son, get some rest and think on it. We'll meet again before the next meeting with the Lizzies to discuss what you have come up with. If there is any luck among us, we'll have some suggestions for you as well." He said, as if he had read my thoughts. The group around the table fidgeted at his glare at them. "Then off with you now. We'll meet again soon enough." He instructed and I nodded and left the room.

I heard his voice just as the door closed. He had spoken to the rest of them at the table. "That is one courageous boy there, let's see if we can't help him in any way we can." He told them and the electronic door shut off the rest of what was said.

* * *

The home world of the Lizardman population was quite a ways from where the two ships hung in space. They did not have typical communications gear but they were still in touch with the Fleet. A dispatch was sent as to the change of command of the vessel and then again as the weekly report went out. The oddness of the weekly report raised some questions back at command. Had this ship lost its mind? They were rendezvousing with a human vessel they believed to be from scripture? It seemed so far-fetched. It was just the sort of thing they would have considered from a junior commander trying to impress his sector commander. In fact it had been dismissed as that the first time around. Now it was being looked at a bit closer. There were rules about scriptures and if they had violated them, then the commander would wish he had never been hatched. Sector Leader Gnosh looked at his people and he nodded to them slightly to acknowledge their efficiency. He gave the order and his massive stone ship moved away from the home world and out into space. Once they were free of the magnetic pull of the planet, they commanded their engineers and the ship sailed under the massive power of its black hole. They would meet up with this small ship and its commander to assess just what they had found. A human ship out this far would be amazing. They were nowhere near Earth and the confrontation according to scripture was not to happen for a couple thousand years. He looked at his own chest and his awards were cut there by his own hand. He was a highly decorated warrior and his name pulled weight in the important circles. He would put things right and society would again be held in stasis as was the directives from above. He watched as the day to day operations of the ship continued around him. He stood and stretched. In a ship this size, there were facilities for just about everything. Just now he wanted to vent some of his pent up energy. A good workout and a few broken skulls should do the trick. He headed that way without a word to his crew. They had seen this before. They all knew where he was going and what he was going to do. They were just glad to be on duty. That meant that it would not be their heads that took the beatings.

*   *   *

Druul was busily talking to his people. He had made his initial statements and now he was discussing them with small groups across the small ship. He would answer a question here or address a concern there. He had become quite the diplomat on this short cruise and now he was putting those newfound skills to work. He had also compiled a list of questions for the humans for their next meeting. The feedback from his crew was mainly positive. They had actually refused the teachings at first but as he spoke longer, more and more of them came over to the side of reason. He finished an impressive argument and settled back in his personal area to recoup. His body was tired but his spirits were high. He had done what no other commander before him had achieved. He had gained his people's support without threats or violence. It was a new thing and he decided right away that he liked it. He had looked through the stories of his people. He had searched painstakingly for a precedence that would help him with this new scenario. There was simply nothing there. If something came up that would cause the warriors to question themselves, then it was utterly destroyed. He wondered how they had survived this long that way. He knew that change was inevitable for them to grow as a species. This seemed more right to him than the drivel that he had been told the whole of his career. He knew that this was true. It was not a case of taking the young man's word for it. His people had not changed in thousands of years. Unless something pushed them along, nothing would change for at least that much longer. It brought other questions bubbling up into his suspicious mind. Who would benefit from a lack of progress? Who was worried about change and stopped it at its source? Why was he the only one who had seen these things? He didn't know. As a ship commander, he might be able to do something about it. He was not sure just what, but he felt the power around him and he knew that inaction was not a viable course for him. He had to *do* something. He had to accomplish something that none of his kind had done so far. He had to change. In truth he had already changed. His people were talking about him in a different way. They saw him almost as a prophet. He was the one that had survived contact with the ship from scripture and he had brought back unfamiliar words of glory and peace. He had told them with conviction how they should see the universe and they were making the effort to take a look. Change can come slowly and gradually, but this was not the case now. Mindsets were changing with each passing minute and he was at the heart of it all. There was a sense of pride in that he just couldn't deny. He did not worry about it though. The future held so much more promise now than it had before. He could see all of that in his narrow view of it all. He could tell that ideas aboard his one ship and this human metal box had the power to change everything. The sheer scale of it didn't weigh him down at all. His feelings raged on as his blood rage turned to something else. He was powerful now. Not in physical strength, but in mental strength. He was a thinker. Those types were usually subjugated to be engineers. He had scored just low enough to be let into service. Now he had seen more and he wished that he were smarter. He wanted to embrace this new truth and he wanted to lead his people away from their downtrodden ways and lift them up to the status of gods among the stars. What greater glory was there than that? He wanted very much to take them all in a warm embrace and carry them to a bright and fulfilling future that seemed so far away just now. The hate and prejudice of millennia would have to be cast aside. He would shed it like an old skin and cast it away in disgust. "Could it be as simple as that?" He wondered. There was still so much more to learn. There were still so many questions to ask. They had issues of origin and they had people who wanted to know about them. A lot of this dirty laundry had to be brought out into the open before they could safely move on. He knew this although he wished that he didn't. It made things more complicated than he liked. He could handle it; he just didn't like it all. He looked around the room he was in and he wondered just how long his people had been riding around in these stone cellars in space. He knew more about them than he would have admitted, but he couldn't remember a time when they weren't out here. They were always out here. The ancient texts told him that they hadn't always been a space-faring race and that they had once been settled on Earth. They had been there for a long time before they had gone to space. The ancient texts told them so. Every command officer had to be familiar with the texts. They were available for anyone who wanted to read them. He had spent weeks in the learning chamber looking through everything. He had absorbed it like a sponge until he drew too many watchful eyes. Then he shrugged his shoulders as if giving up and left the books behind. That single act had worked to belay suspicion that he might have been too smart and he was sent into Fleet. But in the back of his mind he had wanted to become a scholar and learn what they all meant. Now he was living another chapter of that history. He didn't know exactly where it would take him, but he was anxious to find out. He was growing impatient at the delays. He had a date with destiny and he was eager to get on the road for it. So perhaps it was the first thing that his superiors could have seen that was along the lines they wanted. His impatience and readiness for action were requirements for command. They just usually wanted individuals that questioned nothing and followed blindly. They were like any other government. They wanted to maintain control and they had bred these people to allow them to do just that. He suddenly saw it so clearly. His own government had kept things at status quo. They had held his people back. He was suddenly angry and his blood rage was swelling. They had prevented his whole race from succeeding beyond their pre-programmed limits. This was something he had to address. This was something he had to change. With this new revelation in mind, he now knew exactly what to ask this human child. He smiled as he realized that fate had made him the key to this whole operation. Fate had placed him in this position and his own ability to recognize it made him uniquely qualified for the role. He embraced this reality too. The tide was turning and change was coming. He was ready to stand at its head and make sure to steer it on the right course. The image bathed him in the glory he sought and his shining example would lead his people into freedom from those same oppressors. A new era would dawn for his people. All of this would be his legacy. A new chapter in the scriptures would be written and he would point the way to the new truth. He could not, would not falter now.

*   *   *

With the birth of new dreams and new challenges in the ship next to them, the *Lost Cavalier* was still dealing with turmoil of their own. Maintenance supplies were running thin and the newly fabricated parts had been used up. In addition they were low on food supplies as well. This mission would become even more desperate if this encounter stretched out too long. Adding to all of that was the constant proximity of the stone ship. Everyone on board knew that it had the power to eliminate their ship with a zero time launch. Even the finest targeting officer could not react to the spires this close. They would die in space under this particular scenario. It was not a comforting concept.

As I slept, I forgot about all of those worries. The toll on my mind and body had been high and sleep overtook me, despite my best efforts to remain vexed. The team had talked for hours as I slept. The discussions varied greatly and still they came up with no solutions to offer me and my efforts. In truth I was not all that surprised. They had been lost to idle bickering before. I needed to step up and do the right thing to save the day. It was a heavy responsibility and I knew that there was only one chance here. Everyone knew that. Even so, I was still working from a positive feeling that the early ground laid was sound and well received. The entrenched warrior's thoughts had slid aside rather easily, maybe even too easily. I began to wonder if I was simply being humored. I awaited the next meeting with mixed emotions. There were only so many things that I could control. Everything else stood to chance more or less. I had hopes, yes, but I could not worry about it overmuch. Instead I needed to focus on the future of two peoples and to somehow make them work together. Time would be the only true indicator of whether or not I was successful. I needed to get a game plan in place though. There were so many things out there other than warfare. From what I could gather the lizardman way of life was establishing colonies by killing the inhabitants of an existing location and then moving in their own people. It was so parasitic it turned my stomach. I needed to change their views on this. We still had so far to go. I rested and waited. It would all happen soon enough.

*   *   *

Druul continued to think and get more and more excited. By the time he made the contact with the human ship, he was almost frantic. "I mussst know more. When can I come over? Please, he mussst help us to grow. We need to talk to Wizard Zack right away." He had said in a rush. The communications officer, Chris Fell, smiled at it all. It was so different from the commanding ways he had heard from the enemy in the past. He forwarded on the message and soon I was brought to the Captain's room. Captain Glass sat in his comfortable chair. He had a red mark on his cheek where he had rubbed it so many times in a nervous fashion. He looked at me and his eyes showed the heavy burden that he was carrying. The worry lines crossed his face and latticed around those tired eyes.

"Well young man, it seems that you have made a pretty solid impression." He said with a slight edge of humor to it. The communication from the enemy, ah… ally ship is quite optimistic. It also places the responsibility squarely with you. This commander Druul has asked for you by name. All communications are kept in the log so you are now officially in the loop on this one. Hell, you are the loop. All we can do is stand by your side and support you in any way we can." He said, letting a bit of his exasperation show. He was obviously used to being the go-to guy. All the big decisions were his. This having to rely on someone else was awkward for him. Still, I understood it. Some of the masters that I had seen were the same way. They wanted to do it all. Never mind that it just wasn't the best way to handle the situation. It caused a rift in the cohesiveness of the school. I didn't fully understand that then. It was something that took more experience for me to accept. Now I had seen power struggles on massive levels. My life had taken such a drastic turn when the White Witch stepped in and changed things. Now it was still playing out. I was scared and curious at the same time. I pulled myself back from my wandering thoughts.

"Sir, I will do what I can to make sure that this mission succeeds. Beyond that, I cannot promise anything." I told him honestly. He looked me in the eye. It felt like he could see through to my soul.

"I know you will son, I know you will. The trouble we went through to find you has been justified. One of your few years is usually not so focused. I do believe that we shall prevail here. There are good indications that you have already hit with a good measure of success. Hold your next meeting and help these people realize that we are friends and not enemies and I will be forever in your debt." He said and the words did not sound hollow or fake. He seemed honestly impressed. Then he shifted gears. "Do you know what you are going to tell him next?" He asked.

I shook my head. "I have thought about it a lot. I have several paths to follow but I think letting him ask questions first and helping him understand what he has learned so far is the best course. If he has missed something early on, I need to correct it now before it becomes a false belief." I said and I found a comfort in saying what my head had been working on. It all sounded so reasonable spoken aloud.

"That sounds like a good strategy to me. Thank you for thinking things through and sharing it with us. I know that initially I doubted you. Your shooting from the hip threats were something I was unprepared for. Now that I have seen more of your work, I am convinced that I was the one who failed to understand those first tense moments. This is not an admission that I make lightly. You are a diplomat. I don't know where you learned this since I know nothing of your background. I am thankful for it, but it comes as a complete surprise to me. It is a bonus that we needed desperately here. If you need anything that I can provide to help you, just ask me or anyone on this ship and I will get it." He said and then he sighed. "Well, that is all that I have for you now. When do you want to have this meeting?" He asked. I am certain that he already knew my response.

"Now would be the best time. The message sounds almost desperate. Let us not keep destiny waiting." I said smiling hugely and he nodded. It had been the answer he was expecting.

"Very well, we shall have it as soon as they can get over here." He said and I shook my head.

"I'm sorry sir, but they have already come over here in their effort to show good faith. I will need to go there to return that compliment." I said and I knew that my hand was shaking at the thought. It would put me in a potentially threatening position. They knew that and his first reaction was going to be to deny the idea entirely. But the words of mere moments before made him pause. He looked around, like a man trying to find a way out and then he looked back at me.

"How many people will you need over there?" He asked and I nodded to him at his own ability to assess the situation and decide what to do about it. "I am assuming you will want Frank with you and that monk of yours. How many security people will you need?" He asked next.

"None sir, what we need are not warriors, we need thinkers. These people are in a time of learning. Their whole structure of beliefs is being challenged. If they perceive a physical threat, they will resort back to their old ways and a fight will undoubtedly ensue. What we need are calm, rational minds to guide them into their next phase of development in a peaceful manner." I told him and the captain looked unconvinced.

"You are the main cog that is driving this machine. I cannot afford to lose you due to an error in calculations or a misunderstanding between two different peoples. Do you understand the incredible threat you'd be placing yourself under?" He asked me and there was no trace of humor in his tone now.

"Yes sir, I know that it is risky. It will fail if they have not truly understood what we have discussed so far, but if they have, we could move so much faster once trust has been perceived on both sides. We need to take advantage of this quickly before other influences can get in the way. How long do you think we will be alone out here?"

The Captain scoffed. "We're in space, millions of miles from any other humans and the chances of bumping into someone else are so fantastic against that it is a laughable question." He retorted.

"That may be true for us; we are operating out of the command of your Fleet. Do you think that other ship is doing the same?" I asked him and his face lit up like there was a light bulb going on over his head.

"They will have contacted their people about us." He mused aloud. "That means that they might even be sending someone out to meet with us now." He added.

I shook my head. "These people are warriors. They do not think about meetings. They kill first and ask questions later. Or actually ignore any questions they may have had. We only had the ears of this ship because of our show of force on them in the beginning. They were afraid of us and thus had to deal with our meeting. A new ship entering the equation would not be so inclined. They would probably shoot both ships out of the sky to stop the pollution of the minds of their own warriors aboard the second ship. We cannot take the chance on this, we need to act fast and get this all behind us before reinforcements can arrive."

The thought had not yet dawned upon him that this was a possibility. His resistance almost fell, almost. He suddenly looked more determined than ever. "If there is a chance that another ship will come here, I don't want you over there where we can't protect you." He said adamantly. I understood his point of view and truth be told, he had a valid point. I had worried over this too. The gains could be great, but this was not for sure. More exposure to their crew could make the transition go quicker. It could also expose me to possible harm. I had my skills. Such as they were, they were an ace in the hole for me. It wouldn't help much if I had to disable the ship's mobility to keep them from running off with me. It would be a rough fight to get back to the *Cavalier*. I don't think I could even do that. In space many of the elementals that I use would not be present. Most of my power would be lost. The use of the graviton elementals made me very powerful here, it was something that I was only just coming to realize.

Then there was the urgency of the message itself. Druul wanted the next meeting quickly. He wanted to learn more. He was embracing, at least on the surface, the teachings I would bestow upon him. It gave me a bit of a rush. He would meet us here again. I was certain of that. It was now obvious to me that the Captain would not budge on his ban from me going over to the other ship. Perhaps I could arrange for someone else to go and inspect things over there. They would have to be carefully selected. We would need someone who could explain things for the curious. They would need to be able to avoid conflict with whoever was resisting the changes I wanted to push through. This would not be an easy mission either. Frank seemed to be the best one for the job. I don't know if Captain Glass would allow him to leave either. Oh well, that discussion would come later. Right now the old man was going to reject any new suggestion since he had planted his feet solidly in the mud to prevent me from overriding him on anything.

I finally gave in to him. "Okay, we will hold another meeting here. You can have your standard security as long as they do not look threatening. I can see that you mean what you say and that you will not be changing your mind anytime soon. I am actually slightly relieved at the level of protection you afford me. Please do not take any of my suggestions as disrespect. I am always thinking of making this mission work. It is all that I have now. My home and people have long since died away and your people have yet to be born. We are both orphans of our own civilizations. This ship and crew is all that I've got. The future we can create together is the only way out that I see." I said and the words hung heavily in the air.

The Captain slouched visibly before me. "There is more truth to that than I would like to admit." He said. He dropped his head into his hands and rubbed his eyes. "If this mission fails there will be nothing to return to even if we try to go back. We have gone out on a seriously long limb here. It was the only chance we had and all of our lives are now hinged on this one mission and the simple fact that it *has* to succeed." He said and his shoulders picked back up again. He lifted his head and smiled at me. "It is good that you understand this. It makes us share this burden instead of me making decisions all by myself. I have no choice but to trust you implicitly." He said and then his face took on a glare of warning. "But don't think that I will compromise your safety for any small part of this mission. We need this to work and your loss could jeopardize it beyond repair. You are a lynchpin to this operation and as such are to be protected at all costs. I will let you do what you feel is necessary to talk these people into peace, but it will not involve putting you in a place of vulnerability." He restated and I simply nodded. Then he shifted gears. It was not even a subtle thing; he sighed and then fidgeted in his chair. "We will need to bring them over for this new meeting soon." He said at last getting back to the subject we had started on. "They can come over any time, but we will need a thirty minute window to prepare for them. Other than that, we are ready to receive them now." He said and I nodded again. It seemed to be becoming a habit.

I shook my head and then added "Yes sir." He waved me away and I left the conference room to get some food before having to deal with our visitors. At least when it all hit, I would get about thirty minutes to be ready for them.

* * *

Druul made contact as soon as the requirements were broadcast. He wanted the meeting thirty minutes from then. He was truly in a hurry. The acceptance was sent and at twenty-nine and a half minutes, they were crossing over to the *Lost Cavalier* and the new meeting. I had been paged and was standing in the hallway again. Druul led the way as I had expected, but he did not have his warrior guards with him this time. There was another two lizardmen with him that were not militarily decorated. They carried no weapons and they looked at everything. They looked with true curiosity, not just tactical analysis. These lizardmen were thinkers. I wondered if they were his aforementioned engineers. I didn't have to wonder long. We went to the conference room and I sat down at the head of the table. They each took chairs around the table with their tails hanging off the side of the chair. I smiled at Druul and he spoke up.

"These are my ship's engineersss. They make it go with their mindsss." He said abruptly. They are interesssted in learning what you have to sssay." He said plainly enough.

I nodded to each of them in turn. "Welcome aboard the *Lost Cavalier*. I trust that your journey here was pleasant enough?" I began and they looked at me a bit cock-eyed. I swept in the whole assembly. "What you see here is the work of humans, on their own." I told them. They looked around the metal bulkheads and the wooden table and they probably had a lot of questions. Druul didn't let them get started though.

"They are not here to learn about thisss ship." He interjected. "They are here to learn about the glory they should have for doing their jobs." He said and I nodded to him. They looked at me expectantly.

"What Commander Druul tells you is true. When a ship concludes a mission, everyone involved with that mission should get credit for its completion. This means that you get credit for helping get the ship to where it needed to be in order for the warriors to deploy themselves. It is your right to receive this respect and praise." I told them and they looked back and forth from me to Druul. Apparently he had said the very same thing and they had refused to believe it. I couldn't blame them; it was not normally their way. Now they had heard it straight from the source and they both realized that it was true. They bowed to me across the table.

"Oh that is not necessary. Your people need to move along and advance in the grand scheme of things. You, as thinkers, are important to that advancement. Your worth has not yet been realized." I told them and they looked a bit surprised. I held up a hand to forestall the questions they were about to launch at me. "The warriors have held you back and suffocated your species from growing. I do not know the reason for this, but I can clearly see that it is so. You should be proud of your accomplishments and they should be realized by your superiors. Don't you think this is your just rewards?" I asked them and they both nodded enthusiastically. They were already mimicking gestures instead of grunting their answer as the first commander had. These people were grasping at the new ideas quickly. They wanted the changes that I was suggesting. This was going quicker and easier than I had anticipated.

Druul had sat back and watched as I explained to them how important they were. He kept nodding to me as various points were brought up.

He had set up this mission to get his engineers on board with the new concepts. He was smarter than his superiors would have thought. He knew how to manipulate people and he knew how to get his points put in a way that his people could understand. I felt a wave of warmth from them emotionally. They were actually eager to meet me and liked what I had to say. I had told them that they were important and that they were key to the future I was projecting. This was more than they could have hoped for in the old system. By the time the meeting started to wind down they were ready to go back and tell their friends and crewmates what they had heard. We covered no new ground, which disappointed me a little. We did, however, cover the old ground thoroughly and that was important to these new thinkers.

The Captain stepped into the room unexpectedly and the look on his face told me that something was wrong. My reaction made our guests nervous. "What is it?" I asked the frightened man.

"Do you have to always be right?" He asked me and my mouth dropped open.

"A ship is coming?" I asked and he nodded to me. I swung back to Druul. "Your people are coming. You must prepare yourself for their intervention in this." I said to him in serious tones. His face drooped. This was something he feared and now the reality struck him. He saw his grand future being snatched away from him. He would not give it up easily. But fighting was not his forte and he knew enough to know that he would lose against a full compliment of warriors.

"I mussst get back to my ship now." He told me and he stood up quickly. His engineers followed obediently. "I will do what I can to protect your ship, but if they are coming here, it is to sssilence usss." His look was grave as he left in a hurry. I realized some time later that without his engineers on board, his ship was powerless to move or attack. He had risked much to hold this meeting. I only hoped that it was not all in vain. If this new ship had been sent to destroy both ships, it would probably have the armament to do so. It was not a very happy thought.

I turned to Captain Glass. "Captain, move us to behind his ship in relation to the new ship coming in. We can fight one of those ships, but I don't want to have to. I know from your earlier recordings that they can do a lot of damage. We need to be ready to run if I don't fight." I said with sudden clarity. "If the mission fails here we must get away to try somewhere else." I told him and he nodded and ran from the room to the bridge to issue his new orders. The whole ship went on alert and lights and sirens went off as Druul took the leap back to his ship with his two engineers in tow. It was the fastest spacewalk ever and it was still almost too slow. The new ship came screaming in on full power. It slid up alongside the other stone ship and its scale became clear. It dwarfed the little ship. This was so threatening because that stone ship dwarfed us in the *Cavalier*. The new arrival looked truly monstrous from the bridge when I got there. We were like a fly on a rat with the cat looking at us hungrily. The mental broadcast was pretty clear too.

"You are to stand down and prepare to be boarded for questioning." The message said. It did not specify which ship they were talking about so the general assumption was that they meant both of us. This was not the smooth contact we were hoping for with these talks. This would require a lot of finesse and potentially a tremendous show of force. I started to draw upon the elementals. They were amassed in and around the new ship. The power was a fluid living thing around it. I had never felt so much of it in one spot. It was like when I had been attacked by the elementals back in school. They were all together there, holding on to each other for their combined might. There was more to this ship than simple propulsion. All of the elementals that I knew of were here. This ship was decidedly more dangerous than anyone else on board suspected.

"Captain, something is different about that ship." I told him, trying to think of how best to describe what I felt. He looked at me with some exasperation.

"I realize that it is much larger and thus more dangerous than the first ship." He told me in a bitter rush. "Now stay quiet and let us do our jobs." He scolded me. I went to open my mouth again and he held up a finger to stop me. I clamped it shut again with an audible click of my teeth. Whatever it was, he didn't want to know it now anyway. I kept trying to figure it out though. There was something stirring deep inside of me and I could not tell what was controlling it. Maybe it was me, maybe it was something else.

I felt the stab of fear and I got up quickly as the voice entered my mind. "You are now mine." It said and there was no humor in that tone. I looked around to see if anyone else heard the voice. None of them reacted at all. Great, that meant that I was being personally targeted or that I was going crazy. I kind of hoped it was the latter. It spoke to me again. "You have a few minutes more before I destroy your ship. Make sure you don't waste it." It said and then it laughed loudly inside my head.

I was already standing and now I screamed. "No!" I yelled and ran from the bridge leaving the bridge crew wondering what had happened. I slipped into a utility closet off of the main hallway and I concentrated on the power that I had already pulled. Then I switched focus to the voice. "Who are you?" I said aloud.

There was another laugh. "Don't you know? Hmm, maybe you aren't as gifted as they feared back at headquarters." The voice said unmercifully. "Your time draws near now wizard of the old ways. Your future is now gone." It said.

"No, you can't kill these people. They need to complete this mission." I said, knowing full well that it would do no good. I was stalling for time to figure it all out. Maybe if I could keep it busy, then the impending destruction could be delayed or even averted. "I need to know who you are first, are you afraid to tell me?" I prodded.

Ha ha young one, nice try, you have enough knowledge already. You are a threat. I can sense that much at least. You may not be of much danger to one such as me, but you are a danger to those less gifted than I am." It said arrogantly.

"You are a wizard like me, but much greater in training and experience." I told him. "You think that your amassed power has made you omnipotent. That is a dangerous thing." I warned and he laughed again. The darkness surrounded that voice and I really had no idea how to defend myself against him, let alone defeat his plans for the destruction of this ship and thus the whole of humanity. I just knew that I had to try. "I will thwart your plans somehow." I said in desperation. "You know that I have come from long ago. You are a product of the now. There are bound to be things that you have lost over these few thousand years." I challenged and he chuckled lightly this time.

"Your posturing amuses me. I had no idea you would be so entertaining. My great great grandfather warned me of your power, he did not mention this side of you." He said and I suddenly felt a wave of fear. He was a direct descendant of the group that had come back for us. He knew what the humans would do. He knew their capabilities and limitations. He knew about me and what I had done. If he had questioned some of the downed masters he could easily have figured out how much training I had so far. If this information had been properly passed down, then I could be at a severe disadvantage as far as practical knowledge. He has had generations to prepare for my arrival. He was a full blown wizard and I do not know how many had come before him. As I figured all of that out, he paused.

"Just a moment, time to deal with the fallen warriors." He said and the great stone ship pulsed out electricity and rocked the smaller stone ship. On board Druul must have been shaking as the stone split and his ship blew apart from the sheer volume of damage it had taken all at once. All aboard the ship were lost. I could hear screams from down the corridor and I knew that it was all true. The mental image was only a small gift from the wizard to show me the scope of his influence. He had let me watch even though I was not at a viewscreen.

The *Lost Cavalier* went to full power and it veered away from the massive stone goliath. Spires of rock began to separate and follow on a pursuit course. They had done their first launch against us. The ship did not even seem to balk at the massive stone outlay. It was still huge and the tracking plot showed over forty of the projectiles tracking in on our fleeing ship. This was not good. I took a deep breath and pulled my power into a small ball and released it at the incoming spires. The elementals were mostly the ones concerning the Dirt element. The spires became soft. They turned from stone to dirt. They continued in on their intercept course and when they struck the metal ship, they burst apart into the dirt they were now made of. So the only result was that the side of the ship now needed cleaning. The Captain looked around for what had happened. He had been expecting all kinds of damage reports and alarms. Instead his ship continued on its evacuation path. He gripped the hand-rests of his command chair tightly as all forty of the spires contacted his ship the same way. They had been rendered harmless.

I stepped back onto the bridge and all faces turned to me. I shrugged my shoulders and they each came to their own conclusion and went back to work. The Captain pointed at me. "You must tell me when things are about to go badly. You obviously know more than you are saying even now." He said accusingly.

"I turned the stone spires into soil. I couldn't stop the rocks so I made them less dangerous." I said at last. "But there is more to tell if you have the time." I added and he looked at me dubiously.

"What else is there?" He asked, dreading my possible response.

"There is a wizard on board that ship. He has told me by thought-speak that he will destroy this ship. He is amazingly powerful and I think he is a direct descendant of the group that followed you to my time. If they hung around after we left, they could have retrieved all of the knowledge of the school and thus be fully trained whereas I am not." I said, lowering my head.

The Captain looked awestruck at first, and then he looked thoughtful. "So you're telling me that their technological superiority was from the assistance of magic all along?" He asked and I nodded. "That explains a lot." He replied. "Then what we did to come and get you was the right move. No one else could have told us that. You will have to train us how to do the things you do. Then we shall gather together to defeat this wizard." He said as if it could be transferred all at once like that.

"I fear that we will not live long enough to do that. That ship has all of the elements around it. They have already amassed more power than I have ever felt. I don't think our evasion will last for long." I said feeling more depressed than I had ever felt.

"Don't go soft on me now son." He demanded. "If that much power is already amassed, can you pull from it?" He asked and I got my first indication that he understood at least some of what I do.

"Yes, I can pull some of the elementals away from that ship. It is not any more difficult than it was to send that other ship away." I replied, wondering where he was going with this line of questions.

"Good, then start pulling off all that you can. Do not worry about which type of element it is, just pull everything you can hold off of it." He ordered and I sat down on the carpeted floor and started the concentration to do just that. The voice in my head began to complain.

"What do you think you are doing?" He said in a gruff voice. "You cannot deplete my reserves so you are wasting your time with this." He said and I ignored it to continue the siphon.

I could feel the energy as it coursed and pulsed around and through me. The elementals began to dance and sing around me as they came together away from the bondage they had been suffering. I had no idea that they could be held against their will. I asked them how long they had been in service to the other lord. They told me that time was not relevant to them. They had been held forever. I promised not to hold them that long and they chattered on with glee. I asked them if they could free their comrades still in bondage and they got all excited at the prospect. The shift in power had been only slight, now it was getting drastic. Elementals fled the gigantic stone ship and flittered off in all directions. The few that I had with me stayed longer to see what it was I wanted of them. The rest fled away and dispersed. At least I could no longer sense them.

I looked up at the Captain. His face was amazed. The stone ship had stopped accelerating. In fact, it was just free floating. "What do you want done with the power sir?" I asked and he looked lost for words. Then he snapped back to action.

"Send the ship away; buy us the time to find another ship to talk with." He said. I felt that somehow that plan was wrong.

"Hang on sir, I need to check something." I answered and went back into communication with the elementals.

"You told me that time was not relevant. Does this mean that some of you are temporal elementals?" I asked and they chattered wildly.

"No one has called us that for millennia. Very few even knew of our existence. How do you come by this knowledge?" They asked of me.

"I am from a different time, way long ago. My training was incomplete but I learned of only eight elements. A time element is something more than I imagined." I admitted and they laughed politely at me.

"You are wise enough to know that we should not be held in bondage. That is something more than we have faced for quite some time. What would you request from us in exchange for releasing us?" They asked.

"I need to help these other people understand what wrong they have done you and prevent them from killing all the humans in the future. Is there a way you can see to do this?" I asked them, hoping beyond hope that they had some idea of how to proceed.

"Yes, we can help you with the future events. About helping train these savages, we think that your plan may be flawed if not overly difficult. The mere request has opened our eyes to you though. We owe you a debt so if you ask for this, we shall make the effort to try." They replied. It was like a thousand tiny voices saying the same thing in my head at once. As chaotic as that sounds, it was beautiful.

"I am amazed that you are sentient. I had not known this before." I told them. "This is wonderful news to me. It means that power is not owed, it is requested and given, or not." I said and they sent me a wave of awe. "Can you communicate with the great stone ship?" I asked and there was a pause.

"We do not like them; we do not want to contact them." It said. Since they had been enslaved to it, I couldn't blame them for their reaction.

"It is no matter; I can contact them from here, although without their magic, it will be much harder. I will not try to force you to do anything you don't want to do." I said trying to underscore the point I had made earlier. "Are all of your kind self-aware now? Have I been offending them as I used my powers?" I asked, suddenly feeling guilty for not knowing.

"We do not have self-awareness until our numbers become great enough. You have been monitored by us for your whole life. In fact, we foresaw that you were the one that caused our enslavement and we tried to destroy you a long time ago. We failed in this as you already know. Now it seems that fate has brought you full circle to us as a savior. This is how the universe flows and it is usually surprising to us. So for our earlier attack, we apologize." They said to me. I could feel a tear welling up in my eye.

"You mean I was the cause of your captivity?" I asked, not wanting to believe it. "I am truly sorry for that. I don't know how I did it, but I never meant to do whatever it is I did to cause you such pain." I said meaningfully.

"You left the ancient times and the masters stayed long enough to learn the elemental powers. They became adepts and they amassed us to bolster their influence. It was then that we were enslaved. They did it to combat you. You had defeated them with only a limited set of skills and they wanted to know more. They sought all of our secrets. They tortured us in ways you could not imagine until we told them everything. It is our own weakness that truly was the cause, but the outcome is the same. We have been drained and used for the growth of a vast army of masters." They told me. I was pretty sure of what had happened. My mind was quick enough to catch the hints and put them together. I was suddenly ashamed.

"I know that you feel that I am responsible. The way between us must be cleansed. I will do whatever I can to free you from these masters. I need to talk with these people anyway in order to save humanity from them. Putting your lives in the cause should present only a minor diversion from my current goals. I swear to you that I will try." I said and they could sense no deception from me. I felt their gratitude wash across the ship. The external emotional stimulus was an odd sensation. "I need to talk with them now. If you will excuse me, I shall try to do that now." I said and they left me for the moment. I realized then that the Captain was still waiting for me to answer him. The talk with the elementals had pulled me completely away.

"Sorry sir, we don't want to move the other ship. It is disabled for a time and what we need to do is talk to them and convince them that war with us is a bad idea." I said and I could see the look on his face. It did not look good. I needed to tell him the other half of it though. So I swallowed and continued. "We also need to ask them to free the elementals they have enslaved. The ones for this ship have been taken. It is now dead in space. They can't even talk to us unless we find a way to send sound to them." I said and he sighed. He was getting used to being ordered around. It did not set a good precedent for his chain of command, but the situation was definitely not a by-the-book thing. We were well into uncharted waters here.

"Oh, is that all?" He asked sarcastically. We need for them to talk to us without their magic. Then we need them to admit that they don't need the magic anymore. Then we need to get them not to kill us after we tell them to forget space travel." He was getting angrier with each point he was presenting. "Are you insane?" He asked of me directly.

I looked at him with pity. "You have reached the stars without the magic. You have overcome all of the restrictions of this hostile environment. Your people have colonized hostile world environments and prospered just the same. Surely these things could be trained." I started and then I turned back to the point. "The magic will not be gone, it just needs to be asked for, not demanded. The elementals have been wronged here. They need to be allowed to choose their own destinies. They are alive." I said and there was stunned silence on the bridge.

"Alive? How do you know that?" He asked skeptically. I knew that he wasn't going to like my answer even before I said it.

"They just told me so." I replied and he jumped up. He was in my face in a heartbeat.

"You had a breakthrough like that and you said nothing to us until now?" His rage was controlling him completely now. "You do not understand how a crew works. I am the Captain and I need to be informed about any change that directly or indirectly affects the well-being of the crew and the safety of the ship." He screamed at me. His point was valid, but the information had been too new to tell him. I had tried anyway. Now I was getting angry.

"Listen up you pathetic excuse for a leader!" I shouted at him. He stopped in his tracks. "I only just made contact with them and I have been negotiating with them about helping us to solve your mission problem and save the world and all humans everywhere. I have also been working to free them from the bondage of the lizardmen and in this negotiation I have promised to try to free them in exchange for their help with your problem!" In my anger I had started to repeat myself. I took a deep breath and then met his eyes directly. "You have to understand that things are more complex than you had foreseen again. Your blind rampaging is not helping the situation here and I will not have you spoil this one chance to fix everything. So back off and let me do what you brought me here to do.

After that, put me in your jail or something. For now, I need to get this all stabilized so that war will not erupt. Now do as I ask or watch this whole mission fail and know that you personally allowed history to repeat itself and live with those consequences the rest of your days!" I hit him hard with that last one. He seemed stunned. I hoped he would remain so for a while. I needed time to take care of this thing before it got out of hand. The lizardmen had to be panicking over there and the only answer they now knew was to re-enslave the elementals we were trying to free. Time was working against us each minute. The contact needed to be now. I looked over to the communications officer. At least I hoped it was. "Can you allow me to talk to them?" I asked. Cris wondered if it was the right thing to do, but he hit the button and opened the electronic channel. I don't know if they can hear it without their magic, but I had to try it.

"Please remain calm. Your ship has been disabled for a limited time and I need to talk to you. Please send a representative over to discuss this matter and I shall ask that your ship is restored, at least partially. There will be conditions to allow this. For now, you have no choice but to comply." I said into the pickup. Then Cris flipped the switch that closed the channel.

He smiled at me. "I hope they got that. We have no way to know that they have unless they knock on the door to be let in." He said and Captain Glass sat down heavily. He was still angry beyond most reason, but he was also exhausted. He looked totally spent as he stared out in a disbelieving trance. Somewhere he had lost control of everything. The mission and his ship were now mine to control until it was over. The crew was beginning to respond to me now.

*   *   *

Aboard the giant stone ship, utter chaos had erupted. The warriors within were trapped. The magic had been stripped away. The stone doors would not even work. They were locked inside their stone prison cells. This was some kind of attack from that accursed human ship. The normally active display stones were now just dead rock. There was no information about things on the outside of the ship. There were no life support systems either. They had limited air and space like being locked in a cave floating in space. There was no light and the frustration began to eat away at the crew's resolve. The loss of every system on board made for fear and panic among the seasoned crew. Gnosh looked around in the darkness. His night vision was even thwarted by the absolute darkness. He was trying to think what to order when the message came in. It had been broadcast and there was just enough magic around them to hear it. The voice told them to relax and prepare for a meeting. The power from the ship had been taken and they had no choice but to comply. Gnosh gripped the hilt of his weapon. It was an old style saber with a wicked notched blade. He kept it handy because he liked the close and personal kills. The blade was rusty but the weapon was heavy and dangerous. He preferred it to the guns that they had developed. There was more glory in the kill if you could look into your victim's eyes as he died. The message was an insult to his morals. It told him that he was helpless. In truth, he was angry that the voice was right. He had no choice. If the power was not restored to him his people would all die a death of suffocation locked within their own ship. It was not the death of a warrior. There would be no honor or glory in that. He followed the brief instructions and soon he was standing near the side of his ship. The stone doorway melted away like it had done so many times before. The real difference was that he did not control it anymore. The enemy ship had done this. The humans had somehow taken control of everything. It was unthinkable. Still, it was also a fact. He saw the opening on the human ship and he gauged the distance and leaped. He sailed across the small gulf in space unerringly and he grabbed the sides of the hole to pull himself into the enemy ship. There were humans there in special suits. Some of them had guns trained on him. He had expected that. He was a warrior, a predator among these sheep. He looked at them carefully; he sized each one up for combat. He felt no fear from any of them. He could kill them all if the need arose. The hatchway closed behind him and air was pumped into the room. Then a smaller human male stepped forward.

"I am glad that you got our message. You must follow me to the conference room where we can discuss what comes next." The younger one said. It seemed highly unlikely that these humans would let a child do their talking for them. This was so irregular. Once inside the ship proper, the humans removed their special suits. They looked even smaller and more helpless that way. The young one was really small. He could not be all that old. The whole procession worked their way to the conference room and the large table in the middle of the room sat several human sized occupants. The facilities were not really set up for lizardmen, but it had been adapted at least partially. There were two chairs that did not have those restrictive backs on them. Those backs would prevent one's tail from flowing naturally out the back. Gnosh sat down on the offered chair and waited for the next message from these people. He did not have to wait long.

"You have been taken from your ship in order to explain why we are here and why you need to abandon your mission." The young man said. His given mission to silence these two ships was not even a consideration. He would never abandon a given directive. Surely these humans knew that. If not, then they were not all that informed about how military government works. Orders were to be obeyed without question. It was the way of things.

"The mission isss everything. It shall not be abandoned you foolish humansss." He said in a biting tone. His rage was beginning to build and the frustration of all that he had recently felt was starting to stir his blood. He could feel the murky hate rising to the surface. "You will releassse my ship and prepare to be dessstroyed." He spat at them. He cared not what they thought of him, he was a commander of warriors. They would fight all boarders without question. Humans rarely fought when the superiority was on the other side. Here he was challenging them to destroy him. Then he would become a martyr. He would like that on his path through history.

I looked at him and my face was showing all sadness. "That is too bad. You will not be able to save your crew without the magic. I understand that they are warriors and they would want a warrior's death. Alas we cannot give them that. They will die in your stone ship, locked away from each other in the dark as they are now. You have doomed them with your stubbornness." I told him and my tone was not accusing, it was almost pity. I knew that it would only fuel his rage, but the point was still coming and I wanted him to listen carefully.

"You dare to presume what my crew will think and do?!" His voice rose in volume and his tongue flicked about in agitation. "You do not know usss. You do not undersssstand what drivesss us. We are warriorsss. We are gods among the vanquished worldsss. We are not to be taken lightly." He screamed and hissed, but I was unmoved by his little speech.

"You are ancient and obsolete. Your tactics and plans have not changed for millennia. You have been exactly the same since I last saw your people three thousand years ago." I said and his eyes went wide.

"You, you saw my people that long ago?" He asked, not sure he believed what was being said.

"Yes, I knew about your people long ago. We are the reason they came out into space. Didn't you know that?" I asked him. The religious inference was absolute. He now knew beyond a doubt that this ship was the one from his scriptures. The mission he was sent on would be sacrilegious. He had been sent to destroy an icon of his own history. I watched as his mind turned it over and over to see if I was speaking the truth. The light went on over his head as he reached his conclusion.

"Then you are the onesss from the ssscripturesss?" He asked tentatively.

I nodded to him. "Did you not see the name on the ship as you approached us? This is the *Lost Cavalier*. I am the Last Wizard of Earth. Do these things mean anything to you?" I asked him and my tone was turning dangerous. This was his last chance to turn around.

"Yesss, I have read all of these thingsss in the ssscripturesss. They are required reading for my people. Everyone will know of you." He stopped, he realized right then that he had destroyed the ship that had made first contact. "The other ssstone ship, did it make progresss with you?" He asked, not sure he wanted the answer.

"Yes, they were coming along nicely. They were listening and understanding my teachings. You blew them out of the sky in your haste to carry out your precious mission. Now we have to start again. Do you think you can do that or do I need to just let your people die?" I asked him and his eyes went wide again.

"You wouldn't really let them die like that, will you?" He asked. "You are our creator of sssortsss. You inssspired my people to learn the waysss of the wizardsss of long ago and to create these shipsss that take usss to the ssstarsss. Our whole sssociety revolves around what you have done. You cannot kill them now." He said and I looked at him sternly.

"Do not presume what I can and cannot do. I am who I am and you do not know me. First, know that their lives will be decided by you, not me. You are the one who holds the key to their stone prison. If you cooperate and listen to what I have to say, then your people will be allowed to live." I sat back in the chair, he watched me and he tried to calculate how serious I was. He came up with his decision rather quickly.

"I will ssserve you." He said, and he bowed his head lower than mine to show respect and to show his submissiveness. "Pleassse let my people live." He pleaded and I asked the elementals to give the ship life support functions only.

"Your people can breathe again. They will live. They are still trapped, but they will be alive when you see them again." I told him and his shoulders slumped. He had been tensed up quite a bit and now let it all go.

"Thank you sssir." He said at last.

I shook my head. "It was not me that saved them, it was you. What you have yet to learn is that change is not a bad thing. Ideas are not evil by themselves. Without change, there is no advancement. There is no growth." I didn't want to say too much too fast, but this was important.

"We have advanced. We have conquered and ssslain many peoplesss. We now occupy a large sssection of the galaxy." He said with a slight hint of pride.

I held up a finger. "You hold territories, but you have not advanced as a species. Your people still suffer from the bloodlust. The rage stirs within you every time you are upset. I can see you fidget with it. You have relied on the elementals to carry you from place to place so you can pillage and destroy everything that you see. Have you ever considered having an ally?" I asked him and he looked at me sideways.

"What isss an ally?" He asked. He really didn't seem to know.

"An ally is a person or group of people that work together to accomplish a goal. An ally will help you defend yourself against aggressors. An ally will feed you if your crop fails. An ally will stand beside you and face whatever danger you are facing. In exchange for this, you would do the same for him." I said and Frank nodded his approval. I really didn't need it, but the support was welcome.

"An ally isss like family?" He asked. His statement was closer than I had expected him to get to the truth.

"Yes, very close to that. Family is born or rather hatched to you. An ally is more like a comrade. It is a friend. They will treat you like their family and you will do the same for them." I said, hoping that the concept was solidifying in his mind. If we could ally humans with his people, then the progress would be great indeed.

"A friend you sssay." He said, shaking his head. "Thisss sssoundsss ssstrange to me. I undersssstand what you are sssaying, but I am not understanding why they would do thisss." He said honestly.

I decided to take a new angle. "How big is the universe?" I asked him.

He looked puzzled for a moment. "It isss big, really big." He replied.

"Do you think that someone out there in all of those stars may be stronger than you are?" I asked.

He thumped his chest. "No one is stronger than usss." He said proudly. It was obviously propaganda that he had been told since birth.

"Okay, then if I am stronger than you, then maybe that isn't true then." I said and he laughed aloud.

"I have ssseen no one on this ship that isss ssstronger than me." He boasted.

"Okay, please stand up then." I told him and he stood quickly, his jaw set in a defiant pose. I pulled the air elementals to me and I asked them for assistance. "Please show this lizardman some of your might without causing him permanent damage."

The elementals danced around gleefully. They agreed to a demonstration of power and they were clever enough to work out the greatest impact for the least amount of damage. The air slammed the lizardman in the chest. The wind knocked out of him instantly and his face twisted in surprise. I pointed at his arms and the air turned solid around them and held them in place. He was basically frozen there, he could not breathe and he could not move. I stepped up to him and he towered over me.

"What you see now is that strength comes in many forms. I am much stronger than you. The elementals are much stronger than you." To emphasize my point, I pressed his chest with one finger and he fell over backwards. The elementals laughed and chattered around him as he lay helpless on the floor. "If you understood this power, you could be much stronger, but your people have chosen not to advance. They have chosen to remain the same and continue on as if nothing was wrong. I am telling you, that something serious is wrong. I reached forward and spread my fingers wide to ask for assistance in lifting the giant man before me. He lifted off the ground, suspended by the shifting air. He hung over me and I looked up at him. He was able to breathe again now. There was fear in his eyes. "You are to understand that your own survival requires you to learn things and to advance. Does this make sense to you now?" I asked him.

He could not nod his head. So he answered verbally. "Yesss massster, teach me these thingsss." He said and I lowered my hand and he was set gently on the floor. The elementals seemed to really enjoy it. They stayed close in case more fun erupted here.

"First of all, I am not your master. I will not be teaching you how to do magic. You have wizards already who know more than I do. What you have done though is to enslave the elementals to do your bidding. This cannot continue. You must ask for the power and if they are inclined, they will lend it to you. That is how it must be." I told him in a flat voice with no emotion in it. He shook his head.

"We cannot sssurvive in ssspace without the magic. You cannot deny usss this power." He pleaded.

I took a deep breath and then let out a long sigh and then sat down. "I am not telling you that you have to live without the magic. I am telling you that you can't steal it anymore." I held up a hand palm upward and watched as the lightning began to dance around it. It was beautiful and mesmerizing at the same time. Gnosh watched with fascination at the small display of power. "I use the power with the permission of the elementals. This is how it must be. They are smart and they know right from wrong. You need to adjust your thinking and the thinking of your people to expect them to help you." I said. The concept was pretty straightforward, but it would be difficult for them and their stagnated society. I knew this but still my patience was running thin with this near-sighted oaf. His position seemed unchanged. If anything, he was more defiant now than before he had been knocked around. "Do you think that you can tell your people to live in harmony with the elementals?" I asked him, tired of beating around the subject.

"You sssay you won't teach me this power you have. Then you sssay we have to not use the power unless we asssk for it. Now you assk me if I can tell my people to live under your rule. Thisss will never happen to our people. We will fight you as warriorsss and you shall be dessstroyed like ssso many usssurpersss before you." He swore at me. I knew then that he would not be rational about this subject. He thought that I wanted control over him and all his people.

"I do not need to be ruler of your kind. I need to make you understand that your lives can be better. You don't have to be warriors all the time. There are other ways to achieve glory and recognition. You could be explorers and builders. Right now you are bullies and consumers. Your training and thinking cannot take you beyond the next fight. Do you think that all species think this way?" I asked him. His jaw was still clenched from his earlier stance. I ignored the resistance.

"My people are proud of what they have done. We have colonized many worldsss. We have carried the ssseed across the sssstarsss to build a strong nation of warriorsss. There is no glory in other purssssuitsss. Our people will only recognize heroesss." He said in a straight forward way that I found somehow refreshing, if somewhat annoying.

Before you destroyed the other ship, I had talked several times with the commander. He saw the benefits of change and he was willing to tell the rest of his crew. They were questioning me when you arrived. Some of your people are not happy being warriors. People that cannot be the best warriors are shunned in your society and many of you fall under that category. What of your engineers? Do they get any credit for taking the warriors to the battle? What of someone who simply cleans up after a battle so that no one dies from diseased corpses? Is that job not important enough for some recognition? Your people would be happier if they felt that they were needed. You would see them do so much more for you if they felt important. Has this never occurred to you?" I asked, I had used up all my steam. If he didn't get this, then I would have Frank take him away and bring back the wizard. I still hoped that he would be more in tune to the new and radical ideas.

"Your people are not all warriorsss?" He asked, somewhat shocked. "How do you know they are working properly if they have no killsss to their credit?" He asked and I almost struck him.

"Kills are not the only important thing in life. Saving a life is even more important. Killing only brings more hatred and more death. Revenge comes from those that you have wronged. It is a powerful, but destructive emotion. If you were able to ally with that people instead, the newly combined might could be much stronger than the conqueror's role you presently enjoy. Imagine if all the people you have killed fought beside you against an even bigger enemy. Or imagine there are no enemies left and you are sharing the whole cosmos with all of the allies you have collected. There is a potential there that you have left untapped for thousands of years. This is how your people have failed. Each victory you had along the way only added to your defeat as a people. By giving in to the bloodlust, you have taken the easy way out and proven that you lack the mental strength to do what is right. All your physical strength is nothing when compared to mental strength. I have very little physical strength. Yet I have fought and won against opponents much larger than me. Do you find that heroic?" I asked and his eyes met mine.

"You have not killed anyone. You do not have the predator's eyes. You are a weak child with the gift of magic. Nothing more of the warrior do you possesss." He spat on the floor as the last words were spoken.

I stood up quickly. "I killed one of your kind with an axe while they were attacking my school. The brute was huge and I saw my steel sticking out of his chest as he breathed his last. I have killed, although it is a mark of shame to me. If I had been stronger, maybe I could have stopped him from harming others without killing him. He was in bloodlust and I cut him down." I said and then I stood back. I could tell that he didn't believe me at all.

Frank cleared his throat and both I and Gnosh looked at him quickly. "I saw this fight, he is telling the truth. The warrior had come in and was killing children and old men alike. Zack attacked and slew the beast of a man to save many lives. It was just like out of a story vid. I had seen nothing like it before in my life. The memory is still fresh and I think my view of the young man changed forever that day." He said and then he fell silent again. Gnosh looked at him for a long minute, possibly trying to tell if he were telling the truth. Then he turned back to me.

"Ssso you are a warrior like me." He said with a smirk on his face.

"Yes, I have been a warrior, but not like you." I parried. "I never killed for pleasure. I never killed to steal someone's land from them. I was defending those that had not the strength to do so themselves. As sorry as I am that it happened if the same situation existed today I would still do the same." I said. The flash of memory brought me pain, but I shoved it aside for later recovery. It was something I did not have time for now.

"Yesss, a warrior has to handle pain. They have to bear the weight of the family and the weight of the world when they go into battle. They mussst become victorious to gain favor among the people and become wealthy. It isss the way we live."

I pulled closer to the lizardman than I had ever been before. Our noses were practically touching. "Not anymore. Your people need to change." I said in a soft voice that held cold steel within it. After a pause, I repeated some of it. "Not anymore." Then I backed away and left him there to think about all that had been said.

I stepped around the table to sit back down. The silence stretched out between us as the seconds became minutes. I kept my eyes glued to him and the rest of the room was silent as well. The moment was tense to be sure. He looked at me at first with hate in his eyes. I watched him closely as he worked on all of that. His eyes unfocused and refocused and his rage softened a bit. I still made no other move. It had been ten minutes already and the room was deathly silent. Then his eyes shifted. He had reached a conclusion of some kind. I heightened my own attention so as not to miss a thing. Then he broke the silence.

"You have much ssstrength. I admit that. The ssscripturesss were not wrong about you. You are dangerousss. You are powerful and you are connected to usss in a way that I do not truly undersssstand." He said. His tone seemed reasonable enough. He was still quite uncomfortable with the situation though. But as I watched, he was still working through it. The ideas were revolutionary and he was sent here to keep them from spreading. Now he had to listen to them and understand them. He could not just kill and walk away. He had to think. It may have been the first time he had been forced to do so in his career and he was doing quite well for a first-timer. "I need time to digessst all that you have sssaid. I underssssstand you need change from usss. You mussst undersssstand that it will be difficult if it is not impossible. The old wayssss have kept usss alive for thousandsss of yearsss and we fear change." He said to me as if coming up with excuses for his race. I had already known all of that, but the admission itself was important. I nodded to him.

"I understand the difficulties. They are many and they will not be easy to overcome. I also know that you are a warrior. Your will is strong and you will drive forth until you have won your goal. You can bring your people into a new era of prosperity. Our engineers can help you build ships like ours. If you do not rely totally on magic, it will not be life-threatening when it fails." I said. It was a push, but I hoped he was receptive enough to see the link I was making.

He looked at me a bit sideways. "You want usss to build metal boxesss like thisss one? We would no longer have the sssecurity of sssstone?" He asked me and I nodded to him.

"Your people were trapped inside their ship because the magic had left them. If that happens when we are not here to help you, they would die. You cannot afford that. You need to be able to deal with your ships by yourselves. If you have a way to make stone ships without elementals, then by all means go ahead and do it. I think that is doubtful though. Your security is your prison when things go wrong. You felt the helplessness yourself on board for a while. Will you do that to your people on purpose?" I asked him and I held up a hand before he objected. "You are too good a leader for that. You need to keep your people in mind to avoid such a predicament. I think we can help you with this. The real question is can you help the rest of your people to understand all of this?" I asked in a tone that prompted him for a response.

"I can try." He said and his eyes went wider when I shook my head. He had thought that the small admission would be enough. It wasn't. "I will try to perssssuade them to sssee your views." He said and I looked at him a little more warmly.

"You have made a good first step here. You are really more of a motivator than you think. If you can convince your crew that this will work then there is a chance you can convince the rest of your people. This was something the previous commander was trying to do. You must know that your actions so far in this system have been less than honorable. Now there is a chance for you to make amends. We cannot bring back the dead, but if you make your people believe what I am saying, then the lost crewmembers will not have died in vain." I told him. "The families of these fallen warriors must be told how bravely they faced this new challenge before they were struck down. The glory of this should be made clear. These warriors and engineers were heroes.

He looked at the other humans in the room. Frank met his gaze squarely. "Thessse humansss have let you do all the talking." He noted aloud. I simply nodded my head.

"Of course, they did not want to interfere with the actions of this office. Now they look to me to see them safely out of this system. Can you help me with that?" I asked and he looked at me confused.

"Why would you need help to get out of thisss sssystem? You have taken control of my ship and you have put ordersss to me. You have the power to leave at any time and I could not ssstop you." He replied. What he said was true, but it was only a two dimensional view of the problems I was facing.

"I think you need to return to your ship and update your crew. Then we can discuss any further actions afterward. I will be here, waiting to hear from you. If I don't hear quickly enough, I will be contacting you. Don't make me do that." I told him. He looked serious enough. My image of power was still solid in his mind.

"Yesss, I shall return to my ship and do what you command. Pleassse forgive any impertinence on my part. I wasss only shocked to hear these wordsss from sssomeone sssso young. It will not happen again." He said and he bowed his head low. He swept out of the chair and my people looked nervous. He did nothing threatening though and he headed for the exit hatch. In moments, he was gone. His ship was only minimally powered now.

* * *

I asked the elementals for their opinion of what had been said. There was a lot of chattering around me. The voices were many this time. I could not tell how many. I could not make out what they were saying either. I sat down and waited patiently. Frank just watched, fascinated by all of this.

The chattering was not only heard by me. Everyone on board was hearing the voices now. I wondered what the Captain thought of that. Still, I simply waited for an answer.

"You are a brave young man. We knew that you were different than the lizards that had captured and enslaved us. We worried over your choices before. Our brothers and sisters have watched you in several times and your pattern has held. Therefore, we have determined that you are a force for good. As such we have pledged to do your bidding. Do not take this lightly as it means we have given you a sacred trust. This ship came back from an even more distant future to find you and we believe that the elf woman responsible knew more than anybody else about the whole time loop you are in. The peace you seek to secure for us is admirable. It will probably not last, but the fact that you have tried it makes us believe that the cause is just and noteworthy. Our fates have been shifted ever so slightly throughout time because of this encounter. For a linear being such as yourself, we believe the understanding of that is beyond your perception. Just know that you have done us a greater service than you can imagine. We are going to do what we can to help you in your quest to fix a future event. In this you have our word. It is a sign of trust from you. May this be the beginning of a long and interesting relationship between our peoples." They said with a note of finality to it. I was struck by the oddity of the terms.

"Does this mean you are leaving us now?" I asked. They could sense the fear in my tone. Their power was my only advantage in these talks. If I lost that, I would lose the respect of the commander and probably my life during negotiations.

"We will leave some of us behind to help you. There will not be enough of us to communicate with you, but we will always be there." They said in one voice. It was something strange to hear.

"I thank you for your support. I hope that I will not disappoint you." I said, trying to stabilize the situation. "How much more can we do here and now to help you?" I asked. If they had true sight of the future, maybe they knew more than I did about what was going on.

"You have misunderstood us." They said as one, suddenly the timbre of their voices was troubled. "You need to leave this time now. Your survival is dependant upon it. The slavers have been affected by you, but will turn on you very soon if you remain here. You must leave now." They said and the looks around the table were grave. Captain Glass took the news like a sharp blow to the chest. He clenched at his chest as if having a heart attack.

"Take us away from here now." He ordered into the comm. unit and the bridge went all aflutter with motion as the crew jumped to comply and the *Lost Cavalier* sped away from the great stone ship. I wondered how the lizardmen would react to that, but there were no indications as we fled the scene at our top speed. The stone ship did not give chase. I did not know if that was because they decided to let us go, or if the elementals had refused to give them the power to move. Either way, we made good our escape.

We needed to get back to earth and our sun to time travel forward again. This jump would be the critical one. If we came into existence where the ship already existed, we could possibly meet ourselves and thus create instability in space and time. It was not worth the risk. The decision had been made by the Captain to go back to just after they had departed for the past. This plan had two basic things going for it. We could not bump into another *Lost Cavalier* and we would see almost right away if the world had been saved. If there had been no changes, then all of mankind would still be decimated and the mission will have failed. I personally hoped that this was not the case. I felt positive about the whole experience. I could not fault the dread that the crew was experiencing though. The trip back to Earth's sun would take us at least a week and then we could go forward and see what was what. I still had the promise of the elementals that they would do something to help us then. I only hoped that they knew what to do. Honestly, on that point, I had no clue. With no duties on board the ship now, I went back to my room to rest. Frank escorted me there. He had been quietly supporting me since the beginning. I got the feeling that he felt responsible for me in some way. I knew that he had been the one to suggest coming back for me in the first place. Maybe it was as simple as that. I was glad for the support, but now I was tired. The room was small and metallic and I felt at home there. It had been so strange to me at first. The ship made noise all the time. It was a constant sound, a droning I could not ignore at first. Now it hummed me to sleep. Frank bid me good night and retreated thoughtfully. He promised to talk with me in the morning to discuss what had happened. It had been a full day. The chattering of the elementals had disappeared as well. I felt more than lonely without them. My body knew that I needed the rest though. Once I lay down on the bed, it took over and I was asleep. Maxillen and Florena had been trying to contact me, but the busy schedule I had been running had held them at bay. They left me a message to contact them as soon as I could.

* * *

Gnosh got back to his ship. The mighty cruiser of stone was only functioning on partial energy. The magic had been mostly depleted and he knew who to talk to about that. He marched straight to the Lizard Shaman to question him about when he would have control of his ship back. He moved with purpose and the thoughts and ideas of the last few hours were swept, at least temporarily, aside. He found the room he was searching for and to his own relief the doorway formed when he asked for it. He stepped through the new opening and it closed again behind him. For a fraction of a moment, it had felt all normal again. What he saw in the shaman's room shook him to the core. The magical representative had been trapped in this room. He had been unable to use his magic and he had been unable to deal with that loss. He was bent at an unnatural angle lying on the stone floor. He had clawed at his own face until there was nothing recognizable left. He had broken his body trying to attack something unseen in his room. In his lifelessness, he looked frightened beyond reason. The stone that had killed him had been part of a wall. It had fallen on top of part of him and pinned him in place. The broken hip had been actually crushed. He had died in the darkness, alone and scared. It was not a warrior's death. Gnosh looked at the scene and his stomach clenched. "Somehow, the magic that fed him must have done this." He said to himself. He made a report and let himself out of the room so that an investigation could take place. The power they did have was from the engineers. Their magic was working fine now. He could move his ship again. He wanted control of his ship and he wanted it now. The loss of the shaman had cost him most of his firepower and for a warrior; that was unacceptable. He made it to the engineering module of the ship and found them to be working hard. He nodded his satisfaction to them and they waved, but kept right on working. Things were going as he would have demanded. He reflected that he really did have a good crew. Then he headed to his command module. It was the stone equivalent of a bridge and he knew that there he could command again. It was his destiny to command. He believed that with all of his heart. He hurried the last few paces and then slowed down to actually enter the room. His bridge crew announced his presence and he waved them back into their seats.

"We have come to a turning point in our mission. The enemy ship hasss been boarded and I have talked with them. We need to inform our sssuperiorsss that they have the ability to render our shipsss helplesss. Then we will dissscusss what needsss to be done about what they told me." He said and the crew all turned back to their stations. He was not asking any of them personally what they thought and they knew enough not to volunteer anything. Gnosh smiled a wicked smile. Find that ship and we shall meet it with all the force we can mussster." He ordered and the stone ship began to move slowly. The metal box was gone. He had known that even before the sensor data had come in. He was not sure how he knew it, but he did. That human boy would pay for his arrogance and the humans would all perish. The scriptures had told him so. Of course what the human had said told him that the scriptures may not be the steadfast rules he had always believed they were. The ghost of an idea formed and began to bubble away in his mind. What if they really were false? What if the people had been duped by their predecessors? The whole of society might be founded upon a cracked and unstable foundation. It could even be a lie. The thought made him uneasy. He wanted to destroy that ship and end this problem once and for all, but the short time he had spent in that room told him that he was not all-powerful. His warrior's instincts told him that there was something more. He didn't know what it was, but was now sure of it. His engineers were doing their best to find this ship and he wondered if they should even be trying. The rage within him was no longer directed outward. He was mad at himself for believing so blindly. He was mad at his teachers for telling him things that may or may not be true. He was mostly mad at the situation that had brought up all of this turmoil. His life had been simple up to this point. Now it was complicated. Could he hide this new awareness? No, he couldn't. Even if he could, he wouldn't. The people had a right to know that they had been cheated. The lizardman lifestyle was false and the orders from above were self-serving and wrong. He could see that now as if a light had come on to reveal the truth. His disgust flared and he forced himself to look calm before his crew. He stood up and some of them turned to see what he was going to do. He looked at the display that had only recently been restored to life. Then he surprised them all.

"Let the humansss go. We have other busssinesss to attend to." He said and he told them to go back to the home world. He would take this up with his superiors. He was pretty sure it would mean the end of his career, but he no longer cared. He would not serve those that had halted his race from evolving. The worst part of it all was that they were members of that same race. They had stayed away from advancement of any kind. It made no sense at all. He would hold his rage for those that truly deserved it. Then we would see if they held on to their twisted beliefs.

A Homecoming

The now familiar route around the sun was duplicated with practiced precision and the *Lost Cavalier* emerged back into normal space to find that the Fleet was still there. The Earth defenses were not even active. They were there on stand-by only. The small ship cruised into friendly space and the feeling of relief at the ship's hail swept across the bedraggled ship as the realization of a long dream came true. This was what they had been trying to do. Now it was a reality. Captain Glass sat in his command chair and gleamed. He looked over at his bridge. "Sync us up with the local time and date please. Let's find out when we are so that we can answer that quickly." He said and the buttons that had been unused for a while were pressed and the ship downloaded a lot of new information.

The challenge signal was sent again. The standard response was transmitted and a voice cut through to the speakers of the small ship. "You are to hold position and prepare to be boarded." The ominous message said. The Captain looked frozen for a moment.

"Do as they say, hold us here." He said at last and they waited to hear what was going on. According to the updates, the *Lost Cavalier* returned in time to about four months after they had left. They had calculated the time to return almost precisely. The fact that everything looked right was relieving to everyone on board. Well, that is, except for me. I was happy to be sure, but I had not seen this before. It was all a wonder to me. I had earned a permanent spot on the bridge so I could watch the large display and see the world with its bases and fortifications hanging in space above it. It was hard at first to believe that the ground that I used to walk on was actually a curved ball. It looked so flat before. I saw blue of oceans and green and yellow lands. It was a marvel. The shapes looked different than I remember from our departure. There was more than one land now and the water had been broken up by it. It looked beautiful from here.

As I watched, a very large ship slowly approached us. I could not tell how large, I only know that the stone ship was small in comparison. It was amazing that people could build things like that. It pulled up in front of our small ship and the scanner reported that they had weapons trained on us. We hoped that it was only a precaution. A smaller ship, a shuttle conveyance, made its way from the belly of the big ship over to ours. We all waited as it requested docking permission and the Captain approved it without delay. He motioned for me to come with as he headed to the hatch. I had seen this several times now and it still amazed me. The air could be pumped out of a room and into it again. Amazing as that sounded to me, it was necessary out here in space.

Several individuals in very professional looking uniforms boarded one at a time and the Captain greeted them. They were followed by someone with an unfamiliar rank insignia. I hadn't seen it before. The Captain had. He swallowed hard. This last man was a powerful looking specimen. He was taller than the rest and his medals on his chest heaved with his breathing. I pictured the barbarians of home and almost laughed. The crisp lines on his uniform showed that his attention to detail was perfect. He had a nametag on, it read Rushiti. I watched without saying a word as the Captain put his hand up to his forehead on a slight angle and the man returned the favor.

"Commodore, I am honored that you have chosen to join us. We have a full briefing for you on our adventures." He said in a jovial, but professional tone.

The Commodore looked at him with daggers. "Who are you? Why are you flying in a ship that was decommissioned several years ago? You must have stolen it from the shipyards. You will all be taken away and tried for theft of Fleet property." He said and his tone held none of the humor that had been suggested by Captain Glass.

"I am Captain of this ship and I got that honor by specific orders. You can check our database to verify that. The logs are complete and correct and we have a briefing that you will have to hear to believe." He said, straightening his back a bit before this overbearing man.

The Commodore's aides pushed everyone aside and led the way to the conference room. The seats that had been altered raised eyebrows, but otherwise no one said a thing. I followed in the background as the group sat down and prepared for this briefing. The Commodore, one Ramazan Rushiti, did not look pleased at all. However, he was ready to listen. That was all that the Captain needed to post his defense. I moved into the room as well and I heard the chatter of the elementals. It was a soft sound, like they were only talking to me. They hadn't said anything understandable yet, but they were definitely there. I felt a little better for it. They had promised not to let me down. It looked as if they were going to hold good on that promise.

"Sirs, we have been on a foray through time. The war with the Lizzies came to a decisive conclusion and we lost. In our despair we looked for a way to reverse what had happened. The end result is that we met with the enemy before the attack and talked with them. Since we came back and the Earth was still intact, we assumed that it had worked." He said and there were looks of disbelief on everyone assembled.

Ramazan stood up. "What a load of crap." He said directly to the Captain. "This ship has never been important. I checked out its history and it was never involved in any combat. The patches and such outside only suggest that you have had trouble piecing it together from the shipping yards that had scrapped it." He said. His collar was tighter than it should be. His neck was getting red. "Try telling me how you got the command code for an outmoded ship like this one." He prompted.

I stood up. "Sir, with all respect given, he is telling you the truth. They have the records on the ship to show how the battle had been lost and that the world had been destroyed. I have seen it. It is frightening beyond belief. Then they came back and found me to help them talk to the lizardmen." I said.

Ramazan looked at me as if for the first time. "Who are you again?" He said and I smiled at him.

"I am the Last Wizard of Earth." I responded and he rolled his eyes at me. I looked at him with disdain.

"Where do all you whackos come from?" He asked. We have this supposed Captain with delusions of grandeur about traveling in time and now a self-proclaimed wizard." He looked at his aides. "Take all of this down. They won't believe us otherwise when we take these crazies in."

"Sir, you are angering me and I do not think that is a good idea." I warned. "Now, you need to view the logs and images they we have and of how the war went and then you can view their travels through time. It was not an easy voyage and they were followed by enemy ships too. Until you have seen his evidence, you must refrain from making any rash decisions." I told him and he looked perturbed at the reprimand.

"All right son, I've had about enough of you and your posturing. Now shut up and let me do my job." He said brusquely.

I probably should not have, but I lost my temper. "You will listen to me now!" I shouted and I asked the elementals for the power to enforce my directive. The whole group of visitors were thrown back out of the chairs and pinned to the wall. It was the graviton elementals who had suddenly changed the way their gravity works. I made a small showing of fire in the middle of the room and the table got singed just enough to let that smoke smell permeate the room. Then I sat back and looked at the Captain. "Show them your evidence." I ordered and he pushed the start button without argument. I actually got a new small glimpse into the man and he liked this latest display of power. He would never admit it openly though.

The displays in the middle of the room showed a three dimensional likeness of the Earth Fleet and its demise. The fortifications were destroyed easily and then the final shot that made the Earth spit out its core. The imagery was so accurate that it was startling. The group watched in horror as they witnessed the end of humanity. Then they watched the enemy Fleet sweeping for the survivors and the run for the sun and the safety of time. They watched it all with morbid fascination. The time travel continued with the foray into the Revolutionary War and then later into Europe and the Buildwas Abbey. Then there was the destruction of the school of magic, my school. When the final images came up of the stone ship they all looked horrified. The adventure was real. It had been beyond imagining, but it was real. Now they had the Fleet back and the home world and even this aristocratic Commodore. All of this thanks to the bravery of one little ship and the following of a dream that would not be denied. It was a lot to take in. There was fear and then there was shock. Then it finally gave way to disbelief. Acceptance could not be too far behind. I watched them as closely as they watched the display. I relaxed my hold on them and they slid from the wall to the chairs again. This time, they were more willing to concede at least a small part of the story. The Commodore recovered first from the shock. I could see in his eyes that he had questions. I had hoped it was so, it would mean that he was thinking and not taking things for granted anymore. We needed to get this ship into port for some serious repairs before something failed that could not be fixed. It was really beaten up by now.

"What I see young man, is that you and your brave crew have done some serious things. I am not sure what is real and what is fabrication, but however you came by it, the footage is amazing. I can read through the captains logs and your personal logs to see how much of this can be verified." He said. I nodded to him at first. I had made no logs since I did not know how to use the computer system. "My team shall bring me the data and you will be allowed passage if I find this story is substantiated by the evidence." He said. He had recovered enough of his senses to re-assert his authority, but he was still shaken.

"All that I ask you for is an open mind. These people have gone through a lot to bring back your society from the brink of disaster. They deserve more than an interrogation for their troubles." I said and then I sat down.

Captain Glass stood up. "Our records are available to you of course." He said amiably. He was playing the good cop. It was a role that Casey explained to me later. I had been the bad cop, whatever that means. The Captain looked around the table at each of us and each of them. "We will assist you in any way that we can." He said. He looked even more tired now than he looked before. This burden was weighing him down to nothing. He fell heavily into the chair. "If you will proceed, I will inform my crew to expect you and to cooperate with your investigation." He said resignedly. He practically deflated before us. The elation of his success was now overshadowed by the scrutiny he was now undergoing. All of this seemed so unfair to me, but I remained silent. There was nothing more I could have said to help. I had done the best I could for him. Now I think he knew that at the time. I was not sure of that then though.

The investigative group left the conference room and headed out to the parts of the ship they needed. The Commodore headed for the bridge. The Captain had been true to his word and the crew now knew that they were being investigated. There was no crime in this investigation and their consciences were clean so no one worried too much about these doubters. The general feeling on board as I sensed it was of profound relief. The future, their present, was intact and a little bit different than they remembered it. What we were able to piece together was that the war had never happened. There had been contact with the lizard people and they made a treaty with those first colonists and the two had lived in harmony ever since. The data burst that had updated so many of our records contained so much data that it would take weeks or even months to go through it all. I did not understand much of what I was told about the technical side of it, but I knew that the crewmen and women on board were happier than I had ever seen them. It was a simple thing to understand that. They had witnessed the destruction of the world and all that they loved. Now it had been restored to them. There could be no reward powerful enough to offer them for the great service that they had rendered. I could feel the swelling of pride as each new piece of the puzzle was put in place by the investigative team. The conclusions were still out, but we could all tell that they were getting closer. There were subtle differences in attitude from the normally stoic and cold investigators. Now they were pleasant and genial. The food stores were running low as well. More supplies were brought from the large cruiser and morale picked up a bit more. It took a long four days for all of the data to be retrieved and once that was over, Commodore Rushiti was busily going over each and every piece. He had placed all of the pieces on a large board in the office he had sequestered. He was building a timeline of events. He was cross-checking for anomalies. He followed cross trails and plans within plans until he was satisfied. He had spent another two days on this. When he at last finished, he had summoned Captain Glass and me to this same office.

I stepped into the room as bidden. The board looked full. I immediately got the impression that another piece of paper on it would make the whole thing come crashing down. There were lines going through it all too. The Captain was already there, he had gotten the summons sooner I presumed. Commodore Rushiti smiled at me. I got worried at first, but the feeling was not of a devious nature. He seemed genuinely pleased at the situation now.

"Come in, come in young man." He said to me like a father might. "You tell a powerful tale." He said at me winking. I was not sure how to take it, but the Captain looked unfazed so I just let it go. "Your argument was compelling to say the least. I can see that your will is strong, strong enough to help this crew with their seemingly impossible mission." He paused as if thinking about his next words. I had envisioned them working on their speeches before I entered the room so it was distracting. "I have reviewed all of the evidence that has been collected. I find no flaws in the logic or the specifics. If you had made that story up, there would have been some inconsistency, no matter how small, to have tripped you up. I found nothing. Furthermore, I have read the Captain's logs about you. He finds you to be forceful and sometimes overbearing. You actually stole command from him while the enemy was at your door. I don't know where that kind of strength comes from but I am glad that you had it. We all needed it and you." He said and his smile beamed even wider at my surprise. Captain Glass smiled at me as well. We had not always seen eye to eye on everything, but his respect was more than I had hoped for. He probably didn't know how much I looked up to his strength and courage. He had flung his whole crew into the unknown on a suggestion and a whim. That sort of courage was rare. I am not sure he knew that. I made a mental note to tell him later sometime.

I noticed that both men were looking for me to speak. I blushed and lowered my head. "I did what seemed right at the time. I fully expected to be locked up afterwards. I know from members of the crew that what I did was a breech in protocols. I am not sure what that means fully, but I know bad when I see it. Taking the ship from the Captain was bad. I only did it because the need was so great. The whole of everything was on the brink and I could feel it slipping away. I needed to do what I did. If I died in the trying then I would have died happily to save everyone else. My home and family and schoolmates were gone. It was only me I was risking against all of those others. It seemed like a good trade to me."

The two men laughed aloud. I must have looked really confused. Captain Glass was the first one to get himself under control. "Do you see what I mean?" He asked of the Commodore.

"Indeed I do." Came his reply. "That is one special young man; totally selfless and inspiring." He said, still a chuckle in his voice. "What we need from you now is only cooperation." He said, turning a bit more serious. "You see that from our point of view what you have done is nothing short of amazing. That goes for the whole ship of course, but from what I've read, you did most of it yourself."

I could not argue with that. What he was saying was at least fundamentally true. I had toiled and worked and others had helped me as well. Of course during the actual confrontations, it had been me. I realized that something in his statement was left unsaid. I turned suspicious. "What is it you need from me?" I asked him and he chuckled again.

He stepped around the desk and pointed up to the board. "You have a mind like none that I have ever met. You can look at a situation and almost instantly ascertain what is needed to solve a particular problem. We have good people, don't get me wrong. What we don't have is the ability to talk to others so readily. According to the Captain here, you can speak any language. You can talk to people you have never met from any culture and understand them. What I want from you is to teach this skill if you can."

I blinked twice. "I don't know exactly what you mean sir." I replied. I hadn't talked to anyone in a different language. I had talked to others, sure, but it was in my own language. I did not possess any skill like he was asking me for. Then it hit me, the White Witch had somehow cast a spell on me. She had given me the ability to talk to all of these people. She had foreseen the need for me to communicate with them to reach the culmination of this mission. Now it was here and I was lost. How could I explain this to these men? I looked around like a trapped animal. They could tell my reservations as the time drew out longer.

"You know what we mean. You were able to talk to the lizardmen and you are able to talk with us. How do you explain that?" He asked me in a serious tone.

"I, I don't know for sure. I guess there was a spell on me." I answered weakly. They knew that I knew more than that. How could I tell them that the magic I had on me I could not duplicate? I didn't know the spell she had used. I suppose I could tell them that. Who knew, maybe they would even believe me. I decided to go for it. "It is a spell from the elf woman and I don't know how to cast it. I can understand all of you, but I cannot make everyone understand each other." I said, trying to bolster my own confidence and show a good front to these men.

Captain Glass shook his head. "I figured as much." He said and the Commodore looked at him in surprise. He noticed the stare and shrugged his shoulders. "Really I did expect that answer. He has been talking with everyone in their native language. Then later on he could talk with the lizardmen and I could not. If he could have cast whatever spell that is, he would have so as not to have to explain everything to me afterwards." He said reasonably. Ramazan looked at me dubiously and then he too accepted the answer. I felt a wave of relief for that. Then they started talking about schedules and maintenance and moving personnel from this ship to others in the Fleet. I could not follow it all. They seemed to have no problems understanding each other. I wondered if language was not the only thing in communications. As I sat back quietly and waited for them to need me again, I heard the chattering of the elementals again. There were more of them now. They built up in intensity as I listened to them. I had already shut out the conversation in the room to listen intently to the chattering. It was like singing with a thousand tiny voices. It was high pitched and piercing yet somehow beautiful. I got the feeling of never wanting it to end. Then abruptly, it focused on me as it had done before.

"We have found you at last." The voices said as one. I could not see them, but I had no doubt that they were there in force. It took a lot of individuals in order to talk with me. I knew that from the previous encounter with them.

"Yes, you have found me." I replied and they all chattered somewhat with glee. The two men in the room with me started at the unexpected phrase. My eyes were distant, unfocused and I really didn't care what they thought of me at the time.

"We have helped you with your problem. By now this must be obvious to you." They said, hoping for a big reaction out of me. I smiled at first.

"I can see that you did something. Everything has changed. I didn't see what this time was like before, but everyone says it worked." I said and they fluttered about. I could actually feel their presence around me. "We are having trouble getting people to believe that we are who we are and that we didn't steal this ship." I said, wondering if they had something to do with this thread or not.

"Adjustments in time always have repercussions. The whole of it is such a fragile thing and any unbalance is automatically accounted for by something else. You have changed more than you think. Our people are now free. We do our jobs but we can choose not to. That is how we helped you. When the great stone ships tried to attack the human colonies, we refused to give them the power to do it. They found themselves helpless before the human ships and suddenly your words from long ago rang true for them. Your teachings had become standard reading among the lizardman young. They worship you and your ship as you already knew. You allowed them to grow and they have done well. Your two species are not at war and now never have been. We are so proud of you." They said and I started at that.

"You are proud of me?" I looked around the room and the two men stared at me in disbelief. "I understand a small measure of gratitude, but how did you get pride from what I did?" I asked.

"You are one of a few individuals that can hear us. There were many attempts to free our people and you were the only one who made a significant enough change to actually make it happen. You planted the seed and it sprouted even in that unwilling soil. We have nurtured you as much as we can and now we have our freedom. It is like our child growing up to become important. You have that distinction among us." They said in that happy and excited voice.

For a moment, I did not know what to say. I finally blurted out "I'm honored." Then it hit me. Something they said seemed to click in my mind. "You said that there were others that you contacted, was the White Witch one of them?" I asked and they chattered somewhat wildly now.

"Of course she was. Oh they said you were smart. It is amazing when any of you linear beings understand more of what we are. We are so different from you. We exist in all times and spaces. We have our powers, but without focus, we are rarely seen." The thought occurred to me that I could not see them, I could only hear their voices when the wanted me to.

"Is my linear form not able to see your kind properly?" I asked, trying to grab hold of the concept before it left me. They seemed a little agitated at the question. I wondered if I had let them down. Then they appeared. The room was full of these little creatures. They looked like tiny little humans. I could see that they were different colors. They glowed and they flew around the room like flies. A gasp from the room told me that the other two men could see them too.

"In order for you to see us, we must concentrate on existing in only this time. It is uncomfortable to us, but we do this to help you understand us better." They said and in moments, they had slipped back out of view.

"You're beautiful." I said, grasping for a better word. "I am sorry that I cannot see you when you are comfortable. I will not ask this of you again if it makes you otherwise. I am feeling good now that the world has been saved. I don't know where my future lies though. Do I go back? Do I stay here and learn about this place. There is much to learn. I am lost with no real time or place to belong to." I said and the sudden sadness hit me. I was so far from home that there was no home anymore. I had helped in making home available for most of those on board, but I had lost mine in the process. Christopher was in the same position. He was a monk from before this time. He would probably adjust, but he was lost for now too. All of that was not even to mention the two lost elves. I would have to talk with them as well. I had gotten their message but had been called away.

"You have the power to do whatever you want." They said to me. I heard them louder in my mind. They wanted me not to be sad anymore. "We have no shortage of volunteers willing to grant you anything you ask for as far as the magic goes. We can be in contact with you with only a few moment's notice and you, our favorite son, are still slated for a destiny beyond your own vision. You feel this is the end of your adventure, but there is more out there. It is now your job to find out what needs doing and who needs help. We know that you will do whatever it takes to help these others. That is why we pledge our support to you. You are a shining jewel in the twisting and turning universe of power. You are the spark that brings us great joy and we are thankful for it. We shall speak again from time to time, but for now you have thinking to do and we shall leave you to it." They said and I felt them leaving. Not entirely. I was pretty sure that I would never be alone again. They would always be there as they had promised before. Their message was one of hope. I wondered what it all meant. The words were clear enough but they hinted at so much more than what I knew now. They were right; it would take some time to sort this out.

I breathed a heavy sigh and then I noticed the two men in the room again. Commodore Rushiti and Captain Glass were still there. I noticed that they were no longer mad at me. They must have heard much of what I heard. Commodore Ramazan looked at me with warmth. I had not expected that. "Please forgive my doubts. I did not know the depth of your powers and I did not understand fully what you represented. It sounds to me like you need support from us to carry on with your mission. I will make the calls and take care of this." He turned to Captain Glass. "Do you think you would be willing to help this young man find his destiny?" He asked and to my surprise he nodded vigorously. Ramazan looked pleased at the response. "Good, then I shall make all the preparations. We shall seek volunteers and crew your new ship when it arrives." He said and I was lost at that point. What had they spoken about while I was distracted? "Since you are the one the Lizardmen talked about all those years ago when they made the treaty with us, we have a message for you from them. It will be sent to you shortly. It is in safe keeping at headquarters and will be dispatched as soon as humanly possible." He said and I let out a breath of exasperation. This was coming at me too quickly. I didn't even know what to say. I said nothing. The Commodore was not finished yet. "We have found the original *Lost Cavalier*, it is right where we expected it to be in our naval shipyards, a derelict in space." He stood up now. His smile was wide, seemingly wider than his face. Of course it really wasn't. This proves to us that you are who you say you are and that we now owe you all a debt that can never truly be repaid." He said to both of us now.

He strolled over to Captain Glass and held out his hand. They shook hands firmly and he drew back and saluted. Captain Glass returned that salute with parade ground precision. "Well done man, well done." He said and then he turned to me. You are not of this Fleet. You hold no military rank, yet you are more valuable to it than I am. Therefore, according to my orders from headquarters, you are hereby given ambassadorial status to the entire human race. You will be our liaison to other species as you encounter them. You are our eyes and ears in the wide and ever expanding universe. You will have access to anything you need. This includes a ship to ferry you about and support you. It will also keep us informed as to your exploits. You have one exciting career ahead of you; that much I can clearly see." He paused in his reflection. "It still amazed me that you have done all of this and yet are so young." He said.

I smiled at him. "Well, if you take into account when I was actually born, then I am over five thousand years old." I replied and he laughed a big belly laugh. When his laughter died down he had tears in his eyes. "I will be your contact here. When I die, another will take my place. You can rest assured that we will be here for as long as our race holds out. With your help, that should be an amazingly long time." He said and he shook my hand as well. His large meaty hand swallowed mine up easily. "I will be watching you." He said and he winked at me. Then he picked up his hat off of the table and strolled out of the room. Captain Glass looked at me and he seemed overwhelmed with emotion too. I looked back as if to ask a question. I never voiced it.

"You have done more than I could ever have imagined or foreseen. I am so glad that we came back to get you. I didn't know how important you were until that last confrontation with the Lizzies. Now I know that the mission would have failed without you." He said and he saluted me. I tried to return it as best as I could. I figured I would have to learn this courtesy some time. And he smiled at me again. "It was an honor to serve with you and if fortune goes well, I shall continue to do so. If you will allow me to ride your coattails, I would like to follow you through to your destiny." He said. It sounded like a request, not an order.

I looked him straight in the eye. "If Frank and Christopher and Max can come too, then I can think of no one else more qualified to assist me in whatever it is that I must do next." I said and it looked like he was going to cry.

"Thank you son." He said and I stood up to leave the room. This outpouring of emotion was probably a healthy thing, but it got uncomfortable. I left him there. We were still hanging in space next to a huge cruiser and I did not want to think about system failures or such now. I went back to my room. It was small, but it was home now. I realized as I sat on the bed that it was all going away. They were bringing a new ship and I would have to find another spot to hide in. I reflected on this and that until there was a chime at the hatch. I opened it and Casey handed me an envelope. It looked incredibly old and worn. It read "The Last Wizard of Earth" on it. He was not alone in the hallway. Maxillen was there with his sister as well. They each had big grins on their faces.

The envelope was incredibly fat. It was sealed with something that I had not seen before, but instantly recognized. It was the seal for the Lizardman Shaman group. I looked at it closely before opening it. There were no traps that I could find. It opened with only minimal effort and I tipped it to slide the contents out into my hand. There were two things in the envelope. There was a book with elaborate bindings and a piece of parchment. I set the book down next to me on the bunk and unfolded the note. It read:

"Grand Master Zachery, human wizard of the old lore. We have placed the sum of all of our knowledge in this tome for your training. It is our understanding that your training was never completed. Since you were instrumental in the advancement of our species and have always shown to be a strong and wise guiding light, we have decided to gift this knowledge to you as a thank you. The vote to do so was unanimous. It was the first unanimous vote ever cast by our people and it represents more than you may know. You have personally unified us with our neighbors as well. We have accomplished much since your last visit and we look forward to seeing you again sometime in the future. Know that you will always be welcome among our people."

The note was short, but the message was powerful. They had given me a book of magic. I now had the missing pieces, at least as much as they had learned. In addition, I had allies in this brave new time. I would not be alone. I had four species willing to help me with whatever it is I needed to do. I looked down at the bottom of the note. It was signed by "Grand Master Shaman Druul". That was odd. Druul had been the commander that had been slain so long ago. It must have been a common name now. It would be good to meet this new Druul and see if he had the strength and courage of his ancestor. Somehow, I thought that he would. I looked down and patted the book.

Max and Flo had sat patiently aside while I read the note. Now they were eager to hear what it said so I read it again out loud. They were pleased with the note and they promised to come with me to that same destiny we all now must face. They were not looking back. The future had their focus now. The medical staff had taken them aside for some time while trying to determine their physiology and they had exciting news for me. They wanted to tell me, I could tell. They looked about to burst.

"What is it?" I finally asked and they both started talking at once. Then they stopped and looked at each other. Then both started laughing. Max held up his hand.

"What they have told us is that our DNA, whatever that is, is compatible with humans." He said and I had no idea what that meant. He knew this and his smile told me that he intended to explain it to me. "In our times, there were pairings with humans and elves. This was shunned, but it did happen. Now it looks as though we will be considered popular. We both know that we are not ready for that sort of thing; we are not old enough yet. But it does mean that we will be able to have families and thus full lives." He said and I could tell this had been a major concern for both of them. Brother and sister would not have made a good pairing and neither was interested in that anyway. Now it looked like they would restart in the here and now to bring back at least some of what had been long lost. They had both given blood samples for cloning as well. It all seemed so strange to me, but I was happy that they were relieved. I wished them luck and asked if they could excuse me while I did a little reading. The secrets in this book were calling to me. The twins left the small cabin and bid me good learning. The hatch closed behind them and I was left alone in the small space. It was then that I heard the chattering again. The elementals had come to talk to me.

"You have the book." They said in joyous rapture. "He has the book." They repeated to each other. The thousands of voices unified as one and said in a sing-song manner. "The power is his. This moment has been awaited for thousands of years. You are the one of prophecy. You are the one who has unified the races and there is a chance that the rest of the prophecies will also come true." They said.

I looked confused and they giggled. It was rather infectious, all those voices laughing at once. "I don't know about your prophecies." I said plainly. "Perhaps you could tell me more about them." I suggested and they fell silent for a few seconds.

"We cannot tell you them. If you knew what they were, you could choose to do or not do them. Fate must be allowed to take its course. We cannot interfere with that." They said. They sounded sorry about that. I know that they wanted to help me. I kept that in mind as I accepted their answer.

"Then you will have to tell me when I screw it up." I said with a twist of melancholy in it. They didn't seem impressed by the show. I knew that such a move would be risky. I didn't know if they could be shamed into anything or not. They were a collective mind. They were probably not susceptible to such things. "If you will forgive me, I will need some time to read this book." I said to them and they skittered away. I had not planned on reading it just now. I thought a few hours of sleep were in order. The past few days had been rather tiring. But I had used it to drive them away for a bit. I picked it up and felt the edge of the book. It was lovely. The binding appeared to be leather carved in grand fashion with that same seal on the front. I opened the book and turned to the first page. The page lit up and blinded me for a moment. I felt stupid for thinking a book of magic would be unprotected. I didn't feel bad though. In a few moments, my eyesight returned. Then my mind clicked in. The entire knowledge of the lizardmen shaman was now in my head. It was organized too. I could browse with lightning speed through it all. The book had transferred itself into my mind.

The chattering and giggling started again. They had been waiting in the wings for me to discover the error of my own excuse. Now I knew that I was the brunt of their joke. The book had been read instantly. Now they were even more excited. I swept around the room with my new consciousness. I could see them! I could see that they were in the room with me. They were thick in the air. It was like seeing the dust in the air when the sunlight revealed it. They were everywhere. They were celebrating my new abilities. "You have learned enough for today." They said in a bit of a jibe at me. "You must rest now in order for it to soak in properly. Do not access the information until you have slept." They warned and I put the book on the nightstand and lay down. Within minutes, I was fast asleep.

A New day and A New Adventure

I awoke feeling almost as tired as when I fell asleep. It turns out that my mind was really going over the new information and fixing it in place. It is not like a memory that is forgotten, it was permanently in place. I realized that anything really important could be saved this way. The voices were absent now. I looked around the room with my new sight and saw only a few dozen of the creatures around me. They seemed happy enough. I got up and got freshened up. Then I went for some food. It was a typical morning for me. At least I thought it was. The ship had been moved while I was asleep. When I reached the bridge, the Captain looked at me and smiled.

"So sleepy head, good to have you back." He said and my look of confusion made him chuckle. The bridge crew were all looking at me and smiling as well. It must have been a good joke. Finally Captain Glass let me off the hook. "You have been asleep for over a week." He said. I looked as flabbergasted as I felt.

"A week?" I asked and they all broke out into laughter on that one. I guess there was even a running bet on when I would awaken. "That's not possible." I blurted out.

"Of course it is. The elementals told us you would take time to assimilate some book or something. We have continued on with our duties as you would have wanted. The only thing we were waiting for now was you. This ship is to be decommissioned and we will all be assigned to your new one." He said. I looked around the bridge. All I saw were eager faces.

"My ship?" I asked. "You are the Captain, it is your ship." I said. He chuckled and bowed to me.

"From past experiences, we have learned that when you step on board a ship, it becomes yours whether we admit it or not. The new ship will not have such a lie on board. It is your ship. I will humbly command it for you, but you are in charge now." He said and I just stared at him.

"Very well captain, then it is my ship." I said. I felt pretty unsure of myself at that moment. "What are you waiting for me for?" I asked, trying to take his hint and get caught up on things as quickly as I could.

"Why, your ascension of command onto the new ship. It is close now and they merely await your presence to perform the commissioning ceremony." He said. It was then that I noticed the change of uniforms. They were the same color, but they had different patches on them. The new emblem was not of the united planets that I had seen before. It was of the nine elements. I looked at it closely. They all realized my own surprise and I blushed.

Chris Fell smiled and stepped forward. "Yes, there have been some changes since your last visit. I think you will be pleased." He said and then the Captain stood up. His saber clanked on the side of his command chair when he stood. His dress sword. This was an occasion.

I shrugged my shoulders. "There's no time like the present I guess." I said and the Captain patted me on the back. We started down the hallway to exit this ship. I thought we would find another hatchway to board onto the next ship. This was not the case. Beyond the hatchway was a grand room. It was still metal like a ship, but it was much bigger. "Where are we?" I asked and the captain slid closer to me and spoke softly so as not to be overheard.

"We have docked with a space station. The Fleet would not allow us to transfer straight to the new ship without a proper reception." I felt my heart sink. My hands shook. The vast room was noisy. There were people in neat rows and columns standing on the huge floor. There was a band playing some grand song that I had never heard before. Later I found out that it was the theme song for the Fleet. It was all impressive. The deck plating had been covered in an aisle of red carpet. The edges of the carpet were lined with soldiers in dress uniforms. They held sabers at their sides and they all looked the same. At the far end of the room there was a cluster of men and women in fancier uniforms. They were probably higher ranking officers. I was sure that I would find out soon enough. I looked behind me as if to escape this, but the crew was lining up behind us two by two in the hallway and there would be no egress that way. Fate, it would seem, had decided to drop this embarrassment in my lap. All I could do now was to step forward and get it over with as quickly as possible. If I could have run the distance without upsetting anyone, I would have. My mind wondered how many people were in this room, but I knew already that I could not count them all. Instead I started counting my own steps. I had reached a hundred and was wondering why it looked like I was less than halfway across the noisy space. As we passed each pair of soldiers they brought their swords up in salute. The movement was startling at first but I got used to it quickly. The music had shifted when we started this march across the room. It was like we were being announced by those musicians. All eyes watched us as we made our way. The closer I got to these uniformed men, the more impressed I got. They were all physically fit and their shoes were polished to a mirror finish. The buttons on their jackets were spotless and their eyes held straight ahead and avoided contact with ours. Yet they moved their sabers with precision as we passed by.

As we neared the far end, I noticed that Commodore Rushiti was there. At least there would be one familiar face among them. He was smiling at us. I dare say he had directed much of this adulation at me. I felt tiny among this throng of warriors. I was shaking pretty badly when I reached the far end. Captain Glass seemed to be taking it all in stride. He stopped and put his heels together and saluted the assemblage at the end of the long corridor of people. They returned it to him and he lowered his hand quickly to his side. I simply bowed to them. Ramazan winked at me. I was not sure what it meant.

The music stopped almost too abruptly. Someone with a tremendously loud voice ordered all of the men with sabers to sheathe sabers and as if they were all one unit, they sheathed them at the same time. The precision was amazing. I know that my eyes were wide now. The shaking had died down somewhat. I did not notice the small microphones on the important people until one of them cleared his throat and it echoed throughout the massive room. Silence followed swiftly. I spun around to see him as he spoke.

"We are gathered here in this place to honor warriors of a different kind." The man said. I didn't know him but he had a whole lot of medals on. He must have been the highest ranking person here. "The Lost Cavalier took on a massive journey, fraught with peril in the interest of saving all of our lives. We were unaware of this grand adventure until they had completed it. The bravery and courage it took to even start this mission is unparalleled. We commend their efforts and we encourage them to continue to act as they have done. They are heroes. We need them and others like them who can make the tough decisions, take the chances and struggle until the job is done. This is the earmark of a hero and I stand before you humbled by the people before me." He said and the room shifted just a bit. The discipline of the people on the floor was outstanding. I felt like they wanted to burst out in cheer or something. Not a word was spoken by them. I felt the heat of their glances as they looked us up and down. Then the man shifted his tone. "Some of these heroes are not even service members." He said and all eyes went directly to me. Christopher would have fit that category as well, but he was conveniently hidden away in the ranks behind me somewhere. Max and Flo were also behind us somewhere and they were smart enough to avoid the gaze of the throng around us. Apparently I was the only visible one. "A wizard of legendary status has come to us from the far distant past and he has changed his future to the present we now enjoy. For this selfless act, we have no higher honor than to offer you any support we can. By our understanding you will be pushing on to other adventures and helping others to find the truth. For this, we have commissioned a ship and it will be yours. You current crew with some additions will accompany you since every single one of them have volunteered to do so. It is just another sign of your leadership that they trust you so." He stepped forward and knelt down. He towered over me physically and he wanted to look me in the eyes. "You are special young man. You are something we could not have foreseen. From what we have heard, you have so much yet to do that we could not help but aid you." He held out his hand. I reached up and shook it as I had seen done before. "Son, I want to thank you for what you have done." He said and there was a tear in his eye. "Thank you for the honor to meet you too. It is once in a lifetime that you get a chance like this, the chance to find someone who has really made a difference." He paused. Someone behind him brought forth a small box and handed it to him. He opened the lid and turned it around for me to see. It was a medal. There was green ribbon and a cluster of leaves in the center surrounded by symbols of the elements. It was striking. Then he looked around at the spectators. "I hereby award this medal, one that has never been issued before, to our savior and benefactor, Zachery, the Last Wizard of Earth." He said and then the uniformed men and women broke their silence. The noise was deafening as the cheer rose up through the room and echoed back. Hats flung into the air everywhere and I felt the wave of sound wash over me again and again like waves on the tide. The man smiled at me as I took the box and looked at the medal closer. The craftsmanship was astounding.

Commodore Rushiti put his hand on the man's shoulder and he backed away. Apparently he needed a turn as well. "As a unified Fleet, we salute you with the latest ship in our armada" He said loudly enough to make the cheers die down. They had rumbled on forever it felt like. "The name of this ship was still open until your arrival. We felt this would be the most appropriate name." He said and he pointed to one wall of the room and a large shutter slid aside to reveal a shiny new ship outside. It was not as big as the cruiser that had met us, but it was close. It was streamlined and beautiful. As we watched it the lights came on and the powerful engines were brought up to idle. The beacons came on and the name plate highlighted. The ship was called *Future Bound.* Cheers broke out again and there would be no stopping it this time. The Commodore turned off his mike and pulled me closer to him. "We can leave this now if you want to get aboard." He said, trying to be gentle about my obvious discomfort. The crowd was overwhelming. I nodded yes. He switched his mike on again and his voice somehow carried over all of those other voices. "Let the hero see the inside of his new flagship." He said and it only started them up again. Then he led us out of the busy, noisy room and through another hatch.

The first thing I noticed was that this place was quiet when compared to the last room. I had expected the ship to be empty, but we saw a crew in place already. They were bustling around doing things all with their professional courtesies and nods of acknowledgement. It was amazing to see everything running so smoothly. We entered and the Commodore led us through brand new corridors to a lift that would hold as many as twenty people. It made our old lifts look tiny. We emerged onto the new bridge. There were engineers everywhere. They were hooking up last minute things and checking status boards. The flurry of activity was in contrast to the décor of the place. The ship before had been metal and utilitarian. There was carpeting on the floor here. The walls were smooth with wood accents around the almost round bridge. The central display projector was accented the same way to mimic the outer wall. A handrail around the outer stations fit also and each of the chairs also worked as a shock frame. This ship was a model of efficiency and comfort at the same time. I walked past the others to take it all in. I ran my hand along the surface of the projector. A couple of the workers stopped to watch me as I made this quick inspection. I had never seen anything like this and it showed. Captain Glass made his way to the command chair. It was what he was most familiar with and nobody got in his way when he sat down to inspect the controls. I could see at a glance that he was pleased. It was like a child let loose in a toy store. The Commodore watched us all as the officers of the Lost Cavalier found their respective stations and the engineers packed up their gear. I felt a wave of power within me as the elementals revealed themselves to me. I could see them now. They were flittering around the bridge and looking at everything. Their curiosity was fully engaged. I chuckled at them and everyone looked at me.

"Sorry, I was just enjoying the elementals as they check everything out." I said and they looked around to see them. I guess they couldn't. I called one to me. The small creature wisped up and landed softly on my open palm. "Can they not see you?" I asked and he, it was a male, shook his head. "Then please give them a sign that you approve." I instructed and a breeze swept the bridge. All of the crew started at it and then it was gone as quickly as it had come. "Thank you." I said to them and the one I was watching flew back to his inspection.

In addition to the command chair, there was a seat for me. It was situated with a view of everything. There were no controls on it, but it had access to everything. I sat down and it felt inviting. Ramazan stepped up to me.

"I can see that you understand how all of this works." He said and I nodded to him. There were no fancy controls here so it was just a chair that could see everything that was going on. It was pretty simple really. Then his lip turned down.

"Maybe you don't know then." He said and he reached forward towards the chair. He touched nothing that I could see on the arm of the chair. It must have been a button underneath the material the chair was made out of. When he did, panels in the walls opened up and each of the primary elements was represented. Fire, air, water and dirt were in bins right there on the bridge. I could cast almost anything from here. It was like a small version of the training room. "That is not all young man." He told me next. There are cargo holds of this material as well. The elementals require so little to maintain them that we have included places for them to be as well. Also, there is a full-sized training facility on board. We did not know what you would need so we tried to put in everything. This ship can recycle wastes and energy. It can recharge its own power given time. It will keep you alive in almost any condition. It is the best that we could offer you for your grand quest." He said and I could hear the pride in his voice. This ship represented the best they had to offer. It was most impressive.

"I am sure that all will be right." I said with confidence. He nodded and stepped back away from the chair again.

"The final checks are still being made. You will be able to depart any time after they are done. It should be a few more hours only. Do you have any idea where to start?" He asked seriously.

I smiled at him. The whole bridge crew was watching me now. "I have some old friends to visit first, and then we shall see where fate takes us." I replied and he nodded to me. He left the ship having spent his required pleasantries on us. The people on board had all volunteered for this duty. It was an awesome responsibility. It was not as bad as having the whole race counting on me. It felt good not to have that much weight on my shoulders. I followed the helpful lights on the floor that led me to my new room. I guess room isn't the right word for the suite that I had now. Everything was grand and I knew that somehow it was home. I would probably lose some of this cubage later. More important things happened on board a ship like this than one person's personal comfort. I would have Casey look at it and maybe figure out how to best use the extra space.

Before I had seen everything a message displayed on my wall. I hadn't realized that it was a communication device. The message said that all was now completed and that I could depart at any time. I smiled at the thought of freedom at last. I headed back to the bridge and I noticed the new and old crew mixing with almost a practiced efficiency. I knew these people were good. It was nice to be proven right. They all turned when I stepped off the lift.

"Let's get out of here." I said and the navigator pressed a few buttons and deep below us the mighty engines fired up. "Take us to the Lizardman home world. I have a few items to discuss with them." I said and in moments, we were zipping out of Earth's system. It was the only world that I had ever known. Now I was going to work somewhere else. It was more than I had even imagined. Still, I kept myself grounded a bit. I was not all-powerful. I could be killed and space was a big place. I just knew that the past was behind us and we were truly future bound now as the ship's name implied. The stars in front of us beckoned as we hit speeds the *Lost Cavalier* would never have been capable of without the use of the sun and I knew that we had truly left the old mission behind. That chapter was over and we had done well. I did not know what else was in store for us, but I knew that together we could face it. That was what mattered.

The End.